INTRODUCTION

I was a child during WWII and the war dominated our lives. Family members served in the Army or Navy. We followed the faraway course of the fighting in huge black newspaper headlines. Food and gasoline were rationed. We bought war bonds and grew Victory gardens and collected scrap iron. Everything was spoken of in terms of the duration. To a child, the duration was all we knew. We grieved when the lights went out in Paris and when the Luftwaffe bombed England.

The war remained vivid in my memory and, as an adult, I wrote several WWII suspense novels including *Escape from Paris*, the story of two American sisters who risk their lives to rescue British airmen, and *Brave Hearts*, which chronicles the courageous efforts of Americans trapped in the Philippines after the Japanese invasion. Both novels are forthcoming from Seventh Street Books in Summer 2013.

Escape from Paris was originally published in a much shorter version in 1982 and 1983. To sell the book, I had to cut forty thousand words. To my great delight, Seventh Street Books is publishing the original uncut manuscript, which has a newly amended 2013 copyright. It has been thirty years in coming, but now *Escape from Paris* is available as it was written.

I hope readers will share the struggles of brave men and women who defied the Gestapo during the bitter winter of 1940. They knew fear, found love, grieved loss. Their lives and deaths remind us that freedom survives only when the free are brave.

Carolyn Hart

NINETEEN-FORTY

Thursday morning
March 7

He sat alone in his office, his massive shoulders leaning forward, his withered legs covered by an afghan. Slowly, mechanically, he fit a cigarette into the holder, lifted it to his mouth. As he drew the silvery trail of smoke into his lungs, he coughed, the persistent cough of the bronchitic. His pale blue eyes moved from the papers in his hand to the map spread out on his desk. The map was blue, too, the awesome immense blue of the Pacific Ocean. A cluster of silver markers represented the American Western Fleet at its home base of San Diego, Calif. His gaze moved across the map. Other occasional markers represented American ships now at Wake, Guam or Midway, but, in the vastness of the mid-pacific, there was nothing to meet the Japanese immediately should they dare to attack Manila or Hong Kong or the Dutch East Indies as many Far Eastern experts feared.

Roosevelt looked again at San Diego harbor. Taking a red pencil in hand, he scored a direct line from San Diego to Pearl Harbor, Oahu, Hawaii.

Saturday afternoon
April 20

"Oh, Harry, the war's just a joke! Hitler's got what he wanted. Nothing else is going to happen. Why don't you stop taking that gas mask with you? No one else carries them now and you look such a fool."

He moved heavily for he was past his youth, a middle-aged plumpish bank clerk who had waited late to marry and chosen a coquettish ill-tempered girl twenty years his junior. She had snatched him up for he was a social cut above her, but now she was bored and the tight sharp lines beside her mouth grooved deeper every year.

Harry Carlisle stolidly buckled on his gas mask. It was regulations to wear it and it would be a fine thing if the block warden didn't set the example.

Her voice, higher, shriller, followed him down the spotless walk, past the rosebushes he treasured. Time now to spray or the aphids would be doing their work. The aphids were mixed up in his mind with the Germans and the sound of Janet's voice. If there had been children . . .

He opened the gate. She followed him down the walk.

". . . bunch of doddering old men . . ."

He clenched his jaw and kept on walking.

". . . making themselves out to be soldiers and wardens and all those fancy titles and you won't even take time to get out now for a bit of cards. And this silly stupid phony war, that's what they're calling it, I read it in the Daily News, the phony war, it's closed everything down and there never was any fun in this town anyway! I wish we'd never come here."

He lowered his head and walked up the lane, the sweet chill rush of an April breeze cooling the flush in his cheeks. He could still hear Janet.

"Even if there is war, it won't come here. Nothing ever happens in Coventry. And nothing ever will happen in Coventry."

Tuesday morning
May 14

"Boys, I want you to promise that you won't go outside!"

They stared at their grandfather. Jan was blond and blunt-faced like his father. Dirk was small and slight and dark, like his mother.

"Promise me now, boys!" His voice was high with strain. He had huddled near the stairwell with his grandsons since the bombing began shortly after dawn. Radio Rotterdam announced that German warplanes were attacking. All civilians were warned to take cover and all soldiers ordered to join their units.

Jan kept darting to an upstairs window, wriggling away from his grandfather's staying hand.

"Oh, Dirk, the sky is full of them, black planes and silver ones and you can see the bombs falling like black fish."

"Jan, come back down those stairs immediately!"

Just before noon, a piercing shrill whistle shocked them into stiff silence, then Grandfather Groeneveld pulled both boys to him and pressed them against the stairwell wall, shielding them with his body. The explosion rocked their house. Glass splintered and tables shook. A thick grayish dust sifted through the rooms.

The three of them edged to the front window, its glass shattered now and the white lace curtains shredded. Oh, Dirk thought, wouldn't his mother be mad! They looked across the street.

The chimney of the Veelen house stood in a shallow crater. A tongue of fire flickered then whooshed into a fan of flame as a gas line ignited.

Dirk stared at the crater solemnly. Mrs. Veelen always gave him a pastry when he went to play with Conrad. If she and Conrad and Corrie were in the house when the bomb struck . . . His face furrowed.

"Come back now boys, away from the window."

It was one o'clock when the radio announced that the main hospital had been struck. The extent of damage and the number injured were unknown.

It was then that their grandfather, gray faced, his hands trembling, had warned them to stay in the house. He had to go. Their mother, his daughter, was a nurse at the hospital.

Wave after wave of bombers swept over Rotterdam, the bombs falling so fast, the explosions coming so thickly that thunder merged into thunder. Once again, the shrill high piercing whistle warned them a bomb was coming near.

The house shook again. A picture of the Maas River that hung against the wainscoting in the hall tipped suddenly sideways then fell, crashing heavily against the floor.

Jan jumped up. "Dirk, you stay here. I'm going to go down to the fire station. I can help."

Dirk tried to grab his older brother's hand. He did slow him, but Jan was almost fifteen and big for his age, broad-shouldered, strong. He shook Dirk off. "I tell you, Dirk, you stay here. I've got to go and help."

Dirk stood in the empty hallway. He almost darted out the door after his brother, then, again, he heard the pulsating roar of planes, hundreds and hundreds of planes. He turned around, ran frantically upstairs to the window of his room that overlooked the street.

Jan was almost at the end of the block.

"Jan! Jan, come back!"

The roar of the planes drowned his voice. Above the rumble of engines and crump, crump, crump of faraway bombs, Dirk heard a rattling pinging metallic clatter. Little puffs of dust rose in a line down the street. Jan stumbled. The dusty line of the machine gun bullets picked up beyond him. He lay face down, unmoving. Even from where Dirk clung to the second-story window ledge, he could see the stitching of blood across his brother's back.

The Germans. That was what the radio had said. Why did the Germans want to shoot Jan?

Friday evening
June 14

It was a small collection of vehicles. Not nearly large enough to be called a convoy, about twenty men in five light vehicles with only machine guns for armaments. The dusty cars reached Paris in the early evening and drove directly to the Hotel du Louvre. The officers had maps. They knew their way. There was no hesitation. The officer in charge, Helmuth Knocken, was a thirty-year-old athletic university graduate who had gotten into police work almost by accident. He had dabbled in journalism first. He ordered the files carried in, oversaw the setting up of a makeshift office. It was a small group of men, wearing the uniforms of the Geheime Feld Polizei, the secret military police, instead of their regular black SS uniforms, which would have revealed them as members of the Geheime Staats Polizei, the state secret police. Or, as it was usually called, the Gestapo.

Knocken's first act, the next morning, was to send one of his men to the French Prefecture to demand the dossiers of all German emigres and Jews.

Monday morning
October 28

Marie Rothchild set the delicate china pot on the tray, arranged the napkin and salt and pepper shakers. It wasn't the kind of breakfast that she used to fix Max, savory rolls with raspberry jam or strawberry preserves and thick sweet chocolate, but she could still bring him a cheerful immaculate tray even if the coffee was ersazt and the bread a dry piece spread with a thin, thin layer of honey. She did have a precious egg for him this morning. She went through the living room and put the tray down for a moment to pick up the newspaper that her maid had bought at a news stand on her way to the apartment. She sighed, thinking about Berthe. How they could afford to keep her since their expenses had risen so drastically, as had everyone's with the desperate necessity to spend so much just to get a modicum of food? But Berthe had been with them so many years and she was old and had no. . . .

The darkness of the type caught her gaze and the headline. Marie stopped and held the paper close to her near-sighted eyes.

STATUT DE JUIFS

Law about Jews . . . but what on earth . . . her hands began to shake . . . the Vichy proclamation . . . a Jew was a man with three Jewish grandparents or two Jewish grandparents and a Jewish wife . . . her eyes skimmed frantically ahead . . . barred from all government jobs . . . must resign in two months if a teacher . . . oh my God, a teacher . . . or employed in press, radio or cinema . . .

The dainty breakfast tray forgotten, Marie began to run heavily across the living room. She knocked against the end table by the sofa and a Meissen bowl slid and began to fall.

"Max!" her voice was high and frightened, like a child's. "Max, look what they've done!"

He caught her in his arms at the door to their bedroom.

"Marie, what is it? What's happened?"

She held the paper out to him and tears began to stream down her face. "It isn't even the Germans, Max. It's our own government. Oh Max, what is going to happen to us?"

Tuesday evening
October 29

The correspondent waited beside the potted palm at the entrance to the Raffles Hotel Bar. The bar was crowded but then it was always crowded between 5 to 8:30 p.m. That was pahit time, happy hour, and everybody had a gimlet or a stangah and maybe two or three. Many of the men were already in white dinner jackets. You didn't drink or dine or dance at Raffles without coat and tie or a uniform. The correspondent lit another cigarette. He looked sleepily around. He was the only man in a suit. Be damned if he'd wear a dinner jacket. Then he spotted Maj. Caldwell striding toward him. They had to wait a few minutes before there was an open place at the bar. Major Caldwell led the way.

"What would you like, Peterson?"

"Whiskey."

The major jerked his head at the Malay bartender. "Boy, satu whiskey ayer and satu gin. *Lehas*!" He turned toward the reporter. "Well, Peterson, tonight I'd like to get to know you better."

The correspondent nodded and took a long drink.

"Seems that last article you wrote was a bit short on facts."

Peterson smiled his sleepy smile. So that was why the major had invited him out for a drink.

"The one about preparation for war ... or the lack of them?" he asked silkily.

The major's face stiffened. "That one. Lot of damnfoolery there, Peterson."

The correspondent looked lazily around the bar. There was a loud hum of conversation now, a lot of well-bred laughter, a sense of ease and comfort. "Doesn't look like a war footing around here, does it?"

The major slammed his hand on the bar. "We don't need a war footing. The Japs would be fools to try and invade Malaya."

The reporter's tone was mild. "China is crumbling. The Japanese are moving into Indo-China. It's only a matter of time until they move on the Dutch East Indies."

"Let them fight in China. Let the little brown men fight each other. Those Japanese beggars won't attack us. Or if they do, they'll learn a thing or two. They haven't fought Europeans yet."

"You don't think there's any danger to Singapore?"

"Of course not. You newspaper johnnies worry too much. After all, everyone knows Singapore's impregnable. Singapore will never fall."

Sunday afternoon
November 3

She felt a little catch in her chest. It was not the first time. Perhaps she should mention it to Dr. Friedheim. But there was no hurry. Such a lovely afternoon. Not lovely outside, of course. A nasty raw rainy day. But what could you expect in November? Here, in the drawing room, it was so cheerful. Herr Weiss was going to play the piano. She had known him for so many years. He still seemed a youngster to her though none of them were youngsters now. It was hard to believe she had been eighty on her last birthday. Eighty years old. She was so lucky. Her pension from the Berlin Opera and this lovely old folks home to live in here in Mannheim. Everyone was so nice to her. Just yesterday one of the visiting doctors had held her hand and said, "Fraulein Selig, I remember you so well in the role of Erda in *Das Rhinegold*. Such a magnificent voice you had."

Well, her voice had been magnificent. A rich soaring contralto. In her mind she sang again and she could see herself standing on the stage. That last time, that very last time, the entire house had stood and applauded her. She began to smile.

The glass shattered in the French windows that opened onto the rose garden.

Fraulein Selig gasped and clutched her chest.

It all happened so quickly amid the tears and the shouts and the screams, the hard faced soldiers prodding the old people out into the rain toward the waiting line of open trucks.

"Men this way. Women that way."

The Levys clung to each other. Last week they had celebrated their fiftieth anniversary. He was patting his wife on the arm. "Don't cry, Sarah, don't. We must all be going to the same place. I will see you there." But she had clung to him, sobbing and screaming until one of the guards pulled her away, flung her toward their truck.

When they reached the railroad station, Fraulein Selig tried to help look for the trucks with the men. She was taller than tiny Frau Levy, could see farther. Only women stumbled from the trucks lined up by the tracks. The last of the trucks pulled away. They must have taken the men somewhere else. Then soldiers herded them up ramps into open cattle cars. She helped Sarah Levy, kept her from losing her balance. Crushed into the boxcar, they huddled together and late that night the trains began to roll.

"Where are we going?" One of the old ladies cried out into the night.

No one answered.

It took four days to reach the French border. The word rippled through the boxcars from lip to lip.

"France. They've taken us to France. It will be better here. They say we are going to a relocation camp in France."

It was raining again and cold, bitter cold, with the rain sweeping down with the wind off the Pyrenees when the train pulled into the little town of Pau. The train backed up behind another train. Each had a long, long string of boxcars packed with German Jews.

Men. Women. Children.

It was a long wait in the open unheated wet cattle cars before the trucks pulled through the mud to the car holding Fraulein Selig.

"It will be better," one of the old women said, "when we reach the camp."

The road, slick gray clay, snaked up away from the village to a vast swampy plain with the Pyrenees towering above.

The truck slithered through the gate in the first barbed wire fence, then past the second barbed wire fence. Soldiers patrolled between the fences. More soldiers peered down from a dozen round wooden watchtowers. They had to climb down from the trucks and walk across a thick sea of mud toward the barracks. Row after row of low wooden barracks stretched across the muddy plain. Mud pulled at Fraulein Selig, clung to her shoes. Oh, her nice shoes. Her finest shoes. She tottered, would have fallen but Frau Levy caught her arm.

They stopped in front of the barracks that would be their new home. Women's Barrack 17. It was built of uncured lumber that had already warped in the continuing rains. There were no windows, no paint. The shrinkage had left cracks big enough to put your fist through.

The matron of the nursing home looked at the barracks in despair. No heat. No water. No beds. No bedding. It took all of her will to turn and face her old people. "Come in . . . come in. This is where . . . we've been put."

Fraulein Selig was bewildered. Everyone had said it would be better because it was in France. The French didn't hate Jews. She knew that. She had sung in Paris many times. Many times. She looked back at the trucks turning on the road to return to the village. Why, they couldn't go away and leave them here. It was barbarous. There must be some mistake!

It was hard to get to sleep that first night. She was cold, so cold.

She and Frau Levy hugged one another but still they shook most of the night. The rain and the wind didn't stop. It rained and rained. Every day it was harder to cross the thick slimy glutinous stretch of mud to the crude shacks that served as latrines. The steps leading up to the latrines were steep and slick and there was no handrail.

Her chest ached all of the time now and her fine hair, her hair that had always been so thick and golden and she had worn it piled high on her head, her hair hung lank and tangled. The mud pulled at her, clung to each shoe, her big frame straining with effort. She reached the steep uneven wooden steps and started up. She slipped on the third step. Her hands reached out but there was nothing to grab, nothing to stop her. She struck the bottom step as she fell. Pain exploded in her right hip.

Two of the guards did carry her back to Barrack 17. She lay in the corner near the door, unrecognizable with mud streaked over her, even her hair thick with mud.

The matron tried to help her, tried to move her gently, but the pain was too bad and she fell back on the wooden floor. Dimly, she heard the matron arguing with a guard.

"We have to have a doctor. Her hip is broken. It's broken, I tell you!"

Fraulein Selig turned her face toward the wall so the matron wouldn't see her tears. It hurt so badly and she had relieved herself in her clothes and now she was all dirty, so dirty, and her hip hurt so badly . . .

Wednesday morning
December 25

The posters had been put up on Christmas Eve. On Christmas morning the placards were everywhere for early morning churchgoers to read.

ENGINEER JACQUES BONSERGENT OF PARIS HAS BEEN CONDEMNED TO DEATH AND SHOT FOR A DEED OF VIOLENCE AGAINST A MEMBER OF THE GERMAN ARMED FORCES.

Wednesday afternoon
December 25

The boxcars had been shunted off onto a side line two days ago. Only priority goods moved on Christmas Eve or Christmas Day. A skeleton staff stood on duty and the bleak railroad yards were almost silent.

Hans Krueger shivered in his thick overcoat. Lousy luck he had to draw this watch on Christmas Day. Oh well, there would still be plenty of good food when he got back to the barracks. He turned, began the long lonely walk back along the side of the train. The wind gusted suddenly and he gasped. God, what an awful smell! He walked a little faster. The rank odor was what happened with people jammed in the cars like animals with no toilets, nothing. But it wasn't his doing. He felt eyes on him as he walked but he looked straight ahead. That was the only thing that kept them alive, the fact that there were so many of them and they huddled close together like cows for a little bit of warmth. Some were dead, frozen into stiff, hard, brittle clumps. He'd seen one car yesterday with a half dozen frozen bodies in one corner. After that, he knew to keep his eyes straight ahead. It was uncanny how quiet they were, hardly a sound, only the scuff of his boots through the cinders and the icy remnants of snow.

He was almost at the end of the train when he paused, unsnapped his canteen and lifted it to his mouth.

"*Bitte, wasser*. Oh *bitte, bitte.*"

Hans stepped closer, the uncapped canteen in his hand.

Two dark eyes peered out at him.

There was a rustle and a stir within the boxcar. Suddenly a dozen, twenty small faces looked out at him and there was a sound of sighing and hesitant whispers for water.

He was lifting his canteen toward the outstretched hand when a voice shouted behind him.

"Krueger!"

He swung around.

The sergeant major gestured roughly for him to come back up the line. "*Nein*, Krueger, *nein. Juden.*"

Tuesday night
December 31

Rick Stoddard leaned up against the bar and listened to the melodic Hawaiian music. Damn, this was the life. Beautiful girls everywhere, the greatest beaches in the world, shore leave almost every weekend.

He took a deep swallow of his beer. "Hey Al, you gonna re-up?"

Al shrugged. "Maybe. How about you?"

Rick tilted up the bottle, finished the beer and ordered another. He was nineteen but he tried to sound worldly, "The Oklahoma's an all right ship."

"Yeah."

"The Old Man's decent. We get shore leave every weekend when we're in port."

"Pearl's a pretty easy berth," Al agreed.

"That's what I think. Yeah," he said decisively, "That's my New Year's resolution. I'm gonna re-up."

CHAPTER 1

Linda handed her papers to the sergeant. Her hands shook a little but he didn't seem to notice. Perhaps he was used to shaking hands. He read the passes which permitted her to drive, to purchase 10 gallons of gasoline a week and to visit hospitals in a 75-mile radius of Paris on behalf of the Foyer du Soldat.

Linda was ready to explain why it was she and not her sister Eleanor making the visit today, but he didn't ask. He merely nodded, handed the papers back and said, in his heavily accented French, "You may proceed, Mademoiselle."

The sentry pacing back and forth between the hospital gate posts stood aside for the little car to enter.

Linda slowly drove around the side of the hospital, trying, if she would admit it, to put off for another few minutes her entry into the hospital. She had not wanted to come. It was Eleanor who visited hospitals daily, taking Red Cross packages to wounded soldiers and airmen. Eleanor kept hoping, of course, that she would find some trace of her husband. Andre had been missing since Dunkirk.

Today's visit to Douellens had been scheduled for a week or more. When Eleanor was up all night with a toothache, Linda volunteered to go in her place. Linda hated sickness—and wounds—and hospitals—and she was dreadfully afraid of the Germans.

She drove slowly around the west wing to park in the shadow of a huge oak, just opposite a row of bins that marked the kitchen hospital. Linda reluctantly got out of the car. Opening the trunk, she lifted out a picnic hamper filled with small boxes, fifty or more, and walked slowly to the front of the hospital. She climbed broad stone steps into a dirty entry foyer, the marble streaked with grit. The smell in the foyer struck her like a physical blow. She paused for an instant, then, her mouth tight, turned to her left.

"The Commandant's office is just back of the entry foyer," Eleanor had told her. "You must check in there first and show your papers."

A French sergeant perfunctorily looked at her papers.

"Do I just go up and down the halls?" Linda asked uncertainly.

He shrugged, his face weary and bitter. "Do whatever you like, Mademoiselle."

She hesitated for a moment in the main hallway, then stepped into the first ward. She stopped just inside the doorway, appalled. Eleanor had told her the hospitals were overcrowded and understaffed, but she hadn't expected anything like this.

Every inch of space was used, beds jammed so close together there was scarcely room to step between them. The smell of blood, infection, and carbolic acid hung thickly in the steamy air. Linda didn't see a single nurse, only row after row of beds with men lying quietly.

When they saw her, greetings and questions in French spread over the long room like wildfire. "A girl. Look, there's a girl. It must be the Red Cross. Mademoiselle, have you come from Paris?"

She edged her way up and down the rows, answering as well as she could in her far from perfect French, and trying hard not to gasp at the dreadfully maimed. She passed a huge Senegalese soldier, encased in soiled bandages, who writhed in pain, muttering in a language no one could understand. She saw a soldier without a nose, another whose entire face was shrouded in gauze, and so many who were blind.

She walked through two wards, passing out her little packets of cheese, bread, chocolate, and cigarettes. What a useless journey, she thought miserably. Little packets of food for men who needed medicine and clean bandages and good meals. It was worse than useless. It was a mockery of aid. Yet, this hospital was a paradise compared to where most of the men would be sent. As soon as they were well enough, they would be transferred to military prisons.

In the dimly lit hallway, she stood for a long moment, willing herself to enter the next ward. Instead, seeing a splash of sunlight, she turned to her left and went out onto a patio. Ambulatory patients sat passively in the August sunlight. When they saw her, she was instantly surrounded.

Struggling to keep up in her faltering French, she took down name after name and promised to try and get word to families. To at least a half dozen men or more, though, she shook her head. "I'm sorry," she explained over and over, "we can't get word to the Unoccupied Zone. The Germans are not permitting any mail over the frontier."

"Frontier," one of the men repeated harshly.

Frontier. She understood his anger. The conquering Germans had drawn a line across France. On one side, the Germans ruled. On the other, the Vichy government of Marshal Petain ruled. It was now one of the most carefully guarded frontiers in the world. Men died trying to cross it every day and every night. French, English and Canadian soldiers who had escaped the German round-up in the North kept trying to slip across into the Unoccupied Zone in hopes of reaching and crossing the border to Spain. It was easier to get a letter to Minneapolis than to Marseilles.

Linda moved from group to group, taking down names, promising to do her best. Though all of them were hungry to talk to her, each took only a little share of time with a delicacy that touched her.

"Miss . . . Please . . ."

The low whisper came from the shadow of a mimosa. She turned in surprise.

"Are you English?" he asked.

"No. I'm American. Why?"

He brushed back thin fair hair with a hand that trembled ever so slightly. His other hand was swathed in a thick bandage. "I saw you park under the oak tree and you are so fair, I thought you might be English."

"Are you a British soldier?" she whispered.

"Fifth Lancers Corps."

"Why did you ask if I were English?"

He tried to smile. "I thought an Englishwoman might help me escape."

The word hung between them. Nervously, Linda looked around the courtyard but no one was near enough to hear.

He saw the fear in her face. "That's all right," he said quickly and he started to turn away.

"Wait. What do you mean? How could I possibly help you?"

He put a finger to his lips. "I saw your car and I know how it could be done." He explained in hurried jerky phrases.

"Why do you want to escape so badly?" Linda asked nervously.

He held up his bandaged right hand, pulled back the gauze covering. The hand was twisted, the thumb gone, the palm livid with a puckered scar. But it was healed.

He swallowed. "They're taking me to the Citadel Thursday."

The day after tomorrow.

Linda had passed the Citadel, a massive stone prison five miles back toward Paris. She had stopped there this morning and tried to gain entry to give packages to the prisoners of war being held there. The German sentry refused her admittance. She had shown him the permit, signed by the district commander that granted her access to prisons and hospitals to deliver food packages.

"No one enters here without a special pass, Mademoiselle," and she was turned away.

The Citadel was the first stop on the way to prisoner of war camps in Germany. Already, even in mid-August, there were frightful stories being whispered across France about prisoner of war camps in Germany.

Linda stared at the English soldier's drawn face. He was about her age. "All right," she said breathlessly. "I'll help you."

She left him in the shadow of the mimosa tree and circled slowly around the courtyard and went into the East Wing. She didn't think anyone had noticed their talk. After all, she had stopped and talked to so many. That was why she was here. But fear was a hard lump in her chest. She hurried into another ward. She gave away the rest of her boxes and it was time to leave.

In the Commandant's office, the same indifferent sergeant checked her out. She pushed through the main doors and welcomed the heat, the smell of dust and new mown hay and, faintly, lilac. She walked quickly around the side of the hospital to the little car. Swiftly, she looked around. The hospital rose three stories. She stared at the masses of windows with a kind of horror. If anyone looked down when he came . . .

Jerkily, she bent and opened the trunk. It took only a minute or so to take out the empty cartons which had held packets delivered at other stops this morning. She put the cartons in the little back seat then returned to the trunk to push the lid down but, very carefully, not shut it.

She took her place in the driver's seat and waited. She wanted to look over her shoulder toward the kitchen, but she was afraid. Instead she opened her purse and lifted out her cigarette case. She put the cigarette in her mouth and raised her lighter. Her hand was shaking so hard that she couldn't snap the lighter. Calm down, Linda, she warned herself, calm down.

If he didn't hurry, they were going to be caught. That sergeant would walk down the road in a little while to see why she was taking so long. Why didn't the Englishman hurry? Why had she said she would take him? Why had she been such a fool? If the soldiers searched the car at the gate . . . Linda shivered uncontrollably although the late August heat baked the little car, making the leather so hot that her blouse and skirt clung wetly to her. Still she shivered.

She tried again to light the cigarette. The lighter clicked. The pinpoint of flame wavered but she held it to the cigarette, drew deeply. Dear God, why didn't he come?

Her hand reached out, touched the key in the ignition. All she had to do was turn the motor on, put the car in gear and be on her way. She would stop at the gate and show her papers and she wouldn't have to be afraid. The Red Cross pennant on the windshield was her protection.

The pennant wouldn't protect her if they found an English soldier hidden in the trunk.

She turned the key in the ignition. Why should she take such a frightful chance?

The kitchen door squeaked. He dashed across the road, lifted up the trunk lid, rolled inside and pulled it shut after him.

White faced, Linda stubbed out the cigarette. She hunched over the wheel, waiting for a shout, for soldiers to rush toward her.

A wasp buzzed near the window. Far away a dog barked.

Her throat dry, sweat streaming down her face, Linda turned the key and pushed on the accelerator. She backed and turned until the car faced toward the front. She drove slowly, dust rising behind her. Her shoulder muscles were rigid. If anyone had been looking down from a window in the back an alarm would be raised. Surely to God, not every window could have been empty. But those windows belonged to the wards and these were sick and wounded French soldiers, not German.

Still it would take only one voice to stop her and there were many Frenchmen now who hated the English. They heard the German broadcasts blaming the English for the French defeat and believed them. It was easier to blame defeat on others. But the car passed the end of the wing now and no one called out. She drove on to the gate and stopped.

The sergeant stepped out of the sentry box. "Your papers, Mademoiselle."

She opened her straw purse and reached for her identity card and the passes. He had seen all of them earlier but he looked again, reading every one.

She and the sergeant became aware of the smell at the same moment. His nostrils flared and he looked past her, into the car.

The leather seat beside her was empty except for her straw purse. Empty cartons and the picnic basket filled the tiny back seat.

Would he remember the back seat had been empty this morning? She had switched the cartons to make room in the trunk.

The sergeant craned his head to look down at the floor of the back seat. It was the smell, that reek of hospital disinfectant that puzzled him.

The smell clung to the Englishman, the odor of dirt and carbolic acid, and was seeping now from the trunk into the car, worsened by the heat. It would be very hot in the trunk.

The sergeant stared at her right arm.

She looked down and saw the reddish-yellowish streaks on the pale blue cotton.

"You have blood on your dress, Mademoiselle."

"One of the soldiers, he was very ill, and when I tried to help him, I suppose his wound must have been bleeding." Overlaying the smell in the car, she remembered the thick sweet stench from the chest wound of the boy who had lost his brother. "His bandage was old and . . ."

The sergeant wasn't listening. He had satisfied himself about the smell. He closed her papers with a snap and handed them back.

She turned the key, pressed on the accelerator. The engine turned over, once, twice, then died. If the car refused to start altogether, someone might open the trunk. She turned the key again. She excluded everything from her mind, the giveaway smell in the car, the thick suffocating heat as the sun streamed through the windshield, the presence of the sergeant just a foot or so away. She reached out, pulled on the choke button. Just a little. "Don't drown the poor damn car. Just give it a little bit." She could hear Jay's voice, across the years and thousands of miles. Sunshine then, too, but the soft silky sun of California with, always, a touch of coolness beneath the warmth. Jay had taught her how to drive in his old Austin. He had been so proud of that car, the ramrod straight seats, the high roof, the dashboard of tortoise shell. He had shown her, his hand over hers, just how far to pull out the choke, "See, like this, then give the pedal a slow steady push. That's it, that's it, baby, you've got it, hey, you're pretty, you know that?" and his hand had slipped from hers to tilt her face toward him. Sunshine and the smell of roses and her first kiss.

The engine turned over, caught, held, roared, she slammed the car into first and it bolted up the road. She looked in the rearview mirror. The young sentry was watching after her. The sergeant had turned away, to step into the shade of the sentry box.

Linda reached for a cigarette. Funny, she had only smoked occasionally until the Germans occupied Paris. Now that cigarettes were so hard to get, she smoked more and more. Maybe she smoked because she was afraid. She drew deeply on the cigarette. Afraid. Yes. She was afraid but she couldn't admit her fear to Eleanor or Robert. She couldn't tell them because Eleanor already wanted her to go home to America. "Not unless you are coming, too," she told her sister.

Eleanor had shaken her head. It wasn't only that France had been her home since her marriage sixteen years before. It was more than that. She couldn't leave Paris when she had no word from her husband since Dunkirk, and, even if the Germans would permit her to go, they might not be willing to let Robert leave. It was very hard to get permission to leave France now.

Most Americans had left during the year of the phony war and many who had stayed late fled when the Blitzkrieg began in May. There were only a handful of Americans left in Paris.

If Eleanor would agree to leave . . . Linda drew hard on the cigarette. But Eleanor was determined to stay.

The military hospital was out of sight now. Over the next hill lay the Citadel. There would be another stop there, to have her papers checked. If anyone ordered her to open the trunk . . . Her hand trembled and she stubbed out the cigarette.

"I say!"

The wheel jerked a little under her hands. The car swerved but she brought it straight again. There wasn't any traffic to worry about. No one had cars but Germans and their Vichy friends. The Frenchmen walking along the road, scythes over their shoulders, turned hard faces toward her car until they saw the Red Cross flag. She waited until she was past the workers to answer.

"Yes."

"Sorry. I didn't mean to startle you."

"That's okay. Are you all right back there? It's so small."

"Fine, thanks." His voice was muffled but cheerful. "How far are we?"

She realized he wouldn't have any idea how many miles it was to Paris. "About seventy-five miles. But there isn't any traffic." The road began a gradual climb. She could just glimpse the Citadel through the line of poplar trees to her left. "We'll be slowing down in a few minutes. A roadblock."

"Roadblock?"

"Don't worry. It's just to check papers. There are five or six of them ahead."

Not to worry. Unless, of course, they were unlucky. An officious sentry . . . But it was late afternoon now and hot, nearing time for guards to change. They would be thinking of cold beer and food. Why should anyone pay much attention to her?

"Look," and the muffled voice was serious now, almost harsh, "If anyone, you know, makes you open the trunk, if they search the car, well, you just give a little scream, you know, you are absolutely surprised and I'll say I sneaked into the trunk, hid myself."

She blew out a soft little spurt of air. That wouldn't save her. But there wasn't any point in telling him so.

"Okay," she said quietly, "I'll remember. Don't worry. We'll be all right."

"Right-oh. I just meant, well, in case."

The road swung in an arc around the great stone pile that was the Citadel and she spoke quickly now. "Don't say anything again until I knock twice, like this," and she thumped the metal on the dash. She pulled up even with the sentry box.

The guard looked perfunctorily in the backseat, riffled through her papers then returned them.

One down, she thought, as the car picked up speed again. She thumped the dash.

"I say, uh, what's your name?" His voice seemed so young.

"Linda. Linda Rossiter."

"I'm Michael Evans."

"Hello, Michael."

"Hello, Linda." He paused. "That's a pretty name, Linda. You're an American, you say."

"Yes."

"Well, what . . . I mean, how do you happen to be here, in France?"

Linda drove slowly, carefully, and tried to explain. "Last year, just before Christmas, my parents were killed in a plane crash. They were flying up to my college to pick me up for the holidays."

"Oh, I say, I'm so sorry." And she knew he was sorry, that even now when death was everywhere, he had a moment to share her grief.

"Thank you." Linda swallowed. It was still hard for her to talk about that hideous end to her happiest years. "I couldn't go back to school like nothing had happened. My older sister, Eleanor, is married to a Frenchman. She came home to California for the funeral and I came back to France with them."

"Why are you still here?"

"It was just the phony war then and when everything happened so suddenly last spring, I didn't want to leave Eleanor. When Andre didn't come back, he was at Dunkirk, I didn't feel like I could leave."

"Oh, yes. I understand that. So you live in Paris with your sister?"

"Yes, with Eleanor and her son, Robert."

They rode in silence for awhile.

"I say," Michael asked uneasily, "do you suppose she'll mind you bringing me there?"

CHAPTER 2

Major Erich Krause paused long enough in the magnificently decorated lobby to look at his reflection in the ornate mirrors. The death's head on his black cap glittered in the light from the chandeliers. His black boots glistened with polish and his SS uniform, black as death, fit perfectly. He permitted a rare smile that stretched his grayish lips back over yellowed sharp teeth. He nodded shortly at Sgt. Schmidt.

Sgt. Schmidt jumped and stood stiffly at attention.

Krause went into his office, a rare feeling of good humor twisting his mouth into a brief smile. He hung his cap on a coat tree, crossed to his desk. His desk, Erich H. Krause's desk. He'd come a long way since the miserable days during the Great War when he'd been a gassed corporal, struggling back to Germany after the Armistice. Corporals were doing well these days. His smile broadened.

Then he saw the sheet of blue paper slewed almost carelessly in the center of his smooth and bare desk.

He never left loose papers about. Krause frowned. He picked up the blue sheet with a newspaper clipping attached. As he read, his hand began to shake, ever so slightly, until he willed it to be still. His face reddened. A vein pulsed in his forehead. He read the message again: Slackness won't be tolerated. Remedy this.

The insolent scrawl angled across the page. A thick-bodied signature dominated the flimsy sheet. Despite his will, Krause's hand shook again. Helmuth Knocken, chief of the Gestapo in France, second only in power to Heydrich. Knocken had direct access to Hitler. If he thought a man wasn't doing his job, that man didn't have long to live.

The reddish flush died away, leaving Krause's face a sickly white.

He reached down, jammed his finger against the buzzer on his desk.

Sgt. Schmidt came immediately. "Sir."

"Who wrote this article?"

Schmidt looked blank. "It was in the Paris Soir. I saw it yesterday."

"You didn't mention it to me."

Sgt. Schmidt swallowed. He hadn't dared. He knew Krause's temper.

Krause stared at him and, once again, a vein throbbed in his forehead. "You should have told me. You should have told me," and his voice rose to a shout.

Schmidt waited miserably. "I didn't know," he began. Then he said desperately, "I thought it was all a lie."

Krause's ice-green eyes looked down at the clipping. It was all the fault of the clipping.

RAF FLIERS CONTINUE TO ESCAPE

Local authorities in Northern France report a puzzle: RAF pilots daily bail out of damaged aircraft yet German soldiers have captured only three fliers in the past two weeks.

"It is clear," Capt. Bruno Walther, Fifth Army Group, announced Wednesday, "that French civilians are hiding pilots and smuggling them south."

The captain concluded that stricter penalties soon to be enforced will encourage civilians to surrender downed fliers.

Capt. Walther accounted for the disparity in the number of pilots shot down and the number captured by pointing out that once a pilot is picked up and hidden by civilians, it is no longer a military function to discover him, but a duty of the police.

Krause's eyes moved back to Knocken's terse message: Slackness won't be tolerated. Remedy this.

As if he was slack. He worked long hours and he had so many responsibilities, rounding up Jewish emigres, searching out the authors of the new and scurrilous newsletters being published undercover in Paris, hunting for British airmen who should have the decency to be prisoners of war.

He would make sure Knocken had no reason to accuse him of slackness. "Schmidt!"

The sergeant stiffened, then realized with relief that Krause's anger was no longer directed at him. "Sir."

"Establish a permanent checkpoint at the Gare du Nord. The papers of every man of military age must be checked. If there is anything suspicious, accent, clothing, a group of young men traveling together, pick them up." He paused, "Prepare a report for Obersturmfuehrer Knocken on our continuing investigation into the smuggling of British soldiers. Tell him that we are sending out Gestapo agents, who speak English, in captured RAF uniforms. We will soon put a stop to all this smuggling and the damned French will pay for their double-dealing."

The sun shone across the English Channel, too. Picnic weather. Not this August. Jonathan Harris sprawled in the shade of the dispersal tent, drinking a cup of tea but he lay tensely, waiting. The field telephone rang. "Scramble," Squadron Leader Mitchell shouted. "Seventy-plus, angels one-six."

Jonathan and the other pilots jumped up and ran toward the waiting ranks of Hurricanes. He led the dash for the planes, calling over his shoulder to his best friend, Reggie Howard, "Hey Reggie, follow me. I'll show you how it's done." Reggie had shot down three Heinkels the day before. He grinned as he ran past to his plane.

The Hurricanes took off, one after the other, as fast as they could clear the airstrip. But the warning hadn't come in time. The last plane was just airborne when Squadron Leader Mitchell called, "Bandits . . . bandits, 80-plus. Angels one-seven, three o'clock."

The Messerschmitts, slanting out of the early morning sun, peeled down from 17,000 feet onto the hapless Hurricanes.

Jonathan Harris was in the third Hurricane up. He climbed as fast as he could, then at the last possible instant, dived in a tight circle. The ME-110 bearing down on him overshot. For a brief mind-searing instant, Jonathan's Hurricane roared at tree-top level toward an orchard. Jonathan saw the trees in a blur. If the plane didn't lift now, it would be too late. He pulled on the stick with all his strength. He smelled oil and exhaust fumes, heard the squeal of the engine. Abruptly, the nose pulled up and he was climbing. Planes broke away from each other, streaking wildly across the sky, as formless as scattered marbles.

To Jonathan's left, a yellow-nosed ME110 stalked a Hurricane. He turned. Now the sun was behind him. He flew down. Closer, closer, close enough. His gloved thumb pressed the red button in the center of the control column. Bullets curved in a broken white line. The ME110 exploded. Jonathan immediately pulled up, higher, higher. His head swung violently right and left. Was anyone behind him? Anyone? Anywhere?

Another ME110 slipped away beneath him. He veered, was turning to follow when he heard Jimmy Kinkaid shout, "Reggie, Reggie! Bandit . . . six o'clock."

Jonathan looked through the windscreen at Reggie's plane. It didn't take more than eight seconds to happen. The ME110 was already firing. Jonathan had time to think how much the stream of tracer bullets looked like confetti and to see the ragged series of black holes in the fuselage of Reggie's Hurricane before flames puffed up behind the engine. For an instant, there was a thin wavering line of fire, no stronger or wilder than flickering flame in a fireplace. For an instant. Until the petrol tanks exploded and a searing roiling sheet of yellow flame enveloped the entire Hurricane. The plane's metal was dark inside the flames and, dimly, horribly, Reggie shriveled into a blackened mass.

"Reggie . . . Oh Jesus . . ." Jimmy Kinkaid's Hurricane wavered, turned toward the molten fiery tangle of wreckage as the wreckage plummeted mindlessly down. Then the sky was empty of battle, the Messerschmitts pulling away over the gray-blue waters of the Channel, the Hurricanes swinging homeward.

That was the first scramble.

The second sounded at eleven. Kendrick had to ditch in the Channel but he was picked up by a motor launch. Freeman and Croft were killed.

Now they waited again, sprawled in the sun around the dispersal tent. Jonathan finished his tea. He didn't want any bread and jam. Instead, he looked worriedly at Jimmy Kinkaid. Jimmy's mug sat beside him, ignored. Jimmy lay on the ground staring upward, his young face slack and puddly like an old man's.

Jonathan reached into his tunic pocket and pulled out a packet of Players. He fumbled for a minute in his trouser pocket then walked over to Jimmy. "Got a light, Jimmy?"

Jimmy looked up blankly. For a long moment his eyes were unfocussed, then he reached into his jacket, found a lighter and held it out to Jonathan.

Jonathan lit the cigarette. "Thanks."

Jimmy put the lighter back in his pocket.

"What are you doing tonight?" Jonathan asked.

"Tonight?" Jimmy repeated it like a word in a foreign language.

"Porter's taking a car up to London. There's a new band at the Bag O'Nails. It should be quite a bit of fun."

Jimmy Kinkaid looked beyond Jonathan, looked back up into the shimmering blue sky. "Reggie always sat across from me in the mess. Freeman sat on my left."

A prickle of cold moved down Jonathan's back.

Jimmy Kinkaid looked at him now, his eyes wild. "Croft sat on my right. What does that tell you?"

"Not a bloody thing except you're talking like a fool. Like an old woman looking at tea leaves. That's bloody stupid for a man who has to take a plane up any . . ."

The ring of the field telephone turned every face. Squadron Leader Mitchell answered, listened for an instant, shouted to the tense waiting flyers, "Scramble. Seventy-plus, angels one-six," and they were running, all of them, toward the waiting ranks of Hurricanes.

Jonathan reached his ship, the Mad Monk. Right foot into the stirrup step, left foot on the port wing, a short step, then right foot on the step inset in the fuselage and into the cockpit. His rigger, Alfie, passed the parachute straps across his shoulders, then the Sutton harness straps. Jonathan clipped on his mask, slid shut the canopy, gave the thumbs up signal to the ground crew and they pulled away the chocks. Jonathan's was the fourth plane to lift off from Hawkinge Field and turn up and out over the blue-gray waters of the Channel. Up, up, up. As they climbed he scanned his horizon, his eyes flickering back and forth and up, always up. He had learned that. Every flyer still alive had learned that. They hadn't known at first, hadn't realized what an advantage height and sun could be. It didn't take long to learn. They lost six planes on one day in July when the ME's came down out of the sun. They learned, too, that their tight wingtip to wingtip formation was suicidal. They were so busy watching their mates, keeping five feet apart in an air show V, that loosely bunched Messerschmitts ticked them off like ducks in a shooting gallery. Now they fanned out in fours like fingers on an outstretched hand.

The cockpit was hot and stuffy. Jonathan slid the canopy open and welcomed the cool rush of air. The sun hung in the Western sky. If they climbed high enough, fast enough, the sun would be behind the squadron. Then, out of the East, he saw the Germans. Fine black specks came clearer and closer. Now they hurtled through the sky beneath him, coming to be killed, oh hell, yes. Come on now, come on, you bastards. The sky filled with planes, lumbering Heinkels with their bombloads ticketed for the coastal airfields and, above, guarding them, black and dangerous, ME109s.

He saw, out of the corner of his eyes, a flight of Spitfires. Good enough. The Hurricanes would go after the Heinkels, easy meat, while the faster, more maneuverable Spitfires took on the quick and lethal ME's.

Jonathan curved down toward the spreading mass of Heinkels, choosing his prey. Suddenly planes began to climb, fall or twist. There was no form or order left as each pilot fought to survive. Jonathan swerved left, dipping nearer and nearer, then he pressed the firing button and watched bullets stitch across the belly of the Heinkel. The plane flew on for a moment longer then slowly rolled on its side, and, lazily, as if it didn't matter very much, the bomber turned over and slipped sideways down toward the water.

The sharply blue sky was marked with ragged trails of white, curves and curls and swirls of contrails, a ghostly fast fading imprint of the battle, still existing when some of the men who made those trails were already dead.

One Heinkel down, two down. Jonathan talked to himself, shouted when he saw Brewster make a hit. As he climbed up again, searching for another Heinkel, the thick nose of a Messerschmitt sliced by him. Jonathan craned his head to the left. There was no time to radio, no time to shout a warning, scarcely time to see as the ME109 bore down on a Hurricane, machine guns rattling. Jonathan saw, above the Hurricane's wing, the cavorting mouse, Miss Minnie, and knew it for Jimmy Kinkaid's plane even as the ME109's cannon shell struck the cockpit and the Hurricane disintegrated.

Jonathan swung around behind the ME109, dropping just beneath the German's altitude as the plane turned toward France. He hung there grimly, stubbornly, knowing the Messerschmitt was faster, that ultimately he would fall farther and farther behind. But still he pursued. If he could get just a little closer, he would blow him out of the sky. Fritz didn't know anyone was behind him as Jonathan flew in the blind pocket formed by the Messerschmitt's tail unit. If the Kraut slowed down a little bit . . . Then, grimly, Jonathan smiled. A dark slow sludge of oil moved along the belly of the plane. Yes, Fritz was going to slow down. It wouldn't be long. The stain of oil widened, spread, and the Messerschmitt's engine began to smoke.

Jonathan had no thought for anything in the world but the sleek black plane ahead of him. He was gaining on his prey, slowly, ever so slowly. Two hundred yards. One hundred and fifty yards. One hundred yards. His thumb cupped over the firing button. Not yet. Not quite yet.

One instant they flew, pursued and pursuer, almost level, the sturdy Hurricane just below the Messerschmitt, drawing nearer and nearer. The next, the ME109 abruptly slipped sideways. Jonathan, startled, did not follow quite soon enough. The 109 jinked back toward him. He had been spotted. He didn't hear the sound of the Messerschmitt's machine guns but he heard metallic pings against his engine plating. He dropped sideways, trying desperately to regain the offensive. The next few seconds were a whirling buffeting blur, then, straight ahead, he saw the profile of the Messerschmitt. His thumb pressed the firing button.

The Messerschmitt bucked upward, for an instant pointed straight at the sky, almost standing on its tail, before the plane fell backward, streaking flame and smoke.

Jonathan tried to level out. His altimeter wasn't registering. Coils of icy gray smoke swirled from the engine. The white fog thickened. He couldn't see. He released his harness, pushed back the canopy and rolled the Hurricane on her back. He gave himself a shove. As he fell free of the smoking directionless plane, he realized there was something wrong with his left leg. Tumbling backward, he gave a hard yank at the ripcord. It was slack in his hand.

"No. No." He heard his own voice, shouting angrily through the rush of air, then painfully, gloriously, the chute snapped open, jerking him to a swaying rhythmic descent. His leg felt heavy and immovable. Blood was seeping through his trousers. He started at the dark red splotch, puzzled. He hadn't felt a thing, but he was hurt. At least it was a slow ooze of blood, not the swift deadly gush of a severed artery. Gingerly, he tried to move the leg. Pain, for the first time, flamed the length of it. Well, if he didn't bleed to death, he should be all right—if he could inflate his Mae West. He looked down. For an instant, what he saw made no sense at all.

He had begun pursuing the ME109 over the Channel. From that moment on, he had concentrated totally on staying in the invisible pocket just below his prey. Abruptly, Jonathan understood. The 109 had turned for its home base, Jonathan following. Now, instead of the cold blue-gray choppy waters of the Channel below him, Jonathan saw, rushing up, faster and faster, the rolling hilly farmland of Northern France, Nazi-Occupied Northern France.

Maj. Erich Krause ignored the middle-aged man standing tensely in front of his desk. Instead, Krause finished reading the last few paragraphs of the report, initialed it, sat back in his chair. He looked with satisfaction around the high-ceilinged room though his face didn't change at all. His skin tended to a grayish hue, emphasizing his sharply green eyes. His eyes had a peculiar penetrating quality. Sgt. Schmidt once told his wife, "Maj. Krause's eyes gleam like a cat's. I think," he had added with a rush, "they would have killed him for a witch if he'd lived two hundred years ago." Now those pale ice-green eyes studied the rich red of the velvet drapes and the elaborate wheat frond pattern of the molding and the exquisite grace of the crystal drops on the massive chandelier. His office had once served a wealthy Parisian. His nostrils flared just a little, the only change in that grayish still face. He had come a long way from Hamburg and the bitterly cold, filthy cellar. He remembered again, as he had remembered so many times, his shock, the unbelieving shock and horror, when he'd straggled back to Germany, wounded and sick after the War's end in 1918, and found his mother in that cellar, found her only in time to see her die, swept away by pneumonia, her strength gone because she had been too long hungry and cold. He often recalled that cellar, remembered deliberately. The cellar in its chill and filth represented all those lean and miserable and angry years when Germans starved, when a wheelbarrow load of money was not enough to buy a meal, when there was no work, no future, no hope.

He first heard Adolph Hitler speak in Brandenburg on a hot July day in 1931 and he had been caught up by the Fuehrer's magnetism. Krause had followed him, believed in him, first as a hanger on, then as an accepted follower, then as a neophyte in Himmler's SS. And now, not quite ten years later, he sat in warmth and comfort in a Paris office, a sub-section chief in the Geheime Staats Polizei

The Gestapo.

He pulled a stack of folders to him. He was getting quite a good ring of informers together. He had authorized the release yesterday of fifteen more petty criminals from the Cherche-Midi jail. In exchange for their freedom, they would be the eyes and ears of the Gestapo against those foolhardy Frenchmen who dared oppose the New Order.

Like the miserable specimen standing in front of him.

Krause looked up now and enjoyed the quick, involuntary gasp of his prisoner. Krause's pale green eyes stared into the man's brown eyes until they shifted and slipped away. Still Krause stared until finally, reluctantly, fearfully, the Frenchman again met his gaze. Krause felt a quick surge of warmth in his entrails. What a frightened little rabbit. How long would it take to make the rabbit squeal?

Krause picked up a folder from his polished desk, fine walnut from the Louis XV period, opened it and began to read in an almost gentle soothing voice. "Name: Louis Robards. Home address: 7 Rue de Douai. Profession : railroad worker. Born June 6, 1895 in the 13th Arrondissement, Paris. You have worked in the yards at Gare de L'Est for twenty-three years."

Robards listened, his shoulders hunched. He twisted a railroad cap in big work-toughened hands.

Slowly, almost sadly, Krause shook his head. "It is a shame to see a man throw away all those years of good work. Who put you up to it, Robards?"

Robards looked down at his cap.

"Come now, Robards. You didn't do it on your own."

"I didn't do anything."

"No? Then you shouldn't have been so quick to tell your mates that some trains might leave the yards with their brakes filed down."

Robards hunched one shoulder higher than the other. He felt a little prickle of confidence. They couldn't hang a man for big talk. Not even the Gestapo. "I didn't do anything."

"But we know of a train that did leave for Berlin . . . with its brakes sabotaged."

Robards shrugged. "It didn't have anything to do with me."

Krause's eyes flickered almost imperceptibly to the thick-set blond man in a grayish rumpled suit who stood just behind and a little to the left of the prisoner.

With no change of expression, efficiently, almost casually, the man closed his fist, swung.

The totally unexpected blow caught Robards low in his back, just above the kidney. The hard solid sound mingled with his scream of pain. Thrown forward, he slammed into Krause's desk then collapsed on the floor, his breath coming in high sharp whimpers. He was still bleary and sick when his tormentor reached down and hauled him to his feet, gripping Robards's arm viciously.

The worker tried weakly to pull away. The pain in his arm increased. Dimly he heard Krause, "Stand up, Robards. Stand very still and listen to me. I am going to ask you some more questions and this time, this time, I want you to answer them very, very quickly. If you do not . . ." He paused and waited until Robards' quivering face looked at him, "If you do not, Hans and I will take you upstairs to the interrogation room."

It was very quiet in the office now, the only sounds were Robards thin high breaths and the tick of the Dresden clock on the marble mantel and the faraway clatter of a typewriter in an outer office.

"Now," Krause's voice was reasonable, a schoolmaster pointing out the logic of inevitability, "it would be better for you if you do not have to go upstairs. Here," and his eyes once again swept the beautiful room, the Empire breakfront, the long low table with Moorish lines, the Flemish tapestry with a dusty king on horseback, "we can discuss things, talk quietly. Upstairs would not be so pleasant."

Hans loosed his grip and Robards stood on his own, swaying, breathing unevenly. Hans stepped back a pace until once again he stood just behind and a little to the left of the prisoner. Robards half turned to look behind him.

"*Achtung!*" Krause shouted.

Robards jerked forward.

"You are to look at me." Krause commanded. "Only at me."

Robards faced forward, but his whole body trembled.

"Now," once again Krause's voice was smooth, agreeable, unhurried, "where were we? Oh yes, we were talking about your work. Very fascinating work it must be, Robards. Very important work." Krause's face hardened. "Very important work to the Fuehrer, Robards. Nothing must be permitted to interfere with train shipments. Nothing."

Again the blow was totally unexpected, a vicious punch into the same kidney. Robards' scream was a shriek of agony.

This time as Hans hauled him to his feet, he writhed in pain and sobbed, "I will tell you, let me tell you, don't hit me again, I will tell you . . ."

Krause looked at him with a quiver of distaste. What a sniveling weak degenerate. No wonder the French were defeated. There was no room for them in the New World that Germany was building. They were only fit to be slaves.

". . . not a gang. Nothing like that. I was drinking wine, one night after work, and we all got to talking and everybody said how easy it would be to sabotage things, in the yard, and I said, sure, it would be easy, I could do it like a shot. Later, I thought about it some more. Last week I filed the brakes on one of the goods trains going to Berlin. That's all I did. But I did it on my own." He was breathing more easily now, his face still streaked with tears, his mouth trembling, but his voice stronger. "Nobody else was involved. Just me."

Krause stared at him for a long moment, his eyes as clear and cold and green as an ice-locked stream high in the Alps. "All on your own. But you talked about sabotage with the other men."

Robards gave a shrug. "It was just talk over a glass of wine."

"Where do you drink your wine?"

Robards looked puzzled but answered willingly enough. "The Coq d'Or. It's a block from the yards. It's a railroad workers' bar."

"The Coq d'Or." Krause nodded. "Good. Sergeant, this evening we will take M. Robards with us and pay a visit to the Coq d'Or."

"But why?" Robards asked.

"Why? To arrest some Frenchmen, M. Robards. At least twenty men. Anyone who seems to recognize you."

"But why? I told you," his voice rose higher and higher. "I filed the brakes. I, alone am responsible. No one helped me."

Krause's green eyes, cold as death, turned toward him. "The goods train was to slow near Dusseldorf to let a troop train pass. The brakes failed."

It was so quiet in the elegant room.

"Seven German soldiers died. So now, Robards, you will die and for every dead German there will be at least two dead Frenchmen."

"He can't stay here!"

Linda looked at her sister in shocked dismay. She had been uncertain, that was true, of Eleanor's reaction. But she would never have expected this. Never.

Eleanor whirled away, almost running to the windows that overlooked the street. She stood, half hidden by the long green drapes, staring down into the narrow street. Without turning, she asked sharply, "You came here directly from the hospital?"

Linda couldn't answer. She couldn't bear to look at Michael, to see the flush rising up his thin face, and to hear his stuttered, "I'm so sorry, I didn't think. Of course, it is insupportable. I see that now. I'll leave immediately, of course."

He couldn't leave. It was almost dusk. Curfew wasn't until ten p.m., but it wasn't safe for a lone young man to wander about Paris. In the beginning, curfew had been at eight p.m. Since July 5, the Germans, in their kindness, had permitted Parisians to be on the streets until ten.

But it wasn't at all safe. Michael still wore what was so obviously, ragtag or not, a British uniform. He didn't speak French. He wouldn't have a chance, Linda thought, not a chance in a million. Surely Eleanor wouldn't turn him out tonight. Early tomorrow, Linda would take him away, find some place for him, but surely Eleanor would let him stay the night.

Eleanor swung around. "Did you come straight—" She looked from Linda to Michael, then back to Linda. "Oh my dear," and she hurried across the room, slipped her arms around her sister, "I didn't mean we weren't going to help Michael. I only meant we must get him out of here before the Gestapo comes."

"The Gestapo?" Linda repeated. "Why on earth . . ."

Eleanor was impatient with them. "Don't you see, children," and Linda realized oddly that she and Michael, of an age, still seemed like children to her older sister, "when they find Michael gone, and he may be missed by the evening meal," he nodded unhappily, "they will send out search parties. They have dogs. It won't take them long when they realize they can't pick up Michael's scent anywhere around the wall to decide he probably didn't leave that way. They'll try to figure how he could possibly have gotten away. They keep records of visitors." Eleanor's plump dark face was not the least chiding. She smiled reassuringly, "We should at the least have a few hours. We'll . . ."

"My Lord, I never thought!" Michael cried. "Mme. Masson, I'm so sorry. I wouldn't put you and Linda in danger for anything. I just wanted so badly to escape. All I could think of was getting away and, when I saw the car, I knew I could get away in the trunk, but I never thought about their coming after Linda. I'll leave now. If they don't find me here, I mean, it's better that they find me somewhere else."

"They aren't going to find you." It was a statement, final, absolute. Eleanor reached for the huge telephone directory. "First, we'll call . . ." Her words broke off in mid-sentence. She lifted her head to listen. Linda, too, looked toward the door.

Michael looked desperately around, then flung himself the six or seven feet across the room to press against the wall where he would be hidden by the opening door. He grabbed up a knobbed cane from the ceramic umbrella holder.

The door burst open and Robert rocketed into the room.

Linda was so relieved that she didn't even hear his first words, but she heard the last.

". . . and I'm sure it's the Gestapo! It's a gray-green Citroen. The driver's in uniform, a corporal, but one of the men in the back seat has on a dark-gray suit and black hat and everybody says that's how you know the Gestapo, a man in civilian clothes in a German Army car. The car's stopped at the end of our block. Do you suppose they are hunting for the Mayers? M. Caborn told me . . ."

"Robert," his mother said sharply, "are they downstairs here? Outside our building?"

"Yes, and I saw a lorry of troops, at the other end of the block and they are dropping men off."

Eleanor paled. Linda took a deep breath. That was how the Germans searched for hidden soldiers. They surrounded a block and then went into every flat, every room, every closet, the roofs and the cellars.

Michael stepped forward, "I'll go down the back way." He looked at Linda, "Is the garage to the right? I'll try to get back as near the car as I can and, when they . . . if they catch me, I'll say I hid myself in the trunk and had just worked it open. And that you didn't know I was there. I will swear it."

Robert had turned, startled to see him, but he understood at once. "Oh," he said quickly, "Oh, Mama, I see."

So quick, Linda thought, to understand. Thirteen years old and he recognized without any real shock that his mother might help an escaping soldier hide.

Downstairs the entry door slammed. A loud knocking reverberated up the stairwell from the concierge's door.

Skinny, long-legged Robert, all elbows and knees and uneven voice, grabbed Michael's arm. "Quick. I can hide you. Quick."

Michael looked swiftly at Eleanor. Her face ashen, she nodded.

Then they were gone, the door closing quietly behind them. Oh, Robert learned quickly.

Eleanor said brusquely, "I will be in the kitchen, Linda. Pretend you have been . . . " She glanced around the living room as she hurried toward the narrow hall that led to the kitchen. "Pretend you have been writing letters."

Linda hurried to the roll-top desk, pushed up the curving front piece that had such a tendency to stick in wet weather. But, of course, there had been no wet weather. Hot and clear and lovely it had been, this August. She settled into the straight chair, swiftly pulled out a little stock of thick cream-colored stationary, lifted the wooden pen out of the inkwell.

"Dear Frank," she scrawled quickly on the top of the page, "it was so good to hear from you and Betty. I certainly appreciate the work you've done in settling the estate and forwarding payments to Eleanor and me. She is without any other income now. There has been no word from Andre since May. His unit was in Belgium, near Bruges, but she has heard nothing since the Armistice. I am afraid . . ." She lifted her pen, held her head rigid, listening. She had written a letter yesterday to her brother, mailed it in the afternoon, but it was something to do now, words she could scrawl by rote, as she waited for that heavy knock on the door.

She stared at the pigeon holes, bills tucked in one, correspondence in another, Robert's school reports in a third. Why had she been such a fool to agree to help Michael? What would the Germans do to them if they found him? Put them in prison? And Robert—what would happen to Robert if they found him hiding an escaped English soldier?

Even the Germans wouldn't put children in prison. Would they?

She remembered the Petersons' description of their attempt to flee Paris just before the Germans reached the capital in mid-June. The roads South had been clogged, blocked by the thousands and thousands of refugees, families on foot pushing wheelbarrows or baby carriages, others riding in ramshackle trucks, old cars, school buses and farm carts, a few in limousines and hundreds on bicycles, anything and everything that could move and carry a few belongings. There was no food, no fuel. Stops along the way had been stripped of everything. If a car ran out of gas, it was shoved off the road and its owner joined the thousands on foot.

Patsy Peterson's voice had shaken when she told them, "It was just after dawn of the 14th that the Messerschmitts came roaring down along the road, machine gunning everything in their way."

Screams and shouts rose and fell like a long wave across the countryside. People ran off the road, jumped into ditches, hid under trees and bridges. All except those who were dead, of course. That's how the Nazis cleared the road for troops to pass. Stolid-faced, bored-looking soldiers stared without much interest from the trucks that hurtled to the South, chasing the remnants of the French Army.

People who would machine-gun refugees just to clear the road of defeated people, what would they do to a boy, caught helping an enemy soldier?

Frank had demanded in his last letter that they come home to Pasadena, bringing Robert, of course, with them. "You damn fools, don't wait until it's too late and you are trapped."

It had been two weeks before Christmas, 1939, that Frank and Betty put her and Eleanor aboard the Chief, in Pasadena, en route to Kansas City, the first leg of the long journey to France. Frank had been reluctant even then. "Dammit, Linda, there's a war on. Eleanor has a husband there, but you don't have to go."

She was impatient. "No one really expects any fighting now. After all, war was declared September 3 and nothing's happened. Nothing."

He had nodded, but he was still opposed. "Hell of a time to go, anyway. Why don't you spend Christmas here with us, you know the kids love having you, then think about a visit next summer if it's safe?"

But that was just what she didn't want to do and it was so difficult to explain to Frank. Frank, after all, was so much older. He and Eleanor had been almost grown when Linda was born. He was thirty-six and Eleanor thirty-four to her nineteen so both of them were in their college and early married years when she was a little girl. She had clear memories of them, Frank receiving his law degree, Eleanor walking down the aisle at her wedding, slim and dark-haired, smiling radiantly. But Linda didn't actually know either of them well. Frank and Eleanor hadn't grown up in the same way either, though they all had the same parents. Her mother and father had delighted in Linda, the late-come, last child. She had traveled almost everywhere with them. They were on their way to see Linda, to pick her up for a weekend from Mills, when their small plane, lost in fog, had crashed into the Tehachapi Mountains. The loss of their parents had been a grief, of course, to Frank and to Eleanor, but not the devastating loss it had been to Linda. When Eleanor, home for the funeral, urged Linda to come back to France with her, Linda accepted at once.

She couldn't bear to stay in Pasadena, to spend Christmas at Frank's house, and to know that her own home, shuttered, dark, sat silently only ten blocks away. Perhaps, as far away as France, where everything was different, there would not be so many reminders of her parents.

And Paris swept her feelings far from America. Except for the nightly blackout and the colorful mixture of uniforms on the streets, Paris was unaffected by the war. The Phony War. With Robert as her willing guide, Linda learned to know Paris, from the unmistakable ironwork of the Eiffel Tower to the twisty, winding streets of Montmartre. She and Robert and Eleanor were sitting at a sidewalk café in the shadow of Sacre-Couer the Tuesday afternoon in April when the newsboy came up the street waving his paper and shouting, "Germans in Denmark. Germans in Denmark." But it was the horror of Rotterdam, the merciless vicious bombing of a city when surrender was in progress that turned the war from an uneasy rumble in the background of their lives to the all consuming reality that dominated every day. It was then that Linda wanted to go home. This wasn't her war. But, abruptly, Andre was gone, called up with his unit, and she didn't want to leave Eleanor alone.

It was on June 5, when German troops were reported attacking all along the Somme, that Eleanor, her plump face pale and unsmiling, had urged Linda to leave.

"I talked to Patsy Peterson this morning. They are getting ready to leave and they have room for you. They are going to drive to St. Jean-de-Luz and cross into Spain."

"What about you and Robert?"

"I can't leave when I don't know what's happened to Andre. What if he reached Paris and we were gone? But that's no reason for you to stay."

Linda had grown fond, these last few months, of this almost unknown sister with her vivid lively black eyes and good-natured plump face. A good woman, a good mother, a good wife, facing now a bleak and frightening future, but facing that future, Linda realized, with grace and charity. Eleanor didn't know what had happened to her husband, but she worked long hours visiting the hospitals near Paris, trying to help wounded, bitter men get some word of home and some word to home. It was only late at night, when Robert slept, that Linda would wake and hear the soft rustle from the living room, Eleanor pacing wearily up and down, up and down, hoping news would come, dreading what it might be.

So Linda had refused to go home to America. She knew, if she stayed, she could be some help and support. If nothing else, she and Robert could stand in those interminable lines for food, freeing Eleanor for her hospital trips, and help keep up the apartment. At the outbreak of fighting, Eleanor's maid, Marie, had left to go to her family in Toulouse.

It had never occurred to Linda that she might bring danger to Eleanor and Robert.

Linda sat stiffly, listening, hearing the heavy thump of men's feet on the apartment house stairs. She was expecting it, knew it was coming, but, still, the thunderous unremitting knocking on the door shocked her. Her hand closed convulsively around the pen and a thick dark stain angled down the page.

Eleanor stood in the hall doorway.

"Linda, would you answer the door, please. My hands are floury."

Linda pushed back her chair, hurried across the room. Eleanor looked as though she'd been in the kitchen all afternoon, her apron smudged with flour, even a streak of flour across one cheek. A marvelous bacony aroma wafted from the kitchen. Linda knew there hadn't been any bacon in months, not since April at least. But Eleanor was brilliant at improvising. Turning to go back to the kitchen, Eleanor called out something about, ". . . I can't leave the stove or the grease will get too hot . . . fritters . . . do see what all that noise is about . . ."

Linda opened the door, ready to ask with a fine show of innocence what was wanted, but she had no chance to say anything.

"Step clear," he ordered in French.

"Who are you?" she demanded, her voice thin and strained.

The two men ignored her. She saw with horror that the heavy-set blond man held a gun in his right hand. He moved swiftly, almost running, down the hall that led to the bedrooms and kitchen. She heard Eleanor's startled cry and then her sister was in the living room, darting toward the telephone. She grabbed up the receiver, began to dial. The older man caught her by the arm and pressed down the cradle.

Eleanor turned on him in a fury, her words coming so fast she could scarcely catch her breath. ". . . think you are! I'll thank you to get out of my apartment! I'm calling the police. Now. Immediately."

"So you are English. That is very interesting, Mme. Masson. It makes everything quite understandable."

"I am not English," Eleanor said crisply, "though I can't see what business it is of yours. I am an American married to a Frenchman and I have lived in Paris for sixteen years. Now, I will thank you to explain why you have pushed into my apartment. And who is he?" She jerked her head toward the thick-set blond who was coming back into the living room, carrying the gun.

Linda watched, her eyes wide. She had seen scenes such as that in Al Capone movies but she had never before actually watched a man matter-of-factly thrust a hand gun beneath his coat.

"Mme. Masson, my assistant, Sgt. Schmidt. I am Maj. Erich Krause." He inclined his head a little. "Of the Geheime Staats Polizei." He paused, added, "The Gestapo, Mme. Masson."

None of them moved or spoke.

Krause stared at Eleanor. She started to speak. He chopped the air once, sharply, with his right hand. Eleanor flushed but said nothing. The major looked at his assistant.

Sgt. Schmidt shook his head.

Krause frowned, turned again toward Eleanor. "So you are an American. That is no excuse, Mme. Masson."

"Excuse?"

"For harboring an escaped British soldier."

Eleanor gave a sigh of relief. "I can assure you we aren't involved in anything of that sort. And, of course, Sgt. Schmidt didn't find anyone because we don't have anyone hidden here."

Krause's face hardened. "We know, Mme. Masson, that Lt. Michael Evans escaped from Douellens today in the trunk of your car. Now it does no good to make denials. We have an eyewitness. It will only make things go harder for you if you lie. However, if you cooperate, surrender the fugitive to us, and give us your solemn assurances that you will not engage in any such criminal activities in the future, well, I think perhaps my superiors would agree to let the matter drop there."

Linda watched his thin grayish face with a kind of fascination. His head, the skin drawn back tightly over the temples, reminded her of a snake's, the way a caged reptile will lift his head and move it, swaying slowly, from side to side, small eyes glittering. But he was lying to them. How could an eyewitness have seen Eleanor and described her, small and dark and plump, when it had been she, Linda, who drove the car? No one could confuse them. She was a good three inches taller and slender and her hair was red-gold.

"Maj. Krause," Linda interrupted breathlessly, her voice high, "your informant must be very confused. It was I, not my sister, who visited Douellens today. Eleanor had a dental appointment so I went instead. Since this trip was already planned, I took her place. But I certainly didn't bring an English soldier back with me. Why, I've never been there before and didn't know a soul. Besides, the sentry who checked my papers can tell you I was alone when I left."

"She certainly didn't have anyone with her," Eleanor said emphatically. "She arrived here about forty-five minutes ago. Alone."

Krause looked at Linda.

Linda held her face unmoving. Don't let him see you are afraid, she thought, don't let him see. But she was afraid, terribly afraid.

"So it was you."

Her breath caught in her throat. The way he said that . . .

"You won't object then, Miss . . ."

"Rossiter."

". . . if Hans checks your car for fingerprints," and his shining green eyes watched her avidly.

Somehow she managed not to change expression, not to reflect the sudden surge of panic. She had concentrated so hard on not revealing her instinctive, innate revulsion to him that her face was already frozen in a blank emptiness.

"Fingerprints?" she repeated stupidly.

"Yes. If you came home alone from the hospital, then there will be no trace of Lt. Evans' fingerprints in your car or trunk."

"Oh, I see," she said slowly. "I'll . . . I'll get the keys."

The men walked on either side of her down the stairs and out into the street.

She held the keys and looked straight ahead. His fingerprints would be in the trunk. Could she run away? But no, that wouldn't do any good. That would just leave Eleanor and Robert to be arrested even if she should by a miracle escape.

They walked on either side of her, so close. A corporal from their car came behind, carrying a valise. It was an eerie passage. Every door stayed closed. No one walked down the street. No children played on the sidewalks. It was just at dusk on a soft summer evening but the street was as empty as though a plague had stripped it clean. A curtain twitched on the right. All down the street she was conscious of watching eyes.

The Germans seemed oblivious to the deathlike quiet. Perhaps they were used to it.

The garage was empty, too, though she knew Pierre usually sat in the little room just off to the right. The evening paper lay atop a rickety wooden table. A chair was pushed back.

Deny everything, she told herself firmly. That was her only chance. And Eleanor and Robert and Lt. Evan's only chance, too. Deny everything If they find his fingerprints, shrug your shoulders. You don't know anything. Anything!

Schmidt held out his hand for the keys.

She was so involved in her thoughts as he opened the trunk that she wasn't even aware how carefully Krause was watching her and the flicker of disappointment in his eyes. She stood back to give them both room.

The corporal dusted a fine gray powder along the rim of the trunk. Schmidt studied the thin gray film then spoke briefly in German. Krause nodded slowly, his face expressionless. Then he turned to Linda.

"It appears, Miss Rossiter, that we have been in error."

Linda was too surprised to respond.

"We do not, of course, wish to inconvenience American citizens. It was only because of the seriousness of the crime that we have been forced to insist upon an immediate search."

Linda nodded formally, politely, but inside she whistled with excitement. They had done it, they had fooled the Gestapo, the all-mighty, all-powerful Gestapo. And now, the imperious Germans were, for them, apologizing. It was an example of the "correctness" of which she had heard. So far, the occupying forces had been so polite, so correct, in their dealings with the French. If a German officer wanted an apartment, he very politely dispossessed the owner. The apartment was "requisitioned."

But the Gestapo wasn't so smart. They had been bluffing about the fingerprints. Obviously, they didn't have Lt. Evans' fingerprints because, of course, they were liberally sprinkled about in the trunk, but she only nodded soberly, politely, as she listened to Krause.

When he finished, she held out her hand for the car keys. Schmidt gave them to her. Once again she nodded, then she turned and walked steadily out of the garage.

Eleanor and Robert were waiting in the apartment.

"It was a trick," Linda burst out immediately. "They didn't have his fingerprints."

"We should have known that," Eleanor said disgustedly. "That's the trouble with being scared to death, it keeps you from thinking. Of course, they haven't fingerprinted all those wounded soldiers. It's a hospital, not a prison. They aren't fingerprinted until they are transferred to the Citadel."

Eleanor pushed up from the chair, walked to the window and looked obliquely down into the street. "They're standing by their car. Here comes a soldier, a sergeant. He's talking to Krause and there are other soldiers, coming out of the cellar."

Robert came close to peer around his mother's shoulder. "They're alone," he said excitedly, "They didn't find him. I knew they wouldn't. It's a good place, the best place, nobody ever finds me when we play hide and go seek."

"Robert's right. They've given up. Look, there's the truck and the soldiers are climbing into it. Oh, thank God."

When the truck rumbled out of the street, following the sleek gray Citroen, Eleanor hugged her son. "Robert, I'm so proud of you. We wouldn't have managed without you."

He tried very hard to look matter-of-fact, but he fairly glowed with pride. "It's just lucky I came home when I did."

There was an instant's silence.

Some of the elation drained out of Eleanor's face. "Lucky," she repeated. "Yes, we've been lucky so far. But what are we going to do now?"

CHAPTER 3

"**Y**ou're bleeding!"

Jonathan looked down. Blood oozed through his trousers

"Here." The boy worked fast, cutting the tangling parachute loose, thrusting a swath of silk at Jonathan. "Wrap your leg. Fast."

Quickly, grimacing, Jonathan wrapped the silk around his leg. He tried to stand.

"Wait, I'll help." The boy jumped nearer and pulled Jonathan up.

From beyond a nearby hill, smoke rose in a thin plume.

"That's from your plane," the French boy said. "We've got to hurry. The Boche will be here soon."

Jonathan looked around the field where he had landed. "There's no place to hide."

"I have a cart up on the road. Through those trees."

Jonathan's face glistened with sweat by the time they gained the road, his leg throbbed with a hot angry pain. The boy took a moment to look up and down the gray dusty road. Quickly he shifted burlap sacks that looked lumpy. "I've made a place for you. Once you're up, I can arrange the bags to hide you. Don't move. Don't talk. We've got to get away from the plane."

The cart began to move. Jonathan felt pressure against him from a bag, smelled the sweet scent of apples.

Jonathan wasn't sure how much time had passed when he dimly heard a voice. He thought maybe he'd lost consciousness. He understood dimly that the rickety transport was no longer moving. Somebody had helped him . . .

"Is he dead?"

"I don't think so. Hurry up. The Boches are coming."

He wasn't dead, Jonathan thought indignantly. He must tell them so. He wasn't dead. He tried to form the words but they receded in his mind and the gray woolly cloud seeped over him again. He realized there was movement around him and he was dimly aware of hands pulling and tugging at him. He heard whispers and the snap and pop as his parachute was unbuckled.

"My God, it's all bloody."

They were worried about the blood. That was nice of them, he thought fuzzily. He would have to explain, tell them it was a wound, nothing bad, actually. You didn't have to worry about blood, just clean it up. Wipe it up. Everything neat and tidy. He would tell them to relax. Roll me over, roll me over in the clover. He felt a tiny silly giggle forming in the back of his mind. They were rolling him over and over, wrapping him up like a silken butterfly in a cocoon, rolling him up like a sausage in his parachute and dragging him, bumpity, bump, across the ground.

For the first time, he began to feel aggrieved. This was a silly game and he didn't want to play it. What did they take him for? Uncomfortable, too. He was squashed in the folds of silk. He couldn't see and it was hard to breathe. He had a sudden frightening sense of being out of control as he was dragged roughly across the ground, then lifted and swung up into the air. He began to struggle and tried to cry out.

A hand fumbled across the folds of silk and roughly gripped his jaw. "Be quiet. Please. Be quiet."

It wasn't the command that hushed him, it was the desperation in the soft cry. "Be absolutely quiet. Do not move or speak."

Jonathan was fully conscious now and, though he couldn't see, he heard the scratchy rustle of hay and knew when it was smoothed over him. Reins rattled, a horse snuffled and slowly, wheels creaking, the bed swaying, Jonathan felt them begin to move. He was hidden beneath a mound of hay on a wagon. Someone had switched him from the cart to another horse-drawn vehicle.

He was conscious and his head ached. He remembered now the

sudden violent uprush of trees and how he had yanked at his parachute straps but still he plummeted down into an oak, banging his head, crashing heavily through the limbs into a thicket of bushes.

Obviously, he had been seen and rescued.

Why had they wrapped him up like a rug?

The pop-pop-pop of the motorcycle was faint at first, like a string of faraway firecrackers on the Fifth of November. Then the pops sounded louder and nearer until the staccato sound drowned out the muffled clop of the horse's hooves and the sway and creak of the cart.

It roared alongside then slowed to an idle. "Stop." The command was in German. The soldier spoke only a smattering of French.

Jonathan's rescuers made the conversation as hard as possible, pretending not to understand the heavily accented French of the German.

Jonathan knew it was a pantomime, the German pointing at the sky, making the noise of a wounded plane, "*Anglais*," he repeated over and over, "*Anglais*."

"Oh, *oui, oui*," a light young French voice exclaimed finally and there was a rush of instruction and comment and finally, a slow painstaking reply. "To the South. Do you understand? To the South. Four kilometers at least. That way."

"*Danke. Danke.*" The motorcycle revved up, exhaust fumes swirled around the cart, and the cycle turned and lurched off down the road, the way it had come.

The wagon once again began its easy swaying progress up the road. Jonathan felt tension easing out of him. As he relaxed, pain pulsed in his leg. He fought a wave of nausea. It took all his strength not to cry out and he lay weak and sweating, only dimly aware of the moving wagon and uneven jolting ride. The wagon had been stopped for a minute or so before he realized it. Sightless, helpless, he tried to still his uneven breathing to listen.

"Hello, Francois."

"Ah, Maurice, how's it going?"

"So so."

"Lots of excitement up ahead."

"Oh?"

"The Boches are looking for an English pilot. He bailed out somewhere around here. The whole garrison saw it. They've been combing
through the woods and they're beginning to get ugly."

"Why's that?"

"Well, they know he's down but they can't find him anywhere and
they think somebody's hiding him. They're tired of airmen getting
away. There's a roadblock up ahead and they're searching everything.
They'll poke your hay full of holes."

They spoke a few sentences more, then the wagon began to lumber
forward.

Jonathan understood well enough. He couldn't get every word
but he understood well enough. The Germans were looking for him,
looking hard. They would jab and prod this load of hay at the roadblock up ahead. He had to get out of this mummifying wrap and hide.
Nausea swept him again. He had moved his leg. Tears burned behind
his eyes. Goddamn it, he couldn't even walk, much less run and hide.
But he had to do something. He started to twist and turn, trying to
loosen the shroud like covering.

A soft voice called to him, "Be still, Monsieur. Don't make the hay
move. As soon as Francois is 'round the bend, we will stop and hide
you." Then, an afterthought, "Do you understand me? Do you understand French?"

"Yes," Jonathan managed. He lay still, breathing heavily. Where
could they hide him? He felt sweat trickle down his face and back,
not so much from the late afternoon heat, even though it was stifling
beneath the hay, wrapped up as he was in the parachute, but from the
pain, the pain that didn't stop now, that moved up and down his leg
like liquid fire. But fear and a tenacious, intense will to survive made
the pain bearable, an irritant, just one more problem to be surmounted.

Once again, the wagon stopped. Gentle hands pushed the hay
up and he was once again lifted up and out. His rescuers carried him,
running heavily across the road. He was tilted as they half-slid with him
down an embankment.

"This way, Roger, this way."

The pain was too much now. Pain blotted out everything, the movement, their low voices, even, for a moment, the knowledge that he was on the ground and they were gingerly unrolling the thick swathing of silk.

"Monsieur, listen please."

He lifted his head and dazedly looked at them. They were brothers, it was clear, two dark thin faces, watching him, two pairs of worried brown eyes.

He nodded. "Yes. I can hear you."

Quickly, one interrupting the other, they told him they were going to leave him, here, beneath this wooden bridge, hidden by the high stalks of sunflowers growing in the dry creek bed. They would be back. He was to wait and they would come back for him. When it was safe.

It was very quiet after they left. He listened but the only sound was an occasional rustle as some animal moved in the grass and reeds nearby. It was already almost completely dark beneath the bridge. Some faint sheen of light penetrated where the broad boards were laid together but the tall weeds on either side shut away the evening sun. Jonathan wondered if they had left a trail when they carried him down from the road. If the weeds and grasses were bent, the Germans would find him.

There was no point in worrying. He was propped up against the bank which shelved gradually down to the dry rock-strewn creek bottom. It wasn't too uncomfortable, and it smelled good, faintly dusty and grassy. If he could lean back just a little, ease the pressure on his neck. He realized he was still wearing the bulky uncomfortable Mae West. He pulled off his flying gloves, began to unstrap the life preserver. To pull it off, he had to lean forward. That moved his leg. Once again pain made him dizzy and ill. He managed at last to thrust the Mae West away. He clawed at his tunic pocket. He had some aspirin in there. He was sure of it. Last night, he had dropped a tin in his pocket. His fingers touched his cigarette case. Matches. A crumpled piece of paper. That pretty WAAF's telephone number. He had said he would call her tonight. For a moment, he paused. Would she have heard by now that he hadn't come back? Or was she waiting at the barracks for him to call. Funny. He couldn't remember her face very well. Had he even looked at her face? It was her legs he had noticed. Then, at the bottom of the pocket, he found the tin of aspirin. He opened it, touched inside. One, two, three, four. That was all.

His leg hurt like the devil, pain so bad it made him lightheaded. Should he just take one or two, save the others? Two. He would take two of them. It was when he tried to swallow that he realized how thirsty he was, ragingly thirsty. He got the tablets down, then lay back, trembling with pain.

Shouts. Faraway at first, then nearer and nearer. The heavy thump of men running, fanning out, crashing through grass and underbrush, calling back and forth to each other.

He didn't understand German. He didn't need to. It was at least a platoon, the soldiers streaming across the countryside, perhaps twenty yards apart.

Sweat beaded Jonathan's face, clouded his eyes, but slowly, inch by inch, he moved down the little incline until he reached the creek bottom, his right hand levering his body along, his left hand searching. He brushed over the pebbles, the little smooth rocks tumbled along by a spring freshet. Near the center of the dry creek bed, he found a jagged rock as large as a softball. Heavy, sharp edged. A formidable weapon in a desperate hand. Panting a little from exertion, he inched back up the incline so that he was again in a sitting position. The better to throw. He had learned to play baseball his second year at the University. There were two American Rhodes Scholars in his class. He could see their faces so clearly. Paul Weiss and Mickey Jezek. They had delighted in teaching the game to their English classmates. They had told Jonathan he was a "natural." It was dark now beneath the narrow wooden bridge, not even a sliver of the sunset slanting through the cracks, so he lay in a warm dark pocket on the dry rocky ground, screened on either side by head-high cane and sunflowers, waiting, listening to the shouts coming nearer, the clump of boots, the rattle of a truck, remembering the soft silken light of English evenings in May and different shouts, "Strike him out, Jonathan, that's a boy," listening and waiting, remembering, holding the jagged-edged stone.

It didn't take long to gather up a blanket, clothing that had belonged to Andre, worn gray trousers, a blue pullover, sturdy hiking boots he had worn in Zermatt last August, a hamper with a half loaf of bread, a small pot of strawberry jam, a precious piece of cheese and a bottle of sauterne. Robert looked as loaded as a porter when he was ready to start downstairs.

"I'll carry everything," Linda offered. "Robert can go ahead and make sure the way is clear."

Eleanor nodded. "Be sure no one sees you. Explain to the lieutenant that we don't dare bring him upstairs this late in the evening. Everyone is home from work and, if someone should walk out of their apartment, well, we can't take a chance that they might not turn us in." She paused and added grimly. "Especially the Biziens."

Rene and Yvette Bizien had the small tobacconist shop midway up the block. Both had long pale faces and pointed noses and looked uncannily alike. Childless, they always shushed Robert and his friends as they clattered up and down the stairs. They were not particularly likeable neighbors but not offensive. Negligible. At least, they had been negligible until now.

Since the Armistice, everything had changed, including neighborhoods and the way you looked at your neighbors. Every second or third shop was shuttered. They had to walk a half mile to reach the nearest open bakery. They couldn't buy pastries on Mondays, Tuesdays or Wednesdays. There was no sugar, no coffee, no flour, no butter. There were seven kinds of ration cards for everything from meat to cloth. But the biggest difference, especially to English-speaking Parisians, was the division of all France into pro-Vichy, anti-British and anti-Vichy, pro-British. Day after day, the newspapers and radios attacked the British, blaming them for the defeat of France, claiming Britain had forced France into the war then abandoned her.

Some of their French acquaintances looked away to avoid saying hello when they passed in the street.

The Biziens had never been their friends so that didn't matter. But it did matter that they were originally from Alsace-Lorraine and that last week, so the concierge told Eleanor, they had entertained a German officer at dinner. A school friend from Heidelberg.

The Bizien apartment was the second-floor front.

Linda carried a flashlight. Eleanor had taped a piece of blue silk over the lens so it gave just a glimmer of illumination. There was light enough to keep Linda from stumbling on the darkened stairway. Robert was already out of sight. In a moment, he scampered back up the stairs, gesturing for her to come. She passed the third floor landing, waited again in the darkness. When he motioned for her to come, she pattered down the stairs, using the dim light, rushing past the second floor. She was breathless, her legs aching, when she reached the cellar door. They opened the door onto absolute darkness. How horrid it would be to wait in pitch dark, cramped in a hiding place, wondering if every noise, every step, heralded exposure and capture.

Robert carefully shut the door behind them. He began to whistle faintly but clearly, "Oh, Johnny, Oh Johnny, Oh!"

It must, Linda thought, seem like an especially exciting game of soldiers to him. He was showing her the way now, past the huge furnace and a clutter of furniture and tenants' trunks to the coal bin. "There's a little space behind the bin, like a cupboard," Robert explained.

As they came near, a narrow plank of wood creaked open and a dark figure scrambled out.

They spoke swiftly.

Linda turned away as Michael changed into Andre's clothes.

"Hey, these are a pretty good fit? Who do I thank?"

"They belong to my father." For the first time, Robert's voice was strained. "He was . . . his unit was in the fighting around Dunkirk. We haven't heard from him since then."

"I'm sorry," the soldier said. "I'm sorry. A lot of soldiers are still hiding out, Robert, did you know that?"

"A lot?" Robert repeated hopefully.

"Lord, yes. And the Germans took thousands and thousands of prisoners and he may not have been able to get word to you yet. You can't give up hope."

"Oh no, sir. We haven't given up hope. Not at all."

They helped spread his blanket the length of the cubbyhole. They left the little flashlight with him so he could see to eat.

"Don't get out until one of us comes for you," Robert warned. "You'll know it's one of us because we'll whistle, just like I did tonight."

They waited until he was again shut behind the back of the bin, then they closed the lid and began to feel their way toward the stairs. They paused when they reached the top, opening the door slowly, quietly, waiting a long moment, but no one stirred in the corridor. They slipped out, eased the door closed behind them, and moved swiftly toward the front of the house. Once on the stairs going to the second floor, they began to relax.

"Aunt Linda," Robert began, "do you really think my father—"

The bright swath of light from the opening door surprised both of them. They looked up startled.

Mme. Bizien stepped out into the hall. "Who is it?" she demanded. "Who goes there?"

Linda was in the lead. Mme. Bizien peered past her. "Is that a man? Oh, it's you, Robert."

"Good evening, Madame," he said politely.

"Good evening," Linda said formally, but she didn't pause, she kept on walking. She and Robert climbed the stairs in silence. Behind them, Mme. Bizien stood on the landing, watching.

"That woman's a menace," Linda said angrily, when they were safely back in the Masson apartment.

Eleanor nodded. "I'm afraid so. I'm afraid she really is. She must know that we are suspected of hiding a soldier."

"How could she know?"

"The soldiers searched every apartment, Linda, while you went with Krause and his men to the garage."

"You can bet the lousy Biziens couldn't wait to Heil Hitler!"

"Robert!" his mother said automatically, looking toward him. Her face changed. "Are those the lieutenant's clothes?"

Robert dropped the bundle onto the couch.

"Yes. Daddy's clothes fit him."

"Take the clothes a couple of blocks away. Put them in a dustbin. Make sure no one sees you."

"Right now?"

"Yes. We mustn't take a chance that they be found here. Hurry. And Robert, go down the back way. Don't let the Biziens see you."

"Okay."

When he was gone, Linda said unhappily, "I've really put us in a hole, haven't I?"

Her sister, frowning in thought, hadn't quite heard. "Hmm?"

"Eleanor, I'm terribly sorry. I've put you and Robert in dreadful danger."

"Danger?" Eleanor looked at Linda with sudden attention. Linda's slender fair face was pale, her dark blue eyes huge. Eleanor wished abruptly that she knew this younger sister better. But Linda must be made of the right stuff for she had taken the chance, hidden the lieutenant in the car, brought him here. Danger? Who cared about danger after the past hideous weeks, hot and empty and quiet with the somber quiet of death, a dying nation. And Andre somewhere? Or was he anywhere? Was Andre, vigorous, abrupt, forceful Andre, nothing but a memory in her mind? Oh dear God, Andre, where are you?

"I know it was wrong," Linda was saying hesitantly, "If I had it to do over again . . ."

Eleanor said sharply, "If you had it to do over again, what would you do, Linda?"

Linda looked away, looked down. Her shining red-blond hair fell forward, hid her face.

"Well?"

Unwillingly, Linda lifted her head. "I don't know. I don't know."

"Linda, listen to me. You did the right thing. If I had been there that morning, if he had asked me, and it had looked, as it did to you, that the thing could be done, why, I wouldn't have thought twice about it. Of course, you did the right thing."

The right thing, yes, Linda thought, it had been right. But it was still dangerous and she remembered so clearly, with such terrible clarity, those awful moments waiting for him to come, the heat that could not touch the cold chill of fear as she waited. It had been worse this evening. The Gestapo agent, Erich Krause, with his shiny ice-green eyes that clung to her as if he would pry into her mind, pry and poke, pulling out anything he wanted to know. They had fooled him. He would be twice as vicious if he ever knew they had fooled him. And now they were stuck with Lt. Evans hidden in the cellar and the nosy Biziens on the second floor. If she had looked ahead to this . . . Why wasn't Eleanor afraid? Didn't she understand what kind of danger they were in? But Eleanor had never seemed afraid all this summer and now, with a fugitive dumped on her, she looked positively cheerful.

"Yes," Eleanor continued. "It was the right thing to do. This has been such a dreadful summer. No word of Andre and Paris so awful, shops boarded up and everybody staying inside, and the Swastika flying from the Arc de Triomphe and the Eiffel Tower. I hate it. Now, at least we are doing something."

"Yes," Linda said slowly. "But, Eleanor, what are we going to do with him now?"

Eleanor's voice was firm, confident. "We'll figure out some way to get him across the line."

Across the line. Linda lay sleepless in her bed, eyes wide, watching the bright streak of moonlight that slanted in her window, gilding one wall in the narrow room. Was Lt. Evans sleepless, too, in his dark, cramped, hideous hiding place? Across the line. She turned on her side, shielded her face from the moonlight. How in the world could they possibly get him across the line? It took a special pass, the ausweis, to cross the Demarcation Line. Last week Eleanor and Linda had gone to a party, a not-very-gay party, at the Petersons, and Madeleine Lafleur, who worked for Paris Mondiale, the government short wave radio station, was the center of attention, telling how difficult it was to obtain an ausweis.

"My dears, it takes days of standing in line. Weeks, sometimes! The woman in front of me had come every day for two weeks. Her father was ill in Bordeaux and family had been called to come. But they wouldn't give her one. Then he died and she was trying to get one so she could go to the funeral. They still didn't give her one."

"How did you manage?"

Madeleine had, just for an instant, looked a little uncomfortable, then she shrugged. "I had a little influence. My boss gave me a note."

Her boss. He and Madeleine had stayed on at the radio station even after it had been taken over by the Germans. So now they were the ones who put on the programs blaming everything on the English.

"You have to live." Madeleine said.

Madeleine knew how to get across the line. But it wouldn't do to ask her. Anyway, Evans couldn't take the train. Even if he had the right papers, and how in the world could they get them, he spoke no French. He couldn't travel hundreds of miles by train, having his papers checked, being looked at closely because he was young and male, and not know a word of the language.

Smuggle him onto a train?

The trains were carefully searched from the roof to the baggage compartments. Too many had tried to cross that way.

Linda turned restlessly onto her back. Surely they knew someone who could help them. She had met many of Eleanor and Andre's friends, but she didn't know any of them well. There were still a number of Americans in Paris whom they had known through the University.

Still in Paris. Americans who had chosen to live in German-Occupied Paris. Could they call on them to help smuggle an English soldier south?

Eleanor's French friends?

Linda sat up, punched her pillows up behind her. Was there a hospital they could visit, near the line? She would ask Eleanor in the morning.

The truck rolled slowly down the narrow cobbled street, soldiers dropping off every twenty yards. Barricades went up at either end of the block. The few pedestrians coming up to the roadblocks were motioned away. The silver gray Citroen pulled up to the curb directly in front of the Coq d'Or, but the bar's blackout curtains were pulled so no one saw the car. Krause and Schmidt sat in the back seat, Louis Robards slumped between them.

The driver held the door for Krause. He waited on the curb as Schmidt hauled Robards out. The railroad man could not stand straight. He bent forward, his arms crossed over his abdomen, moaning.

Inside the Coq d'Or, Georges Martel picked up his lunch pail and started to push back his chair.

"Hey, Georges, what's your hurry? Martine?"

Georges shrugged. He was newly married and his mates hadn't let him forget it, today or yesterday or the day before. He was good-humored, but he had heard enough of it. "No hurry," he answered, "but I told Martine I'd be home for supper by seven."

"Seven, eh." Pierre wagged his head. "You've got a lot to learn, young fellow. If you tell a woman seven, don't get there before half past. You have to start these new wives off in the right way."

It was heavy handed but well meant, so Georges smiled patiently. "Maybe so, but I told her—"

Alphonse raised his glass. "A toast to Martine! Come on now, Georges, she won't mind if you are a little late—if you tell her we were toasting her. Have one more drink."

Georges hesitated then sat down again. Martine wouldn't mind. He saw her for an instant in his mind, hair tousled, sleepy eyed, reaching out her arms to him. He felt a quickening in his breath. One more drink. Then he would go home. Home was a tiny one-bedroom apartment with a closet-like kitchen but its size didn't matter. Once within, the tiny space was his world and hers. They would have dinner later. When he first got home . . . He took the glass from the barmaid and smiled his good-humored smile for no one could see in his mind. It wouldn't matter if he was a little late.

If Georges had left when he first stood, he would have seen the car and he would have known and, in an instant, the men in the bar, his friends, Alphonse, Pierre, Michael, Paul, Rene, all men who worked together, knew each other well, would have been warned. Or if Schmidt had entered the bar first. Any stranger would have quieted the talk, turned faces wary. But Georges sat down again, smiling, his thoughts his own, and, on the sidewalk outside, Krause motioned for Schmidt to wait.

"Go inside, Robards," Krause ordered.

Louis Robards was a big man, almost three inches over six feet. Bent forward, his head down, he was still an imposing man, looming above his tormentors. He swayed unsteadily. It hurt to stand, to move, to breathe. He was badly injured, his body knew it. He looked at Krause. Pain had smeared his vision but he heard well enough.

"Go ahead."

The day shift was off, Robards knew, for dusk was beginning. Most of his friends would still be inside, drinking pernod or dark red wine, laughing, perhaps, about the train cars where they had switched weigh bills. That would show the Boche. Let them wait for those shipments. And the food cars en route to Germany with the good fresh vegetables. A little acid could do wonders.

"Hurry up, you fool," Krause said impatiently.

Robards took one step forward then slanted to his left and began to run, a heavy, slow lumbering stumble down the sidewalk.

He never had a chance. He didn't expect a chance. In his mind, dazed with pain, he remembered what he had been told, "Don't ever run from the Germans, they will shoot you in the back." Over the agony that jolted his liver with every thudding step, he waited for the rattle of the Schmeisser machine pistol that Schmidt held. "In the back . . . in the back . . . in the back . . ."

Schmidt raised his pistol and the nearest soldier lifted his gun.

"No," Krause directed. He raised his arm and gestured, a short hard chop. The soldier, expressionless, stepped forward.

Robards, his head down, his breath whistling through his teeth, never saw him. The rifle whacked brutally along his shoulder and head and Robards fell heavily to his knees.

The soldier lifted his rifle again but Krause shook his head.

Blood welled from Robards forehead. He wavered back and forth on his knees. A huge man. Too strong yet to fall.

"Grab his elbows," Krause ordered. "Shove him through the door."

Schmidt opened the door. Two soldiers swung Robards to his feet and pushed him forward. He tottered inside, one step, two, then once again sank to his knees, just beside Georges Mantel's chair.

"What the hell!"

"That man's hurt . . . who . . ."

"My God, it's Louis, hey, it's Louis . . ."

They called out and stood and the nearest surged closer. Georges pushed his chair out of the way and dropped down on one knee. "Louis, what's happened to you, man? Who did this to you?"

Abruptly, it was absolutely quiet in the narrow dim bar.

Georges looked over his shoulder. He saw the man in a suit first and then the Schmeisser pistol in his hands.

Krause let the moment expand, let the terrible quiet swell. Finally, his thin gray face as impassive as ever, he began to point. "That one and that one . . . the man trying to hide, there, to the left of the bar. The redhead and the fat one . . ."

Two soldiers closed in on each one named, moved them out the door onto the sidewalk. Thirteen men were taken. Not many were left now, the Devereaux brothers, Fabien, Clause, and Paul, the proprietor, Armand Mongelard, and Louis and Georges.

Georges still knelt beside Louis.

Krause looked down at them. "And that one."

At the door, Georges twisted sideways and called back to the owner. "Please Armand, go tell Martine I'll be a little late."

CHAPTER 4

"Lieutenant! Psst! Lieutenant, are you there?"

Jonathan woke with a start, his heart hammering. The sudden jerk set his leg to throbbing again. His hand tightened around the jagged lump of stone. In the temple, that was the place to get him. He wouldn't make a noise. No noise. Jonathan raised his arm.

"Lieutenant, it's me, Maurice. Are you there? It's so dark I can't see you."

Not a German. Jonathan shook his head, came fully awake. The Germans hadn't found him. He had heard them searching for a long time until it was fully dark then, finally, in the quiet warm blackness, he had fallen asleep. "Maurice." He whispered, too, then he was swept by the strangeness of it all, the dry dusty warm air, the absolute darkness in that pocket beneath the bridge, men whispering though not a soul was about within miles, the stone in his hand. "I'm here, above you."

Maurice scrambled on his knees, one hand reaching out until it touched Jonathan's tunic. "Thank God. We were afraid they'd found you."

No. Not yet.

"I've brought food and medicine. Do you know how badly you are hurt?"

"I don't know. It's my leg. I'll look at it tomorrow. What kind of medicine?"

"A salve. My mother has always used it for deep cuts. Once, when our cow, Georgette, was lamed with a bad cut in her hindquarter, Mother pasted it on, thick, very thick, and Georgette was healed."

Oh hell, Jonathan thought. Cow salve. Every time he moved his leg, it flamed with pain. Cow salve.

"If we can move you, I will try to get Doctor Morissey. They say he will treat wounded soldiers and not tell anyone."

They say. There were so many reminders that he was a danger to everyone who came in contact with him. This boy, he wasn't more than that, not even as old as Jonathan's students, fifteen, sixteen, was risking his life to help a stranger.

"Look," Jonathan said abruptly, "I don't want to be a burden to you. I'll rest up here. Get some strength, then strike out—"

"The Germans would find you. Wait and let us help." He paused, said awkwardly, "I'm sorry I can't take you home with me. But my father, he is so bitter. Don't worry, though, my brother and I will work it out. Now, quickly, for I must start back before the next patrol, let me show you," and he took Jonathan's hand and guided it to a sack. "The salve is here, in this tin, and this is a roll of muslin, to bind up your leg. There is a bottle of apple brandy, a bottle of water, a loaf of bread and some cheese and apples. Our apples. For more than two hundred years, my family has grown apples." He felt about, found Jonathan's parachute, rolled it up. "I'm going to take it a couple of miles south of here and half bury it, just good enough so that the Boche will find it tomorrow, when the search continues. They will think you have gone in the other direction."

Then Maurice was gone, slipping as silently from beneath the bridge as he had come.

Jonathan rummaged in the burlap sack until his fingers closed around the bottle of water. He uncorked it very carefully and raised it to his mouth. He wanted to drink and drink and drink, let the water rush down his throat, swallow until his air was gone, then breathe and drink again. But he took one small sip, a second, then, luxuriously, a third, holding the cool faintly earth-tasting liquid in his mouth for a long moment, letting the liquid trickle down his throat. He punched the cork tightly in the neck and returned the bottle to the sack. The cheese was a round. He took his pocket knife, cut out a thick wedge, tore a heel off the loaf, and ate, once again, slowly. He felt warmth and strength flowing into his body, even the pain in his leg didn't seem quite so bad. He decided to save the apples for his breakfast so he finished with two thick swallows of apple brandy and slowly sank once again into sleep.

Apples and billowing shimmering folds of silk and ripples of moonlit water revolved in his mind, the sharp rattle of machine guns, a long dusty corridor with sunlight streaming through a high arched window, himself strolling, carrying an armload of books, a girl walking away from him, farther and farther ahead, almost out of sight, a desperate panting race to reach her before she was gone. A rumbling thudding shock, bump after bump, bombs, they were being bombed.

He woke, gasping for breath, struggling to sit up, barraged by the thunder overhead. Three trucks rolled heavily across the bridge, shaking the wooden planks, sifting dirt down onto him. Was it the Germans, carrying soldiers out to hunt him?

It was early, the first light of morning just filtering beneath the bridge. Jonathan looked at his watch. Five-fifteen. It was an hour later in France, wasn't it?

He moved his watch ahead, wound it. He smiled wryly. All set up now, wasn't he? Oh well, at least he was still free and maybe the boys would be able to help him.

God, help him do what? How the hell could he hope to get away? He didn't even know where he was. He was lying helpless beneath a bridge near a German garrison and his leg was a bloody mess. Tentatively, he moved his foot. He groaned as his knee twisted and dull throbbing exploded into a knife-sharp sensation of heat.

He must see to his wound. He leaned forward. His trousers were stiff with blood. Worse than that, the cloth was stuck to his leg. Gently, he pushed the outstretched fingers of his right hand down his thigh until it began to hurt. It was all right up to four inches above the knee. That's where he began to saw with his pocket knife, cutting the pants away. It took a long time. He lay back and rested every few minutes, sweat slipping down his face. When he was finished, a rough oblong cut free, the cloth still stuck stubbornly to the flesh. He tugged.

"Oh, God." Fresh blood began to well in the center of the mangled patch of cloth. Whatever had torn into his leg, a part of the fuselage, shrapnel, a bullet, had ripped through his trousers, too, of course, and not only was the cloth stuck to the wound, pieces were embedded.

He stared at his leg for a long time. If he didn't get the wound clean, get those pieces of debris out, treat it, the wound would fester and swell. Already the surrounding skin was puffy and swollen.

Grimly, his face drawn into rigid lines, he began to pull and tease the cloth away. He took the bottle of water, dropped tiny splashes, then, using the tip end of his knife, he lifted up strips and pieces of cloth.

The skin puckered unevenly in an irregular V-shaped wound just above the knee. It should have been stitched, of course, a spread of more than an inch at some places. But he had the bits of cloth out now and it really didn't look too bad. Apparently the piece of metal had sliced over his knee, cutting loose this flap of skin. He couldn't see any shreds of metal and it hadn't cut down to the bone.

He stared at the swollen blackened edges for a long time. Should he spill more water over it, wash it better?

How clean was the water?

He had already used the water to loosen the dried stuck pieces of cloth, so why not wash it out all the way?

Horses. They probably had horses on a farm. It was water from a farm. Horses and tetanus. Something to that combination, wasn't there? Lockjaw. He shoved the cork back in the bottle and took the tin of salve from the bag.

The salve was yellowish-green and smelled like railroad tar.

"Me and Georgette," Jonathan said aloud. Straightening out his leg and pushing the edges of the wound close together, he plastered the gash with the salve, covering the open bloodied rupture with the thick gelatinous medicine. The salve felt oddly cool and warm at the same time, tingly but soothing. He wound a long strip of muslin over and over, fastened the bandage with the two safety pins attached to one end. He was just finishing when he heard the slow clop of horses' hooves. In a few minutes, a wagon trundled over the bridge. He lifted his head, waiting, but no one rustled through the grass down to the dry stream bed. Not Maurice and his brother, then. Or perhaps it was, but they were ignoring him during the daylight.

When would they come? Where were the Germans looking now? Would they beat back this way, knowing they had somehow missed him?

Jonathan drew his breath in sharply. It was stupid to worry over something beyond his control. Stupid and wasteful. It took energy to worry, to be afraid, energy he might need. Now, his leg bandaged, it was time to see if he could walk. There wasn't room enough to stand beneath the bridge. Quietly, pulling himself with no more sound than the scrape of cloth over dirt, he reached the edge of the bridge. He lay there for a long while, listening. A crow cawed distantly, starlings chattered nearby. Some small animal, a rat or rabbit, rustled close by. He listened with the most care to a faint faraway knock. If it was hammering, it wasn't nearby. A hollow but clear-cut knock. He frowned and listened. He listened patiently, five minutes, ten, then, with a flash of memory he was at home again, in his mother's garden, she was smiling, her head turning, saying, "Hear that, Jonathan? It's a woodpecker. Hard at it, isn't he?"

A woodpecker. Not the faraway chop of an axe.

If there were anyone near the bridge and the dry weed-grown ditch, he must be standing as quietly as Jonathan lay. Satisfied, Jonathan sat up and began to push himself backwards up the slope until he could reach up and touch the edge of the bridge. He used both hands to pull up. He hung there for a long moment, his good leg bent and taking his weight, his hurt leg outstretched, and peered over the side of the bridge, looking quickly up and down the road, twisting his neck to look behind him. A forest of oak trees crowded thickly down to the stream bed. The dusty grayish road bent out of sight into the trees. He couldn't see far because of the woods, but he would hear anyone coming long before they would be able to see the bridge or him. It was still cool among the huge trees, the sunlight slanting through the thick green clusters of leaves, the only sound the erratic tattoo of the woodpecker.

Cool and bright and cheerful, and the sky, glimpsed through the tree tops, a clear and vivid blue.

What was happening at Hawkinge? Was his squadron already up? Someone would have packed his kit by now. Group Captain Arnold would have called his mother. Jonathan frowned. His mother had always been a strong woman. She had to have been, to have kept the family afloat after his father's death at Verdun in the Great War. But even a strong woman could bear only so much. His brother, Robin, was posted missing after Dunkirk. Now she must learn that he too was missing.

But maybe she would have faith enough to pull them all through. After all, he wasn't dead. Not nearly. He had felt when he first heard Robin listed as missing that he had been killed, but now, he felt a sudden surge of hope. Maybe Robin was somewhere here in North France, too, hiding from the Boche.

By God, maybe both of them were lucky.

Jonathan was smiling as he straightened up and stood beside the bridge. He kept his weight on his left leg. Cautiously, he stepped lightly with his injured leg. It hurt, it hurt like the very devil, but he could, just barely, manage to walk on it. With a stick or a cane or a crutch, he could manage.

For a long glorious moment , he stayed there beside the bridge, leaning on it, feeling the warmth of the morning sunlight on his face. His eyes moved restlessly around the small clearing and the patch of road he could see and along the wall of trees. No one there, no one coming. He took out his cigarettes, shook one free. Just one. That was all he would chance.

He smoked slowly, drawing the smoke deep into his lungs, savoring the acrid brownish taste. He put the cigarette out very carefully, making sure no spark danced into the dry weeds beside him. Then reluctantly, he swung himself back beneath the bridge, back into dusty dim safety. He stretched out comfortably, ate half the remaining cheese and two chunks of bread, and slowly drank some apple brandy. He lay back and stared sightlessly at his planked ceiling. It was mid-morning now. Thursday, August 15. Last year in mid-August, he had been on a walking holiday of Cornwall, tramping along the rugged rock-hewn coast. At Padstow one mid-week day, it might have been a Thursday, he had bought a pork pie and two bottles of beer and found a faint path winding down to a narrow pocket of sand circled by jagged tooth-edged boulders. The sand was wet as the tide had just raced out. He had spread his mackintosh for a blanket and eaten a leisurely lunch, then rested, hands behind his head, looking up at a milky blue sky and scud-ding clouds, thinking of the first lecture he would give when classes began. Just a year ago. He had thought Hitler menacing and evil, but he had never imagined the mustachioed German would change his life. His life and thousands of lives. But he could still think what he wished. With a slight smile, Jonathan said softly, "Gentlemen, we will consider both Chaucer the man and Chaucer the poet this term. We will begin by recalling the world as it was when . . ."

CHAPTER 5

There had never been a doorman here, of course, but Eleanor remembered the apartment house having a down-at-heels blowsy charm. Now, the entry door moved on only one hinge and she had to lift the door to open it. The foyer was scuffed and dusty. Letter boxes mostly hung open and empty. The Durands, mother and son, had the second-floor back apartment. The smell of cooking cabbage flooded down the stairwell.

Eleanor hesitated. It was so dark and dirty. But if anyone would help her, it would be the Durands. She started up the steps, smiling. Paul was one of her husband's best friends, a fortyish sardonic professor of languages. His mother, Leone, cooked incessantly, talked without pause, welcomed his friends, bemoaned the lack of a daughter-in-law, and continued hopefully to match-make, undismayed by Paul's wry disinterest. Her round, plump face always smiling, tendrils of curls escaping from her bun, her good humor and kindness attracted students of all sorts. Once Paul had put his foot down firmly, "Mother, I know you have a soft heart. I appreciate it, I value it. But, nonetheless, I am not willing to share the front hall closet with that bedraggled girl from Tours. Send her home to her loving family. I wish once again to hang my overcoat in the front closet, place my boots in the corner, tuck my umbrella to one side."

Leone had opened her huge blue eyes wide, tilted her head, and said slowly, "Oh Paul, I'm sorry about the closet. I would clear it out for you if I could. But Paul, Annemarie doesn't have a loving family."

That had been that. Annemarie had lived with them for two years, then married a prim young pharmacist and moved two blocks away to a tiny room in a boardinghouse attic, but she still spent most of her day at the Durands. As Eleanor hurried up the stairs, she was listening. She was almost to the second floor when her steps slowed and she began to frown.

It was quiet. Too quiet.

It was never quiet at the Durands. Young voices, usually raised in excited loud discussion, reverberated until the early morning hours, Leone offering steaming mugs of hot chocolate or glasses of red wine. She knew each student by name, knew his hopes ("Michael, have you been accepted at the Institute, my dear, how wonderful! Dominique, you think twice my dear, don't be hasty. If it is really love, there is no hurry. Tell me your name again? Ralph? How do you say it? Ralph. And you've come all the way from Mexico? No? Oh, New Mexico. Where is New Mexico, Ralph?") Cigarette smoke and the tart smell of wine, the warmth of people, laughter and movement, Paul smiling satirically but always gently.

Silence.

Eleanor almost turned away without knocking. Obviously, no one was home. Of course, the fall term hadn't begun. Perhaps Paul and his mother had left Paris in June, before the Germans came, and hadn't returned. If they had left soon enough, before the German onslaught swept past Paris and turned back the refugees, they might have reached friends in the South and be there now.

Everything had happened suddenly after the Germans stormed into Holland. Andre had only a week's notice when his unit was called up. He had tried frantically to arrange his affairs. That last morning, cramming an extra set of boots into his luggage, he had told Eleanor, "If you need help, real help, go to Paul Durand."

Eleanor stared at the closed door to the Durand apartment. Usually the door had been ajar when they came in the evening, voices and music drifting down the hall. How dreadful that she had not even checked on Paul and his mother since Andre left.

But it hadn't seemed a time for visiting friends, not with half the shops in Paris boarded up and the hated green of the Germans everywhere you walked. It was better to stay home, shades drawn, shutting out all the hurtful sights.

She knocked almost perfunctorily. Once, twice. She turned away. She was midway down the hall when she heard someone coming briskly up the steps. They met at the top of the stairs.

"Annemarie? Yes, it is, isn't it?"

The thin young girl paused, nodded. "You are . . ."

"Mme. Masson. Eleanor Masson. My husband Andre and I used to visit Paul and his mother quite often."

Annemarie smiled. "Oh yes, of course."

"No one's home. I knocked but there wasn't any answer."

Annemarie looked surprised. "Oh, I think you are mistaken, Mme. Masson. Mme. Durand is there. I am living with her now and she never leaves the apartment. I've been out shopping. You know how it is, you have to get to the shops so early. I was at the butcher's at eight this morning. I waited two hours and still there wasn't a scrap of meat left but I told him she was old and needed just a morsel and he found me a soup bone."

Eleanor looked at the basket Annemarie was carrying. Why in the world would she be living with the Durands again? And, even if she were, why would Annemarie be doing the cooking? If ever there was a cook who took joy in her kitchen, who could create the most marvelous meals from the most meager ingredients, it was Leone Durand.

"You say you are living here now?" Eleanor spoke slowly, staring at Annemarie's dark face, hoping, but, in her heart, knowing the answer.

"Yes, since Professor Durand died."

"I didn't know. Oh God, I'm so sorry."

Paul dead. Intelligent, aloof, gentle Paul.

Annemarie was talking on, in that young matter-of-fact voice, ". . . the breakthrough at Sedan . . . a field hospital . . . he had volunteered as an ambulance driver . . . not in a reserve unit . . . asthma. The letter came the next week."

"And Mme. Durand?"

Annemarie looked sad. "It is odd, you know, what happens to people when their world dissolves. She must have cared too much. I would have said, before the war, that she was the strongest woman I knew." Annemarie unlocked the door and held it open for Eleanor. The curtains were drawn. It was so dark that it took Eleanor a moment to find Mme. Durand.

The older woman huddled in the wingback chair next to the fireplace. She didn't look up until Eleanor came and stood beside her.

"Leone."

The once plump high-colored face was sunken and thin. Strands of lank hair hung uncombed. Dark brown eyes looked at Eleanor incuriously.

"Leone, don't you know me? It's Eleanor. Eleanor Masson."

"How do you do." The thin childlike tone prickled Eleanor's back. She looked at Annemarie pleadingly.

"Come now, Mama Leone." Annemarie's hearty voice sounded shockingly loud in the stillness of the dusty dim room. "You remember Mme. Masson. Her husband is Andre Masson. You knew him. He was a professor, too, like Paul."

Eleanor bent down, reaching for the thin hands that lay supinely along the chair arms. They felt cool and dry, scarcely more human than a bird's claws. "I'm sorry." Eleanor's voice broke. "If I had known, I would have come sooner. Oh Leone, I'm so sorry. We loved Paul, too."

"Paul . . ." The eyes flickered with life. She struggled to get up. "Paul will be home soon. I'll start dinner. Whatever am I doing, sitting here like an old woman? And it's so dark. I must have taken a nap. Here, let's get these drapes open and get things straight, well, I've never seen so much dust, and magazines scattered about. It's a disgrace and the students start to come, oh, about four, let me see, what time is it?"

She had slipped between them, darted to the windows, pulled the drapes wide, then turned toward the back of the apartment and the kitchen. Her voice muted now, floated out to them. Pans clattered, cupboard doors banged open and shut.

Then, abruptly, silence.

Leone stood in the middle of the tiny kitchen, clasping a brownish green pottery mug to her chest, tears streaming down her cheeks.

Eleanor recognized the mug. How many cold nights had they sat by the fire, Paul cradling that mug in his hands, sipping strong chocolate with its topping of cinnamon and cream.

Annemarie deftly took the mug, substituting her basket. "Look now, Mama Leone, you won't guess what I've brought today. Look now and give me a guess." She gestured for Eleanor to leave the kitchen.

Eleanor waited in the silent living room. The sharp morning sunlight emphasized the smudged windows, the film of dust in the once immaculate room, the general aura of disuse and neglect.

Annemarie joined her in a moment. "I have her busy now, making the soup. If you don't mind, it would be better for you to go. When she remembers, it distresses her. When she doesn't remember . . ."

When she didn't remember, there was no point in staying.

Eleanor nodded and turned to go.

"Is there anything I can do to help?" Annemarie asked diffidently.

Eleanor wondered if her tension was that obvious. She hesitated, looking again, almost as if for the first time, at Annemarie's young thin face. Dark eyes, sallow skin, a splotch of acne across her forehead. She had, when Mme. Durand first took her in, a hunted badgered look. Warmth and caring had filled out the thin cheeks, relieved the anxious look. Then love had brought a faint glow, a touch of radiance. Now, once again, her face was sallow and pale, her eyes somber.

What was her husband's name?

Annemarie watched her eyes.

Eleanor didn't have to ask.

"Jean-Paul's company was at Lille. The last time I heard."

"Andre was at Bruges. The last I heard," Eleanor said heavily. "So both of them were near Dunkirk."

That was the secret hope, the dream of so many thousands of Frenchwomen. They had heard nothing and they knew, the newspapers and radio broadcasts had told them, that many died on the roads and in the fields as the French and English fell back. But they knew too that thousands of Frenchmen had escaped to England.

Andre and Jean-Paul?

The two women saw in each other's eyes grief and hope and the seeds of despair.

"We don't have much here," Annemarie said awkwardly, "but if you need food?"

Eleanor shook her head quickly. "It's nothing like that." She barely whispered the words. "Annemarie, do you know anyone who could help someone get to the Unoccupied Zone?"

Annemarie looked around the silent living room before she leaned close to Eleanor to whisper. "I have heard, I do not know if it is true, but I have heard that people can go to Saint-Quentin, you know it is a little village just next to the Demarcation Line, and that if you know the right people, you can be taken across."

"The right people?"

Annemarie shrugged. "I don't know who you would ask. It was the brother of my friend Germaine who told me."

"Could you get in touch with him? Find out for me?"

Annemarie shook her head. "He is gone now, too." She frowned. "Perhaps if the person who wishes to cross would go to Saint-Quentin, perhaps ask at the Church."

"That won't do. The person who wishes to cross, he can't speak French."

"Oh, Madame! Oh, you must be careful!"

"Annemarie, Annemarie," Mme. Durand called plaintively.

"One moment, Mama Leone, one moment." Annemarie opened the door, then closed it to whisper quickly, "Madame, do you remember Roger Lamirand? The cocky medical student? The one with the wispy beard who always wore a beret?"

Hazily, Eleanor did. A rasping voice, always too loud. A pugnacious, abrasive not especially likeable young man.

"He lives two blocks from here, the northeast corner apartment house. Just off the Rue Saint Jacques. I think you can ask him."

On the street, Eleanor hesitated then swung to her right. It would do no harm to go by Lamirand's apartment. She didn't have to tell him anything. Why did Annemarie think he could be trusted? She walked slower and slower. The whole area seemed odd to her. It had been so familiar. Andre's offices had been just a half block from here. She had often met him and carried a picnic lunch to the Luxembourg gardens. The Medici Fountain was their favorite spot. They never went there, in the heat of summer or the cool leaf-strewn fall or even occasionally on a brisk snowy winter walk, without seeing some student Andre knew. Now the streets were almost empty and the occasional passerby seemed furtive and wary.

Lamirand's apartment house was in a narrow twisty street where sunlight would touch the curbs only at noon. Even now, at mid-morning, it was cheerless and drab, the bricked facade chipped, the tall narrow windows uncurtained and dirty. In the entry hall, Eleanor paused uncertainly. No letter-boxes here. She knocked at the concierge's door. A middle-aged woman with a flat hard face and harshly hennaed hair stared at her.

"M. Lamirand? He no longer lives here, Madame."

"Can you tell me where he has gone?"

A shrug. Then a flicker of interest stirred. "Are you looking for an apartment, Madame? I could rent it to you cheap, very cheap."

"I don't—" Eleanor stopped, looked up the stairs. Dirty, yes. Cheap. A young man would not be noticeable here, in the Latin Quarter. There weren't many young men these days, but there were some. A place where a young man could hide. Eleanor looked back at the concierge. "I might be interested," she said slowly, very slowly, and emphatically, "in subletting an apartment. I'll pay you in cash and the apartment would still be listed in M. Lamirand's name."

The concierge nodded and answered, as slowly, "It can be arranged, Madame. Of course, I will need a little extra fee to make it possible. Say, 2,500 francs?"

Eleanor calculated quickly, nodded. Not quite fifty dollars. Fair enough. She stepped inside the concierge's apartment and peeled off the bills. She had just enough to make up the sum. The woman gave her the key and pointed up the stairs. "The top floor, back."

It was a small one-bedroom apartment, shabby and cheaply furnished, but cheeringly clean, the living room recently painted buttercup yellow, the floors waxed and swept. Eleanor began to smile. What a perfectly wonderful piece of luck. Now they had a place to hide Michael. Roger must have left in a hurry, the closet ajar, the dresser drawers agape. He had not even taken time to empty out his larder. Eleanor knew then it must have been a very swift departure. The crock of honey would be unobtainable at the grocery and cost up to two hundred francs on the black market. There was half a loaf of moldy bread and, riches, a mesh bag of potatoes. She looked more carefully through the apartment, then. Surely he was coming back. But there were no clothes in the closet, the bed was stripped and bare, the dresser drawers empty. In the small square living room, she was puzzled for a moment by the arrangement of the furniture. There was a worn rocking chair and lumpy sofa along one wall. An armchair sat with its back to the room, facing the one large window to the north. When she leaned against the sill, she said aloud, "Oh, how lovely."

To the left and down the street, old stone, fifteenth century surely, glowed in the hot August noon sun. A crenellated wall with a watchtower and battlements guarded a courtyard and, beyond, a huge Gothic building, the Hotel de Cluny, museum of medieval crafts. Eleanor studied the gargoyles along the balustrade. One of the things she loved the most about Paris was the unexpected glimpses of grandeur, even from the meanest of vantage points. This was where Roger Lamirand had sat, looking up from his studies to admire the pentagonal tower or the incredibly complex frieze that ran along the bottom of the main building's roof or to shade his eyes against the sun reflected from the huge skylights.

Eleanor felt the same surge of excitement she had experienced so many times in Paris, her first view of Sacre-Couer glistening like alabaster in a hard winter sun, the gray magnificence of Notre Dame, the Rue de Conde just after dawn, looking as it must have in 1789, the year the Bastille was captured and the Revolution begun.

A sleek black Mercedes roared down the Rue du Sommerard, the staff flag snapping. The horn blared. Eleanor drew her breath in sharply.

A cart was midway across the street, moving slowly, heavily. An old woman looked up in panic and tried to pull the cart backward. The Mercedes, never slackening its speed, swerved to the left, sweeping past, the edge of its bumper just clipping the cart. The impact shattered the end and dumped mounds of flowers rolled in damp newspapers. The vendor was pulled down. The Mercedes wheeled around the corner.

Slowly, painfully, the old woman struggled upright and hobbled toward her cart. Then, she stood, her shoulders slumped, staring down at the wreckage, the splintered wood, the scattered bright bits of flowers. Tears began to spill down her face.

Eleanor closed her eyes. Damn them. Oh, damn them.

CHAPTER 6

"Didn't you find anyone who can help us?" Linda tried to keep the despair from her voice.

"Not a soul. After I left the Lamirand apartment, I went to the Café Marius, do you remember it? I used to meet Andre there for lunch. I used the telephone and I called and called. Hardly anyone is still in town." She found only a few at home. She told Linda of her guarded inquiry to several, she had a friend, someone she trusted, who knew of someone who needed to cross the line, not openly, and did they have an idea what she might tell them? The cold long empty pauses. So sorry. No idea. None at all. Her stiff good byes.

"What if one of them turns us in?" Linda asked, her voice small.

"I don't think anyone will. They just don't want to get involved themselves."

Linda clasped her hands tightly together. "What are we going to do?"

The heat pressed against them. Not a breath of air stirred, the drapes hanging heavy and lifeless by the open windows. Eleanor leaned wearily back in her chair. "I don't know," she said finally, "I just don't know."

"Mother, I could ask Franz's father—"

"No," Eleanor said sharply, almost angrily. "Don't tell anyone, Robert, anyone at all. I'll think of something. Tomorrow I'll take the train to Senlis and talk to your Uncle Raphael."

Robert looked surprised. "But Mother, I thought you didn't like Uncle Raphael. I thought—"

"Robert."

They sat for a moment in a strained silence.

The clock on the mantel chimed 11:30. "Oh my heavens, it's almost noon. I was gone all morning, wasn't I? Eleven-thirty. We must hurry and get Michael out of the building before the Biziens come home for lunch."

"I'll take him now, on the Metro," Linda offered.

Eleanor shook her head. "We don't dare. I went by the Metro today and I saw the Germans checking papers at three different stations. They come without any warning and check everyone as they go out. We don't have any papers for Michael. Even if we did, he would be lost if anyone stopped him since he doesn't speak French."

"Let's put him back in the trunk of the car, the way I brought him."

"If anyone saw him get into the trunk . . ."

There were so many difficulties. The only safe place to get into the trunk would be in the garage itself but Pierre was almost always there and could they take a chance on him?

"What about riding in the front seat, just like anybody?" Robert asked.

But was there anyone anymore who could be just like anybody? Cars were conspicuous. Only Germans and the friends of Germans had cars. Their car did have the Red Cross pennant, but Michael was young and a man and that just might catch the attention of a German patrol. Would anyone be on the lookout for that particular car with its Red Cross pennant? If Krause were still suspicious of them, they might be under surveillance.

"It's too far to walk. At least we could, but Michael is still weak from so little food."

"My bicycle!" Robert exclaimed. "He can ride my bicycle and I'll borrow Franz's."

Eleanor frowned. "Robert, do you think Franz will loan you his bicycle? You know how hard it is to find a bike and they cost almost 10,000 francs on the black market."

"Franz will help us. You forget, Mother, Franz is Jewish."

"Oh. Oh, yes. But Robert, if," she stopped, took a breath, "if you should be caught with Michael, it would go doubly hard for Franz."

"I wouldn't tell anyone I had his bike. The Germans wouldn't know we didn't have two bikes."

Slowly Eleanor nodded. "That's all right then. That should work. Linda can go by the Metro to meet you at the apartment and bring back Franz's bicycle. Yes, it should all work out beautifully. Hurry now, Robert. Go see if you can borrow the bicycle."

When Robert returned with Franz's bicycle, they left through the alley. Linda followed on foot. They were soon out of sight, Robert riding a half block in the lead, far enough ahead so that if he saw a military roadblock he could turn back and so could Michael while still out of sight of the soldiers.

The Etoile station was the nearest. Linda didn't hurry. The mesh bag she carried, with some necessities for Michael, was fairly heavy. She would reach the apartment before them anyway. She welcomed the shade of the plane trees along the sidewalk. Many of the fine houses along here, sheltered behind grilled fences, looked empty and deserted. There, two doors ahead, soldiers were carrying furniture and paintings out of a gray stone house, filling the Army truck. Some wealthy Parisian would return one day to find his home empty and, more than likely, taken over by a high-ranking officer. She was still a block from the Champs-Elysees when she heard the music, the steady tramp of marching feet, punctuated by drum rolls and the strident blasts of trumpets. She walked a little faster. A parade? Whatever for?

She was struck first by the emptiness of the broad lovely street. No cars, no taxis, no throngs of shoppers or idlers or tourists. Only the wide street and the German band, helmeted, booted, led by a drum major, and behind the band, detachments of soldiers. She knew what it was then though this was the first time she had seen it. The changing of the German guard at noon. The few pedestrians walked quickly, heads down, eyes averted from the street.

Ba-rom-pom-pom, ba-rom-pom-pom, rom-pom, rom-pom, pom.

The soldiers looked straight ahead, their heads held high, chins up, youthful faces cold and arrogant. Their high black boots flashed in the summer sun as their stiffened legs swung up and down.

Linda looked to her right, toward the Arc de Triomphe, at the immense Nazi flag which hung motionless in the summer sun, the Swastika brilliantly red in the white circle against the black background. The band had reached the Arc now. There was an instant's pause, then the drum major raised his baton and the band sung into Deutschland Uber Alles.

Linda turned away, walking toward the Metro steps.

"Stop. At once."

She took another step and her elbow was roughly grabbed. She looked up into the hard red face of a German captain.

"You will wait until the music is finished."

She saw then that German soldiers stood stiffly at attention and the few, very few Frenchman, waited, their faces impassive.

The captain held her elbow tightly until the last chord then loosened his grip and walked away without another word, as if she were too insignificant and unimportant to merit any further attention.

Linda fled toward the Metro entrance, almost running down the broad shallow steps. It was better down here, even though the station was jammed with people. She finally got onto a car on the third train. She would change at the Chatelet station. The car was smelly and hot, claustrophobic, but better, so much better, than standing in the shade of a chestnut tree and watching Germans march past. The subway glided to a stop. Passengers struggled on and off, then it started again. Gradually Linda began to ease her way nearer the sliding doors. Not too far now. Her station was the seventh. She was near the door when the train reached the Louvre station. A young man behind her asked to get by. He was almost out of the door when he saw the green uniforms at the top of the stairs and the line beginning to form as people stopped to show their papers. He stepped backward, his heel coming down heavily on Linda's right foot. She gave a muffled cry. He swung awkwardly around, mumbling, "Pardon." But he still stared at the checkpoint. Behind him, coming into the car from farther up the train, were two men, both wearing hats and unremarkable gray suits, but their eyes darted from seat to seat, from face to face.

If they were looking for the man in front of her, they would be looking for a man alone. She stepped close to him, slipping her arms up around his neck, and buried her face in his neck, her lips next to his ear, "Don't look behind, don't. Two men. Gestapo," then lifting her face she smiled, saying loudly, "Oh Cherie, how wonderful. You are so marvelous to have found us an apartment. It isn't everyone who has such a wonderful husband."

The two men, with their cold searching eyes, were even with them now, and she stood on tiptoe to kiss the stranger's cheek, hiding his face from their view. Then the men were past. She chattered on for a moment more, but let her voice fall lower.

"They're gone now," he said finally.

She closed her eyes and realized she was trembling.

The stranger was trembling, too.

For a moment, they clasped hands, leaned together.

"Thank you," he whispered. "Thank you."

They both got off at the Louvre station, she to transfer, he after a tense searching look, to hurry up the stairs. She looked after him. "Good luck," she whispered. Luck to everyone tricking the Germans. Luck to all of us.

She carried the memory of his face for the rest of her journey. A nice face but remarkable only for its look of strain and tension and fear, a not uncommon look in Paris now. She wondered as she came up into the sunshine and turned toward the Cluny Museum whether her own face had that look. Deliberately, she forced a half smile and swung her arms as she walked. Though if she were stopped now, all she had to do was show them her green identity card. She had nothing to fear. Not right now. But she carried fear with her. My God, what a long way for Robert and Michael to ride. How could they possibly make it without attracting some notice? If they were stopped, surely Michael would pretend he didn't know Robert. But Robert was so young. If he saw Michael stopped, questioned, would he protect himself, realizing that his capture wouldn't help Michael? Or would he give himself away trying to help the Englishman?

Linda paced up and down in the apartment, up and down, up and down. When they finally came, noisily, lugging the bicycles up four flights because they would be a sure loss if left on the street, Linda embarrassed Robert with her hard quick thankful hug.

"My gosh, Aunt Linda, it wasn't anything at all. Nobody even looked at us."

Michael saw clearer than Robert. "Miss . . ."

"Linda."

"Linda. I've put all of you in danger. Haven't I?" His face had that look, too, now. Haunted and drawn and weary. His face and that of the young man on the Metro. Hurt frightened faces. Other faces moved in her mind. Krause's, the captain's at the Arc de Triomphe, those two hard dangerous faces in the Metro. Anger, touched with fear but stronger than fear, stirred within Linda.

"It doesn't matter."

Michael pushed his hand through his thin fair hair. "Look, why don't you go, both of you, and don't come back. Stay away from me. I'll rest up then see what I can do."

Linda smiled. "Don't worry, Michael. We've done all right so far. Haven't we?"

He nodded. "But . . ."

"Trust us a little longer. We don't know what we are going to do with you, but we'll find a way. I know we will. Eleanor's going to Senlis tomorrow. That will probably solve everything."

His face didn't change. That was what was so damnable. It didn't change at all, looking as bland and self-possessed and unmoved as when she had first begun to talk. He was, in a way, so like Andre, intense dark eyes and angular thoughtful face. His fingers lifted occasionally to touch a smooth silky mustache. But Andre's eyes crackled with humor and care and his mouth was broad with deep laugh lines bracketing the corners, not thin and pursed like Raphael's. Raphael didn't like her. Eleanor thought about it without surprise. She had always sensed it, ever since she had come to France as Andre's wife. She remembered her first meeting with Raphael. He hadn't come to the train station to welcome the bridal couple home. It was late afternoon before he arrived at Andre's apartment. Even now, sixteen years later, she remembered the cool dry impersonal touch of his hand, the slight incline of his head. He had said the appropriate thing, welcoming her as a brother-in-law, but his eyes were cold and aloof. His eyes were cold and aloof now as he gazed at the dusty tapestry on his office wall, not at her.

"Raphael." Her voice was louder than she had intended.

"I am listening, Eleanor."

"You haven't answered."

"I don't know what to say." He pressed his fingertips together, then turned his hands palms up. "Even for a woman and a foreigner, I find your behavior surprising."

Eleanor sat very still. A woman and a foreigner. "I am a resident of France. A French wife."

"Then you should obey the law."

She stared at him for a long moment, at his narrow intelligent face, immobile now, empty of all expression.

"Oh, Raphael," she sighed finally.

A tic pulled at the corner of his mouth and a tiny flush of red tinged his cheeks. "The war is over, Eleanor. The Armistice was signed on June 21. France and Germany are no longer at war."

She said nothing.

He said tartly, "The Germans, of course, have every right to demand that the French people surrender to them all English soldiers. Germany and England are still at war."

Eleanor nodded. "The English have continued to fight." She emphasized "English" ever so little.

His fist slammed onto his desk. "The French were betrayed. The

English led us into this war, then, once we were committed, they abandoned us."

"Betrayed? Oh yes, Raphael, the French people were betrayed." She stood up angrily. "But not by the English. The fat generals betrayed the people and the rich industrialists who didn't want the war to destroy too much property and the corrupt politicians, oh yes, Raphael, the French people were betrayed all right." She was trembling with anger now. "But let me tell you something, Raphael, this war isn't over. I heard that French general speak on BBC, that young general, De Gaulle, and he and other Frenchmen who escaped to England, they with the English are going to keep on fighting. And I know that Andre," tears burned in her eyes, "Andre wouldn't give up. I don't know where he is, he may be dead, but if he isn't dead, if the Germans have him in a prison, then every British soldier that makes it out of France is one more to fight the Germans and help free Andre someday."

She was at the door.

"Eleanor, wait a moment."

She stood stiffly at the door, her hand on the ornate metal knob.

Raphael came around his desk and reached out to take her arm. "Please, Eleanor, wait a moment. Don't leave looking angry and upset. You mustn't attract attention. Not now. Not after what you've told me. It could be dangerous, Eleanor."

She managed to speak, though it was hard. "It is good of you to care."

"You are Andre's wife." His hand fell away from her arm. "Have you heard nothing about him? I hoped, when you came, I hoped that you knew something of Andre."

She faced him and recognized the anguish in his eyes. He did love his younger brother. In his own stiff and formal and rigid fashion, he loved Andre, too.

"Nothing," she said somberly. "Nothing. Last week I spent two days on the Avenue de l'Opera, reading the lists of prisoners. But the names aren't in any kind of order. I didn't find his name."

"He might be among those who escaped to England."

"He might." She didn't think so. He might, but she didn't think Andre would have fled, leaving them behind. She didn't think so. She wished she could believe it, hold to it. But she didn't think so.

"If you do hear . . ."

"I will let you know immediately."

"I wish you would join me for lunch before you return to Paris." She tried to smile.

"Please. The café across from the bank still has some food and I've quite a few stamps saved up. Please, Eleanor. You can tell me what it's like in Paris and how Robert is getting along. It has been such a long time since I've seen Robert."

They had watery potato soup and black bread without butter and a leek salad and Raphael tried, not so much to explain, as to share his reasoning.

". . . the Marshal must be given a chance to mold a new France. And, of course, a government cannot survive if its laws are flouted. You see that, Eleanor?"

She nodded. Raphael had spent his adult life practicing law in Senlis, following the rules, accepting his government's dictates. So she nodded.

He even walked to the station to see her off. When the train was pulling in, the wheels rumbling, the black thick dusting of coal smoke sweeping ahead, he caught her once again by the arm. "Eleanor, the chief of police here told me something, I don't know if it is true. But I feel I must warn you."

The travelers were beginning to surge toward the train, but Raphael held tightly to her arm. "He said that if an English soldier is captured in civilian dress, the Germans shoot him as a spy."

"Oh, no." She gasped. "Surely not."

Passengers squeezed by them, carrying parcels and bags and suitcases tied with twine.

"Anyone who helps an Englishman will go to prison."

She was moving away from him now, caught up in the crush of travelers. She twisted around.

He looked out of place standing so formally on the dusty littered platform, his suit carefully pressed, his shoes shiny with polish. His mouth, that thin pursed mouth, moved to form the words, "Be careful, Eleanor. Be careful."

The train was jammed. She stood in the corridor all the way back to Paris, staring sightlessly out the speckled window. The wheels clacked in that unmistakable rhythm of a train. A phrase rang over and over in her mind, "Shoot him as a spy . . . shoot him as a spy . . . shoot him as a spy . . ."

The sun was already hidden behind the tall trees but fiery swaths of orange lighted the high branches though the trunks were hidden in deep shadows. Jonathan held onto the bridge and looked somberly up and down the empty road. The blaze of orange on the horizon was the last brilliant flare of the August sunset. Almost dark now. Another night beginning.

Jonathan rubbed his bristly cheek. Friday night. He had crashed Wednesday. Maurice had slipped beneath the bridge Wednesday night, bringing food and salve and hope. But he had not returned.

Wednesday night. Thursday night. Now it was Friday night. You'd better face up to it, old man. He's not coming back. You're on your own, Jonathan. It's up to you.

The bread and cheese were gone. And the water. He still had a quarter bottle of the apple brandy, but its thick sweetness only made him thirstier. He stood by the bridge as he had that very first morning, holding on, taking all his weight on his good leg.

He couldn't take the bloody bridge with him. Slowly, he let go of the bridge and tried to stand on his right leg. He gasped finally and reached out to catch hold of the uneven wooden edge before he fell. Tears of pain and frustration burned behind his eyes.

He had to walk. He had to walk unless he wanted to rot beneath that bridge, lay there until he was too weak even to crawl.

The shadows of the trees, long and straight as bars, fell across the road now, reached even to the bridge in the center of the clearing. How many minutes of daylight left? Ten minutes. Perhaps fifteen.

Jonathan twisted to look behind him. The dry rocky creek bed curved to the north, then disappeared into the wood. It looked like a fairly wild wood, tangled with undergrowth and thick with broken limbs and fallen branches. If he could find something to fashion into a crutch or cane, maybe then he could manage. He would have to find something. He couldn't walk unaided. And he had to walk.

Darkness came swiftly. Jonathan swung back beneath the bridge. He didn't try to settle into sleep. Not for a long time. He tried to think. He was hungry and a little feverish and very thirsty, but he had to think. First, a crutch. As soon as it was light, he would crawl to the wood, find a broken branch, shape it with his knife.

He uncorked the apple brandy, took a single mouthful, slowly let it seep down his throat. His eyes closed. He slept lightly, waking several times to lift his head and listen. Maurice had said he would come back. Jonathan was sure Maurice meant what he promised. Had the boy been arrested? Or had the search by the Germans frightened him? What was it he had said? That he couldn't take Jonathan home because his father was so "bitter." What did that mean?

Jonathan finally sank into a deeper sleep just before dawn, but he woke at the first thinning of the darkness. He crawled out from beneath the bridge and pulled up to his feet. The dry creek bed was not the most direct route to the woods. The most direct route was through chest-high grasses. A careful man could walk through the grasses, step lightly and leave no trail.

Jonathan couldn't walk. He had to crawl and that would trample a nice wide swath that would catch the eye of even the most incurious passerby.

Jonathan eased back down to the ground and began to crawl up the dry rock-strewn channel, pulling his bad leg along. His elbows and sides began to ache from bumping over the pebbles, some as large as baseballs. It took more than an hour to reach the edge of the woods. He rested for a long time, let the sweat cool and dry. It was dim in among the trees, dim and safe like an empty country church with the sunlight piercing the thick canopies of leaves on a slant like light coming through high deep-set windows.

Dim and safe and silent.

He found a good branch almost at once. Lightning had shattered an old oak, wrenching it almost apart, thrusting one immense limb down into the ground, breaking a half dozen branches into pieces. This branch hung from the limb jammed into the ground. Jonathan pulled and it came away, trailing a long piece of bark. The joint end was about three inches in circumference. He hacked off enough from the other end to form a rough crutch about five feet tall.

It only took him only ten minutes to hobble back to the bridge with his new support, though he could already feel the rub beneath his armpit. He would have to try and shape the top of the crutch better, but, by God, he could move. He was impatient to go but he realized he would have to stay on a road. He couldn't strike out across country on a crutch. On a road, there would be laborers or travelers. Or soldiers. Even without his tunic, he was obviously in uniform. He would have to wait until dark when he could hide if he heard others coming.

He didn't permit himself to think too far ahead. The "others" on the road might easily be German soldiers. Would more than likely be German soldiers. But he had to take a chance. He might as well be in a prisoner-of-war camp as stay beneath the bridge.

Somewhere down that road, though, he would have to take another chance. He would have to ask for help. He had no idea where he was. In Northern France, but that was all he knew. He had no money, no food, no papers. He would have to trust to his luck.

He spent the afternoon, an afternoon that passed slowly in the heavy summer heat, trying to make the armrest of his crutch more comfortable. He hacked about on the Mae West but his knife was not sharp enough or strong enough to penetrate the rubbery covering. Finally, he took off his tunic, cut one sleeve off and wrapped it around the top of the crutch.

Twice he lay back against the bank and looked up at the bridge and listened. Once a horse trotted noisily across. The second time a wheezing charcoal-burning truck labored by. This road wasn't heavily traveled. But it was traveled.

Four o'clock. Five o'clock. Six o'clock. As soon as it was dusk, he would start.

He heard the clatter of the horses' hooves first, then the creak of a wagon. It was getting darker. He was impatient for these late travelers to be on their way, to leave him with the road empty and dark ahead.

The wagon reached the bridge, stopped.

Oh, hell. But it wouldn't be Germans. Not in a wagon. Why had a wagon stopped? He sat up with the stirring of hope, began to twist to get awkwardly to his feet, all the while reaching for his makeshift crutch.

"Lieutenant, it's me, Maurice," and the boy ducked beneath the bridge, carrying an armful of clothes.

Jonathan was sweating and sick to his stomach by the time he struggled into heavy gray trousers. The upper part of his leg was terribly sore to touch, but he didn't need Maurice's whispered pleas for speed to prod him. If a patrol came through the woods, found the stopped wagon, it would investigate. Jonathan stripped off his tunic and his shirt, put on the cotton pullover.

Maurice was scraping out a hole in the dry sandy soil, pushing in the Mae West and the remnants of Jonathan's uniform, spreading dirt to cover them, scattering stones to hide any trace of digging.

Maurice looked curiously at Jonathan's improvised crutch when they stood in the creek bed, ready to climb up to the road. Then he shrugged and helped Jonathan up through the dry prickly grasses to the wagon, talking softly all the while. "Your papers are in your pocket, the back left pocket. They belonged to my brother, Leandre. You are Leandre Martin and you were invalided home from Calais. You were in the fighting at Gravelines."

Maurice boosted Jonathan into the wagon and ran lightly around to climb in on the other side. He took up the reins and the horse began to move. The wagon jolted on bare iron wheels. Jonathan gripped the wooden seat edge, shifted his weight, trying to find a comfortable position. The boy beside him didn't notice. He was too busy looking up the road and to each side, into the dark shadowy woods. "The thing is," Maurice was explaining worriedly, "when we reach the barricade at the crossroads, don't say too much. Leave it to me. The Boche don't usually speak very good French. But occasionally one does."

As the wagon creaked and swayed up the darkening road, Jonathan ran through his new identity in his mind. He was Leandre Martin. God, what a chance Maurice was taking, letting Jonathan use his brother's papers. If the Germans stumbled onto them, there couldn't be any way out. So, Jonathan had better know his story. He practiced out loud, speaking French, saying his little story over and over, a student with an exercise. "I am Leandre Martin. I am twenty-six years old and I live in the village of Ry. My father is Gaston Martin and we have the Martin orchards. I was wounded at Gravelines and invalided home before the war was over."

Jonathan thumbed through the papers in the fading twilight. Identity card, discharge papers, ration books. "I thought your brother's name was Roger?"

"My younger brother, yes, was with me when we saw you in the sky."

Jonathan looked down at the papers. "You have another brother then? Leandre."

"He was seven years older than I. Nine years older than Roger. He was like my father, you see. Tall and very strong. He could work longer hours in the orchards than anyone. Roger and I," Maurice shrugged, "we are like my mother's people, slender and dark."

It was almost dark now, Maurice's face pale and formless in the dusk.

"He was wounded at Gravelines." Jonathan didn't even make it a question.

"My cousin, Michel, brought him back. Leandre did not live quite a week."

The wagon creaked slowly down the road which wound, a dusty gray ribbon in the twilight, alongside the groves of apple trees.

Maurice sighed. "It has almost killed my father. He used to be...such a big man. Do you know what I mean? A loud voice, a strong voice. Everyone heard him and knew who was coming. Now he does not speak for hours and he has grown smaller. He doesn't look so big in his clothes. At night he drinks and then he is angry." The boy shot a side-long glance at Jonathan then fell quiet.

"He blames the British." Jonathan said it gravely.

Maurice nodded. "He says it is all the fault of the English, that they made France get into the war and then, when the Boche came, the English left and Frenchmen died holding off the Germans while the English soldiers escaped."

They rode a while farther in silence. "But you do not agree with your father, Maurice?"

"I do not know what is true, Lieutenant."

A motorcycle popped in the distance.

Maurice lifted his head, listened. "But I know one thing, Lieutenant, I know who is taking our food and telling us where we may travel and hanging their flag from our city hall. And I know who is still fighting. I don't know anything about you, Lieutenant. I don't know what kind of man you are but I know if I can help you escape and you somehow reach England, you will fly again against the Luftwaffe."

Fly again. Oh God yes, he would fly again if ever he reached England. The French boy was right on that. And he was desperately needed. How many planes had the RAF lost this week, this month, this summer? Too many. All the squadrons were down to bare bone. They needed every man, experienced, inexperienced, fresh, tired, it didn't matter. Maurice was right. They needed Jonathan, too.

"Right. I'll fly again, Maurice."

The motorcycle roared up behind them, swerved to pass the wagon on the narrow road. Dust, thick and choking, billowed up, enveloping them. The motorcycle clattered on down the road, the rider not giving them even the slightest glance. Jonathan watched Maurice's face, and he was glad, suddenly, that he was not that German soldier. He hoped no one ever hated him the way Maurice hated the German, impersonally, implacably, not because of who he was but because of what he was. A conqueror. Maurice looked down the road, his face hard and angry, long after the motorcycle was gone.

The air cleared finally and the wagon kept on at its steady even pace. Jonathan began to relax.

"How are you feeling, Lieutenant?"

"Well enough."

"Is your wound healing?"

Jonathan hesitated.

"Do you need to see the doctor?"

The tension in Maurice's voice was clear enough.

"It doesn't hurt as much," Jonathan said slowly. "I think with a crutch I can get about."

"The Boche have started to watch him, Dr. Morrissey. He will come, if we send for him."

"No," Jonathan said quickly. "Don't ask him. It's not that urgent." Funny. He could remember slamming a classroom door on his hand at Oxford and the rush to get to the doctor's and the anxious care to prevent infection. His leg was a wretched mess above the knee but it wasn't at all urgent to see a doctor. The better to live longer. The sun was almost gone, only a faint wavering of pink and orange in the Western sky.

"The barricade's just round this bend. Leave it all to me."

The wagon creaked to a stop at the crossroads. A sergeant stepped out of a sentry box. "Your papers," and he peered curiously at them through the dusk.

Maurice pulled out his papers and Jonathan did, too, slowly, trying to look as though he had done it dozens of times as had all Frenchmen since June 21.

The sergeant turned his flashlight on Maurice's card, turned it briefly on his face, then reached out for Jonathan's card. Jonathan handed it over and found the brief brush of the German's hand against his unnerving. Then it was over and the wagon was moving.

Jonathan knew he was sitting rigidly, his shoulders stiff. He tried to relax. He wanted suddenly to look behind, to see if the sentry was watching them, but he fought the impulse away. He had made it past the first barrier. There would be many more on the road back to England.

Back to England. He was swept by homesickness, but it was anguish for an England that he would never see again, no matter whether he escaped from France. The England of unruffled peaceful days with everyone free to pursue his own vision, long walks on quiet Cotswold lanes, afternoons gliding over pond water as green and still as jade, days made up of small and simple rites, accepted then as normal and ordinary and unremarkable, recognized only now that they were gone as infinitely precious.

"Lieutenant."

Jonathan's head snapped up.

"Round this bend and we'll be there. I'll take back Leandre's papers. You'll get others soon."

There. Jonathan had no idea where he was. He had not even thought about their destination.

The cluster of brick houses turned their backs to the road and looked abandoned with no single flicker of light showing.

"Just past the oak tree, I'll stop for a moment. Walk into the passageway, between the high brick walls. The first door on your left, a huge wooden one, knock three short, one long. Mme. Moreau is expecting you. Remember now, the first door on your left."

CHAPTER 7

The poster was everywhere, plastered against walls and shop windows, wrapped around tall silver lampposts, one to a car in the Metro, slapped every hundred yards along the station wall.

Linda twisted in the packed corridor so that she would not be facing the poster, but the train slid to a stop, and through the fly-speckled window, clearly visible, eye level, she saw another one and read the harsh unrelenting notice again:

ALL PERSONS HARBOURING ENGLISH SOLDIERS MUST DELIVER SAME TO THE NEAREST KOMMANDANTUR NOT LATER THAN 20 OCTOBER 1940. THOSE PERSONS WHO CONTINUE TO HARBOUR ENGLISHMEN AFTER THIS DATE WITHOUT HAVING NOTIFIED THE AUTHORITIES WILL BE SHOT.

The message was clear. No warning of trial or imprisonment. No, it was simpler than that. Anyone hiding a soldier will be shot.

Linda's eyes slipped from the poster to the impassive faces in the car. No one looked at his fellow traveler. If glances crossed, eyes moved quickly on. It wasn't safe. That was the way it felt in the hot close carriage. Who knew who stood beside him? A Gestapo agent? A fugitive? Look down, look all around, but stay aloof.

She hurried out of the car at the next stop, jostling her way through the crowd, and on to the street. She stopped at the end of the line at the control. She had her green identity card in her hand. The line moved quickly enough, the soldiers asking questions of only a few.

The man in front of her wore work clothes, a heavy cotton shirt, dark blue pants. But the hand that held out his papers was unexpectedly smooth, the nails clean and cropped short.

Linda looked up at his face.

So did the German soldier.

It was suddenly very still in the line. No one moved but the circle of space around the man in work clothes seemed to expand. His hair was curly and ginger colored, his face sensitive with deep-set intense eyes. Linda saw him swallow and knew, sickeningly, that he was afraid, though his face still held a sullen impatient look, as any man might when delayed for no good reason.

The soldier's French was thickly accented but serviceable. "You are Jacques Delarue? Your papers say you are a truck driver."

The man grunted assent.

The soldier looked down again at the man's hands and they began to tremble ever so slightly. The German gestured with his head. Two young privates stepped forward and took Delarue by either elbow. He tried to shake free. "My papers are all right," he said loudly. "What's wrong with you? Let me go. I'm a Frenchman going about my business, you don't have any call to stop me."

The control officer ignored him and was already reaching for Linda's card.

She tried not to listen as they pulled him away because she could hear, behind the bluster, the thin note of fear. Oh God, would this happen to her one day? Would strong hands take her arms, hold her helpless, lead her away to . . .

"Oh, you are American, Miss?" The control officer was smiling at her and she managed a stiff smile in return. His English was better than his French. "You are from California?"

Linda nodded.

"Have you ever been to Chicago?"

She shook her head.

He looked disappointed. "I have two cousins in Chicago, Hans and Emil Holtzendorff. I visited them in '36. You have a very beautiful country, Miss."

"Thank you,"

"Have you ever been to Germany?"

Again she shook her head. "I didn't come to Europe until last Christmas, and by then travel was . . . difficult."

He shrugged. "Ah well, this war will soon be over, Miss. Then you must go to Germany." He looked around the dingy crowded platform. "It is clean in Germany," then he handed back her card and she was moving on toward the steps.

It was clean in the Metro until you came, Linda wanted to say. Clean and there weren't any posters, black on white, warning of death by firing squad.

They wouldn't shoot Robert. Surely they wouldn't shoot a little boy. Of course not. The poster said there would be death for anyone harboring English soldiers. A child couldn't harbor anyone. That would be Eleanor and her. Linda stopped on the street, clutching her straw basket.

The leaves rustled gently above her and a squirrel dashed the length of a thick limb, paused with statue-like stillness, then, abruptly, leaped to the next tree and disappeared. So ordinary and everyday. The leaves were beginning to fall now, lying thick and crunchy along the walks, turning reddish and brown, signaling the beginning of fall. The first week in September—and they still hadn't found a way to the Spanish border. No one yet had responded to Eleanor's careful inquiry, "I've a package I need to get across the Demarcation Line. Would you have any idea who could help me?" Three weeks ago today Linda had smuggled Michael out of the hospital. It had become routine now, Eleanor still making trips for the Red Cross, visiting hospitals and prisons, Robert going to school, the Germans in their wisdom had decreed there would be no vacation this year, and Linda every day taking food to Michael, varying her times of visiting and always following a little different route.

Each day Michael looked up hopefully when she came in then the light in his eyes died. He never complained even though this past week she had not had a bite of meat to take to him. None of them had eaten any meat. It was getting harder and harder to find food. Even the vegetables were all gone and there were angry whispers that all the potatoes had been shipped to Germany. Potatoes were second only to wine on a Frenchman's table. They began to call the Germans "polydore" after the little potato bug that could decimate a harvest. The butcher told Eleanor that the Boche had put his second cousin in jail for a week because he shouted out, "Look at the polydore," when passing a café filled with Germans.

Linda paused uncertainly, looking up at the government buildings ahead of her. She wasn't exactly sure where she was going. Elise Barnard had told Eleanor of this café, "It's deep in the Left Bank, my dear, in a narrow little street off the rue de Varenne. The Petit Chat. You just go in and say you are looking for Jean of Amiens. I actually got two chops."

There were German uniforms everywhere. Linda walked briskly, wishing that her chest didn't ache every time a German officer looked at her. Then she missed a step. The Swastika flag snapped in the breeze from the staff of a beautiful pale yellow building, an elegant building with ancient green gates, another public building taken over by the Germans. God, they were everywhere. Every day German military units absorbed more buildings. The Hotel Crillon, across from the American Embassy, was now the headquarters of the local German commander. The Hotel Maurice had been taken over, the Palais-Royal, the Ecole Militaire, the Petit Palais, the Hotel Majestic, all serving as offices for the Occupation Army which every day tightened its grasp on Paris.

She grew nearer the blood red flag with its circle of white emblazoned with the crooked cross. The sentries beside the gate stood at stiff attention. Linda was even with them when she realized she was the only pedestrian on the street. She was the only person the length and breadth of the avenue. She walked in sunlight but the curtains were drawn at every window and no one paused in the shade of a tree or hurried up apartment house steps. Only a Gestapo headquarters could empty a street like this.

She turned off into the first cross street, never mind its name, never mind where the street went. Midway up the block, she found the dark and narrow street she sought and the little café. She pushed in the café door. The solitary waiter, polishing glasses behind the bar, looked up. "We don't open until twelve, Mademoiselle."

Linda held out her basket. "I am looking for M. Jean. From Amiens."

There was a long silence while he studied her, his dark eyes cold and suspicious. "You aren't French," he said finally.

"I am American. I live with my sister whose husband is French. My nephew, Robert, is thirteen and he is very thin. We need meat, M'sieur."

"American."

She nodded.

"Back there." He pointed to a narrow hall just to the right of the bar.

She slipped through the beads that separated the hallway from the dining room. The passageway was very dark. The hall ended at a closed door. Linda took a breath, knocked.

An unexpectedly cheerful voice called for her to enter.

She smelled meat when she stepped inside. Each wall held shelves, stacks of plates and glasses and kitchen implements along one wall, the other three filled with food-stuffs. It must originally have served as the pantry for the kitchen. Now the full shelves indicated another kind of business entirely. Three beef carcasses hung from hooks near a butcher's block. A huge man, he must have weighed almost three hundred pounds, was working on a fourth carcass on the bloodied wooden surface.

"M. Jean. . . . from Amiens?"

"I've heard the name." He rumbled with laughter. "And what would a pretty young lady like you be doing asking after Jean from Amiens?"

Linda felt absurdly at a loss. She had never in her life dealt with someone breaking the law. But she didn't want to think of him as a crook. That brought up different pictures in her mind, dark-cheeked gunmen with tommy guns holding up sleepy small town banks, Bonnie and Clyde laughing with empty eyes, laughing and killing, a blood-spattered sidewalk outside a theater in Chicago. So she swallowed and nodded toward the meat. "May I buy some beef?"

The big man's massive face drooped. "Ah, I would like to help a pretty young lady, but I have my regular customers. Every bit of this," and he slapped the muscle-sheathed ribcage, "is already spoken for." But he looked at her expectantly.

Linda cleared her throat. "Perhaps there would be just a piece from one of those," she nodded at the other carcasses. "I would be willing to pay generously," and she began to fumble in her purse, pulling out a wad of francs.

The big man's face creased again in a smile, but his eyes were cold and calculating.

They settled on a sum finally. She paid twelve times as much as her purchase would cost in a shop. But the shops were mostly closed and those that opened sold out while lines of shoppers stretched the length of the block.

Linda hurried out of the little restaurant. It was open now and two or three diners looked up curiously as she passed. She felt conspicuous as if everyone must know what she carried in her basket.

On the street, she turned right. It would be closer to go back to the rue de Varenne. But she didn't want to be on that street again. She would walk more than a few blocks out of her way to avoid those rigid soldiers and that empty street. Nearby, ash cans clattered. A boy shouted to a friend. Then, everything happened so fast, she scarcely took it in.

Running feet pounded up the sidewalk behind her. She swerved against the wall to make room. A tall, thin priest was coming slowly toward her. He walked with a slight stoop as if he had become used to entering doorways with low lintels. He wore a broad floppy straw hat to shade his face from the September sun and carried an open book in his right hand, reading as he walked. He heard the running steps at the same time that Linda began to step aside and he looked up.

She saw his face clearly, a high forehead half hidden by a drooping shock of black hair, a beaked nose, thin ascetic lips, a firm blunt chin. He was looking behind her and she saw a flicker in his intensely blue eyes. He tucked his book under his arm, reached up and took off his floppy straw hat and thrust out his other arm.

Gasping for breath, the man plunging past Linda was caught up by that long thin arm, swung around to face the way he had come, the straw hat plumped on his head and the priest's wire-rimmed glasses slipped on his face. Then, the priest reopened the book and held it out in front of them and they walked down the sidewalk, the way the running man had come. As they passed, Linda recognized the man in work clothes picked up by the soldiers at the Metro control. He struggled to breathe, his face flaming red from exertion. He ducked his head to look at the book.

The priest pointed to the page. "It isn't as if Savonarola didn't know, my son, what he was doing. It's clear from this passage."

Two soldiers pounded into the narrow street from the rue de Varenne. Their heads swung this way and that, their eyes searching the street and the people, the plump young mother with a baby in arms, the bricklayer on a scaffold, the teenage boys rolling a cigarette, the priest and his companion, Linda, an old lady with a cane.

Everyone continued to walk or work. No one looked at the soldiers. The older one, a sergeant, asked the young mother if she had seen a man running. It took her a moment to understand the question, then she raised her hand. Linda held her breath. The pointing finger reached the priest and his companion, reached them and swept past to stop at an alleyway. The soldiers called, "*Danke, danke, merci*, Madame," and ran toward the narrow cobbled alley.

The priest and the fugitive began to walk more quickly. Linda turned and followed them. Two blocks, three, then near the Rodin Museum, the two men paused. The priest spoke quickly for a moment. The ginger-haired man shook his head. He lifted off the straw hat and the glasses. They talked for a moment more, then the fugitive turned and hurried away. The priest did not look after him but clapped the hat on his head and set off briskly in the opposite direction.

Linda continued to follow, almost breaking into a run at times to keep pace with that swift long-legged stride. Once, twice, she almost gave it up. Did she dare, after all? Then a stubborn almost unformed hope drove her on. The priest had taken a frightful chance on that narrow street. He couldn't know that the other pedestrians would turn blind eyes. But he had taken the chance nevertheless.

He was a half block ahead of her, not quite to the end of the street, when he swerved to his right and disappeared, almost as if he had been swallowed from view. Linda broke into a run. He hadn't turned the corner, she was sure of it. As she grew nearer, she saw worn bricked steps leading down from the street a half level to a heavy oak door. It didn't look like the entry to an apartment house. Puzzled, she looked up. Oh yes, of course. This was a church on the corner, a small church with worn gray stone steps leading up to an arched Gothic entrance. High above, sunshine glistened on the rose and misty blue of the stained glass.

She had come this far.

There was a clatter of footsteps coming around the corner, a bevy of German nurses, chattering and giggling, strode nearer.

Linda gave them one quick look, their soft gray uniforms and wind-blown hair, and rushed down the steps to the basement door. She was, she realized, becoming almost paranoid about German uniforms. She didn't want to be seen by the Germans. She didn't want to see them.

Do you think it makes you safe, like an ostrich, she asked herself angrily as she let the door slam behind her? But she did feel safe in the musty flagstone corridor. It was very dim, only a tiny bulb glimmering near the end of the corridor. She passed a series of closed doors, again of thick and ancient oak, with nothing to hint at the rooms' functions or contents. Her pace slowed even more. Good grief, what if this belonged to monks. She had a very unclear grasp of the Catholic Church, though she had occasionally gone to Mass with Eleanor and Andre and Robert. She had grown up a Methodist and found the Latin Mass, with the smoke of incense and the priests' colorful vestments, beautiful but strange and incredibly distant from the resounding hymns and impassioned sermons of her childhood.

A typewriter rattled furiously beyond an open door to her left and light spilled cheerfully into the hall.

Linda pecked cautiously inside and no longer felt like quite such an interloper. A church office was a church office. A tiny woman with a sharp, thin-featured face frowned at her typewriter, typed vigorously, paused, typed again.

"Pardon," Linda said cautiously.

The woman held up her hand and bent back to work, her fingers flying over the keys, finishing up with a staccato burst. She looked up. "May I help you?"

What did she say now? I followed a priest here, a tall fellow, skinny, with black hair. The woman would think she was demented.

"I'm looking... I didn't get his name. A tall thin priest. He wore a straw hat."

The woman smiled. "Father Laurent. He came in just a few minutes ago. He's upstairs. In the confessional."

"The confessional," Linda repeated blankly.

"Father Lefevre takes the confessional on Mondays, Wednesday, and Fridays and Father Laurent on Tuesdays and Thursdays and Saturdays."

Linda looked at her watch.

The secretary misinterpreted her glance. "There's plenty of time, my dear. You just go to your right from the office and up the stairs. You'll see the confessional when you reach the landing. You've plenty of time. Go right on up."

At the top of the stairs, Linda found a straggling line waiting outside the thick curtain. She almost turned away then, determinedly, she took her place. It wasn't long and she almost fled again when it was her turn. She entered hesitantly, closed the curtain behind her, took a deep breath and knelt. Her fingers gripped the handles of her shopping basket so tightly that her hands and arms ached. She stared up at the wooden grille. Could he see her through the mesh that backed the carved wood? What in the world was she going to do?

"Father." She stopped, swallowed.

"*Ma fille*?" His voice was deep and a little hoarse and very gentle.

"Oh Father, you saved him. The young man in the street."

"Sometimes, my daughter, God sends us down certain streets."

Linda felt safe and warm and secure now. For the first time in so many days, she wasn't afraid. "Father, we need your help. We are hiding an English soldier. If you've been out today, you've seen the posters, haven't you? You know what they say? Anyone who doesn't turn in a hidden Englishman, they'll be shot. So you see, we must find a way to get Michael away." She stared up at the immovable curls and sweeps of shining oak. "You will help us. Won't you?"

It was quiet for so long a moment that a sliver of fear moved again in her chest. Could she have been mistaken? Was the man the priest had helped really been the same one stopped at the Metro control? My God, was this the right priest, listening to her? Or was it one of the Catholic clergy who supported Petain, who saw in the New Order a strong role for the Church?

At first she didn't recognize the sound and then she realized she was hearing a low laugh. She stared up at the wooden grill uneasily. There was nothing funny about being shot by a firing squad.

"Forgive me, my daughter, please. It is only, well, I must make my own confession today. This morning when I arose and made my prayers, I grumbled, yes, I grumbled to God that I was not useful enough in my post here. God is showing me that there is plenty to do, the young man running from the Gestapo, you and your English soldier." He laughed again. "Oh yes, my daughter, everything will be all right now. You have come to the right place."

It was only as she left, repeating to herself the instructions that she had received, that she thought to look back and see the name of the Church. She stared for a long moment. Slowly, she began to smile. The Church of the Good Shepherd.

The photograph spread five columns across the top of the newspaper, an aerial view of London. Much of it was clear, the great lazy loops of the Thames, the distinct lines of streets, larger boxes for buildings, small ones for homes, but the docks were hidden, lost beneath a billowing tower of smoke that coiled thousands of feet into the clear summer sky, thick and dark and impenetrable.

ENGLAND REELS BENEATH THE MIGHT OF THE LUFTWAFFE

Krause smiled. It wouldn't be long now. The scent of victory hung in the air. You could see victory in the eyes of the Luftwaffe pilots swaggering down the Champs-Elysees on leave. There weren't so many of them this week, of course. They were busy this week. His thin mouth spread even a little wider, enjoying his mild joke. Busy this week. Radio Modiale had the reports. The RAF was crippled, their bases bombed. There was a picture yesterday of one coastal airfield after a flight of Dorniers and Junkers 88's demolished the hangers, cratered the field. That was just one field. Now the bombing had spread to London. Soon, as soon as the Luftwaffe had swept the RAF from the sky, the Army would cross the Channel and invade England. Oh, it wouldn't be long now.

Krause studied the photograph intently, the fires in the central business section, what looked like a direct hit on Paddington Station, and, most of all, the roiling twisting plume of smoke that hid the docks. The blazes would be an inferno beneath that smoke. Smoke and flame. The funeral pyre of a decadent society.

He lifted the cup to his mouth, took a final sip of coffee and let his gaze wander slowly up and down the broad elegant boulevard. Parisians were so proud of the boulevard. Actually, it couldn't compare with the Unter Der Linden. The Champs-Elysees looked frowsy this morning, so many shops boarded up and only an occasional car, a German car, to break up the swarms of dilapidated bicycles with their shabby riders. The Arc de Triomphe wasn't a match for the Brandenburg Gate. He was swept suddenly by a wish to be home again, especially now that it was September. Though, once again like last year, the gigantic Nazi Party Rally had been canceled. He had attended the rallies every year since they began in Nuremberg in 1933, caught up in the excitement,

116 ESCAPE FROM PARIS

the glory, the thunderous roar of thousands of exultant supporters. He pictured Nuremberg's narrow streets with their Gothic facades, the tens of thousands of Swastika flags hanging from windows and roofs and balconies, the streets thronged with black and brown uniforms. One year he remembered especially clearly. It was his first time to sit upon the platform in Luitpold Hall. There had been flags there, too, hundreds of them, fluttering above the packed audience. The band played as everyone assembled, then, after the last chair was taken, the last inch of space along the walls filled, the band stopped, a hush fell.

Hitler appeared in the back of the hall.

The band struck up the Badenweiler March.

Hitler started down the center aisle. Goering and Goebbels and Hess and Himmler strode behind him.

Thirty thousand men and women rose. Thirty thousand arms lifted in salute. Thirty thousand voices roared.

Hitler reached the stage. Kleig lights spotted him. The band swung into Beethoven's Egmont Overture. Everyone on the stage, a select hundred of them, party officers, army and navy officers stood, Krause among them, part of them, and everyone shouted, everyone on the stage and in the hall, HEIL HITLER, HEIL HITLER! *Sieg Heil*! *Sieg Heil*!

Krause walked down the Paris boulevard, climbed into the waiting car, the paper tucked under his arm, his breath quickening as he remembered. Thousands strong. They were conquering the world.

He was still smiling as he settled behind his desk. For once he didn't pause to savor the room and its furnishings. Nothing French could be counted as valuable this morning. He dropped the newspaper into the wastebasket and reached out for a stack of papers Sgt. Schmidt had arranged for him.

He skimmed the reports. Ah, activity was looking up in the search for the British airmen. What more could be done? He leaned back in his chair, eyes narrowed. In a moment, he buzzed for Schmidt.

"Sergeant." Krause tilted back in his chair, stared sightlessly at the ornate ceiling, his fingertips pressed lightly together. "Find five Gestapo agents who speak perfect English. Obtain British uniforms, either RAF or Army, RAF preferably. Prepare reasonable escape stories to account for their turning up at various points." He closed his eyes briefly. "Paris, Orleans, Tours, Bordeaux." He opened his eyes, looked thoughtfully at the map opposite his desk. "And St. Jean-de-Luz." St. Jean-de-Luz, just short of the Spanish border. "If only one of them, Sergeant, is helped by the French, we will have a thread to yank. Once we yank, we can unravel an escape line all the way back to Paris."

She awed him as he hadn't been awed since childhood, Jonathan realized. Not since the massive cook, Mrs. Smithson in his wealthy aunt's kitchen, had lifted pale blue eyes one mid-summer morning to remonstrate, "Master Jonathan I do not permit rowdy behavior," had he encountered such strength of personality. Mme. Moreau was not huge, as Mrs. Smithson had been, but she radiated the same aura of power. The very first evening, when he had struggled down the cobbled passageway to knock at the first door on the left, she had welcomed him gravely, helped him inside. Once he was fed, bathed, his wound freshly dressed, she had looked at him dispassionately. "It will be necessary, Lieutenant, that we have a clear understanding of your responsibilities."

He must have looked surprised.

She had smiled a little drily. "Yes, Lieutenant, your responsibilities. It is of utmost importance that you agree to do exactly as I tell you or neither of us will survive. I must request that you do not smoke. My friends know that I am not a smoker. Under no circumstances are you to leave this house. Moreover, during the daytime hours, you must be very careful not to make any loud noise although you may move quietly about the house. I am fortunate in that my home is a single dwelling but passerby must not hear odd noises when they know I am not at home." She looked at him levelly. "This will entail some discipline on your part."

She was right. As the days slipped by, Jonathan was amazed at how desperately he wanted to go outside. Just for a minute. A single minute free of the stuffy, confining, tiny heat-laden rooms. Just one minute. And to smoke a cigarette—his lungs ached, his whole body hungered for the acrid soothing full-throated draw of smoke down deep into his lungs. One day, he took the packet of Players out of his pocket and emptied it, lining the cigarettes in a row. Twelve cigarettes. He picked each one up, ran a finger lightly its length, slipped it back into the crumpled tattered packet. Then, abruptly, violently, he crushed the packet into a ball, crushed and smashed it beyond recall, then shredded the tobacco and paper mixture into tiny flakes and dumped all of it into the garbage pail in the kitchen.

He lost weight, though Mme. Moreau tried, skillfully, to give him the larger portions of their meager meals. His face, that had always been rounded and cheerful, became increasingly lean, his cheekbones prominent, the line of his jaw stark and distinct.

During the weekdays, when she was at the village school, he followed a rigid regimen. From nine to ten, he walked. Five steps forward, five steps back. Five steps forward, five steps back. The first two weeks, he would grimace and hold moans deep in his throat and lean heavily on his crutch. Soon his side and arm would begin to ache. But, day after interminable day, he walked back and forth across the tiny living room in the dead hot air, sweat streaming down his face and back and legs for the windows were shut and the curtains tightly drawn. From nine to ten he walked. From ten to eleven he read. It was hard at first. He had not read in French for many years but there was the excitement of struggle and success and the peace when time was suspended and his mind delighted in the clarity and grace of that clearest and most graceful of languages. Mme. Moreau's bookcases filed one wall in the tiny dining room. The light was poor, the bindings old, titles often almost illegible. It was the second week that he found, tucked toward the back, a modern day English version of Beowulf. That first afternoon he never looked up from the book until he heard Mme. Moreau's key in the lock at six o'clock. After that, he was more sparing. If he worked hard at his walk and his French and his afternoon exercises, he permitted himself to read Beowulf. Lunch was soup and a piece of bread. From one to two, once again he walked. From two to three, he studied the 1919 Atlas, learning the track of the narrowest country road, the belts of forest, the rivers. Les Andelys was near the Seine. How big was the river here, Jonathan wondered? What kind of boats still moved? Was there a chance to escape in a boat? From three to four, he exercised, mostly pushups in the beginning for he could just manage those with his injured leg. From four to five he rested and read. At five, he began to straighten the house, picking up his books, putting the chairs back in place in the living room, setting the kitchen table.

Days slipped by. The heat lessened and the leaves began to flame orange and red. From the attic window, he could look out and see an ancient oak. Every day a few more leaves drifted down into untidy autumnal heaps.

Each night, when Mme. Moreau returned, he looked up hopefully, then turned away.

He was beginning to be able to walk with only a moderate limp. The wound was closed but the skin felt strange around it and he had noticed last night during his first bath in a week, for there was so little soap and water had to be heated in the kitchen and fuel was too precious to waste, pinkish streaks radiating downward from the lumpy discolored scar. The wound no longer hurt, unless he bumped against something, but he didn't feel well. And he was always hot.

Today he felt awful. He kept to his schedule but he did his exercise grimly, mouth tight, and his thoughts were as dark and murky as water in a stagnant pond. He was just beginning to pick up his day's litter, a stack of books by the couch, the cup with dregs of ersatz coffee, yesterday's Paris newspaper, the Atlas, when he heard, clear and distinct, familiar after these three long weeks, the brisk clatter of Mme. Moreau's sturdy shoes against the cobbled stones.

Jonathan came to life, grabbing up the paper and the book and the cup, lunging hurriedly toward the dining room and the narrow steps that twisted up to the single bedroom and higher yet to the tiny attic.

It was only half-past five. What had happened? What was bringing her home early?

The key scraped in the lock. No time to get to the attic. Was anyone with her? Was something wrong? He dumped his armload on the dining room table and grabbed up a straight chair and waited, pressed against the wall.

The door slammed behind her. He heard her uneven breaths. She must have hurried awfully fast. He lifted up the chair.

"Jonathan? Jonathan, where are you?"

Slowly he put down the chair.

She swept into the dining room. A smile softened her severe face. She held up her school satchel. "I have them here," she said excitedly. "Your papers. Everything's set, Jonathan. You leave tonight."

CHAPTER 8

Eleanor kissed Michael's cheek. Robert shook his hand. Linda smiled and realized she was holding back tears.

Michael looked at each of them. "I can't thank you enough." His voice broke a little at the end.

"No thanks," Eleanor said quickly. "We thank you, Michael. Go to England and keep on fighting them and someday you'll come back to Paris and we'll have a grand reunion. You and Linda and Robert and . . . and Andre, he'll be home by then, and myself. We'll take you to a fine little café, La Bonne Franquette, up in Montmartre. That's a promise."

He nodded, pressed his lips together.

Linda said it. "It's time now."

Michael took the little mesh bag that Eleanor had fixed, a loaf of bread, cheese, a bottle of wine. A little slowly, he also picked up a thick woolen jacket, red-and-black checked. "I hate to take this, Mme. Masson. Your husband will need it when he comes home."

Eleanor didn't look at the jacket but Linda saw the imperceptible change in her sister's face and realized with a cold horror that Eleanor didn't expect Andre to come home again. Ever.

Eleanor looked at Linda. "The priest said they cross the Pyrenees into Spain, didn't he?"

Numbly, still shaken by her sudden insight, Linda nodded.

"Well then, Michael, you will need it more than Andre. By the time you reach the border, the weather will be turning very cold up in the mountains. Soon the snow will begin. You must take the jacket. Andre would want you to have it."

Father Laurent had instructed Linda to bring Michael to the Medici Fountain in the Luxembourg Gardens between 10 a.m. and a quarter past.

Linda was reaching for the door knob when Eleanor asked, "Do you think it would do any harm if Robert and I followed along? We'll pretend we don't know you, of course."

Linda hesitated for an instant. But it couldn't make any difference that she could see.

They walked down the Boul' Mich', Eleanor and Robert trailing about twenty yards behind. They passed bookstores and cafes. Every day a few more shops opened, though the boarded-up windows on every block still reminded of those who had fled in June and had not returned.

Linda and Michael didn't talk. She was tautly conscious of him beside her. She wished they had given him a cap to cover his thin blond hair. A long strand fell over his forehead. He looked so English. Linda began to walk faster. If she could just get him to the park and to the fountain. Once he was delivered to Father Laurent, they would be safe again. Eleanor and Robert would be free of the danger she had brought to them when she smuggled Michael out of the hospital. Ever since the posters had gone up, the black-and-white posters announcing death for those who did not surrender Englishmen, Linda passed each German soldier with a sickening sensation of dread. Firing squad. To be lined up in front of a firing squad, to stand, blindfolded, and wait. To hear, in that last instant, the guttural command to fire.

Linda saw the gray-green of a German staff car approaching and she stumbled.

Michael looked down. "What's wrong?"

"Hush. *Ne parle pas anglais.*"

"Sorry," he muttered and she could have screamed at him. The instant the car passed, she was filled with regret. For God's sake, even the Germans couldn't tell a man on a sidewalk twenty feet away was speaking English. But she was afraid, afraid all the way through. They were so near now to safety, she and Eleanor and Robert. Just a few more minutes and all the strain would be over. They could walk away, leave the apartment empty. They wouldn't have to be afraid again.

She might even go home. Oh God, what she would give to go home. It would be all right to go home now. There wasn't anything more she could do to help Eleanor. And, if she sensed the truth, Eleanor no longer hoped for Andre's return. Perhaps Eleanor and Robert would come, too. They could all go home. Pasadena would be lovely now, anemones blazing against the wall in the backyard, the sweet smell of hibiscus, soft cool air and nowhere the sharp green of Army uniforms or the soul warping black of the SS.

The air was cool on the path leading to the fountain, huge trees blocking the thin September sun. Red and yellow and brown leaves crackled underfoot. It was beginning to feel like fall, a cool edge beneath the morning warmth. The path was wide enough here for four to walk abreast. Room, then, to pass the couple walking toward them. Once again her legs were leaden, felt clumsy and unmanageable. Michael reached out, gently, to take her arm.

The German soldier and the girl with him didn't look at Linda and Michael as they passed and Linda was ashamed of the way her arm trembled. She pulled free from Michael. "It's all right," she whispered. "I'm all right." Soon she would be all right. The constant pressure was going to end, no more tension and danger and, worst of all, the insidious unending fear that turned her mouth to chalk and tightened her chest until it hurt to breathe.

"Look for the artist," Father Laurent had said.

The easel sat to the right of the fountain. The artist stood in front of it, as tall and angular as she remembered. Somehow, she was surprised when she saw him. She had not thought he would be there in person. Slowly, casually, she and Michael strolled toward the easel, stopped to look at the drawing.

It was a penciled sketch, not quite finished, but with only the contrast of soft lead against the creamy manila paper, he had caught the essence of the fountain, the slender and young and graceful bodies of Acis and Galatea, each absorbed, consumed by the other, Galatea lying back against Acis, cradled in his arm, looking up into his eyes, and, above them, driven by jealousy, implacably dangerous, the huge Cyclops, Polyphemus, crouched, forever captured in bronze in the act of rolling the huge boulder down upon the lovers.

Linda looked from the drawing to the fountain, at the pale clean-limbed lovely bodies of Acis and Galatea. So beautiful and so vulnerable. "*C'est bon.*"

"*Merci.*" Father Laurent deepened a shadow, murmured, "There is a woman with a boy. Behind us. They seem to be watching."

Linda bit her lip. "I'm sorry. That's Eleanor and my nephew, Robert. They wanted to see Michael off."

"That's all right. I just wanted to be sure." The priest half turned, smiling at Linda and Michael, as a painter politely would respond when his work was admired. "Michael?"

Michael nodded.

"Take the path to your left. Follow it to the lake. There is a boy in a yellow sweater, sailing a red toy sailboat that is almost a half meter long. Go up to him and say, 'That is a handsome boat, Claude.' He will take you from there." The priest repeated the French sentence twice.

"That is a handsome boat, Claude." Michael managed the French well enough. After a swift glance at Linda, he turned and walked quickly away.

Linda was ready to leave when, to hide the almost overwhelming surge of relief that swept her as Michael was lost to sight, she said abruptly, "I didn't expect you to be here, Father. I thought, when we talked the other day, that one of your helpers would meet me."

He frowned at the drawing. "I had not intended to come." He paused and looked around the clearing, at Eleanor and Robert, dawdling now on the other side of the fountain, at a student stretched out on a bench, his sweater over his face, at the old woman walking slowly down the path, her head bent, stopping to pluck up any broken twig or piece of bark. "You came to me for help and now I must ask you for help."

Linda looked at him, startled.

"Please, look at the painting and do not appear worried."

Linda leaned forward, as if to see the drawing better. "What is it, Father?"

"I did not tell you, for there was no need, but the reason I could take Michael was because I am a part of a chain that helps English soldiers reach Spain. It began in July when a priest I knew at seminary dropped by to see me. He lives in a village in Northern France. There are thousands of English soldiers hiding in the woods up there and he is bringing them, in groups of four, to Paris. He turns them over to me and I see them on their way to Bordeaux. A former student of mine picks them up there and takes them across the Demarkation Line. He has a friend who sees them on to Hendaye. From there . . . But you see how it works. It all began a little blindly. My friend came to me, I went in search of a friend in Bordeaux, he found a friend in Hendaye. I have also been the one who obtains the necessary papers. That takes time so sometimes it means the men that come to Paris must wait a while before leaving. That brings me to my difficulty today."

"Yes." Her throat was dry.

"The home where I had arranged for the men to stay tonight . . ."

"Yes?"

"A Gestapo agent has moved in upstairs."

But you know so many people, Linda wanted to cry, all the people in your Church, hundreds of them, and others, people you've known for years. In all of Paris, can't you ask someone else?

"Four soldiers," she whispered.

"Yes. They may need to stay for several days, perhaps until next weekend. When I heard that we needed to find another place, I thought of you immediately. An apartment in the student quarter. Oh, it couldn't be better."

"The apartment is empty," she said slowly.

ALL PERSONS HARBOURING ENGLISH SOLDIERS . . . NOT LATER THAN . . . WILL BE SHOT . . .

She could see the edge of the poster from where she stood. The old familiar tension tightened the muscles in her shoulders. He was so sure of her answer. That hurt almost as much as the fear flickering deep within her, like a banked fire that would explode at any time.

"But the apartment is leased by my sister, you see, and I will have to ask her."

"Of course. I understand. It isn't your decision to make." Father Laurent looked toward Eleanor and Robert, sitting now on an iron park bench. They were smiling, excited and happy, Linda knew, that Michael was safely on his way. Eleanor looked so young. She was much thinner because of their limited diet. Her face was slender, almost ethereal, the face Linda recalled from her childhood. Eleanor bent close to her son, speaking rapidly, one hand gesturing toward the pond. He nodded and their laughter rang across the dusty clearing.

It was Robert who first felt Linda's glance. He, then his mother, turned suddenly still faces toward her.

Linda gazed at the priest. When he nodded, she waved for Eleanor and Robert to come.

Father Laurent took both Eleanor's hands in his. "My daughter, I am delighted to have this chance to meet you."

"Is it all right?" Eleanor asked uncertainly. "Michael?"

"Everything is quite all right about Michael." Father Laurent looked at Robert then back at Eleanor. "You are very brave, Madame."

Eleanor shook her head quickly. "Such a small thing, Father."

"To risk your life and that of your son's?"

"It is worth a risk to feel alive again." Eleanor's thin face looked suddenly bleak. "But now it's done. Over. While we had Michael, while we were searching for a way to help him, it wasn't so hard, being without Andre, being here with the Germans all around us. Now it will be like that awful summer again, Paris dreary and empty, day after day of nothing."

Linda listened with the dreadful sense of knowing what was going to happen without being able to do anything to prevent it. It was like foreseeing an avalanche, the first tentative shift, knowing that tons and tons of snow and rock and rubble hung by a thread, knowing that it would be too late in an instant more.

The priest said quietly, "There are people here in Paris and across the country, who are cooperating to help Englishmen and Jews escape."

"I know," Eleanor said unhappily. "It was frustrating when we had Michael. I kept trying to find people who would help, but I couldn't. If I just knew how to help." She looked intently at Father Laurent.

Like an avalanche, obliterating in an instant all safety, all security.

Eleanor began to smile. "I thought, from what Linda told me, that you were just helping us with Michael. But that isn't right, is it? You are a part of something bigger."

The truck rumbled along the rutted narrow country lanes until dark then stopped for the night because of the curfew. The driver had bent down by the rear tire, thumping it, and warned Jonathan not to stir. "There's a garrison three doors down. But this is where I always stop. That makes it safe, you know. They searched the truck a few times, but not any longer."

Jonathan lay on his back in the narrow cramped space, boxes of apples stacked around and over him, forming an oblong space, big enough to hide him. From the tail gate, the truck bed looked fully packed, every inch taken. He slept some but kept awakening with the cold and the unaccustomed hardness of the frame and the rich, fruity, suffocating smell of the apples. The truck left Gisors just after dawn. It stopped twice at control points. Each time, Jonathan lay rigid, straining to hear, wishing he could speak German. Everything the German soldiers said, in guttural harsh tones, sounded threatening, but once the driver laughed and the sentry joined him. Each time the truck started up again and the hard jolting uncomfortable passage resumed.

Hours later, the truck swerved off the road, bumped over cobblestones, then, after a quick and hurried exchange, pulled into a garage. The door was slammed after it. The back end of the truck was lowered and two men began to shift the heavy crates out until one end of Jonathan's oblong space was open.

"Hurry up, mate."

Stiff and sore, Jonathan twisted onto his hands and knees, wrenching his injured leg. He grunted with pain but kept on going. Helping hands pulled him up and lowered him over the tailgate to the hard-packed ground. They motioned Jonathan out of the way. The apple crates were quickly rearranged until the narrow space was gone. The tailgate was swung up and closed, the garage door pulled wide, the truck backed out and the door shut again.

It had not taken more than ten minutes.

Jonathan leaned against the stone inner wall, waiting passively for his new protectors to attend to him. He felt the familiar sensations of uneasiness, helplessness, uncertainty, and a kind of embarrassment. He was handed along from person to person, a human burden, unable to fend for himself. He hated it, yet he had to accept it.

He had never even known the name of the truck driver. Now he looked around in the gloom of the unlighted garage. The only illumination came from a faint glow through slits high in the side stone wall. Two men walked toward him. One was old, unshaven, squinty-eyed. He moved on past Jonathan, hurrying, one shoulder lower than another, toward the back of the garage. The other man, short, stocky, unsmiling, stopped and faced Jonathan. "The train to Paris will be at the station in about forty-five minutes. If it's on time. Here is your ticket. In forty minutes, walk out that door," he pointed to a wooden door just past Jonathan, "turn to your right. To your right. Have you got that?"

Jonathan tucked the ticket in his pocket and nodded. Goddam, did the man think he was a fool?

"Turn to your right. Walk two blocks. You'll see the station. Go in. There will be some German soldiers waiting. Don't act nervous. Walk to the second barrier. When the train arrives, go into the third compartment. Do you understand that? The third compartment. Look for a baldheaded man, about forty, in a blue-striped shirt. He wears glasses. He'll be carrying a Bible under his right arm. Don't speak to him. For

God's sake, don't. Don't try to sit by him. Follow him off the train in
Paris. Discreetly."

Jonathan was still nodding. He would have enjoyed punching this
patronizing son of a bitch right in the mouth. How stupid did he think
Jonathan was, that he had to repeat every instruction, put it on a child's
level? Jonathan felt the tightness in his chest, the rising flush of anger,
felt it and realized he was close to erupting, he, who had always been
equable and balanced, almost phlegmatic in his acceptance of circumstances. What was wrong with him?

He shook his head, realized he had missed part of the instructions.
"Sorry," he muttered, "What was that?"

"In Paris, after you arrive at the Gare du Nord, follow M. Paul
outside. He will lead you to the guide who will take you to a safe house.
You will stay there until the next leg of your journey is arranged."

Jonathan frowned. "What if I should lose sight of M. Paul?"

"Don't." Then he looked down at the hard-packed floor and
frowned. He hesitated, then said unwillingly, "If anything goes wrong,
if M. Paul is picked up or if you should lose him, you may go to the
Church of the Good Shepherd." He looked at Jonathan doubtfully. "It
is a long way from the station. Five kilometers or six." He pulled a piece
of paper out of his pocket and a stub of pencil and, slowly, carefully,
drew a map. Jonathan looked at it and at the street names, names he
had never heard before, rue de LaFayette, Boulevard Madeleine, the rue
Royale, the Boulevard Raspail, the rue de Naveau. Jonathan took the
map. Five kilometers or six. He couldn't possibly walk that far. "At the
station, couldn't I catch a taxi?"

A look of disgust settled on his companion's blunt heavy face.

Jonathan, hot already, felt his face flame.

"There are no taxis in Paris, M'sieur. Perhaps it would be best if you
made an effort to keep M. Paul in sight."

Jonathan's hands balled into fists. He looked away from that
swarthy contemptuous face, looked at the dirt floor. He had to keep
calm. It didn't matter that the Frenchman thought him a fool. Why was
he letting the man's disdain upset him?

"Do you have a watch?"

Jonathan held out his wrist. "Yes." He set his watch as the man directed. Ten-seventeen. He was to leave the garage at five minutes before eleven.

The stocky man picked up a basket that had been tucked into a corner. He held it out to Jonathan. "My wife fixed this for you. She thought you would be hungry. I'll leave you now. Be sure to keep track of your time." He started to turn away then paused. "Good luck," then he was gone.

The gruff sincerity of the salutation stayed with Jonathan long after the man was gone. Jonathan awkwardly lowered himself to the ground, sitting with the stone wall at his back. Everyone in France these days had a story or a memory or a pain. If this was the stocky man's garage and it must likely be, he was risking imprisonment to help a stranger. Who knew what feelings he harbored? Distress that his country had given in while Jonathan's fought on? A brother or a cousin lost in the delaying circle thrown up by the French around Dunkirk? Was a daughter or a sister or a cousin smiling at the German soldiers? They were men, weren't they, and not grim and poor and emasculated. Did the stocky man envy Jonathan's chance to rejoin the battle? Or was he angry, angry with a deep and abiding and unforgiving anger at what had happened to his country and ashamed that a stranger should see it?

"*Bonne chance.*"

Good luck from a stranger, a basket of food fixed by a woman he would never see. The roll was crusty and still warm with a trace of marmalade inside. The small bottle of wine was wrapped in leaves and it was cool and fresh. He ate too fast then fought a rush of nausea. Groggily, he shook his head. He felt like the very devil. He must wake himself up. He had to be alert. He started to get up, forgetting for a moment to favor his right leg. The wound pulled and split. Pain seared his thigh and he felt spreading warmth. He pulled up to his feet , clinging to the wall. He leaned against the stones for a long moment until the pain began to ease. Then he saw, with a feeling of sickness, the dark stain on his pants, and noticed the smell, sweet and noxious.

Like a dead animal. He stared down at the slowly spreading patch of dampness and began to shudder. Blood had always smelled unnatural to him, but this was worse than the smell of blood. Much worse.

Panic swept him. He had to walk to the station and board the train. He took a step, then another, then a series. Oh God, he could walk, though his leg hurt, but the dampness, whatever it was, some thick and viscous fluid from his wound, was sliding down his leg now and soon, soon, his pants would be wet enough for everyone to notice . . . and smell.

Jonathan stumped down the center of the long garage peering through the gloom. A pair of coveralls hung near a work bench. Jonathan snatched them down then looked desperately at his pants leg. Almost sodden.

Hurrying, even his fingers awkward now, he pulled off his trousers, stepping out carefully. He could see where the wound had split and the oozing stream. He grabbed up a pair of shears, cut off the unsullied trouser leg and used the cloth to make a wadding of a bandage, to stop the flow, hide it, absorb it.

When that was done, he rested.

Hot. God, he was so hot. He wiped the back of his right hand against his face then jerked his hand away. That smell. The odor would nauseate a horse. He bent nearer the bench. Nothing, nothing. A can of turpentine, a barrel of vinegar, a vat of paint, nothing to help. He searched the near end of the garage. He stopped to pick up the basket that the stocky man's wife had fixed and his hand felt the faint coolness of the bottle. He hadn't quite finished the wine, had he? Jonathan tilted up the bottle and heard the faint slosh. Not much wine, but a little, an ounce or two. He cupped his hands, poured out a meager teaspoon, rubbed his hands over and over. The sour smell of the red wine wafted up and soon he could no longer smell the sweet sickish odor of the discharge from his wound.

He poured the rest of the wine in tiny driblets onto the coveralls, just above the wound. Some wine soaked through the wadded bandage and touched the newly raw edges like liquid fire, but he clenched his teeth and kept on pouring. The odor of wine clung to him, hung sourly.

The Gestapo wouldn't arrest a man because he smelled like he had drunk too much. The smell of a rotten wound was another matter entirely. He was exhausted when he finished. Slowly doggedly, he folded the napkin, put the basket on the workbench. He had fifteen minutes before it was time to go.

He closed his eyes and repeated in his mind his new name, Michel Beauvais, and his history: A Parisian returning from Clermont where he had gone in search of his girlfriend. They had quarreled. You know the kind of thing? You say things you don't mean. Somebody had told him she had gone to Clermont to stay with her sister. But the Tillon family here had never heard of Genevieve. Or said they hadn't. Now, disgruntled, sullen, hostile, he was returning to Paris. He lived in the 13th Arondissement, in a room above a cleaning shop.

Ask me your questions, Jonathan thought wearily, I can answer a few. But only a few. If the questions delved very deep or if a native-born Frenchman heard him speak, he would be caught. But there was no point in worrying about that. Not now.

It was time.

The garage opened onto a dusty courtyard. The hulks of two burned-out cars sat on one side. The old unshaven man who had helped shift the crates of supplies was dismantling the motor of a pickup truck with a broken axle. He kept working as Jonathan walked by, not looking up.

Jonathan turned to his right. It was a rocky village street with a mild uphill gradient. Two blocks. It seemed a long way, a long bloody way. For a moment, he hesitated. He was tired, so tired. Two blocks. Just two blocks then he could rest. His head down, moving with a stiff uncertain gait, Jonathan started up the street toward the station.

CHAPTER 9

They had to walk faster. This slow pace was making the others conspicuous. Already, the chunky blond and the tall emaciated man were waiting at the corner, each trying to ignore the other. Across the street, waiting, too, was the third man, his face turned toward them, a pale blob in the dusk.

Don't look at us, Eleanor thought angrily. I told you what to do. And they all, each of the three, looked so foreign. For just an instant, the thought hung in her mind. Andre would love that, she thought. I think they look foreign. Andre would . . .

Tires squealed behind them.

Eleanor's hand tightened on Jonathan's elbow. Oh God, a car. That meant Germans, more than likely. Sometimes they stopped pedestrians on the street, checking papers at random. If it were Gestapo agents on the prowl and if they had seen three young men, moving slowly and uncertainly down the street, they might very well be suspicious.

The car picked up speed, roared by in a blur. It was a German staff car. Eleanor caught a flash of a green uniform but a touch of color, too. She began to breathe again. High ranking officers with their girlfriends. They wouldn't be interested in pedestrians on the shabby street. Probably they were on their way to Maxim's for a night on the town. Gay Paree. For some.

"No."

That was all he said, but it was a guttural sound of defeat..

"It isn't far," she said quickly. "Only five more blocks. You've come this far. You can make it a little farther."

"I'm too slow. Take the others. Go ahead." Jonathan swayed perceptibly. "I'll start up again in a while. If . . . maybe come back for me . . ."

Oh God, Eleanor thought. Did I say it out loud? Did I tell him we had to go faster? I was trying to hurry him and I pulled on his arm. I can't leave him here. We're almost to the apartment. "Five more blocks. Oh please, just five more blocks."

He didn't shake his head, didn't move at all, didn't say a word.

It was getting darker every instant. Now, all three of the Englishmen in their ill-fitting civilian clothes, were looking back, obviously tense and afraid. Eleanor had warned them. Walk easily, slouch a little bit, you're on your way home, you just got off work and you're tired, looking forward to a bit of supper. Now, close to safety, or at least the illusion of safety, they waited on street corners, strangers in a dark city, dependent upon her to guide them.

A sliver of light flashed for an instant near the corner. Before the door shut, Eleanor heard a snatch of rollicking can-can music. She remembered a party one night years before in Montmartre and a thin silver quarter moon hanging behind Sacre-Couer and the laughing giggling group, arm in arm, singing and swinging their legs.

She gestured for the men to come, short quick imperative waves. Each turned, stepped indecisively, stopped. She waved again. As they walked toward her, Eleanor quailed for a moment. Did she have any right? She was gambling their safety for the man beside her.

The tall thin man, Kittredge, that was his name, reached Eleanor first. "What's wrong? Are we lost?"

She shook her head, waited until they all had gathered round her. She whispered. "I need your help. This man," and she nodded at Jonathan, "is very ill. He can't make it any farther. I want—"

The chunky blond, Jamison, interrupted. "Leave him. Let's leave him here. The bloody Germans are going to catch all of us if we stand around on the street having a bloody meeting."

"Hold on, Jamison," the third man said quietly. "We can't go about dumping people. Tell us, now, ma'am, what do you want us to do."

Jamison shook his head. "Don't be such a bloody hero, Miller. We don't know this man. Why should we stick our necks out for him?"

"Jamison's right," Kittredge chimed in.

"Hush, all of you." Eleanor glanced up and down the street. "We can't afford to stand here and quarrel."

"That's what I'm saying," Jamison said, his voice rising. "Let's get on with it."

"Yes," Eleanor said crisply. "Let's get on with it. Mr. Miller, you and Mr. Kittredge put Mr. Harris between you, his arms over your shoulders. That way you can carry him. If a patrol comes around the corner, we will sing."

"Sing!" Jamison exploded. "You crazy old . . ."

"Mr. Jamison." She grabbed his arm, pulled him along beside her. "You will walk with me. All of you, listen," and she began, very softly, to sing the bawdy lighthearted lyrics to the can-can.

Jamison tried to shake off her hand. "We don't have to do this. You can't make us."

She stopped. Once again the whole group stopped. "It's five more blocks to our destination, Mr. Jamison. I'm the only one who knows the way."

They crossed the Seine into deep shadows by Notre Dame, walking several blocks out of their way to avoid the German-occupied Palais de Justice and the Prefecture de Police. They reached the Boulevard Saint-Germain, coming up behind the Hotel de Cluny, only a block from their goal.

A car came around the corner.

Eleanor tightened her grip on Jamison's arm, lifted her head, and began to sing. One by one, they joined in, the words blurred but the tune distinct.

The car slowed, stopped beside them. A spotlight beam circled them.

"Keep singing. Keep singing." Eleanor laughed, waved one hand in the air, kicked out her legs in a mock can-can.

"Mademoiselle! Messieurs!"

Still laughing, Eleanor swung around. "Yes!"

"Can you tell us," the French was labored and slow, "how to find the Café Rotonde? In Montparnasse?"

For an instant, Eleanor had trouble drawing breath into her lungs, then, dropping Jamison's arm, she stepped nearer the curb.

"Why, of course. Go back to the Boul' Mich'. Do you know it? Yes, turn to your left. When you reach the Boulevard Montparnasse, turn right."

"*Merci. Danke.*" As the car began to make its U-turn, the German soldier called back, "A good night for a party, isn't it, Mademoiselle."

"Oh yes, yes indeed."

Even Jamison helped carry Jonathan the final block.

"Phew. He stinks," Jamison muttered, but he grabbed Jonathan's legs.

"He's out cold," Miller said. "What's wrong with him?"

"I don't know." Eleanor almost ran as she led the way the last long block. They struggled up the four flights, breathing heavily by the time they reached the top floor.

Linda was holding the door for them. "What's taken so long? Oh Eleanor, I was so afraid you'd been stopped. What's wrong with that one?"

"Put him in the bedroom," Eleanor directed.

As the men half-carried, half dragged Jonathan across the room, Linda ran to open the bedroom door.

Eleanor pulled down the spread, eased a pillow behind Jonathan's head.

"My God, if that doesn't take the cake." Linda exploded. "Here we are taking a chance on a ticket to a firing squad and you come dragging in with a red-faced drunk. Eleanor, we'll have to tell Father Laurent, we just won't be involved with someone like this."

"Shh, Linda. He's not drunk. He's sick. Awfully sick."

In the afternoon, after it had been decided that they would take Father Laurent's group, Eleanor and Linda and Robert had worked hard, making several trips between their apartment and the empty one in the student quarter, outfitting it for its coming occupants. They brought in bedding, what food they could muster, and even a few books.

Now Eleanor stood tensely by the bed. "Linda, there isn't any medicine, is there?"

Linda shook her head. She couldn't take her eyes off the flushed beard-stubbled face. "He looks awful."

Eleanor leaned close to him, touched one cheek. "His fever is too high. We must get a doctor."

"We don't dare," Linda whispered. "How can we take a chance like that?"

"I think I can trust Dr. Gailland."

"Think? Eleanor, we can't take the chance."

"We must."

"But Eleanor. . ." Her voice was rising. Linda heard it herself. She clapped her hands over her mouth and turned and rushed from the room.

The other men looked up as she burst into the room.

Miller, the slow-voiced Scot, bent solicitously toward her. "What is it, young lady? Has the young man . . . Is there anything I can do?"

Get out, Linda thought hysterically, if you would all just get out of here, leave us alone. The three of them stood looking at her and she could see the weariness of weeks of danger and privation, the slump of Kittredge's shoulders, the desperate light in Jamison's eyes, the droop of Miller's mouth.

Wordlessly, she shook her head.

Jamison tried to help. "It's the smell, Miss," he said awkwardly. "I smelled them like that in the hospital." He held up his left hand. Three fingers were missing, sheared off at the knuckle. "I was lucky enough. Gangrene didn't set in. When it does it's pretty bad. Anyway, Miss, it's enough to turn a man's stomach."

"Yes," she said quickly, "that was it."

Eleanor came out of the bedroom, shut the door softly behind her.

Linda rushed ahead, "The rest of you must be very hungry. We don't have much but I'll get it ready. Some potato soup. There aren't many potatoes actually, a few for flavor, but we have bread and applesauce."

When they were seated and had begun to eat, Eleanor came to

stand by the table. "Gentlemen, as you eat, let me explain what we all must do to avoid capture. Walk around the room as little as possible and do not wear your shoes. Keep away from the windows when the curtains are open in the daytime. Speak softly. We want at all costs to avoid attracting any attention. Any attention. In line with this, we must ask you not to leave the apartment. We know it is very confining, very boring." She looked at each of them in turn. "But it is much more comfortable than a prisoner-of-war camp."

"We understand, ma'am. We'll cooperate." Miller looked at Kittredge and Jamison.

They nodded.

"Hopefully, you won't be here too long. A week at the most and then you should be on your way."

It didn't take them long to eat. The men very carefully did not look toward the kitchen as they finished. Each bowl was absolutely empty. Not even a crumb of bread remained on the platter.

"I'm sorry we don't have more," Eleanor said quietly.

"That's plenty, ma'am," Miller replied quickly. "That's more food and better than we've had in a while. It was wonderful."

"Thank you. I'll see if I can't bring back more tomorrow. It's hard to get food now in Paris."

Eleanor and Linda helped the men arrange their beds, the couch and two pallets in the living room. Then Eleanor took Linda with her into the tiny kitchen. As they washed up the dinner dishes, Eleanor said abruptly, "Linda, what upset you? In the bedroom?"

Linda rubbed the tea towel around the lip of the blue pottery soup bowl. She didn't look up though she could feel Eleanor watching her. Why was it so hard to be honest with Eleanor? Why couldn't she just tell her? I'm afraid. I'm afraid of the Gestapo. I'm afraid and I don't want to—her mind shied away from putting her thoughts into words. To think about what might happen would make the possibility more real, more threatening.

"Linda?"

The bowl was dry now but still Linda rubbed the dish towel against the smooth pottery. "It's just that—" She broke off and put down the bowl, picked up a glass, began to dry it, to hide the sudden trembling in her hands.

"Linda, is it the sickness? Does it upset you, to be close to someone who is very ill?"

Linda did look up, finally. Eleanor was looking at her with such kindness, such concern. Why couldn't she be brave like her sister? It was so much more of a gamble for Eleanor. She had her son to lose. Linda felt the hot rush of tears behind her eyes. Why did she have to be such a coward? She widened her eyes, making the tears stay back. "I'm sorry, Eleanor, I'm sorry to be such a fool. It will be all right. I promise you. I'll help you take care of him. I won't act like such a baby again."

"Oh, Lindy," and the old childhood familiar slipped out so easily, "don't be hard on yourself. It's no crime to be squeamish. And if I could figure out any other way, I would, but Robert is back at the apartment, waiting for us. I told him to stay home and not to worry if we were a little late. Anyway, I don't think I should send him to ask Dr. Gailland to come. It's a job for an adult. I couldn't blame the doctor if he wouldn't listen to a child. It's too serious for him and for us to take any chances on how we contact him. I can't send you because he doesn't know you and even with a note he might be suspicious that it was a trap. I must go myself."

Linda nodded, not quite seeing where the rush of words was heading. At least she wouldn't have to cross dark Parisian streets to ask help of a man she had never met.

"But someone has to be here to let Dr. Gailland in and hear what he wants us to do—"

The other Englishmen, Linda thought.

"—and it obviously has to be you because none of the Englishmen speak French." Eleanor tipped over the dishpan, let the water trickle down into the sink. "Dr. Gailland may not need you to help him so maybe it won't be difficult at all."

Linda nodded again and hung up the dishcloth, shielding her face for a moment, for long enough. Oh no, it shouldn't be difficult, just waiting for a knock on the door and not knowing, not really knowing, whether it would be a doctor willing to treat a fugitive or the Gestapo. Nothing difficult at all.

It was very quiet after Eleanor left. The men went to bed and were almost at once asleep. Linda could hear their deep uneven breathing as she waited in the rocking chair near the door. Twice she checked on the sick man. She carried a candle. Their blackout curtains weren't good enough to risk the lights. His breathing was slow and labored. The second time, Linda approached the bed and resolutely touched his cheek. She yanked back her hand. His hot, dry skin felt like metal under an August sun. For the first time, she felt a pang of concern for him. He was something more than a problem, an inert foul-smelling burden.

His face was turned toward her on the pillow and he looked defenseless as do all sleeping creatures. His blond hair was thick and curly. Longer now, she would guess than was his custom. The stubble on his face had a reddish cast. He would probably, Linda judged, have blue eyes. His face was thin and drawn but had once been heavier, a full stubborn chin, broad cheeks. A nice mouth, wide, full-lipped.

He opened his eyes suddenly, looked directly at her. Not blue eyes at all. Brown. Rich dark brown, almost black. He stared at her, his mouth moved, but there was not even a whisper of sound. He stared and tried to raise up his head then, as quickly as a light dims, his face was empty, his head fell back, his eyes shut.

For an instant, Linda was rigid with horror then, with a rush of relief, she saw the slow rise of the bedclothes over his chest and heard again that stertorous breathing.

Linda picked up the candle holder and returned to the rocking chair. The flickering of the candle threw her shadow against the wall. Eleanor had been gone more than an hour now. Of course, the doctor might have been out, seeing another patient. Perhaps she hadn't found him yet.

Dr. Gailland. Linda had never met him. She did recall Eleanor mentioning an appointment with him, oh, it must have been March or April.

Eleanor had an earache. She had come home and talked inconsequentially with Andre about the visit, the waiting room had been full, Dr. Gailland's sister had joined him in his practice, her specialty was pediatrics, Dr. Gailland and his wife were planning a trip to Nice in May.

Now Eleanor was hurrying to put their lives in his hands. It would be easy for him to turn them in. So many Frenchmen accepted Petain, supported him, considered the English their betrayers.

How could Eleanor be sure?

Linda rocked, back and forth, back and forth, then she stopped and put her hands against her mouth. She was going to be sick.

The tapping was so soft, Linda scarcely heard it. She sat up straight, bent her head forward. Through the open bedroom door, she heard three quick taps, three slow taps on the apartment door. Numbly, her lips pressed tightly together, Linda rose and walked to the door. She listened once again.

Tap, tap, tap. Tap . . . tap . . . tap.

She opened the door a scant inch and wished she had blown out the candle. "*Oui?*"

"Mlle. Rossiter?" It was a woman's voice, soft and clear.

Linda hesitated.

"Mlle. Rossiter, your sister, Eleanor, has sent me. I am Dr. Gailland. Marie Gailland."

Dr. Gailland's sister. Well, surely it was all right, but still Linda stood stiffly at the door.

"Your sister told me to tell you that she was born in Santa Barbara. And you were born in Pasadena."

Linda held the door open.

A small slight woman stepped inside. She carried a black leather satchel.

Linda picked up the candle holder and led the way to the bedroom. Linda waited at the foot of the bed as the doctor made her examination.

In better days, Marie Gailland's face had a tendency toward laughter. Curved lines at the corners of her mouth and eyes testified to good humor. Now fatigue had slackened the muscles in her face, made pouches beneath her dark intelligent eyes. She took Jonathan's pulse. Quickly, efficiently, cut away the coveralls over the improvised bunched bandage. Her eyebrows drew together. "Would you get me a basin of some sort? And some hot water?"

Linda brought a steaming tea kettle and a small blue enamel basin. Linda very carefully didn't watch but she knew when the wound was opened. An indescribably vile odor swept the room. He stirred and moaned once, a deep weary unconscious sigh of pain. His head twisted on the pillow. His face was young and defenseless and still as the cold marble on a crypt.

Dr. Gailland cleaned the wound. "Mlle. Rossiter. I have drained some of the infection. Every four hours you must take a fresh swab and insert it, thus," Linda watched in horror as the doctor thrust the white-tipped cotton into the wound and gently pressed forward and backward and a yellowish thick liquid oozed from the opening. "Here." She handed Linda a fresh swab. "Let me see you do it."

Linda held the swab in a hand that trembled violently.

"Don't be nervous. It isn't difficult." Dr. Gailland placed a firm brown hand over Linda's and gently guided her hand forward. Linda resisted as the swab was next to the wound. "It's all right," the doctor said, "you won't hurt him. The nerve ends have been cut. There won't be any pain. Besides, he is unconscious."

The swab slipped into the wound, moved back and forth, pushing out more of the pus.

"Very good. Each time, after you finish swabbing, reinsert the tubing so that the wound will continue to drain." She looked down, frowning. "I hope you understand, Mlle. Rossiter, he is very ill. It would have been better if I had seen him sooner."

Linda looked up, shocked. "But he'll be all right, won't he?"

The doctor shrugged, an infinitely French shrug. "He is suffering from blood poisoning, Mademoiselle. Do you see the reddish streaks here, on his leg, above and below the wound. If I could take him to a hospital, perhaps he would get well. But we can only try."

"You think he's going to die."

Slowly Dr. Gailland began to gather up her equipment. She opened her bag, stared down into it for a moment, then turned to Linda. "I have something new here. I've not tried it on any of my patients so I can't be sure of it's worth. But I may as well use it." She opened the container, lifted out a vial and a syringe. "They say it's a miracle drug. He needs a miracle." She upended the vial, pulled down the plunger to draw the liquid into the syringe. "It's a sulfanilamide," Dr. Gailland added almost absently.

When the doctor closed her valise, she gave a tired sigh.

"Would you care for a glass of wine?" Linda asked tentatively. "If it won't run you too late?"

The doctor smiled and looked, suddenly, years younger. "Oh, I have a special permit. I don't have to worry about the curfew. I'm even allowed to keep my car and receive ten gallons of gasoline a week. It isn't enough but it's better than nothing." She glanced down at her watch. "If it won't keep you up too late, Mademoiselle, I would very much enjoy a glass of wine."

Linda led her guest into the tiny kitchen and closed the door, explaining softly, "There are others, asleep in the living room."

Dr. Gailland nodded. "Of course. Things are irregular in many homes these days."

When the wine was poured and they each had lit a cigarette, Linda raised her glass. "You are very good to come, doctor."

"It is my job." She drew deeply on her cigarette. "I don't know how long I can manage all of it, my brother's practice, my own. And those like you, who need me in the night."

"You're working alone? I thought you and your brother were in practice together."

"Claude and Annette were in Nice when the Blitzkrieg began. I have not heard from them since Paris fell. My brother called, a few days before the Germans reached Paris, to tell me they would not be coming back." She took a sip of wine. "So I am trying to take care of all of his patients who are still in Paris. Today I had no time for lunch. A bowl of soup for dinner."

Linda popped up, began to open the cupboards. "Here are some biscuits. I'm sorry I don't have more."

The doctor tried to refuse, but Linda insisted and she saw, finally, how quickly and hungrily her guest ate.

"Did your brother expect you to manage all of his patients, too?"

Dr. Gailland shot her a quick perceptive look. "You think he did not much value his patients?"

Linda tried to protest but Dr. Gailland rushed on. "He is the kind of doctor, Mademoiselle, who did not bill his poor patients, who stayed through the night with a sick child. Oh, yes, he cared. He cried that day when he called to say they were staying in Nice." She tipped up her glass, finished the wine. "My sister-in-law, Annette, has never been strong. They have no children. I know that is a grief to them. Annette is about your size, and blond, as you, but she has dark eyes. She is very beautiful and very kind, a gentle creature. And Jewish."

Long after the slender dark-eyed doctor had left, Linda rocked sleepless in the chair, rocked and smoked. When it was time, wearily, her face drawn, she walked to the bedroom, carrying the clean basin with tepid water. She gave him a sponge bath to try and lessen the fever. When he was clean and cooler to touch, Linda gently loosened the bandage, slipped free the tubing and reached for a clean swab.

CHAPTER 10

"**U**ncle Erich." The young voice was eager and happy.

"Fritz." Erich Krause pushed up from his chair and rushed around his desk to grab up his nephew in a warm embrace. Then he stepped back to look at Fritz. The first thing he saw was the eagle above the right breast pocket of the blue-gray gabardine uniform. "The Luftwaffe. Fritz, I didn't know. When did this happen?"

Fritz smiled proudly. "I didn't let Mother write you until I was sure I had made it. I transferred from the infantry to the Luftwaffe in July. They needed more pilots."

"July?" Erich Krause frowned. "And you already have your wings?"

"It's a new accelerated program, Uncle Erich. There's a great need for more pilots."

For an instant, it was silent in the shining elegant office, then Fritz said quickly, "Of course, the air war's going splendidly. They say the RAF is barely operational. I expect I'll just be part of the mop-up before the invasion. I wish I could have made it here sooner."

The Paris newspapers daily carried estimates of RAF planes downed in the previous day's raids by the Luftwaffe, but there was no corresponding list of Luftwaffe losses. Every evening the BBC broadcast the estimate of losses for both sides. Paris drew its shades and clandestinely listened.

"How long will you have in Paris?"

"Until morning. I'm sorry I couldn't let you know I was coming, but my travel plans weren't definite until yesterday."

"It doesn't matter. God, it's so good to see you, Fritz. How long has it been now?"

"Two years ago, after the Party Rally in Nuremburg, you came to Berlin to visit Mother and I was home on leave."

"Have you seen your mother recently?"

Fritz nodded. "She told me to bring you all her love."

Krause smiled thinly. His sister Marta was always ebullient, irrepressible. She had teased him, that last meeting, "All right, Erich, if we're going to have a policeman in the family, we might as well get some use out of it. I want Gertrude Friedrichs arrested. At once." He had lounged back in the huge overstuffed chair, his shining black boots crossed. "Oh, and what has Frau Friedrichs done?" "She took my best torte recipe and gave it to everyone in her sewing club." Everyone had laughed. The next Monday he had Gertrude Friedrichs arrested. He held her for two days. When his sister called, he had laughed. "I did you one better, Marta." "Erich, I was only joking. I never meant for you to arrest her." "I thought you might like to know that I can arrest anyone. Anyone at all." "Yes," Marta replied, "I see that you can," and there had been no laughter in her voice.

Marta had always been so pietistic. He controlled the rush of anger. She always irritated him because she was unimpressed with his success in the Party, disdainful of the bully-brown shirts, as she called them. Well, of course, the Brown Shirts had had to go, but they had been useful in their time.

Krause looked at his nephew with approval. Marta had never deserved to have so fine a son as Fritz. He should have had such a son, clear blue eyes, stocky muscular build, hair as bright and shining as a golden helmet. None better in all of Germany. Krause forgot the anger that always stirred within him, moving dangerously close to the surface like the molten surge of lava pressing ever upward. Instead he enjoyed the moment as he rarely enjoyed time. To be with Fritz, that was enough for now. "When does your train leave?"

"At nine."

"We have plenty of time. Come, I'll take you on a tour of Paris. You've not been here before, have you?"

"No, sir, but do you have time to spare? I didn't mean to break in on your day. I know you are very busy."

Krause frowned at the piles of paper on his desk. "Nothing I do is as important as your task, Fritz. Though I do my part for you and the other fliers."

"Oh?" Puzzled, Fritz asked uncertainly, "Are you associated with the Luftwaffe in some way?"

"Nothing direct. It's my job to round up these English soldiers who are hiding in the North and the RAF fliers who parachute into France. Every English pilot less, the better for you, right, Fritz?"

His nephew nodded vigorously. "That's true, but I shouldn't think you'd have too much difficulty finding them. Are there still soldiers hiding near Dunkirk?"

"Almost ten thousand. We pick them up every day in the northern woods. We use dogs, you know, and motorcycle units. But some of them still manage to escape us." Krause's eyes narrowed. "The damned French. We've defeated them and we've treated them very gently. We have strict rules on the treatment of civilians, you know, unless they are involved in a crime against the Reich. Still, they don't honor their agreements. Sly. Just like the French. But we put out a new directive the first week in September—the death penalty for anyone who is hiding an Englishman and doesn't surrender him by October 20. It's time to stop treating these criminals so gently." He reached for a stack of manila folders. "Look at these—you wouldn't believe the time and manpower it is taking to try and break up these subterranean rings of people who are smuggling Englishmen into the Unoccupied Zone." He flipped open the first folder. "This is one of my successes. I'm putting some of my men out into the field who speak good English. They are my decoys. We've broken up two escape routes through them this last week. One in Bordeaux and one in Nantes. I'm getting a network of informers established. It's like a game, Fritz. A little bit of information here, a little there. You put it together and sometimes it makes a picture, a very interesting picture. People talk." Krause smiled. "What the fools don't realize is that we are listening. Here's this report, for example, from a farm laborer. We picked him up at a control. His papers weren't quite right. Well, we told him that he could prove to us he could be trusted.

All he had to do was tell us if he heard anything strange about anyone in town, a doctor calling at a house where no one was known to be sick, too much food being bought on the black market by a small family, an unusual amount of activity in a house. That kind of thing. He is to report to our office weekly." Krause smiled again. "That puts pressure on him to tell us something every week. Much of it will be meaningless, but some of it will be helpful." He skimmed the page, flipped to the second. "A parish priest, Father Peridot, has been buying quantities of work clothes. A druggist rumored willing to provide morphine without prescription. A man seen leaving the home of a widowed schoolteacher, Mme. Moreau, in the early morning hours." He snapped the folder shut. "That's just one village, Fritz, Les Andelys. Soon we will have listeners in every village." He put the folder down, looked again at his handsome nephew. "But that's enough about my dry old desk work. Tell me more about your posting."

Lieutenant Fritz Weber didn't quite hide his smile of pride. "At Guines, near Calais. I've been posted to the 26th Fighter Group, Third Wing at Caffier's airfield." He paused, then added, "Maj. Galland's unit."

Maj. Galland was Germany's premier air ace, the veteran of 280 Spanish missions, 87 Polish missions. By early August, he had already been credited with 17 victories against the RAF and had been awarded the Knight's Cross.

"We have much to celebrate. Come now, Fritz, I will show you Paris. We will have dinner at Maxim's."

Eleanor paused in front of the art store window to study the display. The Romanesque steeple of the Church of St. Germain-des-Pres dominated the small watercolor on the easel, giving the painting a lop-sided look. The initials SW were clear and distinct in the lower left-hand corner. In front of the easel, in two uneven rows, was a collection of small matchboxes. Eleanor counted the boxes. Five in the first row, five in the second. Ten. The Englishmen were to be taken to the Southwest corner by the Church of St. Germain-des-Pres on September 10. Tomorrow was Tuesday, September 10. The rendezvous hour was always 5:30, no matter the date or the place, as the train for Bordeaux left the Gare d'Austerlitz at 7 p.m.

Father Laurent had arranged for the display to be made by the shop owner in order to avoid so much traffic in and out of the Church. If, however, Eleanor or Linda needed to talk to him, it could be arranged. Tomorrow he would be expecting four Englishmen, but there were going to be only three.

Eleanor pushed in the shop door. A bell tinkled. After a moment there was the sound of slow heavy footsteps. Eleanor peered through the gloom. Paintings hung from the walls, were propped against tables, stacked in corners. A dark velvet curtain at the rear of the shop swayed, parted, seemed to move toward her. Eleanor blinked. The curtain was coming forward. Then she realized it was a mountainous figure swathed in dark velveteen. The woman moved ponderously, the floor creaking beneath her weight. Her face was immense, too, bloated, the chin lost in rolls of fat that swelled in creases down to the huge yet shapeless chest. She stared blankly at Eleanor. "Yes?"

Eleanor cleared her throat. "Is Mme. Lisette here?"

"I am Mme. Lisette." A deep throaty gruff voice.

Eleanor looked at her searchingly. "I am interested," she said slowly, "in paintings of medieval churches. Especially those by Laurent."

The woman nodded heavily. "I am a connoisseur, too."

At that correct response, the tension eased out of Eleanor's shoulders.

"I do not have any in stock," Lisette continued. "If you will leave your name, you will be contacted when a painting is available."

So that was done, Eleanor thought, as she walked up the Boul' Mich' toward the Hotel de Cluny. She did need to talk to him. Not just to tell him there would only be three travelers tomorrow. That wasn't a problem, merely a matter of information. But she did have a problem if the fourth Englishman died. Harris, that was his name, Jonathan Harris. Perhaps Father Laurent could help her get some papers in the name of Roger Lamirand. The apartment, of course, was still listed in his name and the concierge, in the official domicile records, carried him as the renter. Father Laurent might know specifically which papers would be needed.

Would it take cooperation by the concierge?

Eleanor recalled her face, middle-aged, hard. Which way would she jump? But she might go along with the story. She had, after all, been willing to sub-rent the apartment to Eleanor without any questions. She must have known, would surely have known, that there must be some compelling reason for someone like Eleanor to go to such trouble. Something more than just a love affair, in times such as these.

Eleanor walked a little faster. She was willing to gamble. She must be catching something of Father Laurent's spirit. What was it he had said Saturday? "There will be plenty to help us. We don't need to be afraid, almost all Frenchmen will help, if we ask."

She didn't subscribe to that. There were too many who had turned brusque when she had called, hinting at her need for help. But there had also been Annemarie and now Madame Lisette and Father Laurent and all those who had helped the men who were hiding now in the apartment

The apartment door opened before Eleanor reached the top of the stairs. Robert poked his head out and looked disappointed. "We thought it might be Dr. Gailland."

His mother put a finger to her lips. When they were inside, the door closed, she cautioned. "Don't use names, Robert, in a hallway. The doctor is taking a risk to help us. Let's not take any chances on endangering her."

"Do you think someone here in the apartment house would turn her in?"

Eleanor said gently, "We don't know, Robert. But we must remember to be careful. With every word and every action. So many others are depending upon us now."

He nodded solemnly, his thin face grave and adult.

Oh Robert, Robert, his mother thought, I am so proud of you. I love you so much.

His shirt was too small. It stretched across his chest and shoulders. He was beginning to grow from a little boy into an adolescent. He was shaped so much like his father. He was going to be thick-chested like Andre. Funny, they had never foreseen that when he was small. His school trousers were short, too. How he had grown since last spring. Andre had not seen him since May 19. Oh Andre, are you somewhere? At this moment are you picturing me or Robert, tracing in your mind where we would be, what we would be doing on a sunny September afternoon?

"Mother, do you think the doctor can do something more?"

"Is he worse?"

They spoke in low voices. Funereal tones. It was quiet, Eleanor realized, throughout the apartment. She could see Kittredge, standing to the left of the window, staring down into the street. One of the men, sat with his back to her, reading. The third was asleep, sprawled on his stomach on the sofa.

"He lies too still. He looks like wax."

"Where's Linda?"

"She stays with him. He makes too much noise when he is alone. He mumbles and thrashes and sometimes almost shouts and tries to struggle up. But he hasn't done that since early this morning. Now, he doesn't move. Aunt Linda bathes his face and talks to him, just gently. He rests better when she is there."

Early this morning? "Robert, didn't you go to school?"

Robert avoided his mother's eyes. "Aunt Linda wants to talk to you. She thinks we ought to try and call Dr. Gailland."

Eleanor wasn't deflected. "Robert, did you miss school?"

"I thought Aunt Linda might need me. I knew you were going to be visiting the hospitals all day and I thought I should stay here."

"Robert." She tried to be stern. "You mustn't miss school. It's part of what we talked about. We must try to keep our usual schedule. That's why we are going to have Linda stay here at the apartment. Our neighbors won't notice her comings and goings but you must keep to your school schedule and I will continue to work for the Foyer du Soldat. We mustn't do anything out of the ordinary."

"Sister Colette won't turn us in."

"Petain is currying favor with the Church, Robert. He is easing restrictions on the clergy so many of the Church leaders are supporting Vichy and that means they won't work against the Germans."

"Not Sister Colette," Robert said stubbornly.

"Robert, I don't want you missing any more classes."

He didn't answer.

She slipped her arm around him, hugged him close to her. "There will be plenty for you to do, my dear. You won't be left out." She felt his shoulders relax. "Right now you can go get some food." She opened her purse. "I went by the bank earlier." She drew out a wad of banknotes. "I understand there's a new black market behind the Broken Lance restaurant. Buy whatever you can, anything that we can fix for dinner."

When Robert was gone, Kittredge called out to her. "Mme. Masson, have you heard anything?"

"Yes. I have news."

Miller put down his book and Jamison struggled to a sitting position on the sofa.

"You leave here tomorrow evening for Bordeaux."

"Bordeaux? Where's that?" Jamison asked.

"Southwest. It's still in the Occupied Zone, but you will cross the Demarkation Line there and travel on to a little town near the Spanish border."

"Who's taking us?" Miller rubbed his chin nervously.

Eleanor smiled. "One of us will take you to a certain point. We will do it in the same manner that we walked across Paris Saturday. One of you may walk with me, one of you will follow a half block behind and the third will follow on the opposite side of the street. When we reach our rendezvous—the southwest corner in front of Paris' oldest church—I will leave. You will follow a man carrying a plaid valise. He will take you to the railroad station, buy the tickets and travel in the same car with you to Bordeaux."

"What if we get stopped, here in Paris? Or what if they ask to see our papers on the train?" The questions spurted out of Miller.

"Just be relaxed," Eleanor urged. "Don't look frightened or worried. When they ask for your papers, '*Vous papiers, s'il vous plait*,' hand them over. Look tired, maybe a little surly. There's no reason for anyone to ask you any more questions. Your papers will look good."

He nodded and turned away, walking swiftly to the window.

I hope your papers look good, Eleanor thought, but there isn't a thing in the world you can do or I can do to make everything go perfectly. But, later this evening, after Robert came back with something for dinner and after she had seen to Linda and her patient, she must remember to come and sit with Miller, talk to him, teach him a few more words of French, try to give him the confidence to make the journey.

Eleanor sighed. She was tired, very tired. She had visited four hospitals today. At each one, she couldn't help looking for Andre among the still forms who lay unconscious, unknowing on the high narrow beds in the surgical wards. Down every corridor as she carried food and took messages, she looked for Andre. Then she had made the long walk to the bank and taken the Metro to the Latin Quarter and the art shop. She didn't use the car except for the hospital visits to save the precious gas. Now she and Robert needed to get home, resume their regular schedule. Linda must be tired, too, and tired of dealing with that dreadfully ill airman. Eleanor turned toward the bedroom.

"Why can't we go today?" Jamison demanded harshly.

Eleanor turned back to face him. He was glaring and once again his eyes were wild.

"That decision isn't mine, Mr. Jamison. I'm sure there are good reasons why Tuesday was chosen."

"Isn't there somebody who can change it? Make it today?"

"Mr. Jamison," she struggled to keep the irritation out of her voice, "you leave tomorrow. Not more than twenty-four hours from now. Why are you complaining?"

He took a deep breath. "I can't stand it here. I've got to get out of here. Tell me how to get to the Church. I'll meet you there tomorrow. I'll find someplace else tonight." He started for the door.

Kittredge caught him by the arm. "Don't be a fool, Frank. You'd be picked up for sure. There's the curfew."

Jamison struggled to break free. "I don't care." His voice rose. "I can't stand this place. It stinks. It smells like death."

"Lad, be quiet."

"Oh Eleanor, hurry, come quickly, Eleanor, hurry!" Linda's voice sounded above Jamison's, cut through the scuffle at the door.

"Don't let him leave," Eleanor said sharply. She turned and dashed for the bedroom.

Linda was bending over the bed, clutching Jonathan's shoulders. "I fell asleep for a little while," the girl cried, "just for a little while, then, when I woke, he was so still and white. Oh my God, he died while I was asleep, oh Eleanor, I just slept for a little while." Tears streamed down her face, her whole body quivered.

Eleanor gently pulled Linda away from the bed. She reached down, picked up one of those flaccid hands. In a moment, she spoke. "Linda, listen to me, there's a pulse, I tell you, I feel a pulse."

The slender reddish blonde girl, her face streaked with tears, her hair rumpled with sleep, whirled back to the bed and reached out to touch Jonathan's face. "But his face is cool, almost cold."

"Mme. Masson," the soft Scots voice called. "The doctor is here."

"Oh, thank God," Eleanor breathed.

"Is he still alive?" Linda asked anxiously.

Dr. Gailland listened for a heartbeat. "Yes, Mademoiselle. However, the crisis is near. I will give him another injection of sulfa, but I will tell you honestly that I have little hope of his recovery."

"But he is alive now," Linda said steadily.

The small doctor nodded. "That he has lived this long surprises me. Every hour, Mademoiselle, that he survives increases his chances. If he makes it through the night I think he will live."

"Tonight," Linda repeated. "Tell me what to do. Tell me."

"Continue the alcohol baths. Continue to drain the wound." She shrugged. "And pray, Mademoiselle." She stopped at the doorway, "I will return tomorrow."

She stepped into the living room, motioning Eleanor to come. In a low voice, she said worriedly, "I hope you understand, Mme. Masson, I cannot give you a death certificate."

"I understand. If I can obtain a French identity, the identity of the man to whom this apartment is rented, could you then give us a death certificate?"

"If his papers included discharge from a military hospital, to account for the wound," the doctor said carefully, "then perhaps I could risk it."

Eleanor nodded. "I will see to it. But, whatever happens, Dr. Gailland, we will make sure you are protected. I promise you that."

The doctor smiled. "I trust you," she said simply.

Jamison waited until the door closed behind the doctor, then he confronted Eleanor. "What was all that jabber about? What did the lady doctor say?"

One more problem to deal with. She had to settle Jamison down. If he burst out onto the street, wandered around, he would certainly be picked up and in his present emotional state, he would be an easy mark for the Gestapo. That was the first moment Eleanor realized how vulnerable she and Linda and Robert were to the men they were trying to help. There was always the chance the men would be picked up somewhere down the line of the escape route. It would take only one of them to talk, to tell all he knew, to lead the Gestapo to the apartment just off the rue Saint Jacques. After this, they must not reveal their names to the soldiers. There was no way, of course, that they could hide their nationality. It wouldn't take the Gestapo long to sift through the Americans still left in Paris and find them. Eleanor pushed a hand against her temple. So it didn't matter much if they remained nameless, though it might be a little protection.

"Mme. Masson," Jamison persisted, "Did she say he was dying?"

Eleanor managed a smile. "He's doing much better. She expects to see a marked improvement by the time she comes again tomorrow. So you see, you can relax. I will fix some dinner for all of us soon. That will make you feel better. Until then, why don't you rest?"

He rubbed nervously at his unshaven chin. "Rest. I can't rest. I haven't slept in nights Every time I go to sleep, I see bodies, all stiff and hard, arms and legs sticking in funny shapes, and I smell that rotten stink, then I wake up. I can't rest."

"Frank, come look at this."

Jamison half turned.

Kittredge was gesturing for him to come. "This magazine has a map, lad. Come let me show you. It even shows the way the railroad line runs to Bordeaux. That's where we're going. Come here and I'll show you."

Jamison moved heavily across the room, his head and shoulders rigid with strain, but, in a moment, he sat down beside Kittredge and bent over the map.

Wearily, Eleanor turned toward the kitchen. She began to set the round wooden table. She had just put a saucepan of water on to boil, surely Robert would bring back something to cook, when he banged in the front door.

"Hey, Mother," he called excitedly, "Look what I have." He emptied out the mesh bag onto the counter top and unrolled several sheets of the Paris Soir. "Look at these."

"How marvelous." A year ago, she wouldn't have considered buying these lamb chops. They were thin and small and the meat looked more grayish than pink, but now her face lighted up. She unrolled the last sheet. One, two, three, four, five.

"I could only get five, mother. I'll share mine with you."

Five. Three soldiers and Linda and Robert and herself. Hunger was constant these days. She woke up hungry. She went to bed hungry. She turned to reach for the skillet. "Oh no, Robert, that's all right. The five will do perfectly. I ate earlier. At the hospital."

It was a cheerful dinner for the three Englishmen and Robert. Robert described a vacation the Masons had taken in Bordeaux and the magnificent forest of pine trees, Les Landes. Eleanor carried Linda's dinner to her and watched her sister eat. Linda left an edge of crust on her plate. When Eleanor was back in the kitchen, she took the crust and slowly, carefully rubbed it in the skillet, absorbing the grease. She ate the scrap of bread very, very slowly and drank a half glass of wine.

She warned Linda, before she and Robert left, to tell anyone who asked that Jonathan Harris was improving. "One of them, Jamison," Eleanor gestured toward the living room, "is upset. Battle fatigue, I suppose. He threatened to leave, wander the streets when he thought Jonathan was dying. We can't afford to have him on the streets."

Linda's pale face flushed. "Let him go," she said angrily. "Why should we care what happens to anyone who is selfish enough to—"

"Hush," Eleanor said sharply. "Please, Linda, do as I ask. I have to think of everyone, protect all of us. If he were picked up by the Gestapo, we might all be lost."

Slowly the flush faded from Linda's face. She looked down at Jonathan, lying so still on the narrow bed. "She said the crisis would be tonight."

"Linda, you go home with Robert, I'll stay. You have done more than your share."

"No."

Later, Linda wondered why she had not accepted. She still fought waves of nausea every time she opened the dressing, pulled loose the tubing and reached for a swab. Her lips pressed tightly together, her hand tensed to still its tremors, she edged the swab into the open wound and carefully pressed it forward. Only a trickle of pus appeared. Had she pushed it deep enough? Gingerly she moved it again, the breadth of the opening. Almost nothing. Was that good? She looked up at his face. His features were as distant and unmoving as marble effigies she had seen on medieval caskets. She tossed the swab into the wastebasket, gently redressed the wound.

"Live, Jonathan. Live. Do you hear me?" She bent near his still face, felt his breath touch her lightly, lightly as the ripple of water beside a swan.

She knew his face now, knew it as she had never known another face, the curve of the forehead, the strong sharp line of his nose, the fullness of his mouth, the almost unnoticeable indentation in his chin, hidden now by the growth of bristly reddish beard. She knew his hands, long slender hands that looked both strong and oddly helpless as he lay so quietly. The fever was gone. Surely that was an improvement. But he lay so still.

Linda straightened the sickroom. It was quiet throughout the apartment now. They turned off the lights at dusk, of course, because of the blackout. They had not yet had time to cover the windows with blackout-proof curtains. Eleanor had promised to try and get the material tomorrow. The drawn curtains weren't sufficient to hide a light so the men dropped off to sleep soon after sunset.

In the bedroom, Linda had covered the window with towels. She didn't risk the electric light. The wavering shine of the candle gave her enough light to tend to Jonathan but wasn't bright enough to penetrate the towels.

She lay down on the pallet she had fixed beside the bed, setting the candle holder beside her. She lit a cigarette and slowly smoked it, staring into the wavering darkness, watching the flicker of the candlelight against the ceiling.

Jonathan Harris. Jonathan Harris. A nice name. He looked nice. He looked kind. What did his face look like when he laughed? What made him laugh? Chaplin films? Did he roar at the Little Tramp or was his humor quiet and subtle and wry? Jonathan Harris . What was he like?

When she woke, the candle had burned down almost to a stub. She checked her watch. Time again to tend to Jonathan. She struggled up to her feet, stiff from sleeping on the floor. It was getting so much cooler at night now. What were they going to use for fuel and warmth this winter? Their coal allowance, 55 pounds a month, was only enough to heat one room in the other apartment for two hours daily. There wasn't any extra to bring here. They would have to bundle up.

She put a new candle in the holder and set the light on the table beside the bed. She would have to get fresh water. She reached out and gently touched Jonathan's face. Oh good, the fever hadn't returned. His face felt cool and normal and he was still breathing.

His head turned on the pillow, turned toward her. His eyes opened. Dark brown eyes, defenseless and trusting.

"Jonathan."

He stared at her with a kind of wonder in his eyes.

"You . . ."

She smiled at him, smiled and leaned closer and the candlelight turned her reddish blond hair into shimmering gold. "Jonathan, can you talk? How do you feel? Oh my God, you're awake. That's wonderful."

He smiled a little too. "Who are . . . you?"

She laughed, a tiny soft triumphant laugh. "I'm Linda."

"Linda."

"I'll get you some water. I'll go get some fresh—"

"Wait." His voice was thick and rusty and dry. He reached up to gently touch her sleeve. "Linda. I thought you were a dream."

CHAPTER 11

Jonathan turned his head to smile as Linda came in the room.

"Hello. Jonathan. I've brought you some books."

Jonathan struggled up on an elbow. "Oh, I say, Linda, that's kind of you. I didn't mean to put you to the trouble when you have so much you must do."

"It was no trouble," she said quickly. And it hadn't been. It had been fun to look through Eleanor and Andre's library and select books she thought might please him. She crossed to the bed and smiled down at him. He looked better. Every day he looked better, his color ruddier, and his eyes brighter. He was too thin. Painfully thin, but so were they all. Hunger was constant, a dull gnawing ache that never left. She put the books down beside him and her hand brushed his.

"Linda, sit here by me and show me what you've brought."

She perched on the edge of the bed. "It won't crowd you?"

"No." His dark eyes watched her steadily.

Her hair fell softly around her face. A soft flush touched her cheeks. She pointed to the first book, "It's a French translation of Sir Gawain and the Green Knight."

His hand covered hers as she traced the title. "Sir Gawain. Linda, you could not have brought me a better book."

She smiled. "Oh Jonathan, you are pleased, aren't you?"

"Pleased," he repeated softly. "Yes, I'm pleased." Then in a rush, he said, "Linda, you are beautiful, so beautiful," and he reached up to pull her down to him and his mouth found hers.

Despite the sharp icy gusts of wind, a little crowd gathered to watch the itinerant artist. He hunkered down, his ears red with cold beneath the black beret, his thin shoulders shivering under the frayed gray jacket, but his hand moved in short sure strokes, drawing in chalk against the sidewalk the twin towers and huge rose window of Chartres. Robert edged in beside two teenage girls. Robert didn't even look at the artist, instead, his gaze swung up above the center spire of the drawing. In blue chalk, a flock of birds rose. Five birds. So there would be five Englishman to meet today.

Robert looked beyond the drawing of the Cathedral at a red chalk portrait, half hidden by a Pomeranian on a leash. Robert waited patiently until the dog moved a few steps. There, partially smudged, of no interest to anyone, was another drawing of a squat figure wearing a monocle and carrying a cane.

Whistling, Robert turned and strolled away. Five Englishmen shepherded by a plump man wearing a monocle and carrying a cane. Robert grinned in delight. This was fun, more fun than school, more fun than anything had been since the war started. He loved picking up fugitive Englishmen right under the noses of the Germans, leading them safely across Paris to the apartment. He looked forward to his days as the guide. They took turns, he, his mother and Aunt Linda, to avoid attracting the attention of Germans nosing around the railroad station. It wouldn't do for anyone to notice that one of them came, for example, every Monday and Thursday. But he wished he could meet the train every time. When he saw the black uniform of an SS officer, Robert grinned to himself, oh haven't we fooled you, haven't we done it.

He broke into a run then slowed again as he realized he was crossing the rue de Rivoli. He looked down the arcaded street. More Gestapo offices in there. That's what Franz had told him. Franz's family knew where the Gestapo offices were, from other Jews in Paris. Robert didn't understand the ins and outs of it, but Franz had told him that when France surrendered, she had agreed to give up to the Nazis any refugees who had fled Germany to France before the war. That included Franz's family. His father, Karl Glickman, had been manager of a furniture factory in Frankfurt, but, after the persecution of the Jews worsened in 1938, Herr Glickman had gathered up Franz, his two sisters, Hilda and Gertrude, their mother, Margret, and fled to Paris. He had not, of course, been able to get as good a job as he held before. He had, in fact, been forced to work as a turning lathe operator. But they had found a tiny apartment and made themselves a home.

Now they lived in fear that the Gestapo would find them.

Robert frowned and kicked a stone. He had to kick the stone straight down the sidewalk. If he kicked too hard and the stone skittered into the gutter, the Gestapo would catch him. He had several very near escapes, but, each time, he caught the stone on the side of his shoe, throwing it back toward the center of the sidewalk. The game lasted for three blocks before he tired of it. He found a short thick stick and ran the length of one block, banging it against the pointed tips of the black iron fence, making an exciting rat-a-tat-tat. In the next block, most of the shops were boarded up, but midway up the street, a German staff car, with two pennants fluttering from its staff, waited outside a fur store.

In the window, a white ermine coat hung from a manikin. Black velvet served as a background.

Robert approached cautiously. Usually, there would be a driver waiting in a command car, such as this one, but maybe not this time. Robert walked very softly up behind the car. He looked all around. Across the street was a café. The driver must have received permission to go for coffee. Robert looked at the fur store. Only Germans or Frenchmen who were helping the Germans could afford to buy fur now. In the shop window, a card stated, Man spricht Deutsch.

Robert's face hardened and looked, suddenly, much older than thirteen. Once again, swiftly, he glanced around but the street was empty.

He bent down, grabbed up a sharp stone, ran to the driver's side of the car and scored, deeply, harshly, an immense V. Dropping the stone, he began to run. He didn't slow until he was three blocks and an alley away from the fur shop and just a block from the railroad station. He began to whistle again. Maybe Mother would let him spend the night at the Latin Quarter apartment. Sometimes she did. He liked to talk to the English soldiers. He always asked, "Did you ever meet a French captain named Masson? Andre Masson? His unit was in the fighting near Bruges."

Eleanor gently massaged her temples, lifted her index finger to rub at the bridge of her nose. In her memory she could hear her mother's light voice. "Ellie, you mustn't frown as you work, (or read or sew or think) it will make the deepest indentation there, between your eyes, and you know you don't want to look like a cross old woman when you are still young." Eleanor smiled. For an instant her face looked so different, cheerful and amused, almost impish, and, since she had lost so much weight since summer, quite young. But the line was there, a deep crease, and growing deeper every day. Oh Mother, she thought, if that was all I had to worry about now, looking young, fighting lines. Then, with a rush of remembered affection, she was fiercely happy that her mother was safely dead and couldn't know, couldn't dream of the fears and worries that peopled Eleanor's days and nights. Eleanor's brows drew together again as she frowned at the check book.

What was she going to do? For an instant, she fought a flood of panic. She had never before in her life been afraid because of money. Because of not enough money, actually. There had been, when she was a girl, the security of being Eleanor Rossiter. Of the Pasadena Rossiters. Her great-grandfather had come west from Pittsburgh to California, one of the faceless thousands joining in the Great Gold Rush. He had found gold, as had so many. Justin Rossiter was not only lucky, he was canny. He sent for his three brothers and they established banks in the raw mining towns and the family wealth began to grow.

After her marriage to Andre, she had never thought of money either. Andre didn't earn a great deal as a professor, but the money from America always came, the income channeled to her from family investments and trust funds. There had always been money. The payments came quarterly, dependable substantial checks every four months. Then came the shocking deaths of her parents and the subsequent probate of the estate. Frank, as an executor, had arranged for her income to continue. She would be, when the probate was completed, a very wealthy woman. But that money was in America and she sat in her unheated Paris apartment, bundled up in a fur coat, hunched at her roll-top desk, frowning at the checkbook.

There had been so many expenses since the last check from America. It cost 500 francs a head for each soldier to cross the Demarkation Line, and 7,000 francs to cross the Pyrenees, about $140 a man. That didn't include the money it took to feed the men coming to the Latin Quarter apartment twice a week. They had now, she made hatch marks on her pad, been responsible for passing along fifty-four British soldiers. For an instant, the tight line between her eyes eased. Fifty-four men safe from the Germans. Or, possibly not safe, who could know how far along they were on the way to freedom, but they were started, they had a chance and some of them, perhaps all of them, would struggle through the high reaches of the Pyrenees into Spain, and, if luck touched them, they would make it to Gibraltar and sail for England.

Oh, it was worth it. It was worth the danger and the strain but none of it was going to be possible if she didn't get more money, money to buy black-market food and gasoline, money to give to Father Laurent to help pay for forged papers, train tickets, money to meet their own expenses, including the rent on two apartments. And, God yes, money to buy an adequate winter coat for Linda. She had come to Paris last winter with her spring coat, suitable for California. There had been plenty of coats in Paris stores then, but, somehow, they had never bothered to shop for one. This winter there were no new coats. No buttons. No needles. No cloth for sewing. The polydore at work, Parisians said. Everyone knew where the coats and dresses and peacetime goods had gone, along with the food. The trains, laden with scrap iron, oil, food, and plundered art works rolled eastward every day.

Money, money, money.

Eleanor pulled open the lowest shallow drawer and picked up her address book. In August, she had called almost every person in it. Most of the telephones had rung unanswered, but, every day more people returned to Paris She flicked slowly through the pages, saying names aloud, "The Arbeufs . . . Paul Bidault . . . Paul might help but I don't know how much money he has. Yves Callet. No. Rene Christen. Maybe. Armand Galois? I don't know. Oh the Leclercs . . . I will call Jacqueline. She will help if she can and they are quite rich."

The Leclercs were older than most of their friends. They lived in an elegant private house in the Roule district. Felix Leclerc owned a chateau in the Loire Valley which he permitted the public to visit twice yearly. He and Andre had met at a philatelist congress and, since they both were interested in the same kinds of stamps, early issues in Africa, they met again in Paris and gradually, over the years, became friends. Their wives had enjoyed each other and it was one of those easy relationships which can sometimes develop between couples distant in age.

Eleanor reached for the telephone then let her hand drop. It would be better, safer to drop by unannounced. If the Leclercs weren't in Paris, well, then, she would have to think of someone else.

Panic flickered again. She couldn't write another check without being overdrawn and no more money was due from America until November. If she wired Frank . . . All wires would almost surely be read by the Germans. She couldn't afford to attract their attention. If she wrote Frank, well, all letters leaving the country had to be cleared through censors. Of course, a request for money wouldn't excite anyone but Frank might wonder why, might write back and urge Eleanor to be more careful of her expenditures and inquire what she was spending so much money on in a war-repressed economy, might even list sums. A smart German, and God knew there were too many smart ones, might wonder too why an American-born French resident with only a son and a sister to support needed so much money.

Eleanor massaged her temples again. She had to stop worrying. The thing to do was to get up and go hunt for help. It didn't do to be proud, not in circumstances such as these. But she hated to think of asking anyone for money.

She struggled to open the ground-floor door. She pushed out into the wind and stopped for a moment, shaken by the onslaught of cold. It was the coldest November in years. And they had no warmth to come home to. The Germans had all the coal. The only way to have a warm apartment was for a member of the Gestapo to move in. That brought the coal trucks. But they were better off cold. That would be all they needed now—to have someone associated with the Gestapo living in their apartment house. She pulled her fur coat around her more tightly, ducked her head and plunged down the steps into the windy street.

Yvette Bizien peered down from her front window. "I wonder where she goes every day. In and out. In and out."

"Who?" her husband asked absently, not looking up from his morning newspaper.

"That Masson woman. There's something odd about those people. Always going in and out and it isn't just for shopping. They don't have packages or bags when they come home. Half the time that boy doesn't go to school but off he hurries in the mornings. What are they up to?"

"Who cares?" Rene folded the newspaper, put it neatly down on a doily-topped table. "I'd best be getting on to the shop. Will you come in this morning?"

Yvette turned away from the window, her thin pale face petulant. "It doesn't matter, does it? We don't have enough business for me to come."

She began to clear the breakfast table. "What are we going to do, Rene? We will have to close by Christmas if something doesn't happen."

He was at the closet, getting his overcoat. "I don't know. Why ask me? I didn't start the war. I can't help it there aren't any customers."

"I've heard there's money in the black market. If we could get a truck—"

"A truck? You might as well want the moon. It couldn't cost much more." He slammed out the door.

She washed the dishes, her pale face drawn in thought. They had to do something. When the apartment was straight, she walked again to the window, stared down into the empty street. All the little shops in their neighborhood had closed one by one, except theirs. No one around here had any money. The Germans had all the money. If only she and Rene had one of the expensive restaurants or a shop dealing in antiques. If only they had something they could sell to the Germans.

The front door to the apartment house slammed shut.

She craned her head, looked down. Oh, that was Mme. Masson's sister, the American girl. All huddled up because of the cold. Not dressed for it either. So why was she going out on such a bitter day? What was she carrying so carefully? Something wrapped in paper? It would be interesting to know where she was going in such a hurry.

Jonathan heard the slight click of the key in the lock and swung to face the door, his hands loose at his sides. When he saw Linda, his dark eyes lighted, he smiled and began to limp toward her. "What a nice surprise. I didn't expect you today."

She came up to him, her cheeks red with cold and something more. "I wasn't supposed to come today. But I have something for you and I had to get it here before Robert comes with the new batch of men. There wasn't enough flour and sugar to make more than one.

It's just a little something." She held out the clump of tissue paper. As he unwrapped it, she said breathlessly, "My mother made them for us when we were little—it's a sugar crisp."

He held the small pastry in his hand, a thin curl of dough baked in the shape of the letter J, sprinkled with precious sugar.

"Happy birthday, Jonathan."

He stared at the pastry. His birthday. Yes, it was. November 23, 1940. He was twenty-six years old today. When had he told Linda his birth date? During one of those long restless nights when he was mending and she sat by the bed? She had talked to him, giving him by her very presence strength and will to survive. They had talked and talked and talked, of England and America, of Chaucer and medieval romances, of sea sides and mountains and cities, of Jonathan and Linda.

And she had remembered. She looked so young, standing there in that pale blue coat, her face thin and too pale, her eyes smudged with fatigue, young and a little frightened and uncertain.

He tried to speak, stopped.

"I'll make some tea," she said, as the silence stretched. "I've saved a little bit."

He followed her to the tiny kitchen and watched as she measured the water, set it on to boil.

"A clandestine tea party," she said and laughed, but there were tears behind the laughter.

He insisted that they share the crisp. They sat close together at the little white wooden table and ate the delicacy and drank the steaming cups of tea and watched each other with eyes full of emotions they weren't free to express.

"You're walking better."

"Much. My leg's stronger every day." When his leg was strong enough . . . but they didn't talk about that either.

He was helping her wash up the little pile of dishes, standing close to her in the tiny kitchen, so close, when they both heard the rise and fall of the siren.

Linda lifted her head to listen.

He saw the flutter of a pulse in her throat and realized she was scarcely daring to breathe. He reached out, took her in his arms and she clung to him, burying his face against his shoulder.

"It isn't coming here, love. It isn't coming here. Can't you tell? It's turned away. Linda, don't be frightened, it isn't coming here."

It was a long time before she would look at him and when she did her face was streaked with tears.

His hands tightened on her shoulders. Such small shoulders. "Linda, listen to me. Apply for an ausweis. You can get one. I'm sure of it. You're an American national. Your Embassy is still here. They'll help you."

She pressed her lips together to keep them from trembling and shook her head.

"Why not?"

"I can't. It isn't fair."

"What isn't fair?"

"For me to go home when Eleanor and Robert can't." She paused, said miserably, "Why don't we be honest about it? Eleanor wouldn't leave if she could. She wants to stay here and keep on helping the soldiers escape. I think she feels like it is something for Andre."

"That doesn't have anything to do with you," he said gruffly. "You've done more than was ever your share anyway."

"You don't think it would be deserting Eleanor?"

"No. And she wouldn't see it like that, either."

She looked up into his eyes. "Jonathan . . ."

He smiled at her. "What?"

"You don't despise me?"

"Despise you?" He looked startled. "Is that what you think? My God, Linda, don't you know how much you mean to me? Don't you have any idea how much you've done for me? How much I admire you?"

"Even though I'm a coward?"

"A coward? You little fool," he said angrily, "Don't you know we're all afraid? Don't you know that you're braver than any of us? Because you know what can happen. You can imagine it in your mind and know it and yet day after day you walk across Paris with men who will only go to prison if they are captured but you will die. Despise you? Linda, don't you know how much I—"

"Jonathan?" Robert's clear young voice called softly. "Jonathan, I've five of your 'chaps' today. Come meet them."

Jonathan and Linda looked at each other, then he sighed and turned toward the living room.

The butler began to close the door. "Madame is seeing no one."

Eleanor startled him and herself as she pushed against the closing panel, slipped into the hall.

He drew himself up, his dark face reddening. "Madame is seeing no one," he hissed.

The cavernous hall was achingly cold. The marble floors looked dull and dirty. Eleanor could remember another November evening, years before, when she and Andre had come to a formal dinner. Eleanor had worn an evening dress and a light shawl over her bare shoulders. Sleet had hissed against the dining room windows but fires flickered in every grate and every room had been warm. Past the archway to her right she could see the long formal dining room. The furniture was covered, the fireplace grates empty. No lights had been turned on though it was almost dark now.

"Tell Mme. Leclerc that I am here, that Eleanor Masson needs to see her. Tell her that it is very important."

"Mme. Leclerc is seeing no one. I must ask you to leave."

Why was he so determined? And so angry about it? Yet, at the same time, he gave an impression of furtiveness.

I don't like you, Eleanor thought, I don't like the way your eyes move. I don't like your face, the pasty look of your skin or your thin weak mouth or the sound of your voice.

"I must talk to her." Eleanor was almost shouting now and the sound of her voice shocked her as it echoed in the huge hallway.

They both heard the door close above and the slow sound of steps. "Jules? Jules? What is happening?"

The man gave Eleanor such a hostile glance that she was startled. He turned walked midway up the stairs. "I am so sorry, Madame, but this person has pushed her way in, even though I told her you were resting."

Resting? That wasn't what he had said. Eleanor came up the steps, too, stood just behind him, called out. "Jacqueline, I'm sorry to disturb you, but I must speak with you."

"Eleanor? Is it you, Eleanor Masson?"

"Yes."

The old woman stood at the top of the stairs. "My dear, forgive me if I don't come down to greet you properly. Please come up and we will go to my room. Eleanor, how kind of you to come."

Eleanor was shaken by the change in Mme. Leclerc. They had to stop twice for the old woman to rest, the long way down the hall. However, the sitting room was warm. A good fire crackled in a little monkey stove. Madame Leclerc waved Eleanor to a seat beside the stove.

Eleanor held out her chilled hands. "This feels so good. How wonderful to be warm for a little while."

Madame Leclerc smiled wryly. "I never thought it would ever come down to breaking up my furniture to keep warm. But it has."

Eleanor was shocked. "You are burning your beautiful furniture?"

The old lady was calm. "Not the fine pieces. Not yet. All the servants are gone except for Jules and his wife, Margot. We've been breaking up all the wooden things in the servant's quarters. We may reach the salon eventually. I would rather be warm than have lovely furniture." Jacqueline looked incredibly old and shrunken.

Eleanor started to speak, stopped. How could she involve this old, old lady in her problems.

Mme. Leclerc smiled at her kindly. "I've thought of you and Andre so often. I tried to get in touch with you, but there was only a small memorial service. There isn't any family left now, you know. No one."

Eleanor reached out, touched those old gnarled hands that lay quietly on Mme. Leclerc's lap. "I'm sorry, Jacqueline, I didn't know."

"He died the day Petain said he was asking for peace—June 17." She looked at Eleanor steadily, but tears brimmed in her eyes. "We listened on the radio and then, without a word, he picked up his walking stick and stormed out." She looked across the crowded room at a portrait above the mantel. It was scarcely visible in the early darkness of the winter afternoon. He was in uniform in the portrait and the brim of his cap shadowed his face. A World War I uniform, Eleanor realized. He looked toward them, out of the portrait, with unseeing canvas eyes, but they could each of them see him again, a slight but dignified man with bright and lively dark eyes and a firm but gentle mouth.

"We were at the Chateau. We had gone down in late May, after the blitzkrieg started. Felix felt we should see to our people. So we were there the day Petain said it was over, that France wouldn't fight on." Tears trickled slowly down her face. "Felix didn't wait until the speech was over. He slammed out. I went after him." She stopped then, looked down at her legs with a bitter face. "But I can't walk well and he wouldn't wait for me. He walked faster and faster along the line of poplar trees. That was the last I saw of him, striding, his head down, and the poplar trees stretching out ahead of him, green and gold in the sunlight. I sent Alphonse, the head gardener, after him. He found Felix at the cemetery."

At the little village cemetery where Leclercs had been buried for three hundred years, they found Felix lying there beside the graves of his sons.

The old woman saw the surprise in Eleanor's eyes.

"Yes, we had three sons. You would not have known them. We lost all three of them in the first War. In the Great War. Rene was twenty-one when he died at Verdun. Henri was twenty-four when he was killed at Reims. Fabien was twenty-five when he died at Ypres."

The fire crackled in the monkey stove. "I didn't know. Forgive me, I didn't know."

Had she ever heard it mentioned, in the casual way that mutual acquaintances do, that the Leclercs had lost their sons in the Great War? If she had, it hadn't touched her. But now, in the dim sitting room with its crowd of furnishings, it touched her with horror. Andre, where are you? Are you anywhere? At least Robert is still a little boy. At least I still have my son.

"You are grieving too, aren't you?" Madame Leclerc asked.

Eleanor told her how they had received no word of Andre. "We still hope."

"And I pray."

"I will pray, too," the old lady said simply.

Eleanor started to gather up her coat.

"Eleanor, you haven't told me why you came."

"Oh, it's nothing really. I came for help but I didn't know Felix was gone. I'll be all right."

The old woman caught her by the hand, pulled her down again on the sofa. "I told you, Eleanor, there isn't anyone left for me to care about. I haven't a child or a cousin or a sister or a brother. I can still care for my friends."

Eleanor hesitated, leaned back. It wasn't taking advantage. Mme. Leclerc was old but she was still alert and capable. And if she would want to help, she could make such a difference.

The old woman listened intently. She clapped her hands in excitement when Eleanor told her how many soldiers had been saved so far. "Want to help? Eleanor, I would be honored, deeply honored, to be a part of this wonderful effort. What can I do?"

Eleanor rubbed her temples. She hated to ask for money. "It's money," she said miserably. "I've run out of money. It takes so much, you see, with the black market and the train tickets and the necessary sums to pay the guides." She spread her hands. "I've run out of money."

"I have plenty of money," Madame Leclerc said simply. She rose, pulling herself awkwardly up, and walked slowly toward the ormolu desk in the corner. "I'll write a check. Perhaps we should do it on a monthly basis rather than one huge sum."

Eleanor came behind her. "Jacqueline, if I might suggest, it will be safer if it were handled in cash. You don't want a check written out to me in your records. If the Gestapo discovers me you will be safe." If I can manage not to tell them what I know, Eleanor thought. Please God, I will try. I won't tell them. I won't. Somehow I will manage not to tell them.

"I see," Mme. Leclerc said slowly. "I appreciate your thinking ahead for me. Not," she added wearily, "that I find this life too much worth preserving now. But perhaps this is why I am still here." She frowned at her checkbook. "I will get a fairly large sum, to begin, 50,000 francs. You can let me know when you need more."

"Fifty thousand francs! Jacqueline, that will be marvelous. I will be very careful with the money. I'll give most of it to Father—to the man who is running the escape route. I'll just keep enough to tide us over until my next check comes, then I can give that sum to the escape route, too." Eleanor leaned down and hugged Mme. Leclerc and felt the cool softness of her cheek and caught the delicate sweet scent of violet. "Jacqueline, you are wonderful."

The old lady smiled and there was a bright spot of excitement in each cheek.

Then Eleanor frowned. "Jacqueline, you are sure now that this won't be a hardship for you. Are you still in a position to give away such sums?"

The old woman laughed grimly. "I have money, Eleanor. Most of it will go to the Church when I am gone. I have promised Jules and Margot a nice sum when I'm dead. To make sure that doesn't tempt them," she added dryly, "I've made it clear they will receive an extra 25,000 francs for each year they are in my employ. It's to their advantage for me to live a bit longer."

Eleanor looked at her with shocked eyes. "If you don't trust them, you could come and live with us."

"I trust in their self-interest."

The door to Mme. Leclerc's sitting room was open just a trace, just wide enough for their voices to be heard by Jules, who knelt in the shadows of the hall, his head resting against the creamy white wooden panel.

Fifty thousand francs!

How often would this woman come and ask the mistress for sums of that kind? Even Mme. Leclerc didn't have untold wealth. If these demands went on, month after month the money would dwindle. He strained to hear. How dare she give money such as this to a stranger. He and Margot took good care of Madame, they were earning their money. Another year or two, if they kept her alive that long why, they would be rich when she died.

But not if she gave all her money away beforehand.

The first sum would be handed over . . . He inched the door a little wider.

"I'll have half of the money by next week. I'll meet you on Monday. At the Arc de Triomphe."

Krause was almost dressed. He buckled his belt then sat on the shabby overstuffed chair to pull on his sleek black leather boots.

The bed springs creaked. She pulled up on one elbow, hugging the covers to her breasts. "Major, are you leaving already?"

"Be quiet." He was sick of the sound of French. He was sick of French faces and French places. He looked at her with distaste, at her stringy black hair and sallow face and bony body. A French woman was scarcely a woman at all. All bones, no body to her.

Though she hadn't been too bad. Mechanical. Did she think he didn't know it? And ignorant. It had been amusing to turn and twist her and see the fear in her eyes and deep flicker of hatred. But she had performed.

"Major, please," she whispered.

He stood and reached for his tunic.

"Major!" Her voice was hoarse, pleading. "I haven't told you yet where they are holding my brother. You promised if I . . . you promised to get him released."

He pulled on the jacket, began to button it, his grayish face remote, uninterested. "Write it down."

She rolled out of the bed, awkwardly dragging the chenille spread after her. She searched hurriedly for some paper, then, seeing him reach for his heavy green overcoat she tore a piece from a sack, grabbed up a stick of mascara and scrawled, "Jean Massu, The Citadel," on a piece of brown paper and thrust it toward him.

He took it and tucked it into his coat pocket, paused. "The 10,000 francs."

Wordlessly, she bent and knelt, an awkward unlovely figure, and wormed her hand between the mattress and the springs and, finally, pulled out a worn greasy envelope.

He took the envelope with a grimace and turned toward the door.

"Major, when will Jean—"

The closing door shut off her words. She stared at the dark wood for a long moment, then tears began to stream down her face and she stumbled blindly toward the bed, thin and young, hugging the worn chenille spread to her chest.

On the street, Erich Krause paused to light a cigarette. He wiped his hands against his great coat. A greasy feel to that damned envelope. He walked moodily down the street, glaring at the passersby. They all looked worn and cold and dirty. What a depressing people. The cold was vicious. Despite his warm lined coat, he was uncomfortable. A damp penetrating cold, not invigorating like the sharp cold of Bavaria. He walked faster but his humor didn't improve. No matter how fast he walked, he would still be in Paris.

It was better when he reached his office. The coal stove in the corner of the room glowed cheerfully. There was the smell of thick strong real coffee and the comfortable sound of German being spoken. He hung his coat on the tree in the corner behind his desk. Reaching into the pocket for his cigarettes, his fingers touched the greasy envelope and the scrap of paper torn from a sack.

As he settled in his chair and lit another cigarette, he looked at the scrap of paper for a long moment. He picked it up, began to crumple it into a ball.

Sgt. Schmidt sat a tray on his desk with a mug of coffee, a pitcher of cream and a bowl of sugar. He poured cream until the coffee turned the color of honey and added two heaping spoonfuls of sugar. Krause stirred it, drank a huge mouthful and smiled. The little ball of paper, half-crushed, lay on the desk. He picked it up, started to throw it into the wastebasket, stopped. After a moment, he shrugged, pulled a sheet of paper toward him and began to write: Orders for Release of Prisoner Jean Massu on the authority of Maj. Erich Krause, GSP, Amt. Iv, D-4, Paris

Humming a little under his breath, he reached for the papers in his in box. He flipped open the first folder, began to read.

Dossier: Helene Moreau, 57, schoolmistress, Les Andelys. He skimmed the single spaced typewritten report: Daughter of Jean and Marie Bizet Moreau, b. June 16, 1883 in Vandreuil... educated... married to Pierre Moreau December 5, 1903... taught... no children... intellectual, aloof... widowed August 9, 1930... reputation of the highest respectability, no history of criminal activities, no known association with undesirable people.

Krause frowned. Why had he asked for a report on this so respectable Mme. Moreau? He pulled open the deep desk drawer to his right and thumbed through the index tabs to the folder marked Les Andelys. As he read that summary of village gossip and speculation he began to nod. Oh yes, the village school-teacher who had entertained a male visitor late at night.

Krause's eyes narrowed. He looked back at the new report. Reputation of the highest respectability. No history of romantic liaisons. A fifty-seven year old widow. Not too old to be sexually active but could a middle-aged woman in a tiny village escape the notice of observant village eyes until now? Krause leaned back in his comfortable swivel chair and stared at the ornate molding that encircled the ceiling, delicate fine-edged fronds of wheat.

Why, other than sex, would a man slip from a widow's house late at night?

Krause sat up and energetically began to read every detail of the report on Les Andelys. Toward the end, he smiled, a thin satisfied smile. A man had been seen leaving the widow's home early one morning in September. Two men were glimpsed at the end of her street just before dawn two weeks later.

Two men. Men do not visit a widow, no matter how active, in pairs. A British soldier and his French guide? Her house was probably a way stop for escaping soldiers. She would take them in for a night or two while papers were prepared, travel plans made.

He would have her arrested, brought to Paris for questioning. He learned long ago there were few, very few, who could withstand arduous questioning. His hand was on the telephone receiver when he paused. Instead of calling, he picked up a cigarette, lit it, blew a narrow stream of smoke toward the ceiling. There were always those who were stubborn. It might be better to be clever.

"Sergeant."

Sgt. Schmidt got up from his smaller shabbier desk and hurried across the room. "Major."

"Didn't Kurt Heimrich pass himself off successfully as an RAF pilot in Bordeaux?"

Schmidt nodded. "Yes, sir. So far we've picked up fifteen people involved in that circuit."

"Get Heimrich for me. Immediately."

CHAPTER 12

"It's a lovely city. I know you will like it." Jonathan's voice was eager.

Linda sat close beside him on the lumpy couch. Robert had gone to pick up another batch of soldiers, but, until they came, Jonathan and Linda had the apartment to themselves. They clung to a warm circle of happiness. The cold weather, the hunger and the dreaded Germans seemed far away.

Linda smiled up at him. "Oh, Jonathan, it does sound lovely. Tell me about your office."

"I'm one of the youngest dons so it's just a little cubbyhole tucked behind the stairs in a building put up after the Great War."

"The Great War?"

"The first world war, you know, from 1914 to 1918. That was the Great War. Until now."

War. For a while, listening to Jonathan's descriptions of Oxford, the world had seemed a lovely place, with students in caps and gowns walking at a leisurely pace between ancient buildings and, on weekends, boating on the river, pausing sometimes at deep green pools to watch their shimmering reflections. "It would have been so wonderful."

"Would have been?"

She didn't answer. Tears welled in her eyes.

Gently, he took her face in his hands.

"I shouldn't speak now. I have no right. We don't know what lies ahead, but I can't wait any longer. Linda, someday, when all of this is over, will you marry me?"

Eleanor hurried, her fur coat drawn tightly around her. She was late. It seemed that she was always late these days. Everything took so much time and it was damnably hard to get around with no taxis and the Metro jammed. Especially now that the weather was so bitter. Tomorrow was Saturday. She and Robert would go to early Mass again unless there was another surprise group. Twice last week, Father Laurent had sent soldiers unexpectedly. One night there had been eleven men jammed into the little apartment. It was cold there, too. My God, it was cold everywhere. The cold made everyone hungrier as if they all were not always hungry enough. Robert was very thin. Perhaps she would be able to get some eggs this afternoon. But there were always the hungry men to feed, too, and many of them had been on much less generous rations than Robert. She couldn't save the eggs for him.

For an instant, a sob hung in her throat. Hunger and cold were wearing her down. She would have to eat something today. She had been lightheaded at the hospital this morning and had almost fainted when she was passing out the cartons of food. A nurse had led her to the corridor and brought her a cup of hot sweet tea and a croissant. Just this one more stop to make and she could go home.

She reached the corner and the wind howled down the cross street, tearing at her coat, snatching her breath away. She paused to pull her muffler up over her mouth.

If she hadn't paused, if the gust of wind hadn't buffeted her at just that instant, she would never have noticed the black car sitting in the wintry shadows of the cross street.

She was so tired and cold, in such a hurry to be done, to dash into the shop and ask if the shipment of Cuban cigars had arrived, that she would never have noticed the car if she hadn't stopped at just that spot.

The car glistened with polish. It sat in the side street, its motor running. Cars belonged to Germans and the friends of Germans. No one but a German had the gasoline to let a motor idle.

Eleanor retied her scarf with hands that suddenly shook. She looked up the street now and saw a man in an overcoat standing across the street, standing in the November cold, watching the Duquets' tobacco shop. Now he had seen her.

Eleanor bent her head and began to walk toward him, her hands jammed deep into her pockets. She walked quickly, almost running, but everyone moved quickly in this cold. She passed the shop, her face hidden by her scarf. She was just a few feet farther on when she heard harsh words in German and the scuffling of feet. At the end of the block, the long dark car passed her and she could see, a momentary unforgettable harrowing glimpse, the faces of Emile and Lucie Duquet. Then they were gone.

She wanted to run but, even after the car was out of sight, she continued to walk, head down, coat drawn tightly to her. There would be a Gestapo agent left in the shop, to gather up all those who wandered in. There would be another agent, the one across the street, to watch and see if anyone started to enter then swerved away. As soon as she turned the corner, she broke into a run. She had to warn the others. She ducked down into the Metro, packed now as the work day ended, and elbowed and wormed her way across the jammed platform, ignoring angry mutters, to get onto the first car. As the train rocketed across Paris, filled to the last inch with weary workers, smelling of sweat and wool and garlic and wine, Eleanor closed her eyes and tried to decide what to do.

She had to warn Father Laurent. The Duquets knew him. If they talked, if they were forced to talk—Eleanor opened her eyes, willing away the images that flashed before them. Everyone knew what the Gestapo did. The whispers floated around Paris, hung in the frosty air, obscene visions of terror.

They made you kneel on a bench then an agent would climb on your shoulders.

They filled a bathtub with ice water then, your hands handcuffed behind you, plunged your head beneath the water until you almost drowned, pulling you up, struggling, choking, hysterical, at the last possible instant.

They took away your clothes and attached an electric wire to your ankle and to your nipple or your penis, then turned on the current.

They filed your teeth, tore out your nails, burned you with a soldering iron.

They beat you with their fists or clubs, kicked you with their boots.

She fought a wave of nausea. If she changed lines at the next station, she could check at home first, get Robert to safety, see about Linda. But the Duquets didn't know her. They knew Father Laurent. Even if the Gestapo had broken into the escape line, they had no direct link to Eleanor yet. She had to warn the priest first. It was he who was vulnerable.

What if Father Laurent had already been arrested? What if a Gestapo agent waited in the Church, sitting behind the heavy oak door in the cellar offices?

She rode on to the Vaneau station. On the street, she turned and began to walk up the rue de Varenne. A block from the Church of the Good Shepherd she walked more slowly, looking from side to side, searching the street, checking the windows. The Gestapo often took over an apartment across the street from their quarry's address, the better to watch and see all who approached a particular door. It was a long block. When she heard a car coming up behind her, she fought the desire to run. It wouldn't do any good to run if the car were coming for her. It would be a certain giveaway if it weren't.

The car roared past, then began to slow near the Church.

Eleanor watched tensely. It was a German staff car. She could see the green of uniforms. The car stopped at the corner, the back door opened and a group of laughing German nurses clambered out. One of them bent near the front window. "*Danke*, Eric."

Eleanor continued to walk. The ache in her chest eased a little. It wasn't quite so hard to breathe.

The nurses had already disappeared up the steps by the time she reached the Church. She walked on, to the corner, and looked up and down the street. Just a few pedestrians. Mostly old women. A few men, none of them young. A boy on a bicycle.

No men in thick overcoats wearing hats.

Gestapo agents who made arrests were always dressed in plainclothes. Parisians weren't sure why. One rumor had it that the Army didn't like the Gestapo, either, and didn't want it in France any more than ordinary Frenchmen. But the Gestapo was there, scattered about the city, at the Avenue Foch headquarters, at the rue des Saussaies, at the Hotel du Louvre. Anyone taken into one of their buildings had little hope of leaving except to go to either the Cherche-Midi or Fresnes prisons.

Eleanor turned and walked back to the Church. After one last searching look up and down the street, she darted down the basement steps. The hallway was quiet and dark and cold. The Church office was closed.

Eleanor looked at her watch. Almost six o'clock. She walked on to Father Laurent's office. Instead of knocking, she opened the door, very slowly, very softly.

The cold draft of air from the hall rustled the papers on his desk. He looked up inquiringly, his hand holding his place in a book.

She shut the door behind her, leaned against it. "The Gestapo has arrested the Duquets. I came to warn you."

He closed the book, laid it gently on his desk. "When did this happen?"

She told him what she had seen. "I came directly."

"I will warn the others who were linked to the Duquets. Perhaps some of them will wish to leave Paris. I will send them to you. I'm not sure how many there will be. Perhaps as many as seven."

"We can manage." She hesitated. "And you, Father Laurent. Will you leave?"

He shook his head.

"The Duquets know you. If they are tortured, they may not be able to hold out."

"We don't know yet why they were picked up, my daughter. It is possible that they have been arrested only on suspicion. That does not mean they will be released, but, if the Gestapo does not actually have all the facts from an informer, then a brave man when tortured can confess in such a way that he does not name others. I do not believe Emile or Lucie will name me."

"Father," she could scarcely manage a hoarse whisper, "you do not know what the Gestapo does to people. No one can be expected to keep silent."

"I know what the Gestapo does. I also know the human heart and the Duquets. No matter what they tell the Gestapo it will not include my name because their only daughter is my secretary and they would rather die in agony than endanger her."

Eleanor nodded slowly. If it were to protect Robert . . .

The priest sighed. "We have been, I suppose, a little too trusting, a little too careless. I understand your fears, my daughter." He frowned. "I must devise a way to protect you and your family. If I am arrested, it will happen here at the Church, of course. Unless all of us have been betrayed, you should have nothing to fear. But, since I too, know what the Gestapo does and, to be truthful, my daughter, I do not know how courageous I am, it would be well for you to escape. If I am arrested, I will have my verger, Father Franciscus, contact you. He will call or in some way get this message to you." Father Laurent thought for a moment. "'The curtain is down.' That message will be the signal for you and your son and sister to take the escape route yourselves."

The first surreptitious knock woke Mme. Moreau. She sat bolt upright and listened. Someone was knocking on her front door. She slipped into her robe and picked up the candle holder. She didn't light the candle for she knew her way, every inch of it, down the narrow hall with its worn carpet to the twisting stairway. She stopped on the landing to listen again. Knock, knock, knock. Louder now. Soon it would wake the young soldier asleep in the attic. Would he have sense enough to stay where he was? Mme. Moreau hurried on down the stairs. She pulled back the bolt, but she didn't loosen the chain. She opened the door just an inch or two. "Who's there?" Her voice was sharp, irritated.

"Please. I need help. Will you help me?"

English!

Mme. Moreau stood very stiffly.

"I'm RAF. My plane crashed, just a few miles from here. Could you help me? Or direct me to someone who would help?"

She lit the candle then opened the door a little wider and held up the candlestick.

He was a little older than many she had helped. Nearer thirty than twenty, handsome with thick blond hair and deep blue eyes. He smiled.

"I couldn't hear what you said," she said in French. She leaned forward and put a hand behind her ear.

He answered in easy fluent excellent French. "Madame, I am a pilot. I've crashed just past the village and I am looking for help."

She hadn't heard any planes overhead tonight and she had very good ears. If a plane had crashed, just past the village, it would be closer to seek sanctuary at a farmhouse. And, if he were going to chance the village, why had he come directly to her door and why, if he spoke such excellent French, had he first spoken in English?

She repeated slowly. "A pilot?" She put the candle near him, close enough to see the Mae West and the blue of the uniform. But the Germans would have no trouble getting an RAF uniform. She pointed at his sleeve. "*Anglais*?" She repeated it several times, her voice rising excitedly, "*Anglais*? *Anglais*?" She began to shut the door, crying, "It's against the law. They will shoot me. I will have to call the police."

He continued to knock as she rang the home of the police chief, Jean Boulanger. It was Jean who found rides for the English soldiers to Gisors. When he sleepily answered, she deliberately broke into a torrent of speech. Jean had known her for more than forty years. When she had told him to come, come quickly, there was an English soldier on her doorstep and she wanted him picked up because she certainly didn't want the Boche shooting her, he said, "An English soldier?"

"Ersatz, Jean," it was a whisper, "an ersatz English soldier."

"I understand."

The knocking had stopped by now. She looked out her shuttered front window and in the vague grayness of dawn saw the soldier walking down the street. When the car came, throwing him into clear relief in its headlights, he stopped and held up his hands.

Mme. Moreau ate very little that day and scarcely slept the next night. It wasn't until Sunday morning, when Jean bowed over her hand at Church, that the ache in her heart eased.

"You were right, Helene. I called the Germans. They picked him up in just a half hour and, when he got into the back seat of the car, one of them slapped him on the back and laughed. When they drove off, he was laughing, too."

As she knelt for prayer, she was torn between relief and anger. "Thank you, God."

Damn the Germans, damn them.

Dr. Gailland gently touched his thigh, pushing, and moving the muscles and ligaments. She looked up and her tired face broke into a smile. "I pronounce you well, Lieutenant. You were my first miracle patient. Since then I have seen sulfa do many wonderful things but I still feel your cure is the most miraculous of all."

"It wasn't just the medicine, doctor," Jonathan responded. "It was your skill and the care I have had." He looked at Linda and there was no mistaking the love in his eyes.

Well, well, the doctor thought. Probably not all the credit should go to the sulfa.

Jonathan turned back to the doctor. "I can travel?"

Dr. Gailland looked thoughtful. "It is not a good time of the year to go into the mountains. But you are as strong as you will become,

Lieutenant, until you can get more exercise and better food. If possible, take another week or two and go up and down the stairs as often as possible."

Another week or two. Linda kept her face unmoved but the pain within her was so intense that her chest actually ached. Another week or two and Jonathan would be gone. Would she ever see him again? Oh God, more important than that, would he be safe? Please God, take care of Jonathan, please take him safely home. I love him so much. Please God.

At the door, Dr. Gailland shook hands with them both. "I may not see you again," she said soberly. "God be with you."

When she was gone, Linda and Jonathan looked at each other.

He was frowning.

Linda began to gather up her coat.

"Linda."

"Yes."

"I want you to apply for an ausweis."

They had been over this before. She turned away. "Eleanor needs me."

"Eleanor should apply for one also. She is still an American citizen."

"They might not let Robert leave. So she won't even think about it. It's too late."

"It's not too late for you."

She didn't answer.

He came up behind her, gently turned her to face him. "Eleanor knows time is running out. It's running out for everyone. Last week Father Laurent sent word to six people who had been helping in the escape line to leave and save themselves. How long will it be until—"

"Until what, Jonathan?" Eleanor interrupted from the door.

Jonathan turned and looked at her gravely. "Until the Gestapo catch all of you, Eleanor."

She stood by the door, her face white with fatigue. "I don't know, Jonathan. But we have to keep on as long as we can. Every man we send back is another to fight for England and France's only hope is that England will continue to resist."

"I can't quarrel with your trying to save other Englishmen. That would be a little bit much, wouldn't it? I can't say, well, save me, but don't help any other chaps. But please, Eleanor, send Linda home."

"Yes. It's time."

"Are you going to talk about me like I'm a child? Not to be asked but merely to be told? What if I don't want to go home?" To go home. Home. She could see the house suddenly, the way it had always been, a long creamy adobe house with pepper trees and eucalyptus and tall slender palms. The grass was always trimmed just perfectly and, even in November, it was a cool green carpet that smelled like spring. But it isn't that way anymore, she thought confusedly. Mother and Daddy are dead and Frank has probably sold the house by now and there isn't any home for me, anywhere.

"I don't want . . . I want . . ." She began to cry and that infuriated her. Why did she cry at everything anymore? Jonathan must think she was the biggest sop in the world. Oh Jonathan, you will leave in two weeks. Only two more weeks.

Eleanor touched her shoulder. "It's all right, Lindy, don't cry. I know you don't want to leave. But none of us can do what we want these days. Jonathan is right, it's time for you to go. Relations between Germany and America are getting more strained every day. You are so transparently American. That attracts attention. Yes, you must go. I want you to apply for an ausweis tomorrow."

Linda stood in line for three hours at the rue Galilee office to apply for an ausweis. She was applying for permission to cross the Demarkation Line and travel through Vichy France to Spain then Portugal. And sail for home.

Would Jonathan reach England? Could she go to England? She would try, when she reached Lisbon. But would Jonathan want her to come? It was cold in the barren waiting room but the offices where the German officials worked were almost stuffy with warmth.

The woman in front of Linda asked, "How many times have you been here?"

"This is my first."

"Oh well, it takes months. Where do you want to go?"

"Home. To the United States. My sister is married to a Frenchman and I was visiting her when the Blitzkrieg started."

"Ah well, they'll likely let you go. More likely than they'll let a Frenchman go to Bordeaux," she said bitterly. "This is the fourth time I've been here in two months. I first came the second week in September. I'm from Limoges and my family got word to me that my sister was dying. The Boche said to come back in a week. I did, but they still put me off. Then she died. I tried to get permission to go to the funeral. They said funerals didn't matter. Now I've had word my mother's in the hospital with a heart attack."

The line crawled slowly forward. It was very quiet in the waiting area, a sullen angry quiet.

I'm glad I'm not German, Linda thought. I would hate to be surrounded, enveloped by this unspoken but seething hatred. It didn't seem to bother the clerks who took the applications. A sergeant major in one corner heard special pleas. Linda overheard the exchange between the woman who had spoken to her and the sergeant.

"Please. Let me go this time. My brother doesn't think my mother will live."

"Is he a doctor?"

"No, but she is so ill and he says she has lost her will to live. He doesn't think she will last the week."

The sergeant riffled through a small pile of slips on his desk. Then he shook his head. "Request denied. All the special permits for this week have already been given." He looked past her, at Linda. "Next."

"Please," the woman cried, "one more couldn't make any difference. Why won't you let me go?"

"Your brother is there. She has a family member in attendance."

"I am her only daughter left. She is calling for me."

"Next," he said again, ignoring her.

Linda handed the sergeant her completed application form, her identity card and her American passport.

"American. Pasadena. I've never been to California but I visited St. Louis during the World's Fair. I have a cousin who lives there. Do you know St. Louis?"

Linda shook her head. "I've never been to St. Louis." What kind of person was he? He was smiling at Linda, eager to talk to her in English. Why had he treated the Frenchwoman so peremptorily?

He stamped her application and handed it and her papers back to her. "Take these to the third desk from the left, Fraulein, and your application will be filed."

"How long do you suppose it will take?"

He smiled. "Not long. Perhaps next week it will be ready."

She felt a wave of distress as she moved across the room. She heard the little ripple of words, oh, an American, stamped the first time, that's why. She didn't look at any of the tired faces of the people still waiting. At the third desk, she once again handed over the application and her identity papers.

A pudgy private with a perpetual worried frown took them. He looked to see if the application bore the official stamp, flipped open a ledger with narrow lines and laboriously began to write her name and age and residence, her destination. He looked up. "When do you want to leave, Fraulein?"

To leave. It sounded simple, easy. Was it really going to be this easy to leave France? "As soon as possible."

He thumbed through a card index, rubbed his nose in thought. "You understand, Fraulein, there are many ahead of you. December 13 is the first open date." He looked up and laughed and the laughter sounded strange in the sullen quiet. "It's Friday the 13th, Fraulein. Are you superstitious?"

Superstitious? Linda shivered as she stepped out into the biting cold. She pulled the inadequate blue spring coat closer against her and began to walk swiftly toward the Metro. It would be a lucky Friday the 13th if she could start home. But it was hard to believe she was going to obtain her ausweis so easily. The private had added another stamp and told her to return next week to pick it up. Today was Friday, November 8. She could pick up her permit next week and then it would only be a little more than a month and she would leave.

Jonathan would be gone by then.

One more dreary month, fighting the cold and the constant gnawing hunger. There was never enough to eat. One more month to be afraid and then she could go home.

All the way across town on the Metro, she hugged a leather strap and rode with her eyes closed and permitted herself to think of home because, for the first time n so long, it didn't seem an impossible dream. She would spend Christmas with Frank and Betty. Betty always fixed Posadas, the long row of paper sacks with candles glimmering inside, along the sidewalk leading up to the house. The Christmas tree, an Oregon fir, would sit in their living room. She would go to Mother's, or wherever things were stored, and get out the box of Christmas decorations. The same ones they had used ever since she was a little girl. Frank and Betty would love them, too. The wooden gingerbread man with black jade eyes. The delicate glass redbird that she always put on a branch next to a popcorn ball. The tiny church her grandfather had carved and painted. To sit beneath the tree, loveliest of all, the wooden crèche that her parents had brought back from a trip around the world.

Linda had always loved the crèche best of all and it was she who laid the Christ child in his manger bed on Christmas Eve. The figures were carved from a darkly golden wood and every tiny detail was perfect, Mary's smile, Joseph's awe, the portly dignity of the Three Wise Men.

She could see her Mother, reaching up in the basement closet to lift down the box. Every year, she had said the same thing. "Just think, Linda, this has come half way around the world to be part of our Christmas, all the way from a little Bavarian village to Pasadena."

Linda's eyes opened. She had never thought before that the figures came from Germany. They were so beautiful, so lovingly done. By a

German. By a German. By a German. The words rolled over and over in her mind to the rhythm of the train. By a German. She shivered.

The walk from the Metro station seemed longer than ever. It was getting dark. The Arc de Triomphe loomed behind her, dark, massive. Pedestrians hurried, heads down against the cold wind. At the beginning of their block, Linda paused and looked up. All four shades across the front of their apartment were down. Eleanor had devised a signal to prevent all of them from being arrested should the Gestapo come and find only one of them home.

At any unexpected knock, a lighter-colored shade, which Eleanor had installed in the second window, could be pulled down instead. They had experimented and the lighter shade was distinct, even at night, but not noticeable enough to attract the attention of anyone not looking for it.

The four shades were uniform in color.

Linda walked a little faster. The apartment would be cold, but not quite this cold. She could wrap up in a blanket and there would be hot soup for dinner. And in a month, just a little more than a month, she could start for home. She might be home by Christmas.

CHAPTER 13

It was icy cold in the dining room but Eleanor smiled happily at her son and sister. Robert wore his heavy plaid jacket. Linda was bundled in a wool blanket and Eleanor wore her thickest tweed suit.

"Tonight is going to be a very happy night. We are going to have one rule at the dinner table. No one will talk of the war. Not one word. We are going to have dinner and later, over coffee—"

"Coffee?" Linda exclaimed.

Eleanor nodded. "Coffee and some other marvelous surprises. The black market is richer tonight but we are going to have a fine meal." Her tone was almost defiant.

Linda wondered how Eleanor had come up with the money but she wasn't going to ask about it or worry. From the minute she had come home tonight, she had smelled the most marvelous aromas. It had been so long since they had eaten anything but watery soup without even potatoes. They hadn't had any sugar for almost a month. Linda felt a twinge of guilt. She had used up almost the last of their sugar to make Jonathan's birthday crisp.

Robert was excited. "What other surprises, Mother?"

"We received a letter from Uncle Frank today. He sent some money. Thank God he did. Though I'm going to be able to get some money next Monday to help us with our soldiers, but we needed money, too. I went out and bought wonderful food. We are going to have a lovely dinner, thanks to Uncle Frank. I have saved his letter for all of us to read together tonight."

A year ago, none of them would have thought this a fine dinner. It would have been a nice supper, but nothing remarkable. Tonight they ate almost in silence, slowly, slowly, savoring every bite, puffy sweet omelets with bits of cheese, potatoes fried very crisp and brown, and, unimaginable luxury, thick slices of ham.

After dinner, they sat closely around the potbellied stove in the living room. Robert stuffed it full of the paper balls they used for fuel. "We're almost out, Mother. I soaked all of last week's papers and mushed them into balls, but this is the last of them."

"That's all right," Eleanor said recklessly. "At least we will be warm tonight."

The balls were more show than substance. They crackled and flared into a brief bright flame, dancing inside the enamel panels of the stove. There was a tiny flash of heat, then too quickly, the fuel was gone and the penetrating cold seemed worse.

Linda and Robert shared her blanket.

Eleanor brought them each a slice of yellow cake, sprinkled with sugar, and a cup of coffee with hot milk. Draping an afghan over her feet, she sat in the cane rocker next to the stove and began to read Frank's letter.

"Dear Eleanor,

"We were delighted to receive your letter today. It took three weeks to reach us, but I guess that's not bad, considering how far it had to come. Did you realize it went by way of Alexandria and Rio? We hope you have had some word of Andre by the time you receive this."

Eleanor took a deep breath, continued.

"I've been hard at work settling the estate. The final papers should be approved soon. We have, to put it simply, split the estate three ways. I did take as my share mother and Dad's house. If Linda should want it someday, we will certainly be willing to talk about it. I would doubt, though, that a girl her age would be interested in maintaining such a huge place. She is, of course, always welcome to come live with us. It is her home."

"They didn't sell it," Linda said softly. "I was afraid they would."

Eleanor shook her head. "There was no danger of that. Frank has always loved that house."

High on a gentle hill. Green grass and eucalyptus trees. Soft brown adobe and faded red roof tiles. Her home. It would be there, waiting for her. She wished Jonathan could see it. She would send him pictures, tell him about it. About the stream that curved slowly through the rose garden to empty into a broad shining green pond and the geese who ruled it. They had been Christmas presents, tiny golden balls of fur, the year she was ten. They had grown into huge imperious geese, especially Caesar who considered humans interlopers to be tolerated only if familiar. His head outstretched and lowered, his huge wings flapping, he would immediately attack any stranger, hissing viciously. Caesar liked Linda. When she fished, he would float gracefully on the water, only a few feet away, his dark beady eyes watching her.

"We should soon receive under separate cover a copy of the final probate decree from the estate attorneys, the firm of Marshall, Levy and Jensen. Eleanor, you will remember Earl Jensen. He was in my high school graduating class. He is active in city politics. Some think he will soon run for the Assembly. His wife is Janey Morris. Remember her? A tiny redhead. Not so tiny now. Betty and I play bridge with them."

Linda hugged the blanket a little closer. It sounded like life on another planet. Estates and pleasant gossip and evenings playing bridge. One more month. One more month and she would be on her way there. The Christmas decorations would be up by then. Silver bells, bright red holly berries, strands of lights twinkling downtown.

"I decided to forward a sum of money to you. In times such as these, you might find ready cash helpful."

Eleanor paused and laughed. "Frank can't imagine how helpful. The first thing I did was pay the rent."

"We hope Linda will soon come home and, of course, Betty and I will be delighted if you and Robert can join us, too. Do think seriously about coming, Eleanor. We understand your concern for Andre but I know he would wish for his family to be safe, if at all possible.

"Our love is with you. We think of you often. Come home to us. Your loving brother, Frank."

It was very quiet for a moment. The fire began to fade. Robert opened the little door, pushed in two of the dried paper balls. The flame leaped high.

Eleanor looked at her son. He was so handsome. His face was just now beginning to take on some of the character of maturity. It would be, when he was a man, a strong face. The high bridged nose, Andre's nose, was just a little too large. His dark eyes were deep set, his skin a clear smooth olive, his dark hair thick and curly. "What do you think, Robert?"

"No. It wouldn't be right." He reached out, impulsively squeezed his aunt's hand. "You don't understand, Aunt Linda. I'm French. I can't run away. It wouldn't be right."

Linda looked at Robert then at Eleanor. "If you stay, if you keep on smuggling airmen, the Gestapo will catch you. They can't help but catch you. How does that help France?"

Eleanor closed her eyes. If the Gestapo took Robert . . . Even to a child, the Gestapo would be vicious. She looked at her son again, her face was white, sick. "Linda's right. Someday they will catch us. Robert, promise me solemnly, if I am captured or Aunt Linda, whichever of us might be free is to immediately take the escape line. Promise me, Robert."

"Oh Mother, Aunt Linda's just a scaredy cat. She always thinks everything's going to go wrong. Look how well we've done. Jonathan's gotten well and we've passed along almost sixty—"

"Promise me, Robert."

He shrugged. "I promise. But they won't catch us. Everybody along our escape route is cautious. None of them will betray us."

"I don't think so either," his mother said quickly. "But it does no harm to think ahead. We have a lot of planning to do. Robert, what are we going to send to your cousins for Christmas? Since Aunt Linda will be going home, we can send presents after all this Christmas."

Frank's sons, Peter and Bobby, were fifteen and thirteen. They had visited the Massons in Paris three years earlier and Robert and Bobby liked each other immediately. They had corresponded irregularly ever since.

Robert frowned. "There isn't anything in the shops."

"I thought it might be nice if you made something for them," his mother suggested. "You haven't used your woodworking iron for some time."

Robert leaned toward the stove, stretching his hands toward the heat, shielding his face from view. Andre had bought the woodworking outfit for him last Christmas. They had worked together, their grandest project a somewhat lopsided vision of Sacre-Coeur for Eleanor's birthday.

"Your father would like to know that you were using it."

"Do you think so?"

"I'm sure of it."

Robert stared moodily at the stove. "I was going to wait until Daddy came home."

"He will be excited to see how you've improved."

Robert jumped up. "There is a special one we talked about doing," and he hurried off toward his bedroom. In a few minutes he was back, carrying a rectangular wooden case. He put it down on the floor beside the stove and opened it. "Here it is." He held up a thin piece of wood with ink markings. "What do you think, Mother?"

Eleanor smiled. "The Eiffel tower. Could there be a nicer gift from France? Robert, it will be a lovely present."

Robert lifted up the iron and set out the tray with the different points. "I'd better get right to work on it. We don't have much time. When are you supposed to leave, Aunt Linda?"

"The thirteenth. December thirteenth." It still seemed impossible, but every time she repeated the date it took on a little more reality.

They stayed up later than usual, enjoying a rare glass of wine, watching Robert work on the picture. He held the tool carefully, delicately edging the main outline of the Tower. The acrid smell of burning wood overlay the light scent of wine and peculiar odor of the paper balls. Eleanor and Linda talked softly, cheerfully, watching Robert, remembering years ago the doll house that Frank and Eleanor had built together for Linda's fifth birthday.

"We had so much fun with that." Eleanor smiled. "Frank built the house and I decorated it. Do you remember the rumpus room? He paneled it with tiny pieces of pine and even built a little pool table."

"And you painted two little miniatures of Mother and Daddy and hung them in the dining room. It was the most marvelous fifth birthday any little girl ever had." When she got home, she would search the attic for that dollhouse. She wanted, suddenly, to see it again. Oh, it would be wonderful to be home. She hated Paris now, hated the dark gray cold streets, the tired and anxious faces of the passerby, the sleek, well-fed, well-dressed Germans. If only Robert and Eleanor could come, too. She almost brought it up again, but Eleanor was smiling and she looked young and unworried. For the moment, her eyes had lost that haunted look. She wasn't thinking of Andre or the War or what had happened to her adopted city. She was laughing and bending forward to look at her son's handiwork. Linda folded her lips. Not tonight. She wouldn't mention Eleanor and Robert leaving Paris again tonight. This evening was happier than any she could remember since Andre went away.

The last puffy ball had burned to a crisp of ashes. "You've made a good start, Robert. We'll help you put it all away for tonight."

"Must I stop now, Mother?"

"It's getting late and I have to start out very early. I have several hospitals to visit." And Mme. Leclerc to meet at the Arc de Triomphe. But she didn't say so aloud. The less anyone knew, the safer they were, all of them, Linda, Robert, Mme. Leclerc. But the meeting mattered. With the money from Frank and the help from Mme. Leclerc, there would be money enough to pump a new vigor into their escape line. The count of soldiers passed through stood at sixty-two. Sixty-two men sent toward England, back to their families.

Would someone, somewhere help Andre?

When the apartment was quiet, Linda and Robert settled in their rooms, asleep, Eleanor wandered slowly about the icy cold apartment, hugging her fur coat to her. She should sleep. But it was no pleasure to sleep alone, to wake in the night and reach out to nothingness. She walked into the kitchen. There was half the small pound cake she had made that afternoon. She reached for the cake knife then let her hand drop. It seemed another world, the life when she had been plump and a midnight snack nothing special. She would save the cake for Robert and Linda. She turned back into the living room. She was very tired. She must go to bed. The alarm would ring at six and it was past eleven now. She walked restlessly to the front windows, pulled the shade out a little to look down into the darkened street and saw the hooded lights of a car. Germans.

For an instant, her breath held in her chest. The car slid past their apartment house. But it was stopping. A truck of soldiers followed the car. Soldiers dropped off, one by one, at twenty-yard intervals.

Oh, God.

She stood, rigid with horror. This was the hour when the Gestapo struck, while people slept, battering down their doors, pulling their victims out into the night, just partially dressed, their minds fuddled with sleep, their hearts racing with fear. She craned forward, trying to see. Cautiously, slowly, so that it wouldn't squeak, she raised the window, leaned out into the night.

Not their apartment house. Thank God, it wasn't their apartment house. She could see now. The troops were surrounding the smaller apartment house at the end of their street. There was a narrow alleyway, oh perhaps three or four feet wide, that divided that building from their own. A German soldier stood at the entrance to the alley, another soldier plunged into its dark depths. Two men in plainclothes, heavy overcoats and hats, walked up the apartment house steps. At one's nod, a soldier began to pound on the door with the butt of his rifle.

When the door opened, the two plainclothesmen and four soldiers went inside. Eleanor waited until she began to shake with cold then pulled down the window but still she stood and watched. Were they searching the apartment house for someone? Or was one particular apartment their objective? Were they even now pounding on an apartment door and, within, were people waking to the violent knock, waking to terror?

Five minutes passed. Seven. Ten. The door opened again. Eleanor pushed up the window. A soldier came out first. Eleanor strained to see. Two more figures, one supporting the other. A man and a woman? Another soldier. Then a single slender figure wearing a scarf. It must be a girl. She paused on the top of the steps to look back. One soldier motioned with his bayonet. She hesitated. He poked her with the blade and she started down the steps. Two soldiers appeared with someone struggling between them, struggling and screaming. The thin screams cut through the heavy silence of the icy night. A girl or a young woman. She struggled and kicked and screamed. The soldiers paused at the top of the steps then, together, they lifted the struggling girl high into the air, swung her back and forth, back and forth, threw her out into the night. She flew up, trying desperately to turn herself so that she could land facing forward but her balance was gone. She went so high that Eleanor knew she must be small, must weigh very little. She seemed to hang in the air for a long moment, a pathetic flailing figure before she plummeted heavily down, crashing into the back of the Gestapo car, then slipping sideways to land heavily on the pavement and lay inert.

"Hilda!" The woman cried. She tried to push through the soldiers to reach that still figure.

"*Nein, nein.*" A soldier herded the woman and the others to a paddy wagon waiting just past the car. When they had been pushed up the ramp, two of the soldiers picked up the girl and tossed her in after them and slammed shut the door.

The Gestapo car left first. The paddy wagon followed. The last of the soldiers climbed aboard the open truck and it slowly rumbled away.

The street was silent now, dark and cold and silent. Not a light showed. Not a voice sounded.

Eleanor still stared downward. The back of her hand, balled into a fist, pressed against her mouth. Dear God, she was so afraid she knew what had happened. Hilda. That was what the woman had called. Hilda. But there had only been the two older people and two girls. God, please, don't let it be Franz's family. But he did have a sister named Hilda. And another sister. Please God, please don't let it be Franz's family.

Eleanor was slumped in the rocking chair, her hands clamped onto the arms, staring sightlessly into the darkened room, when she heard the knock.

It was such a small sound that she thought for a moment she had imagined it.

A dull tentative ghost of a knock. Almost like an animal scratching to be let in. Eleanor jumped up, ran across the room, undid the bolt and yanked open the door.

He was huddled on the floor in front of the door. She heard the uneven hiccups of his breathing, saw him shaking. Kneeling, she slipped her arm around his thin shoulders. He was shaking with cold and more than cold, wearing only his worn flannel pajamas.

"Franz."

His hands shook, his body shook. He tried to speak but his breaths fluttered in his throat.

Eleanor bent, scooped him up. He was so much smaller than Robert. Near in age but still a little boy in frame. Tonight he felt heavy, leaden. Eleanor pushed the door shut with her foot and carried him to the rocker. She picked up the afghan and wrapped it around him. She sat in the rocker and held Franz in her arms.

"My . . . uh . . . my . . ."

"Don't try to talk, Franz. I saw. From my window. Don't try to talk."

Finally, he did stop shaking, but every so often a shudder racked his body and Eleanor's arms tightened about him. "You're safe now, Franz. Please don't worry. We'll see that you are safe. We know a way to escape from France. Rest now, Franz, rest."

He slept finally. Eleanor held him, rocking back and forth slowly. Beneath the blanket she could feel the rise and fall of his chest, warm and alive, safe for now. She stared into the darkness. Finally her eyes closed but even in her sleep, she saw it all again, black and silver images against her mind, soldiers in silhouette swinging, back and forth, back and forth, then throwing their captive high into the air. That thin and pitiful twisting body. That anguished cry of a mother for her child. "Hilda!"

Eleanor jerked awake, hearing that cry once again.

It was Franz crying out in his sleep. "Hilda!"

She shook him awake, gently, gently. "Franz, you're dreaming. I'm here. Robert's mother."

It was dawn now, a cold gray dreary dawn. He looked up at her, his thin childish face blanched and stricken. In a mixture of German and French, he told her what had happened. "We were asleep. I didn't know what was happening. There was banging, like sledge hammers on stone. Hilda was yanking at me, shaking me. I didn't understand but she made me help her move the chest against my bedroom door and then we heard a crash, the door to the apartment breaking." His eyes were wide and dark. "Hilda screamed at me to hurry. She shoved up the window and put me on her shoulders. She held onto the side of the window and made me jump up and catch the fire escape. I could hear the crashes against my door and she screamed at me to hurry, to run, and she pulled down the window. I heard her screaming and fighting. I hid there on the fire escape. They didn't know she had opened the window and she struggled so hard they didn't even think to look for someone else. When they had pulled her out of my room, I went on up the fire escape to the roof and ran across it. I could jump down onto the roof of your building. It wasn't far."

Eleanor's arms tightened around his shoulders. She didn't speak. What could she say? When a child is hurt, you hold them, say, "It's all right. It's all right." But it wasn't all right. It would never be all right. And how could a little boy, oh God, just twelve, a year younger than Robert, how could he understand the evil that would wrest away his family in the middle of the night, crying and screaming, carrying them off to concentration camps and for only one reason. Because they were Jews.

It made the world hideous.

"Mme. Masson."

"Yes, Franz."

His mouth quivered. "Did you see what they did to Hilda?"

"Oh, Franz." She met his imploring eyes and tears welled in her own. "Oh Franz, my dear, my dear, I'm so sorry. I'm so sorry, Franz."

He buried his head against her and rackingly, harshly, began to cry.

CHAPTER 14

Linda tucked another blouse into the suitcase and a packet of sachet. A little smile tugged at her lips. Did she think the faintly sweet scent would matter to Jonathan? She knew it wouldn't. But, it was funny, the things you do when you are in love. She was still smiling as she closed the suitcase. She heard the front door of the apartment slam.

"Eleanor?"

Her sister came to the bedroom door and Linda felt a pang of concern. Eleanor was so thin, so weary. For an instant, Linda hesitated. Would it be better for Eleanor if she stayed here? Not really. None of them spent much time here now. She had been alternating between this apartment and the one in the student quarter, staying at the latter when there was a group of soldiers to prepare for escape. Eleanor spent so much time at the hospitals that she was scarcely ever home.

Eleanor began to slip off her gloves, her gaze abstracted. "I'm glad I caught you. On your way back from the apartment tonight, could you stop by a pawn shop near the metro?"

"I'm not coming back tonight," Linda said hurriedly.

Eleanor frowned. "We don't have a group tonight."

"No."

"But then it would just be . . ." Eleanor trailed off. It would be just Jonathan and Linda. Alone.

Linda lifted her chin. "I've decided to stay there now, Eleanor. For the rest of the time." She didn't have to explain. The rest of the time until Jonathan left.

Eleanor smoothed her hands on her fur coat. A year ago, it would have been unthinkable for her unmarried sister to spend the night alone in an apartment with a young man. That was a year ago. A great many unthinkable things had occurred since then. This was a long way from the day when appearances mattered. A long way from Pasadena.

Slowly Eleanor nodded, "That's a good idea. All this running back and forth, it's such a waste of time, isn't it?"

Linda smiled tremulously, picked up the suitcase and started for the door. When she reached her sister, she stopped and gave her a hard hug and left without another word.

Eleanor walked slowly to the kitchen. She was so hungry. She looked dully at the cabinets. Nothing there. She heard the front door slam behind Linda. It would be lonelier without Linda, but she wouldn't call her back for the world. Eleanor closed her eyes. Love him, she thought gently, love him.

CHAPTER 15

"**I**t's today, isn't it?"

He nodded nervously. "There isn't anything we can do about it, Margot," Jules said. "You know that."

Her heavy mottled face turned toward him and, as always, he couldn't meet her eyes. Something in her eyes that made him quiver inside. He had never crossed her. Never. It didn't pay to anger Margot. There had been the kitchen maid, oh it was years ago, a little Breton kitchen maid. Stupid, of course. But sassy for all of that. She had laughed at Margot, called her Old Fat Legs. He had never forgotten the look on Margot's face, almost the same kind of look she had right now. Implacable. The little kitchen maid had lived in the smallest room just at the top of the twisty attic stairs. When they found her dead at the foot of those stairs early one morning, her neck broken, Margot had said calmly. "She was clumsy." Her mouth had curved into a tiny satisfied smile. Now Margot stared at him.

"When are you taking her?"

"Just after lunch."

"The Arc?"

He nodded.

"Don't leave here until one-thirty."

"But Madame said one sharp."

"The motor won't start. Come down the Avenue Hoche. I will be watching."

He started to ask Margot what she intended to do, but when she looked at him once again, he nodded his head quickly and turned to leave.

She stared after him contemptuously. How had she ever married such a bungling inept weak little man? Her mouth turned down and she moved heavily about the kitchen, getting out the implements she would need to fix lunch. Madame still had a good lunch. There was money enough to pay whatever it cost on the black market, 300 francs for a chicken, 120 francs for a dozen eggs. But how long would the money last if she persisted in this madness? Madame had promised the foreign bitch 50,000 francs. Madness. To throw money away to help English soldiers who meant nothing to Madame. And she had promised them an extra 25,000 francs a year for every year they were in her employ. She and Jules were taking good care of Madame, Madame had promised. The money belonged to them.

Margot's face grew heavier, more sullen with each passing moment. If she were married to a man, he would do something. It was going to be up to her. She would manage. No one was going to rob her of what belonged to her.

After lunch, Margot normally moved heavily, slowly up the back stairs to their bedroom for an afternoon nap. Today, she didn't even wait to do the dishes. As soon as Madame was served, Margot walked to the cloak closet and pulled out her heavy dark brown coat and a thick woolen scarf. The Metro was crowded but she planted herself solidly near the exit. It was only after she had left the train, climbed laboriously up the steps to the thin gray winter sunlight that the first sense of unease stirred within her. Why were there so many people streaming toward the Arc? She stopped and looked to her left, toward the Champs-Elysees. Hundreds of young people walked quietly, groups of two and three merging into clumps of twenty, thronging into a solid dense moving phalanx walking determinedly toward the Arc.

Mounted German troops reined their horses in a circle around the Arc. More troops were arriving by truck.

How would she be able to spot the car and Madame and that woman Madame was meeting? "What's happening?" Margot asked a woman that had stopped too at the top of the steps to look at that silent awesome crowd.

"Don't you see?" The woman asked quietly. "The young people are carrying flowers. To the Tomb. It is Armistice Day."

November 11, 1940. The Great War had ended on November 11, 1918. Margot turned her heavy face toward the Arc de Triomphe which stood over France's Tomb to her Unknown Soldier.

They were coming by the hundreds now and the flowers were piling into a soft white and pink and red mound. Students wearing black ties, mourning France's Occupation, middle-aged women in shabby coats, some old men with ill-fitting ancient military caps, quietly they came, inexorably.

A German major shouted orders to the soldiers climbing down from the trucks. Students near him looked up with hostile faces.

"There's going to be trouble," Margot said sharply. The fools. They were silly fools. Their stupid little flowers didn't matter. Did they think flowers could hurt the Germans? That major had an ugly look in his eyes. Somebody was going to get hurt. How stupid it was to irritate the Germans. She began to move to her left, toward the Avenue Hoche and already the crowd was so thick that she had to struggle against the press of people moving toward the Arc. She used her bulk to push her way nearer the street. These fools were going to keep her from finding Madame.

Then, over the dull sound of shuffling feet and the soft rustle of cloth, she heard a car, a recognizable familiar throaty purr.

Thank God nobody but the rich and the Germans could drive cars. In the old days, cars would have been whizzing around the Arc, clogging the streets in mid-afternoon. Now, a single car could be heard.

Others heard the motor too and turned, looked back, their faces tight and angry. Only Germans and the friends of Germans had cars.

Margot was only ten yards away when the car eased to the curb and Jules hurried around to help Madame get out, then handed the crutches to her. "Madame, there is some kind of demonstration. I don't think you should get out now."

"Return to that end of the block." Mme. Leclerc pointed away from the Arc. "In half an hour. I will be there." She turned and began to stump toward the Metro exit, her thin aged face held high. People made way for her. No wonder she had a car. She was old, crippled. She stopped once and turned toward the Arc. She bowed her head and closed her eyes and made the sign of the cross, then resumed her slow steady progress toward the Metro.

She and Eleanor met at the top of the Metro steps

Margot, her scarf wound round her head, obscuring much of her face, moved up behind them. She strained to hear but they spoke softly, quickly. Margot saw the younger woman take a soft leather pouch, slip it into her purse.

Mme. Leclerc smiled tremulously and pointed toward the Arc. Her companion nodded somberly, quickly embraced the older woman.

Margot pushed her way closer, closer, keeping her head averted.

"Take care, Eleanor. I'll bring the rest of the money here next week."

"Thank you, Jacqueline." Eleanor hesitated, then suggested. "Let's meet down on the platform next week. Oh no, no, what am I thinking. You can't manage the steps with your canes. We will meet here again. God bless you, Jacqueline," and she turned and moved off into the crowd.

Margot was caught by surprise. The woman moved so swiftly. And Madame was turning this way. Margot didn't dare push after the woman, not until Madame was past. Oh move, you old fool, move!

The old woman stumped along, moving jerkily, tiredly, then, once again, she paused to look back toward the Arc and the dark mass of people surging slowly, quietly, determinedly toward the Tomb, flowers in their hands.

Margot veered to her left, her back to Mme. Leclerc. She forced her way through the crowd, trying to keep Eleanor's brown fur coat in sight. Soon Margot was panting. She never moved quickly in her kitchen. She had not walked this fast in years. She drew a deep breath. Fifty thousand francs. She forced herself to move faster. There she was. Not too far ahead now. If she could just keep her in sight . . . Damn the woman, she was plunging deeper and deeper into the crowd. Was she trying to go up to the Tomb, too?

"Break it up there. Move along." A German MP plowed his horse into the crowd, shouting at the people to leave. "We're closing the Avenue now. Disperse. All of you."

"Who are you to close the Champs-Elysees?" shouted a voice from behind him.

The German twisted on his horse. "Who said that?"

Another young man, off to the side, yelled, "Guess who, Fritz? Guess who?

The crowd began to shove. Margot was pushed hard from behind. She stumbled, and in a swell of panic, turned and struggled toward the sidewalk, trying to move against the flow of the crowd. By the time she broke free onto the sidewalk and turned to look frantically about, the brown fur coat was nowhere to be seen.

Jonathan held a finger to her lips. "Franz just fell asleep."

"How is he?" Linda asked.

"He's very subdued. He doesn't say much. I'm glad he finally got to sleep."

She started to take off her coat.

"Wait. Let's go up on the roof. So we can talk."

"Do you think that's safe?"

He nodded. "Robert went up every night for a week. He never met anyone going up or coming down. And God, it's great to be outside, even if it's only on a roof."

Linda felt a surge of sympathy. How long had Jonathan been cooped up in the apartment? Seven, eight, no, it was nine weeks ago that they had carried him, unconscious, into the apartment.

"All right," she said quickly, though she was still cold from the long walk from the Metro. "Let's go up."

He led the way, walking softly up the steep narrow stairs that led to a trapdoor. He pushed it up, stepped out onto the roof then turned to help Linda up the last steep step. They picked their way among the chimney pots to the far edge of the roof.

"There's a clear space here. I walk up and down, about fifty times each night. It's getting my legs back in shape."

"Oh, Jonathan." She spoke his name in a half cry.

"What's wrong, Linda?"

"Could you wait a little longer to leave? It will be so dangerous in the mountains now."

He slipped his arm around her and they began to walk up and down the roof. He didn't answer until they had made the length and back again.

"You see how well I'm walking now?"

"Oh yes," she said happily. "You are so much better. You almost don't have a limp."

"Yes. That means I've stayed too long already. It's my job to get back as soon as possible. I've been able to travel for several weeks now. But so much has been happening. The scare when the Duquets were picked up. But somehow they managed not to reveal anything about Fr. Laurent. And now Franz. I wish I could stay and help you and Eleanor. But I have to go soon, Linda."

"I know." He was right. He had to go. It was time.

They turned around and began the long walk back along the side of the building. The feeling of his arm across her shoulders was reassuring, strengthening. So much like Jonathan. They had come to depend upon him in so many ways. Ever since he had started to mend, he had taken charge of the incoming soldiers at the apartment, smoothing over the anxieties and tension that developed among frightened men cooped up together. Just meeting him there calmed many of their escapees.

When he left things would be harder.

"Have you picked up your ausweis yet?"

"I get it Wednesday."

He heard the noncommittal tone in her voice. "Linda?"

"Yes."

"You will go home. Won't you?"

She wanted to go home. She wanted so much to go home. But how could she leave Eleanor and Robert alone to run the escape route? "I don't know," she answered slowly.

"Eleanor will manage."

He reads my mind, she thought without surprise. And he was right. Eleanor would manage. Eleanor was a remarkable woman.

"Did I tell you that she's found funding to help run the line?"

"You said she had hopes. It is working out?'

They reached the end of the roof, turned again, and the icy air rushed into them. Linda shivered and his arm tightened around her.

She had thought, growing up, many times, of what it would be like to fall in love. There had always been the soft rustle of surf in those dreams and palms dark against a moonlit sky and the scent of jasmine floating on balmy air.

It was cold, so cold, but she would stay forever on the icy roof as long as Jonathan walked with her.

"An old friend is helping. Eleanor hasn't said who. They met yesterday and the woman gave her 25,000 francs. She will have another 25,000 next week."

"25,000 francs?"

"I know, isn't that wonderful? Eleanor had the most exciting time making contact with her friend. Did Robert tell you what happened today at the Arc de Triomphe?"

"No, he spent all of his time with Franz. They drew routes on a national Geographic map across the Pyrenees."

Oh God, Linda thought. Franz was so small and this was the worst winter in years and years. How could he keep up with grown men, make that tortuous secret dangerous crossing? He was too small for Robert's hiking boots. Eleanor was going to try and find some better shoes for him before his group left tomorrow night.

"What happened at the Arc?"

"Hundreds of people came. That's where France's Unknown Soldier from the Great War is buried, you know. Today is Armistice Day. Most of them were students, Eleanor said, and almost everyone carried a little bouquet. They piled the flowers on the grave until the flowers made a huge mound. It made the Germans mad, of course. Finally, they sent in troops to try and move the people away and there was some pushing and shoving and the Germans started to arrest people. Eleanor said she ducked into a side street when she saw the soldiers piling out of the trucks."

"It's a good thing she didn't get picked up carrying that much money in cash. They would have thrown her to the Gestapo for sure."

"Yes." That was all Linda said.

"Linda." He stopped and pulled her gently around to face him. "Please forgive me. Damn stupid thing to say."

She shook her head and tried to smile but couldn't. "They're going to catch her. One day, Jonathan. One day they will."

"No." He said it heartily, wishing he believed it. He almost believed it. "Eleanor is careful. She isn't a daredevil. One day she will look around and weigh up the risks and decide it's time to get out. She's doing it for Andre. But one day she will decide she owes him the safety of his son."

Linda looked up at him. "Do you think so, Jonathan? Do you really?"

"I'm sure of it. Eleanor isn't a fool." If Linda believed Eleanor and Robert would follow her out of France, she could in good conscience leave. "She'll leave, Linda," he repeated emphatically, "I know she will."

Linda shivered.

"You're too cold. Let's go in now."

"Not yet. I like it up here. With you."

"Oh, it's a fine place. Come over here and I'll show you my favorite view." He took her hand and led her between chimneys. "Watch out there. There's a skylight."

"You certainly know your way."

"I know it by heart. Here, around this chimney."

They came out into a flat bare space on the northwest corner of the building. He pointed and in the faint thin moonlight she could see the dark immensity of Notre Dame and its thin unmistakable spire.

"It's lovely," she said softly. "Even now."

"The Germans can't ruin Notre Dame."

"Just everything else."

"Not everything."

She looked up and wished she could see his face in the darkness.

"Linda."

"Yes?"

"I don't want to frighten you, but I want to show you something."

For an instant she had felt safe but the nightmare never ended. What did he want to show her, an apartment rented by the Gestapo?

"Come this way. See, you go around this chimney. Over there's the trapdoor. Do you see which way we are coming?"

"Yes." She stumbled along with him, ready now to go downstairs. At least it would be warm. But she walked with him, his arm guiding her.

"See." They stopped by the coping. "The corner building is only one floor lower than this building. I checked it out once in the daytime, too. You could jump—"

"Jump?"

"Like Franz. That's what gave me the idea. Robert told me how he did it. If the Gestapo came, you could come up here and stand just about here, see Linda, and jump. There's a clear smooth space down there, looks like the roof's been tarred at some time or other so it wouldn't be too slick, unless there was ice. If you could make it to that building, you'd have a chance to get to the street and get away."

Linda clung to his arm. She looked where he pointed, at the opposite roof. She didn't look down into the crevice between the buildings.

"It isn't too far, is it?" she asked coolly and she was proud of her voice. It sounded as though she really didn't think it much of a distance at all. She had been frightened too many times with Jonathan. This once he was not going to know that the hand tucked through his arms sweated inside its glove, that she didn't look into the alleyway between the buildings because she couldn't bear heights, that it might as well be five hundred feet as five.

He was strikingly handsome. A thick black brush mustache, a bold nose, bolder eyes. He loved champagne and pretty girls, and most of all, he loved to fly. But tonight his face was grim, his full wide mouth compressed. He reached for a cigar, then lay it back on his rickety desk. He had no appetite for a good cigar now. No appetite at all.

In the mess tonight, his men had raised their glasses and laughed heartily, but their eyes were strained. It wasn't good form to notice the men who were gone, but tonight had been the worst night yet.

Seven pilots lost. Seven. And they had already filled places emptied in October and September and August. How many men were they going to lose?

Adolph Galland slammed his hand against his desk. Goering's directive was insane. Tying the ME109s as escorts to the slower bombers was like putting brakes on a sled. Often the bombers were late to the rendezvous, making the fighters use up too much of their fuel so that by the time they were over England, their reserves were down to nothing and they had ten minutes to fight then had to start back across the Channel or be forced to ditch midway because they had run out of fuel.

How many of the men lost tonight had run out of fuel? Maybe most of them. He looked down the list of names. All of their families would be notified but he felt as their commanding officer a duty to write to their nearest relative. He would wait a day or two to be sure none of them had been picked up by a seaplane. But there were two letters he must go ahead and write. He had seen both planes go down and the pilots had no parachutes. One pilot would have had no hope in any event, the plane breaking up.

That newest young man, God, what was his name? Fritz. Lieutenant Fritz Weber. A nice boy. Though he'd scarcely had a chance to get to know him. Fritz had been so polite, so careful of protocol. He had lost some of his reserve though that one night, talking about his visit to Paris. He had an uncle there, a major.

Galland pushed back his chair and went to the baggage piled in the corner of the office. Yes, this was Weber's. He riffled through the gathered-up odds and ends until he found a pile of letters. He received letters from his mother, Frau Marta Weber, and from his uncle, Maj. Erich Krause.

Galland sighed. He'd better write both of them.

Krause picked up the letter with a since of anticipation. A letter from Maj. Galland, Fritz's commanding officer. Had Fritz been commended for gallantry? For an instant, Krause pictured his nephew, standing rigid in his uniform, his head high while Goering slipped over his head the sky blue ribbon with its dangling Iron Cross. It wouldn't be anything that spectacular, of course. Not yet. But Fritz had written him the week before and, modestly, quietly mentioned that he already had three planes to his credit. Fritz had a great future.

The words leapt up at him, brutally, flattening his face in shock.

". . . Fritz fought gallantly. He had dived on a Spitfire, but the Spitfire timed it well. It waited until the last instant then made a tight turn. Fritz tried to follow but the ME109 couldn't take the stress. The Spitfire came around and its shells caught Fritz's plane amidships. The plane exploded. It is an unhappy duty to be the bearer of such news but I do assure you, Maj. Krause, that your nephew gave his life in the . . ."

Krause blindly put the letter down on his desk.

Exploded.

Fritz seared by flame, his flesh burning, his body turning black, shrinking.

Krause pushed back from his desk, walked unsteadily across the room. He grabbed up his overcoat and turned toward the stairs. Fritz, Fritz . . .

CHAPTER 16

"Franz, I've found a perfect pair of boots."

Franz was standing by the window of the Latin Quarter apartment, looking down into the bleak wintry street. He turned slowly to face Eleanor.

She was smiling, pulling off her fur coat and wool scarf, fumbling to open a package wrapped in newspapers. What luck, she thought. Father Laurent seemed to be able to manage everything. "Look, Franz, they are thick leather. With some wool socks, you will be very well outfitted."

The slight dark boy walked reluctantly across the room. He didn't reach for the boot that she held out.

Slowly, her hand dropped. "Franz, what's wrong?"

He spoke very formally, his voice stiff. "I thank you, Mme. Masson, but I do not need the boots. You must give them to someone else."

"Franz, of course, you need them. The snow is very deep in the mountains now."

"Mme. Masson, please, I won't be going to the mountains." He gazed at her with desperate stricken eyes. She laid the boots to one side and looked at Robert, who had come to stand beside his friend.

"Franz can't leave Paris, Mother. Not when he doesn't know what's happened to his family. He can't do that."

Eleanor looked at the two boys, one beginning to grow so tall, beginning to look like a young man, the other still as slightly built as a child. But they were both just boys. How do you tell boys of evil? Of hopelessness? "Franz, Robert, we must talk."

"Ma'am?" A white-faced English captain jumped up from the couch. "Ma'am, you aren't intending to send a child with us? It's madness. A child can't keep up."

Eleanor lifted her head. "Captain, you are here by our grace. It isn't for you to choose who travels with you. We help anyone who needs help to escape the Nazis. That includes children, Captain."

"But you can tell he's a Jew just by looking at him."

"Captain." Her voice was steely.

"I'm not going," Franz cried. "You don't need to worry, I'm not going."

Jonathan was beside the captain now, pulling his arm to turn him away from Eleanor and the children. "Captain, you are a guest."

Eleanor bent near Franz, pulled him close. "Come, my dear, you and Robert and I will go in the kitchen. I have a little bit of cocoa. Come, now."

Franz's small hand was icy in hers, icy and trembling. He came unwillingly, his back stiff, his face white and fearful.

She brewed the chocolate and talked the while of the weather, so cold, and the hospital she had visited that morning, so many shell shock patients still, and of the busy day ahead, of course it was always a busy day when it was time for one of the groups of soldiers to depart. She poured the cocoa and watched as the boys started to drink.

Franz took a sip, put the mug down.

Oh my dear, she thought, don't look so at bay, please.

"I can't go." His voice was a whisper. "My mother, my father . . ." Tears welled in his eyes. "Hilda and Gertrude." He looked at her imploringly. "What have they done with them? Where did they take them?"

They. The enemy. The Germans. What have they done with them?

Eleanor looked down at the table. "I don't know, Franz." She frowned thoughtfully. "I will ask Father Laurent to see if he can find out anything. He has friends in the Prefecture and sometimes they know what has happened to people. Or can find out."

Franz's eyes lit up.

She wanted to cry, oh my dear, don't hope, there isn't any hope, not anymore, but she just watched him silently.

"Oh, Mme. Masson, would you please. Maybe it is a matter of the proper papers. Maybe they will let them go. I mean, this is France. Maybe. . . ."

"Maybe, Franz."

She left the boys in the kitchen and they were cheerful now, pulling out the checker board to play. She joined Jonathan in the living room. All of the men, there were four Englishmen this time, looked up, then quickly away.

Eleanor ignored them. "Jonathan, I'm going to let him stay for now. We will send out the usual group next Tuesday, the 19th. Perhaps then."

Jonathan nodded grimly. "I'll stay until the next group leaves. Four days can't make any difference to me and I can look out for Franz if we travel together."

Eleanor smiled at him. "We will all be glad to have you stay longer, Jonathan. You know that."

Jonathan nodded and abruptly turned away. It was hard to be honest even with oneself. He had been quick to offer to stay and, by God, he would look out for Franz, but in his heart he knew why he delayed. Linda, where are you? When will you come? You think I'm leaving today. Linda, where are you?

She was breathless as she hurried through the door, still remembering to shut it softly behind her, never forgetting for an instant to be careful. She looked quickly around the dim room until she found Jonathan. "I hurried. I was afraid I would miss you."

Jonathan knew he wouldn't have left without seeing Linda one more time.

Eleanor looked from one to the other. "I'll be in the kitchen. I'm going to pack some sandwiches."

The apartment was cold but stuffy. Every window was taped shut and newspapers were crammed along the sills to keep out drafts. Stuffy and full of people.

"I brought—" Linda began.

"Let's go up on the roof," he said quickly. "We've time."

The white-faced captain looked after them as they went toward the door. "How is it that he gets to go up on the roof and the rest of us have to stay shut up in this damned little room?"

Robert and Franz were resetting up their game on the living room floor. Robert looked up and said coolly, "Maybe it's because he was wounded and has been here since September. Maybe it's because he knows how to handle himself and some others don't." Robert looked down at the board, ignoring the captain's scowl.

It was already dusk on the roof, the early dusk of winter.

"Over here, Linda, behind this chimney. It's not so cold."

"I was afraid I had missed you," she said and her voice was uneven, breathless. "I hurried so fast, Jonathan." She held out a thin flat packet of newspapers to him. "Open it," she urged.

The gloves were oddly shaped but thick and covered with fur inside and out, a kind of grayish white fur.

"Where did you find them?"

"A little shop on the Boul' Mich'. I'm afraid it's some kind of odd fur or fake fur, but they will keep you warm."

"Anything will do." He laughed and she joined him and they stood, laughing, touching the gloves, touching each other's hands, and then they were quiet, their faces so close together.

"Oh, Jonathan."

He bent his head and his lips found hers and they drew together and for that moment there was nothing else in the world but the two of them, not time or danger or despair or grief, only Linda and Jonathan.

"I want you so much."

"Jonathan, Jonathan . . ."

"Linda, listen, my dear, my love, listen, we've time yet, a little time."

"Minutes. Oh God, Jonathan."

"I'm not leaving today."

"Not leaving today?" She stopped and pulled back a fraction to look up into his face, the face that she knew so well.

"I'm going to stay over until Tuesday. Because of Franz. He refuses to go today. He wants Eleanor to try and find out where his parents are."

"Tuesday." Today was Friday. That gave them Saturday and Sunday and Monday and most of Tuesday. Until five o'clock Tuesday when the group would begin its long walk across Paris to the train depot. Long time. Short time. Some time. Time. Oh Jonathan, my dear, my love. Kiss me, Jonathan, again and again.

"Redouble the checkpoints at all incoming train stations from the North and East."

"Yes, sir."

"Increase street patrols. Pick up any suspicious looking men in their twenties. Set up spot paper checks on all the main streets. Tell them to be on the look out for men who are walking and who aren't warmly dressed."

"Yes, sir."

Krause lifted up the thin black cigar. He rolled it between his fingers, lifted it to his nose, breathed deeply. The box of cigars had arrived yesterday with a note in it from Fritz. Krause didn't need to look again at the note. The words would always be in his heart: Dear Uncle, it read, please accept these cigars as a small gesture of appreciation on my part for the truly enjoyable tour of Paris. I am looking forward to returning, perhaps in December, and visiting you again. I'm finding the flying a great challenge and I feel very honored to be a part of Maj. Galland's wing. Just time for this short note. I'll write a longer letter next week when I have a day off. Best regards, your loving nephew, Fritz.

Krause lit the cigar, drew in the fragrant smoke. Fritz would never smoke a cigar again. Fritz would never come back to Paris. Krause slammed his hand down on his desk.

Sgt. Schmidt jumped.

"I want more done. More," Krause said loudly. "I want every damned sneaking craven English soldier caught and the people who are helping them. Check daily with the Prefecture to see if they have received any information on Englishmen or those hiding them." Krause paused, frowned, blew a thin blue stream of smoke at the ceiling. "Sometimes I think our French colleagues do not pass on to us all the information we would like." Krause smoked in silence. "We can remedy that. Post one of our men who speaks French well at the switchboard in the Prefecture. Then we will be sure we receive the names of those who are hampering us. After all, not all Frenchmen love the British."

The four narrow flights up to the Latin Quarter apartment had never seemed so steep, so difficult. Eleanor climbed a little more slowly with every step. How could she tell Franz?

No matter how slowly you climb, you must eventually reach the top. She paused at the door. At least there would not be any strangers at the apartment. Robert would at this moment be walking toward the train station to pick up this day's new arrivals.

Jonathan was there, of course, and Linda. Linda had stayed at the apartment over the weekend and would stay tonight, Jonathan's last night.

Poor Linda. But at least Jonathan is this moment alive and here. While Andre . . . but she and Andre had so many years, so many wonderful years. They fell in love so quietly, taking long walks in the Tuileries, laughing at Punch and Judy shows, eating roasted chestnuts in the winter, looking at their shimmering reflections in the Luxembourg pond. Slowly, sweetly, completely, and all the years of love, tender and passionate, exquisitely sensual, unchanging but never the same. Oh Andre, we had such fun.

She still stood by the door. She had to go inside. She had to tell Franz. She had to do that and then so much else this raw gray wintry day. It was such a cold day. A bad day for the old to be out. Should she call Mme. Leclerc, say she would come by to pick up the money? But it was better to keep to their meeting at the Arc, safer for Madame. The money was a huge help. They could keep the apartment going and their twice weekly groups of Englishmen at least until spring with that much money. Thank God for Madame.

Footsteps sounded on the stairs below her. Eleanor opened the door and entered the apartment.

"Eleanor?" Linda poked her head out of the kitchen. "Jonathan and I are making some bread for them to take tomorrow."

"Good." Eleanor looked around. "Where is Franz?"

He poked his head up over the couch, then flung himself up and around it to race toward Eleanor. "Madame, Madame, have you found out anything?"

"I found out." She stopped, swallowed. "I talked to Father Laurent and he asked his friends in the Prefecture. They knew. It seems there was a huge roundup all across Paris . . . of families. Most of them had fled Germany in '38 or '39."

Franz nodded, his head jerking up and down, his dark eyes never leaving Eleanor's face. "Where did they take them?"

She forced out the words. "The trucks went directly to the Gare de L'Est. The trains left the next morning for Germany." Hundreds of people of all sorts, old women, babies, children, mothers and fathers, crammed fifty or sixty to a car. Open cattle cars. In the coldest November in modern memory.

"Left for Germany?" Franz repeated numbly.

"Franz, I'm sorry. But you had to know."

"Left? Mutter . . ." His thin narrow face quivered. "Where did they go?"

"Father Laurent said his informant thought the trains were scheduled to a camp named Buchenwald but he wasn't sure." She watched Franz's face but it didn't change when she said Buchenwald. He didn't know then what they said of it, what Father Laurent had told her of it. Oh Franz.

"Mutter will be worried about me."

"Franz, I'm sure she must guess that you escaped and that will give her something to hold on to. She must be so happy that you are not with them."

Eleanor began to open her purse. "I want to show you something, Franz, something very important. Father Laurent has a friend who can make the most beautiful official papers and I've had him draw up papers showing that you are mine and Andre's adopted son."

She slipped her arm around him, drew him toward the couch. "Let's sit down here. I want to show you. Now, these papers are very important to you, the papers and the letter I've written to my brother, which will make it possible for you to go to America."

"America? But that's so far."

Eleanor nodded soberly. "I know, Franz. But you will be safe there. Someday, when the war is over, we will find your family."

Bewildered, he looked down at the stamped notarized adoption papers and the letter, folded very small. "You must leave with the group tomorrow night, Franz, when Jonathan goes. He will take care of you and make sure that you reach the right American officials in Spain."

He listened intently as she explained it all to him. When she left, he was reading her brother's name, "Mr. Frank Lassiter of Pasadena, California, Mr. Frank Lassiter of Pasadena, California."

She didn't go in the kitchen to talk to Linda and Jonathan. This was their last day. Let them have every possible instant together. She only poked her head in the door. "I'm on my way now."

Linda turned toward her. She looked very young and happy, her face flushed with exertion, a smudge of flour along one cheek, her eyes smiling. "We have some ersatz coffee."

"I don't have time. I have to meet the lady who has the money and I've just time to get there. I won't see you until tomorrow. You and Robert will be staying here tonight, won't you?"

Some of the light left Linda's eyes. "Yes. Oh yes."

"It will be Franz's last night, too, Linda. Try to console him. His family is already on its way to Germany so I'm sending him home to Frank. Tell Franz you will be starting home, too, next month."

Tell it to a little boy who must cross the Pyrenees by stealth in

November. Tell it as if it were so certain you will be seeing him again, Eleanor thought, as she started down the stairs. But it was better for Franz to make the dangerous journey than to stay in France. There was no hope for Franz here. If he could reach Spain, and Jonathan would see that he reached Spain if he humanly could, then Franz might have a chance to make the long difficult journey to America.

More chance than his family had.

The cold was bitter when she reached the street. Eleanor bent against the wind, stayed close to the walls of the buildings, as she walked to the Metro. As the train rattled across Paris, jammed as usual, hot with the body heat of travelers, she thought about the Glickmans. They had been arrested a week ago on Monday night. The train, cattle cars, had left Tuesday morning. Tomorrow it would be a week. Surely they had reached the camp by now. If the train hadn't been shunted to a side rail while troop or goods trains passed. Were there other families like the Glickmans still in Paris whom they might be able to help? She would have to ask Father Laurent. With the money Mme. Leclerc was giving, they could handle more travelers.

The people streaming up to street level at the Etoile stop didn't seem as numerous as usual. Eleanor remembered why as she neared the top of the Metro steps. She could hear the loud clear overweening blare of the brass and the dull heavy beat of the drums. She didn't look at the goose-stepping band. Like all French, she had learned to ignore what she would not see. Halfway up the steps, Eleanor hesitated. Had they been foolish to pick this hour when the Champs-Elysees was almost deserted? But then she saw Mme. Leclerc at the top of the steps. Eleanor hurried up to her.

No one was paying any attention to them. Mme. Leclerc stood as if about to descend the steps. They didn't speak, but brushed close together and the small square packet slipped from the elderly woman's hands to Eleanor's. For an instant, Mme. Leclerc's hand patted Eleanor, then she turned away, walking slowly toward the waiting car. Eleanor stood for a moment at the top of the steps, shrugged, as if she had changed her mind and turned to walk back down into the Metro.

A heavyset woman with a mottled face followed her. Margot moved quickly for her bulk, keeping only a few feet behind Eleanor, pushing into the same car when the right train came. They got off at the next stop, Eleanor first, Margot following.

She's not noticed me, Margot thought. She's too busy thinking about the money. If I hadn't lost her last week, she wouldn't have the money. Twenty-five thousand francs. Money that should belong to Jules and me. I won't lose her now. This is the last time she will get money from Madame.

Eleanor huddled in the dark living room in the plum-colored overstuffed chair that had always been Andre's. It was too large for her but it gave plenty of room for her fur coat and two blankets and an afghan. She was warm for the first time in days. She should go to bed. It was almost eleven. But there never seemed any reason to go to bed any more. No one there to talk to, to share her day. No one to hold her. She didn't sleep well alone.

Andre, Andre . . .

She opened her mind, calling out to him, willing him to answer. There was nothing, nothing, nothing at all, just the silence of the empty apartment and the still night, Parisians barred from their own streets, nothing to give her hope that Andre lived.

If he lived, she would know. She would feel his thoughts, feel his care across miles and time. There was nothing, nothing, nothing.

Eleanor pushed back the covers, got up from the chair and crossed to the malachite-topped table next to the fire place. She grabbed up the crumpled packet of cigarettes, wrenched one free, put it to her lips. The cigarette lighter flickered on and shadows rippled around the walls. She drew deeply on the cigarette. She was smoking too much. Her throat burned raw and a deep-seated achy cough had begun. But cigarettes helped fight the constant dull pang of hunger, made it easier to take small portions for herself and give more to Robert.

If only Robert could be safe... That was what every mother wanted, of course. Franz's mother, the mothers of all the young men she was helping escape from France. Most of the fliers weren't more than a half dozen years older than Robert. They were still boys to their mothers. So that at least was good in her life now. No matter what else she lacked, had lost. If Andre never came back, she had Robert. But she wouldn't think about that now. It was at night that it was hardest to will away depression, hardest to keep a semblance of hope, hardest not to despair.

Eleanor whirled away from the table, paced toward the windows. She must get to bed. It was foolish to waste energy. She didn't have enough food to waste energy like this. She must sleep.

She stopped by the middle front window and pulled the shade back just far enough to peer into the street. A week ago tonight the Gestapo car had slipped, its lights hooded, down the street, stopping in front of Franz's apartment house.

The car came slowly around the corner, eased to a stop directly beneath her window. Eleanor's hand tightened on the wooden frame. The driver jumped out to open the back door on the sidewalk side. Two men in civilian clothes, with trilby hats and heavy overcoats, got out and turned toward the steps. One of the men, the second one, carried a bulky automatic weapon. Robert would know its name. He had talked about them before. Schmeisser, that was it, a Schmeisser pistol. Then the men were hidden by the overhang and there was just the dark car with its uniformed driver standing by.

It was so quiet, so unemphatic, that she stood a moment longer, staring numbly down into the street.

They are coming for you Eleanor.

Still she stood, unable to move, unable to breathe, her mind racing frantically. At least, thank God, Robert and Linda aren't here. Oh God, had they already raided the Latin Quarter Apartment? Did they have Robert? Oh Robert, Robert my son! But they might not. Perhaps it was something else, not a leak in the line. If somehow they'd found her another way, there might still be hope for the apartment. But they would leave a Gestapo agent here after they arrested her.

She could hear them on the stairs now, coming up to their floor.

The shade, Eleanor, you fool, the shade. Hurry, hurry now, before they were here. The second window, that was the one. She moved to her right, reached up and pulled down the lighter shade she had installed over the darker one. She pulled it down. Now, if Linda and Robert came home tomorrow, and if they looked up, please God, make them look up, they would see the second shade, so much lighter, clear, distinct, blazoning a warning, please God, make them look up.

They were pounding on the door now, a heavy reverberating knocking. She lunged away from the windows. She mustn't draw attention to the windows. Was there anything incriminating? Nothing written down, of course, nothing. That had been the rule from the very first.

The money. Twenty-five thousand francs.

Eleanor stood in the middle of the floor. The knocks were thunderous, obscene in the still of the sleeping apartment house. Her neighbors would all be awake now, huddling fearfully in their cold apartments, wondering if their door would be battered next.

Eleanor scooped up her purse, pulled out the packet of bills and ran toward the kitchen. She hadn't examined it earlier. Surely to God, Mme. Leclerc hadn't left any identifying mark inside. Eleanor turned on the kitchen light, tore open the packet. Money, just money. Frantically, she opened the mesh bag full of potatoes. She drew the cord tight again and plumped the bag back in the pantry. Turning off the kitchen light, she hurried toward the door.

"I'm coming, I'm coming," she called out. "Wait. What is the matter? What is it?"

She undid the chain and opened the door to peer sleepily into the hall. "What's wrong? Who are you? What do you want?"

"One side." They brushed past her. As the second man came in, he shut the door behind him. Eleanor had time to see Mme. Bizien, her pale yellow hair in tight sausage curlers, peering avidly up the stairs.

Bitch.

She drew herself up, stood as tall as she could. "I demand to know by what right you are invading my home?"

The first man turned on the living room light, reached into his coat pocket to pull out a badge. "German Secret Police." His eyes darted around the living room. He reminded Eleanor unpleasantly of a ferret with a sharp-featured face and slick brown hair that lay close to his skull. Heavy lidded eyes gave him a malevolent sleepy look. "Where are the others, Mme. Masson?"

It shouldn't have shocked her, hearing her name in his thick German accent. But it was one more unmistakable signal that this was no accident, that it was she they wanted. "Others?"

"The others who live here. Your son." He looked down at a sheet of paper in his hand. "Your sister."

"They've gone to Rouen. On a visit."

"When did they go?"

"They left yesterday."

He pulled a pen out of his pocket and a small notebook and slipped it open and began to write.

Rouen, Eleanor thought frantically, where can I say they are? What's the name of that hotel where Andre and I stayed that weekend? Le Royal, that was it.

"Give me their names, Madame, and the address where they are staying."

"What business is it of yours?"

He looked up at her, the thick lids dropping over his black eyes. Inwardly she flinched. His eyes were sickening, she thought, sickening and evil.

"Their names and the address, Madame."

"Robert Masson. Linda Rossiter. Le Royal Hotel."

"What was the purpose of their trip, Madame?"

"To visit military hospitals on behalf of the Foyer du Soldat."

It was so quiet she heard the scratch of his pencil as he wrote. When he finished, he slapped the little notebook shut and returned it to his pocket. "We will give you time to dress." He turned to his subordinate. "You may begin the search."

"Search?"

He looked at her again and the same sickening sensation swept her. "You have very little time, Madame. If you waste it talking, you will have to come along dressed as you are."

"Where are you taking me?"

"To our office, Madame. For questioning."

"Questioning about what? I haven't done—"

He looked at his watch. "You have three minutes, Madame."

Eleanor averted her eyes and hurried toward the bedroom. She dropped her fur coat on the floor and shut the door behind her. For an instant, she hesitated, then slipped off her flannel gown and pulled on the skirt and the sweater she had worn that day. The window? No, it gave onto a narrow ledge, too narrow.

A heavy knock on the bedroom door.

"I'm almost ready," she called irritably. She was pulling on woolen socks now and heavy walking shoes.

The door opened.

So there had been no time to try an escape. And that would be a confession, wouldn't it? If she had tried to escape, they would be certain that she had some guilty knowledge. It would make her that much more vulnerable. Now, she could continue to proclaim her innocence. She picked up her fur coat and slipped into it.

As they walked through the living room, she risked one quick glance around. Yes, the shades were just as she had left them. All four were pulled down and one was a distinctly lighter shade. It would be meaningless to anyone else.

She didn't look back at the apartment as the car pulled away. The second Gestapo man stayed behind. When they left, he was sitting at the roll-top desk, methodically emptying every drawer, looking at its contents. He would have no reason to raise the shades.

Please God, don't let him raise the shades.

They rode in silence. When the car began to slow, Eleanor looked ahead curiously. She saw sentries standing beside a gate and beyond the gate, a graceful, dignified building, another elegant private residence converted to an office by the Germans.

The first floor was almost dark, only an occasional dim wall sconce breaking the gloom. Wooden doors were closed on either side. Her escort took her elbow and pushed her toward the stairs.

"Where are we going?"

He ignored her.

When they reached the third floor, he guided her down a narrow corridor to the third door on the right. He took a ring of keys from his pocket, opened the door and stepped back for her to enter. "You will wait here."

"Wait for what? Why am I being held? I demand—"

The door slammed shut.

Slowly she turned and looked around. A single bright bulb, covered with a guard, dangled from the ceiling. Its glare illuminated every corner. The room wasn't large, perhaps ten by fourteen feet. There was one window, boarded over. A straight chair sat against one wall. A huge Paris telephone directory, its cover splayed and ripped, lay in the middle of the floor.

Her eyes moved, stopped.

It was such a homely sight to be so frightful. A white porcelain claw-footed bathtub. That was all. Slowly, unwillingly, Eleanor walked across the room toward it until she saw the streaks of blood that had dried along the bottom.

Quickly, she turned and walked away. That was probably why she had been put in this room, to frighten her. Her heart thudded and her breath came in gasps. She made herself breathe deeply, quietly.

How long would it be before someone came?

She walked up and down, near the door. Finally, achingly tired, she went to the straight chair and sat down. A half hour passed. An hour. An occasional noise sounded in the hallway. Each time her head would snap up and she would wait.

No one came.

It was almost three in the morning and she had dozed into a half sleep, awkwardly bunched into the chair, when she heard movement in the hall, footsteps, voices.

She sat up, brushed her hair with her hands and looked toward the door.

The door opened to the room next to her. The door slammed. There was a long moment of indeterminate noises, a scrape and a shuffle, a dull thumping noise.

The scream started high and rose higher, thin, shrill, piercing.

Eleanor bolted to her feet and stared at the blank wall.

The scream broke off. "Non, non, non, non, non . . ." Over and over again, the noises, the scrape and the shuffle and a dull thump and another scream, sobbing, racking, laced with agony.

As she heard the high piteous screams of agony, Eleanor sank to her knees on the cold linoleum floor and buried her face against her legs and wrapped her arms around her head and rocked back and forth. Oh God, she couldn't bear to hear it, not any longer. Please, God, make them stop it, make them stop!

CHAPTER 17

Linda hurried, her face red with exertion as she struggled for breath against icy wind. It got colder every day. Never had the three blocks from the Metro to the Masson apartment seemed so long. She would put on another sweater before she started back. She came around the corner. Only a half block more. Eleanor would be surprised to see her. But Franz had to have a pair of gloves. How had they overlooked them? It was hard to remember everything and there had been so much to do, getting the right kind of papers for Franz. That posed a problem but Father Laurent, as always, had a friend.

The wind wasn't quite so bad after she made the turn so she walked a little faster. The sooner she picked up the gloves, the sooner she could get it back to the Latin Quarter apartment. Jonathan had still been asleep when she left. She had paused and looked down at him. He slept on his back, his arms flung wide. She wanted, so terribly, to touch him, just to touch him. But Robert had been behind her, ready to leave for school, so she only looked. She hoped he was still asleep, perhaps in a dream of a canoe gliding over still green water. He needed sleep, he and the soldiers and Franz. They needed all the rest they could get today. She looked down at her watch. Seven-thirty. In less than ten hours, they would leave.

Tomorrow, Jonathan wouldn't be there. But it wouldn't be too long before she could leave. December 13. Less than a month now. She was going to try to go to England. She and Jonathan had planned it. She hadn't told Eleanor yet. But she must guess. Perhaps she would tell Eleanor this morning. No, it would take longer and she wanted to hurry.

Linda looked up. No light in the front room, at least the shades had no glow this dark and gray . . .

Linda stumbled, almost stopped.

Lighter. The second shade was lighter. The second shade!

The sidewalk stretched away empty. A man slammed a door a few feet from her and walked briskly out into the cold. Nothing else moved the length of the street, the iron spike fence dark and gray, the uneven pavement dark and gray.

Linda started up uncertainly. The second shade was light, the signal they had planned. Only Eleanor had been home. Eleanor wouldn't have pulled the lighter shade down by mistake. But anyone can make a mistake. Linda fearfully looked up and down both sides of the street as she continued to walk forward.

A man stood up at the top of the stairs of the building across the street, shielding himself from the wind and the cold in the entryway to the building.

The man stood, made no move to go down the steps.

Linda walked on. Her legs felt leaden and old. Her heart thudded with a sickening unevenness. I'm going to faint, Linda thought, with horror, I'm going to fall down and then they'll know. Somehow she kept on walking, not looking at the Masson apartment house as she passed, not looking again across the street. Shrinking within her coat, her shoulders drawn tight, her head ducked forward, she waited to hear a shouted command to stop. The street seemed so long now. How far to the end of the block, then she would turn to right. Thirty feet, twenty, fifteen. Had the man waiting in the entryway seen her look up toward the Masson apartment, seen her stumble and almost stop?

Ten feet, five. She plunged around the corner, then, still fearful, walked faster and faster but didn't dare to run. One block. Two. Three. No one paid attention to her. The streets were beginning to be populated now as people started to work, pedestrians, occasional bicycles, a few rattly cars running on charcoal. A small café on the next corner was opening for business. There would be a telephone.

She ordered coffee and a brioche and asked to use the telephone.

As she dialed the number, her hands began to shake. In a moment, Eleanor would answer and it would all turn out to be a mistake and they would laugh about it, how Linda had crept by the apartment house and walked so fast to get away..

"*Allo. Allo.*"

Linda closed her eyes. My sister. Oh, Eleanor, my sister.

"*Allo. Allo.* Who is calling?"

Linda pressed down the cradle bar, cutting off that harshly accented stranger's voice. Blindly, she turned away from the telephone, moved toward the door, not even hearing the proprietor's voice. "Mademoiselle, don't you want your coffee and sweet roll?"

She stopped on the sidewalk. Father Laurent, she must tell him. Perhaps he could do something. Robert. Oh my God, how was she going to tell Robert? Robert! What if the Gestapo was looking for him? They would come for him. They would be searching for Robert and for her. If they asked the neighbors most of them wouldn't know anything about them, some who did would pretend ignorance, but the Biziens knew where Robert went to school.

Linda walked faster and faster. When had Eleanor been picked up? Was it this morning? Was a Gestapo car even now going toward Robert's school? Or was the car already there?

Linda ran the seven blocks to his school. The school was around the corner from St. Ferdinand's. Her chest ached, her legs hurt. She hadn't run this far in years. She slowed just before she reached the block and cautiously approached the intersection. The street looked normal, no cars, three pedestrians. She slipped unobtrusively into an alleyway that bordered the east side of the school and entered through the kitchen. A lay sister looked up from a mound of potatoes and smiled "*Bonjour*, Mademoiselle."

"*Bonjour.*" Linda walked down a narrow dark hall to the central stairs. Robert's classroom was on the next floor, three doors to the left. The classroom door was ajar and she heard the soft murmur of Latin declensions. Linda edged up to the door and looked down the rows. Oh dear God, what if he had disobeyed and gone home and not to school as he had promised? What if the Gestapo has already come and taken Robert away?

Robert stood at the blackboard, his back to her. He was reaching up, straining to reach the very top of the marking space. He looked so young and so vulnerable.

The teacher looked up and saw Linda. She spoke quietly to the class then rose and moved toward the door. She stepped out into the hallway, closing the door behind her. "We have met before, I believe. I am Sister Marie Angelique.

"I am Robert Masson's aunt, Linda Rossiter."

"Something is wrong?"

Linda nodded heavily. "My sister . . . Robert's mother . . . the Gestapo . . ."

"Oh, my dear. Wait here. I will get him."

In a moment, she and Robert stepped into the hall. "What is it, Sister?"

"This way, Robert. Come, we will go down to my office. Your aunt and I must talk."

He saw her. "Aunt Linda, what's happened?"

"Robert." The words hurt her throat and her voice sounded strange. "Robert, I went to get the gloves. When I looked up, the second shade was light."

"Mother," he whispered. "Have they arrested Mother?"

She couldn't answer.

His face whitened and his eyes looked suddenly enormous. He turned away from them, moved unsteadily down the hall, stopped. He turned back, stared at Linda in despair.

"Robert, my dear, we will hide you. And you, too, Mlle. Rossiter. We know a way."

"Oh thank you, sister, but we too know a way. But we must hurry. Someone might tell the Gestapo where Robert goes to school."

"Aunt Linda." His voice was strained but steady. "Have you thought, if they've arrested Mother, they may know about the other apartment. Everyone there may have been caught."

Her heart twisted. Jonathan. She had left him sleeping, his fair hair tousled, his arms out flung. And Franz and the four soldiers.

"Robert, you go to Father Laurent. Be careful going in the church. If he is there, if they haven't caught him, he will know what to do. I will go to the apartment and bring Jonathan and the others to the Church now—if they are there. We won't wait until evening."

Eleanor woke with a stiff neck and aching head. She stared uncomprehendingly around the stark room with its tan walls and boarded-over window and glaringly bright light. She remembered when she saw the claw footed bathtub. She half lay, half-sat in the corner of the room farthest from the door. The night had passed. The screaming had, finally, terribly, stopped. An occasional heavy boot had sounded in the hall way. Once there was a clatter and the low rumble of several voices. Toward morning she smelled coffee and the thick sweet scent of frying ham. It was the smell of food that brought her fully awake.

Clumsily, she began to get up. When she stood, she leaned against the wall. She was so hungry and thirsty. Water. She moved unsteadily toward the bath tub. When she leaned over it, she once again saw the rusty dried stains down the side and across the bottom. But she must have water.

She turned the tap on cautiously and let a little trickle of water spill down. She splashed water into her face and then, filling her hands, began to drink, quickly, thirstily. Her purse sat next to the straight chair. It seemed odd to see her purse here. It was a beautiful purse, fine grained leather from Spain. Andre had given it to her last Christmas. She walked across the room and picked it up. It gave her a sense of orderliness to comb her hair, apply lipstick, a bright dark red, and a fine dusting of powder. Then she sat on the straight chair, folded her hands in her lap, and waited.

She hadn't been gone an hour. Not even an hour. Linda ran the last block, not caring that early morning pedestrians watched her curiously. She dashed around the last corner. No cars. Not a car in sight. No huge black German car. No Army trucks. Just a bicycle padlocked to the fence across the street. Oh God, thank you, God, thank you. They are all right. I'm sure they are all right.

She clattered up the stairs and burst into the apartment.

Jonathan hurried out of the kitchen. "What's wrong?"

"Eleanor's been arrested."

"When?"

"I don't know. Either last night or this morning. The lighter shade was pulled down in the second window. Eleanor said we should pull it down if the Gestapo came. I went to a café and telephoned the apartment and a man answered."

He gripped her arm. "What about Robert? We have to get him."

"I did, Jonathan. I went to his school. I've sent him to Father Laurent and told him to say we would all be coming now."

Jonathan talked fast. "I'll get the men. You see to Franz." Before he moved away, he reached out and took her hand. "I'm sorry, Linda."

Major Krause didn't look up as Eleanor was brought in. His head was bent as he read.

The guard nodded at the chair sitting in front of the desk.

Eleanor sat down, and unobtrusively, looked about the office. An elegant office. A Persian rug with tones of ice blue and shadow gray on the floor, dark heavy velvet curtains, an ornate ceiling and sitting behind the desk a man wearing the black of an SS officer.

No one had hurt her yet. That gave her a little courage. She had tried hard to keep her face unmoved when the door finally opened this morning. It must be mid-morning now. She looked to her left at the Dresden clock on the carved mantelpiece. Ten-forty-five. She had waited hours for someone to come, dreading for the door to open, yet welcoming the break in the fearfulness of anticipating horror.

A single soldier had entered and ordered her to come. Now again she waited.

But they hadn't hurt her yet.

What was she going to do if they did to her whatever hideous thing they had done to the man who had been in the room next to her last night? Her hands tightened on each other. Don't think, Eleanor, don't think. Just say you don't know anything at all about anything and maybe they would believe her.

He was writing now, his pale hand moving the pen sharply across the paper. He paused, made a final brief note, laid down the pen, and looked up.

She knew him at once. It was the same officer who had come to the apartment in August after Linda had brought Michael.

He stared at her, his green eyes, a peculiarly piercing green, bored into hers. "You would have been advised, Mme. Masson, to have turned over Lt. Evans last August. We would have forgiven one mistake. But, as it is now, you are guilty of many crimes."

"I don't know what you are talking about."

"It won't do any good for you to deny it, Madame. It will only make things harder for you. We have all the evidence, you see. We know that you have been hiding soldiers in your apartment," his eyes never left her face, "that you are part of a conspiracy to spirit English soldiers out of France."

Eleanor was tired, so tired. How long had it been since she had really slept? And she had not eaten since supper the night before and that was only a cold potato and a glass of wine, but she heard that one telling phrase so clearly, your apartment. Your apartment and he meant the Masson apartment. He didn't know anything at all, he really didn't. And Germans responded only to strength.

She began to shake her head. "Major, this is all some great misunderstanding. I know nothing of any such activities, and I can't imagine why I have been brought here." She pulled herself up straighter, lifted her head. "I really must demand some kind of information on the charges against me. After all, I am an American citizen. I want the American Embassy informed that you are holding me. I also wish to call a lawyer."

His thin mouth spread in a smile. "You forget where you are, Madame."

"I certainly know where I am."

"And where is that?"

She stared at him coldly. "In offices," she looked around, "that used to belong to France but have been taken over by the Germans."

His face flushed. "Not just Germans, Madame. You are in the offices of the Geheime Staats Polizei and we do not permit lawyers to interfere with our investigations or foreign embassies or anyone. Here, Madame, you are in our power until we choose to release you or condemn you. So you should make an effort to cooperate."

"I am making every effort, Major. But it is difficult to show one's innocence when one is ignorant of the charge."

"The charge? Conspiracy, Madame, to flout the law by helping fugitive soldiers escape. We know you are a part of a ring. We know you have received huge sums of money. Twenty-five thousand francs yesterday. Who gave you that money, Madame?"

Eleanor looked at him blankly. Money. Mme. Leclerc wouldn't betray Eleanor, it just wasn't possible. But Madame didn't know about the Latin Quarter apartment. She might well think Eleanor had hidden soldiers in the Masson apartment. But Mme. Leclerc wouldn't betray her.

Jules face flashed in her mind. He had tried to keep Eleanor from seeing Mme. Leclerc. Could he be the one who had betrayed her? If it was Jules, he didn't know anything about them. If it was Jules, the others were safe, Robert and Linda and Jonathan and Father Laurent. Safe, all of them.

Eleanor relaxed in her chair and smiled at Maj. Krause. "No one has given me money, Major. No one."

He sensed the change in her. The woman wasn't afraid. All of a sudden, when she realized of what she had been accused, she wasn't afraid. He frowned and looked back down at his sheet of paper. An anonymous tip. She had been arrested just before midnight and brought here and kept in a third floor cell. Sgt. Friedland has searched her apartment and found nothing incriminating. The neighbors had professed ignorance as to her activities, though, one, a Mme. Bizien had volunteered that there was certainly something funny going on with those people because they were in and out, in and out, all the time. Krause's frown deepened. There were certain ways that would, ultimately, make most people talk. But she was an American citizen.

Abruptly, he picked up the telephone and dialed the number of the Masson apartment. "Sergeant? Maj. Krause here. You have found nothing?" He listened, nodded heavily. "Search again, sergeant. Search everything." He hung up and studied Eleanor again. An attractive woman, though too thin. Curly dark hair. Large brown eyes. And she didn't look frightened.

"All right, Madame. Tell me what you did yesterday. Start with your breakfast. I want everything you did, everywhere you went."

They went over it and over it and over it. His face wavered in front of Eleanor's eyes and her tongue seemed too thick to talk. Over and over and over again, until her voice was a dull monotone," . . . took the car to the hospital. I spoke to Sister Marie Therese and visited the wards on floors three and four . . ."

"Madame!"

Eleanor's head snapped up.

"Earlier you said floors two and three. Which is correct?"

She looked at him blankly.

"Floors three and four or floors two and three," he shouted.

"Three and four," she said slowly.

Was it there that she had received the money? He wondered. Or was the whole tip a lie? Did she have an enemy? There had been no 25,000 francs hidden in her apartment. Perhaps it was all a mistake.

His telephone rang. "Ah yes, Sgt. Friedland." Krause listened, then, slowly, cruelly, he began to smile.

Instinctively, she drew back in her chair.

"You have accepted no money, Madame?"

She shook her head.

He slammed his hand down so hard on his desktop that a coffee cup rattled in its saucer and fell sideways. "Then Madame, how do you explain the 25,000 francs hidden in the bag of potatoes?"

Father Laurent's wavering candle threw a misshapen shadow of his billowing cassock ahead of him. Linda saw the shadow against the bricked tunnel wall, beyond the dim radiance of the kerosene lamp. She struggled to get up. "Father Laurent?"

"My daughter, I have news, not all of it bad. It is true that Eleanor has been arrested. My informant at the Prefecture says she was reported to be trafficking in sums of money that were being used to aid English soldiers. She was taken Monday night to a Gestapo headquarters on the rue de Varenne and, as far as he knows, she is still there."

"What does it mean, Father?"

"I'm not sure, Linda. The good news is that no one else in our circuit has been picked up and that means that our escape line is still operating. We can even use the Latin Quarter apartment."

Linda rubbed at her cheeks. "Does it mean Robert and I can go to Eleanor's apartment?"

"No. The Gestapo has sent out a pickup order for you and Robert. Apparently, Eleanor told them you had gone to Rouen on a visit."

"What happens when they don't find us there?"

The priest spoke quietly. "It will be better, far better for Eleanor if the Gestapo does not find you. If they had you and Robert in custody, they would be able to apply a great deal of pressure. No, my dear, I believe you and Robert should leave tonight with this group. I have papers for both of you. I will keep track of what happens to your sister, through my friend in the Prefecture. If she is released, I will see to it that she too escapes."

"That's the only sensible thing to do, Linda." Jonathan stood beside her, his arm around her.

Linda buried her face in her hands. Too much had happened in too little time. Eleanor arrested. The nerve wracking walk across Paris to the church with Jonathan and Franz and four English airmen. The day-long, interminable wait in this subterranean tunnel with cold damp curving brick walls and, beyond the pale glow of the lamp, the stealthy skitter of rats and the rumbling echoes from the street above when a truck passed overhead.

Eleanor in the custody of the Gestapo—everyone knew what the Gestapo did to people. Oh God, Eleanor, my sister, it's all my fault, I brought Michael home and that's how all of this began and now my sister is at the mercy of sadists, Eleanor with her thin hands and gentle face . . .

Jonathan was somber. "Linda, listen to me, you can trust Father Laurent. If there is anything he can do for Eleanor, he will. She asked you to promise her that you would leave. If the Gestapo caught one of you, the other two were to escape. Please, Linda, it's what you must do."

"What if Mother gets out and tries to find us—and there's no one home?" Robert asked. A child's nightmare made real.

"She will be glad, Robert," Jonathan said gently. "She will know then that you and Linda escaped. Besides, the first thing she will do, if she gets free, is contact Father Laurent. Then he can help her escape."

It all sounded so reasonable, so easy but Eleanor right now, this moment, was held by the Gestapo. Linda pressed her hands harder against her face.

"Linda."

She looked up at him finally. Dear Jonathan. He wanted her to come. He loved her. She knew that, was sure of his love when nothing else was certain. Slowly, with finality, Linda shook her head. "I can't leave without knowing what has happened to Eleanor. I can't."

Jonathan looked much older suddenly, his thin face drawn and weary. He started to speak, didn't. If it were his brother, if it were Robin, he couldn't leave either. Wordlessly, he reached out, pulled Linda close to him, her face against his chest, his arms around her, then he spoke to Father Laurent.

The priest looked thoughtful. "My children, you can't know what tomorrow will bring."

Linda's voice was clear and firm. "But we will have this moment."

Slowly the priest nodded.

Father Laurent insisted they all come up into the church. Linda stood with Jonathan's arm about her. She would not have the wedding she'd always imagined, with the scent of gardenia and walking down an aisle on Frank's arm. But she would be Jonathan's wife.

Father Laurent called his secretary and some of the sisters and the little group stood around in a semicircle as they spoke their vows.

Then it was time to go.

Linda and Jonathan clung to each other for one last embrace.

"Linda, come as soon as you can."

"I will. I promise."

He kissed her as the others picked up their bundles.

This one time Linda didn't care how long it took to walk to the train station. They walked close together, Jonathan's arm around her, Robert and Franz on each side.

The last time, Linda thought, the last time, but I will follow as soon as I can, as soon as I know about Eleanor. It will work out, I know it will. In her purse, she carried their marriage certificate. If she could reach the British Embassy in Spain, she could get a visa to England.

At the train station, she bent to kiss Franz and Robert goodbye. "Robert," she whispered, "try to get word to me on the BBC if you reach London."

He nodded. "Tell Mother . . ." He swallowed. "Tell mother I love her."

Tears burned behind her eyes. She gave him a last hug then turned to Jonathan. Somehow, she managed not to cry until the train was gone, until she was standing on the icy platform, waving, but knowing they could no longer see her.

She rode the Metro back to the Latin Quarter apartment, climbed the dark stairs and let herself into cold emptiness. She walked to the pallet where Jonathan had slept the night before. She reached down, touched the cold wrinkled covers, and, bitterly, quietly, began to weep.

CHAPTER 18

Maj. Krause's face was flushed with irritation. All day long and she hadn't changed a word of her story. But the 25,000 francs came from somewhere. "Who gave you the money?"

She looked at him vacantly. "I told you," she said dully. "My brother sent extra money to me."

"Madame, don't lie again. Your brother sent you 10,000 francs two weeks ago, not 25,000."

She nodded slowly, her head going up and down so wearily. "Yes, you are right. But I had other money, other cash, and I didn't want to trust the banks, I had cashed out other sums of money."

That was true enough. He was looking at her bank balance. Heavy withdrawals, starting in September.

"Don't you think it is too much of a coincidence, Madame, that an informer should guess the exact amount you have hidden," he paused then added sarcastically, "in the cleverness of a potato bag?"

Eleanor didn't answer. You almost didn't find it, you bastard. You can guess all you want but there isn't any proof. And the others are safe, oh God, they are safe, Linda and Robert and Jonathan and the men and Father Laurent. Keep me here forever and I will answer as I have because the others are safe.

It was dark now. They would be on the train by now. Oh Robert, bless you. You and Franz and Linda will go home to Pasadena and be safe. The train must be almost to the outskirts of Paris now. She closed her eyes.

Krause frowned. He could send her upstairs, put Schmidt to work on her. But she was an American citizen. She was a rich woman, obviously. Spoiled. Look at that fur coat. Well, a little taste of prison might make her more willing to cooperate. And there was something odd here. His instinct was sure of it. When the sister and the son were picked up, that would give him some leverage. Something might turn up at the apartment. Friedland would stay there and arrest anyone who came.

"Madame."

Reluctantly, she opened her eyes.

"You are making yourself needlessly uncomfortable."

She didn't answer.

His thin mouth tightened. "If that's what you want to do, we are quite agreeable." He pushed a buzzer on his desk. When Sgt. Schmidt came, Maj. Krause was shutting the folder. "The Cherche-Midi. The charge is suspicion of harboring English soldiers."

As Eleanor pulled herself to her feet, he said softly, "If convicted Madame, you will be shot."

It was a fifteen minute drive to the military prison of the Cherche-Midi. Eleanor looked across the bulk of the Gestapo men on either side of her to glimpse familiar landmarks. She felt as if she had not been outside, smelled fresh air in days. She was dizzy and weak from lack of food. Krause had eaten, of course, at his desk, had soup and a sandwich for lunch, coffee in the afternoon. She had eaten nothing, had only the handful of water upon awakening, nothing since.

The ride across a darkened Paris in the back of the heavy car didn't seem real. It was the grudging sound as the heavy door opened at the prison that made her realize what was happening to her.

It was an old prison, massive, its walls feet thick, its cell windows nothing more than narrow slanted openings cut through rock.

Eleanor clutched her fur coat tightly about her as she followed the sergeant down narrow twisting stairs. At the foot, he turned her over to a huge woman guard who took her impersonally by the elbow and led her to an empty room. "Take off your clothes."

Eleanor looked at her in dismay.

"You must be searched. Hurry now. All your clothes off. Everything."

The woman watched stolidly.

When Eleanor was nude and shaking with cold as she stood barefoot on the icy floor, the woman slowly, methodically, picked up each item of clothing, shook it, explored the pockets. She lingered over the fur coat, stroking it. When each piece had been checked, she turned toward Eleanor.

Oh no, surely she wasn't going to have to be touched by this monster. When it was over, the guard wiped her hand against her skirt, nodded down at the heap of clothes. "You can dress now."

The next stop was for her picture to be made. Eleanor stood against a wall. The photographer, who smelled of cough drops and had dirty hands, fastened her head in a metal clamp, pinned a placard with a number on it to her coat, took a full face picture, then a profile.

When her fingerprints were taken and a sheet fully filled out, the chief guard, a sergeant major, rang a bell. "Take her to the third floor," he told the middle-aged guard who answered the bell.

The guard looked at Eleanor without interest. "Follow me, 1887."

They started up a winding stone stairway. At each landing, there was a fully armed soldier, a bayonet on his rifle. It was cold, filthy and very dark, only an occasional dim bulb lighting the way. And it smelled. Eleanor had noticed the smell, a disagreeable odor of sewage, in the basement. The higher they climbed, the more intense the odor became until the stench was so thick and rank she wanted to gag.

On the third floor, her guard led her midway down a corridor to an ironbound door indistinguishable from a dozen others up and down the hallway. He pulled open a sliding piece of metal that covered a peephole and looked in. Then he turned the key, which stood in the lock, opened the door and motioned for her to enter.

It was pitch-black in the cell, the only light filtering in from the open door. She tried not to gag from the nauseating, overwhelming, suffocating smell.

When she hesitated, he said, "That's your bed, 1887," and gave her a push.

She stumbled inside. The door swung shut and she stood in absolute darkness. She had glimpsed four iron beds. They filled the cell except for a small table in the center with a tin canister on it.

The canister smelled horribly.

"You have to go to bed now." The voice was light and cultured. "If they open the peephole and you are still up, they will put you in solitary confinement."

Eleanor stretched out her hand, moved uncertainly to her left, toward the empty bed that the guard had indicated. "Is it always dark?" Eleanor heard the tremor in her voice. She couldn't bear to be shut up, crowded up in this filthy airless room, blind, not knowing who was near her, not being able to see.

"Oh no," another woman answered. Her voice was deep, almost rough. "It's just another little torture from the Boche. The light goes off at eight every night. They turn it back on in the morning."

Eleanor sank down on the bed. "That smell is awful."

"That's our toilet, love. The bastards haven't emptied it tonight. Some nights they don't. But, that's the war."

There was something in this woman's deep voice that cheered Eleanor, something buoyant and indestructible.

"What are you in here for?" the deep voice asked.

"Oh, for helping English soldiers escape."

The silence in the cell was suddenly absolute.

"But you can get the—" The lighter, cultured voice broke off.

—the death penalty, Eleanor finished in her mind. Yes.

"Is it true?" a third voice asked. "Did you do it?"

Eleanor started to answer but before she could utter a sound, a hand gripped her arm, tightly, painfully, the fingers digging harshly into her despite her coat, a warning.

"It's a mistake of some kind," Eleanor answered unevenly. The thick fuggy air pressed against her and the darkness crackled with tension. The deep voice and the cultured one spoke together, quickly. They had so many questions, was England still fighting, did it really look as though Germany was going to invade, what was the weather like, and food, did she know anyone who would bring her food packages?

Eleanor answered as well as she could though now she was so tired that despite the smell and the uncomfortable bed, she wanted desperately to sleep.

"What did you do that made them suspect you?"

Again, there was a little circle of silence until the cultured voice spoke, "Don't talk about it, my dear, if it's upsetting to you."

Eleanor knew the voices now. The cultured voice, the deep buoyant voice and the third voice, an almost nondescript voice, dull, lifeless.

"I am tired," Eleanor admitted. "I believe I will go to sleep now. We can talk in the morning."

"That we can, dearie," the buoyant voice said humorously. "We'll all be right here."

It was abruptly quiet then, though the breathing of each was distinct as they struggled for air in the fetid closeness.

Eleanor was tired, tired to the bone. But she lay quite still on her cot and stared sightlessly into the dark. The third voice . . . something wrong there. Why else had a hand gripped her so painfully when she started to answer? But it didn't matter much now. Robert and Linda were on the train, the wheels were clacking, carrying them farther and farther from Paris. Robert . . .

Eleanor bolted upright, her heart hammering.

A dim light flickered on above.

"It's all right, dearie."

The thunderous knocking that had shocked her awake was repeated like an echo, moving farther and farther away.

"That's how they get us up in the morning. Right on the dot, Fritz is, seven-thirty every morning." She was a big woman to match her deep voice. A crest of iron-gray hair puffed up like a cockatoo's comb above a square, resolute face. She was bending over her cot now, shaking the grayish blanket, smoothing it up. She looked at Eleanor and nodded, almost formally, "I'm Eloise Cottin."

Eleanor smiled. "I am Eleanor Masson."

"I am Simone Bernard." Eleanor half turned. The cultured voice.

Simone had a slender aristocratic face and faded red hair. She held out her hand and Eleanor took it.

Eleanor looked at the third cell mate.

Her face was pale and her hair pale, too, a pale dull gold. Her light green eyes darted over Eleanor and looked longest at her coat. She realized suddenly that the three of them were watching her. "Marie," she said shortly. "Marie Leroy." Then she too began to straighten her cot.

"Hurry," Madame Barnard said. "The beds must be made and everyone dressed before he comes back or they put you in solitary confinement."

Eleanor did as she was bid, recoiling in disgust from the filth of the covers in which she had slept. Soiled, smelly, odorous. She finished just in time.

The cell door opened and the guard stepped inside.

After a quick glance, Eleanor followed the lead of her cellmates and stood stiffly at the head of her cot.

The guard looked under the beds, in the corners, nodded and turned to leave.

"We need a fresh canister," Mme. Cottin boomed.

"Tonight."

"But it's almost full."

The cell door slammed shut.

The other three then sat on the edge of their beds.

Eleanor looked at her cot. It was so dirty. But she felt dizzy and weak. She started to lie down.

"Oh no, Madame. You can't lie down during the day. You have to sit on the edge of your bed."

"All day?"

"When you aren't too tired, we take turns one at a time walking up and down."

Eleanor looked at the cramped cell, scarcely a foot of space between the beds and the table with the evil smelling canister.

Eleanor sat down on the edge of her bed.

No one talked now. They all seemed sunk in apathy though it was more than that, there was an air of tension and reserve.

Eleanor's eyes closed. It took every effort of will not to sag down on the bed. Today was . . . Her mind felt dull and fuzzy. Was it yesterday . . . no, the day before, that had been Monday and she was arrested Monday night, then Tuesday at the Gestapo building and now today, today must be Wednesday.

The cell door creaked open.

An incredibly old man shuffled inside, carrying a tray. He handed each of them a mug, three-fourths full. Then he sat a small basin, half filled with water, on the table.

The others were all reaching beneath the pillows on their beds and bringing out variously wrapped small lumps.

Mme. Bernard's was wrapped in wrinkled brown paper, Mme. Cottin's in a piece of cloth, Mme. Leroy's in a piece of silk. She looked up and saw Eleanor watching. "I tore it out from the lining of my coat."

Mme. Cottin looked up then. "It's our bread ration. They give it to you at night and you have to save enough for your breakfast and lunch."

Eleanor hadn't realized until she saw that small piece of dark bread how ravenously hungry she was. Eleanor lifted up her tin cup. "Is this all we get?"

The others nodded.

Eleanor sipped from the cup. It was supposed to be coffee, she could tell that, but it had an oily bitter taste. She drank another mouthful. It was foul. For an instant tears burned her eyes. It was just another German trick to make you miserable. She started to put the cup down, then, desperately, she drank again. She had to drink. She was so thirsty and hungry.

Mme. Cottin leaned toward her. "How long has it been since you've eaten?"

Eleanor tried to think. The days slipped in and out of her mind. "Monday," she said finally. "I ate Monday."

Mme. Cottin handed her piece of bread to Eleanor.

"Oh no," Eleanor began. "I can't take your food." The bread was in her hand and her fingers were closing around it and she was bringing it up to her mouth.

"Of course you can." Mme. Cottin laughed and that booming laughter sounded odd but triumphant in the cold filthy cell. "I've been trying to lose weight for years. Didn't think I could do it. And, believe me, I've still lots of extra."

There was a little burst of animation after breakfast. The basin of water, all they would get for cleaning purposes, was passed from hand to hand. "Goes in order of seniority," Mme. Cottin explained.

By the time the bowl reached Eleanor, the water was gray but she splashed her face, washed her hands, then once again joined her cell mates in sitting on the edge of the bed.

Hungry, hungry, hungry. The foul tasting lukewarm drink had only made her hunger worse. It was a live thing, her hunger, a coil of pain inside her. Time expanded to incredible lengths. Twice Eleanor looked at her wrist before she remembered that her watch and wedding rings and money had been taken from her when she was admitted to prison. What difference did it make? She was no longer Eleanor Masson, free to determine her day, free to choose where to go, how much time to spend. She was Number 1887, sitting on the edge of an iron bed on a dirty ticking mattress covered with soiled coarse linen and one thin wool blanket. The cell was bitterly cold. She wrapped her arms around herself. At least she still had her fur coat. Andre would never have imagined, when he gave it to her, how much it would someday mean. He had been pleased with her pleasure. "Oh Andre, it's too extravagant," she had objected. He had smiled. "The coat will keep you warm." She hugged the coat tighter to her.

It was only midmorning, but already to Eleanor it seemed as if she had been forever in the ill-lighted cold and airless cell, when the slide scraped open, then a moment later the door swung in.

"Number 1843."

Mme. Leroy looked up, then rose and leisurely moved toward the hallway.

"Hurry, 1843."

When the cell door slammed shut, Mme. Cottin and Mme. Bernard both watched it close with grim silent faces. When a long moment passed, they nodded at each other and both of them moved closer down their beds toward Eleanor.

Mme. Cottin leaned across the narrow space where the table sat and the sickening canister. She ignored the smell and whispered, "Madame, last night, it was I who grabbed your arm. I was afraid you were going to speak, to say that you were involved in the escape line."

"That woman is a plant," Mme. Bernard hissed. "They move her from cell to cell and she tries to pump new prisoners. We knew we were going to get a new prisoner yesterday when they took two of our cellmates away and sent her in."

"Don't say anything incriminating. Not a word," Mme. Cottin warned.

Eleanor looked toward the door. "Where has she gone now?"

"She'll pretend she's been had up for interrogation," Mme. Bernard said disdainfully. "Instead, she's in the guard room, eating a good breakfast. It's warm in there, too. They have a stove and plenty of coal."

Eleanor reached out, touched both of them. "Thank you."

Mme. Cottin shrugged. Mme. Bernard smiled shyly. The smile transformed her thin ascetic face. She started to speak, hesitated, asked, "Are you English?"

Eleanor smiled. "No, Madame. I'm American."

"American," Madame Cottin exclaimed, "but Germany isn't even at war with America. Why are you in France now?"

Eleanor explained that her husband was French and that she had lived in France since her marriage sixteen years ago. "Andre has been missing since Dunkirk. I stayed in Paris with my son and my sister, who was visiting me. I've been working with the Foyer du Soldat and in other ways."

Her new friends nodded understandingly.

"Have you been charged yet?" Mme. Cottin asked.

Eleanor shook her head.

The big woman frowned. "That's too bad. They don't permit extra food, say from a friend, while you are under examination."

"They will call you up for questioning after you've been here a while. They like to give you a taste of prison. Some people will confess to anything if they think they can get out," Mme. Bernard explained.

"Are you still under examination?" Eleanor asked.

Both of them shook their heads.

"Two years sentence," Mme. Bernard said.

"Six months," Mme. Cottin replied.

Eleanor hesitated, asked, "Why are you here?"

Simone Bernard told her story first. She was the wife of a banker. He was really too old to go to the front, but he had rejoined his unit when the fighting began. He was wounded at Lille and taken prisoner. Mme. Bernard had attempted to bribe a guard at the military hospital to gain his release. She had been betrayed by a second guard who was jealous of the money received by his co-worker.

Mme. Cottin smiled hugely. "My big mouth cost me six months in prison, but I've never regretted it once."

Eleanor couldn't help but smile in anticipation. "What did you do?"

"They made me take a sergeant major as a lodger. I have a boarding house, a nice little house, in the Porte d'Orleans quarter. Well, I took him in. I had to. But I kept having a little trouble with his name."

"You did?"

She nodded her head emphatically. "It always seemed to slip out when I saw him. Good morning, Sgt. Maj. Polydore. Good afternoon, Sgt. Maj. Polydore. Good night, Sgt. Maj. Polydore."

Eleanor was still laughing when they heard the peephole scrape open.

The cell was silent when Mme. Leroy returned. No one spoke. She tried twice more to pump Eleanor. Each time, Eleanor responded volubly, complaining about the damned Boche, how a woman's own money could be held against her. Her eyes wide, she demanded, "I don't trust the banks. How can anyone trust the banks? Do you trust the banks?"

Mme. Leroy tried one more time, the next day. "It must have been very exciting, to be part of an escape line."

Eleanor was sharp. "I wouldn't know. I've heard about things like that. Actually, I think it would be pretty foolish, don't you? I mean, with the death penalty and all that?"

When Mme. Leroy was called up for examination that day, she didn't return.

They had a new cellmate that afternoon. They heard soft stricken moans before they saw her. The three women sat on their beds, turned toward the door as it opened. The guard shoved a young girl inside. As the cell door shut, she wavered unsteadily on her feet then began to fall forward.

Mme. Cottin, moving quickly for a woman of her bulk, caught the girl before she reached the floor. When her hands touched her, the girl writhed in agony.

"Don't touch me, oh God, no, don't touch me."

Mme. Cottin lowered her slowly, carefully toward the cot. She didn't lay the girl down. Blood seeped through the girl's blouse from her back. The soft material was torn, ripped, some of it embedded in puffy bloody welts.

They used what was left of the morning wash water to clean her back as well as they could. She lay on her side, hands clenched, face rigid as Mme. Cottin worked.

Eleanor took off her coat, her thick wool sweater, and then the soft cotton blouse she had been wearing when she was arrested. Her nose wrinkled a little in disgust. She had worn these clothes, the long days sitting on the edge of the cot, the interminable nights, lying wrapped up in the filthy blanket, ever since her arrest. The cloth must smell hideous, but it was a blouse, something to cover that lacerated back and thin bruised shoulders.

The girl didn't complain. Later that day, after she had managed to eat lunch, the whale bone soup, a gray jellied mass that tasted like Vaseline, and two slices of fake salami, she lifted up on one elbow and told her story, her tear-streaked face pinched with pain. Her name was Angelique Fornier and she was seventeen years old. "It wasn't organized, nothing like that. It was just the spur of the minute thing. Jean—"

Mme. Bernard interrupted, "Don't tell us anyone's real name, my dear. It isn't wise."

Angelique nodded. "A boy I know. We were taking a walk. You know that's almost all we can do anymore. The movies are all German films and who wants to see them? My brother was killed at Houthen. I didn't want to see a German movie about how wonderful they are and how they've come to save us. Save us from what? Being happy and free? So we take—took walks and sometimes there were more of us, a group. Lots of kids." She paused and gave them names and they all knew these weren't really their names, "Claude and Henri and Jacques and Paulette and Marie and me. There is an overpass on the boulevard in our neighborhood and sometimes we stop there and look down and watch the cars."

Soon they began to notice that prisoners being taken to a Gestapo headquarters on the Avenue Foch were driven beneath the overpass. They just noticed that. Talked of it some. Didn't really make much of it. "Until Paul was arrested. Paul is the older brother of . . . of my friend. They found Paul passing out copies of the new underground newspaper."

All of them came alive at that. What newspaper? When had it begun? What did it have in it?

Angelique had not seen a copy of the paper. She had just heard about it. The Resistance, it was called. Anyway, the Gestapo arrested Paul. His brother and Angelique and their friends made a plan. Paul was being transferred to the downtown Gestapo quarters that morning. They had taken turns on the overpass. When Claude spotted the Gestapo car coming, he had motioned to the others, waiting in the nearby alleyway with bricks and two musket balls they had wrenched from a statue.

They waited until the Citroen was just nosing beneath the underpass. At Claude's signal, they dropped their weights. The windshield shattered, the car swerved out of control and slammed into the brick center span.

Two others waiting below had dashed to the car and smashed the rear door window. One of them slammed the plain-clothes man then reached inside to try and pull Paul out.

Everything went wrong. The driver was unconscious but the Gestapo agent on the far side wasn't hurt and he had a Schmeisser pistol. When the shooting was over, the two who had tried to get Paul were dead. Those on the overpass started to run.

"I twisted my ankle."

They looked down. Her ankle was swollen twice its size and was a darkening purple over the instep. "I couldn't run. I had gone the opposite direction from the others. It was getting dark when it all happened so I don't think they realized I was caught." She began to tremble. "Now they want the names of the others." She looked up at the three older women fearfully. "I didn't tell them. I didn't." Tears began to trickle down her smeared and dirty face. "But it hurts so much. It hurts so much."

The next morning when the peephole slid open, Eleanor was sure it would be her turn.

"Number 1889."

Angelique didn't move.

The guard jerked his head at the pale girl. "You. 1889."

When they brought her back, late in the afternoon, she was unconscious. They dumped her on her bed. She moaned all night.

Eleanor pulled her coat up over her head, squeezed her eyes shut. They were going to call her one of these days. One of these days, it was going to be her turn. But Robert was safe. Andre was safe. For the first time, she thought it in her mind. Andre is dead. No one can hurt him now and Robert is safe. It doesn't matter anymore what happens to me. I must fool them, lie, never give the others away so that Father Laurent can keep on saving lives, just as he saved Robert and Linda and Jonathan and all those soldiers. Seventy-three soldiers, the last time she had added up. That was a fair exchange. More than fair. Seventy-three men and those she loved, all safe, so somehow, she would manage not to tell them. They weren't sure about her anyway. If she could not be afraid, if she could keep them from sensing her fear, they might not torture her. Weakness drew them, as a carcass draws flies.

The days passed, day after day after day, the foul smell, the cold, the debilitating unending gnawing hunger, the fear, the tedium, the dreadful mind-numbing fatigue, day after day.

The posters were put up all over Paris on Saturday, November 23, black letters stark against white cardboard. They were signed by the Kommandant of Paris, Otto von Stulpnagel.

> 10,000 FRANCS REWARD FOLLOWING THE DECREE ESTABLISHING THE DEATH PENALTY FOR ALL THOSE WHO HIDE ENGLISH SOLDIERS OR AID THEM TO ESCAPE, THE GERMAN HIGH COMMAND ANNOUNCES THAT IT WILL PAY 10,000 FRANCS REWARD TO ANY PERSON PRO-VIDING NAMES AND ADDRESSES OF THOSE ENGAGED IN THIS CRIMINAL ACTIVITY.

Yvette Bizien saw three of the posters on the short walk between the apartment and her husband's tobacco shop. Ten thousand francs. If they had 10,000 francs, they would be able to buy a used truck. If they had a truck, there was a fortune to be made in the black market.

Maj. Krause put half the sandwich down, uneaten. He'd scarcely had any time for lunch the past two weeks. The fox had found the chicken coop. Escape lines were cracking under Gestapo pressure everywhere, from Rouen to Toulouse. More than forty people had been rounded up in the last few days alone. The arrests were all due to Maj. Erich

Krause and his English speaking agents in their tattered RAF uniforms. That would show Knocken that he, Erich Krause, was succeeding. Knocken was having his own troubles with the Army but no one could complain about Maj. Krause's efforts. He had a good relationship with the military police. They were only too happy to raid when he ordered it. Krause smiled. This would show Knocken.

Slowly his smile eroded. It might be better to be tactful. He could see Knocken suddenly, trim athletic figure, mop of auburn hair over a high, domed, intellectual forehead, emaciated unpleasant face, and gray blue eyes that never changed expression. Or perhaps it was his mouth, with its noticeable twist to the left that gave him such an intimidating expression. Or perhaps it was the knowledge, throughout the SS, that those whom Knocken favored prospered, and those whom Knocken opposed, disappeared.

But it wouldn't hurt to make a good report. He could put it tactfully.

"Sgt. Schmidt, take a letter to Obertruppfuehrer Knocken. 'In accordance with your previous instructions to pursue with vigor the criminals who have persisted in hiding and passing fugitive Englishmen, I am happy to report . . .'"

It was the loneliness that hurt. As much as anything, Linda hated the apartment when it was empty. The silent rooms were dull and dead and gray. Even the yellow walls seemed dingy in the thin winter sunlight. There hadn't been much sunlight. The days when the soldiers arrived were tense and busy and that day and night and the next day when they left always flew by.

The days in between were hard. She stayed in the apartment and there was nothing to do, nothing at all. She wrote one letter to Frank and had one of the soldiers carry it with him with a promise to mail it from England. In it, she told Frank that Robert and Franz were coming, that Eleanor was in prison and that she, Linda, would come when she knew Eleanor's fate.

She lay curled up in bed. She must get up soon. Soldiers would arrive today. That was something. Their accents reminded her, achingly, of Jonathan. Was Jonathan safe? Had they crossed the Pyrenees, reached sanctuary in Spain? Or had they been gunned down along the frontier or captured by the Spanish and thrown into prison?

Jonathan had promised to try and get word on the nightly BBC program if they made it. They had planned the sentence that would signal the safe arrival of their group. "Robert is halfway to Pasadena." If she heard it, she would know. Father Laurent had found a radio for her. Theirs, of course, was still in their apartment.

Did the Gestapo agent find the apartment to his liking? Had they already stolen Eleanor's antiques? Or was the apartment empty now, dusty, unlit, a ghostly place that once had been a cheerful home. How long would the concierge keep it for Eleanor? She would have to clear out their things, rent it eventually.

There was something about today. Something she had forgotten. Wearily, she pushed back the covers. She wore her clothes to bed now. She had one change of clothing, again, the gift of Father Laurent. She was always cold with only her pale blue spring coat and no coal for heat. It had been so long since she had been really warm. What was it about today?

She shuffled around the kitchen, boiling water to make a cup of the odd-tasting coffee substitute, halving one roll and cutting a small piece of cheese. Like an old woman, she thought, moving so heavily. She sat down at the table which seemed large with only her there to eat. She was hungry but food had no savor. She chewed halfheartedly on the roll. If Jonathan were here, she wouldn't shuffle. She would have brushed her hair and straightened her clothes. She would smile and the hard roll would taste delicious. Loneliness makes you old, she thought, even if you're young. Loneliness takes all the light and color out of life, reduces every day to mechanical, spiritless, dull drudgery. Oh Jonathan, would she ever see him again, ever touch him, hold him?

She cupped her hands around the mug, teasing a little warmth through the pottery. That was what it was about. Today was December 13. Friday the 13th. This was the day she would have left Paris on her ausweis.

Linda stared somberly at the mug. She wouldn't leave Paris today. Not today. It was time now to leave for the train station and the new batch of airmen. But she wouldn't be leaving Paris.

Father Laurent greeted her openly, at the station. At Linda's frown, he had chided gently. "A priest can still say hello to his parishioner. Even in Nazi Paris."

"You take too many chances," she replied, unsmiling. "You should have just sent me a message."

"I wanted to talk to you." He took her arm and they walked along the platform.

Peripherally, Linda could see the airmen falling in behind them. None of these looked English. That was good. She hated leading them across Paris when one of the men was a carrot top or had a broad fair typically British face.

"It's Friday the 13th," she said as they reached the main lobby of the station.

"Next Sunday will be the third Sunday in advent."

It all depended upon your perspective, she thought wryly. How could he always be so equable, so positive? Didn't the man have sense enough to be afraid? His collar wouldn't save him if the Gestapo found him. How could he stand in the middle of this teeming lobby with two Gestapo agents manning a checkpoint only feet away and seem totally unworried?

"One of the men speaks good French. I've sent him over to get some food for the others. You and I can have a minute here to talk."

It came to her abruptly. "You've found out something about Eleanor?"

He nodded. "She's still at the Cherche-Midi. A colleague of mine, a Mr. Marvel of the American Quakers, is permitted to visit American prisoners. He saw Eleanor yesterday."

Linda swallowed. "How is she?"

"He was able to see her for only a few minutes. They couldn't talk about the charges against her. Actually, there are no charges yet, she is still being held on suspicion. That's too bad in one way. Prisoners under examination are forbidden extra food. Mr. Marvel said Eleanor is very thin and weak but apparently hasn't been tortured. More than likely that's because she is an American. I notified your embassy and I know they have lodged a formal protest. That won't free her but it may give her some protection."

"Is there any hope she may be released?"

The priest smiled. "There is always hope."

CHAPTER 19

"**1**887."

Eleanor hadn't looked round when the peephole scraped open or even when the door swung in. She didn't respond to the command. She sat, her head slumped forward on her neck, eyes closed, the fur coat bunched tightly around her. Inside her mind, a room glowed with color, the bright green of a fir tree against the deeper green of the velvet curtains, garlands of red and white and pink and green and blue lights that winked on and off, a glisten of snowy white cotton bunched around the trunk, and packages, gold and red and green and white, tumbling out around the tree. Andre was smiling as he knelt by the mounds of gifts, picking them up to hand out. He was leaning toward her . . . She tried to ignore the tug on her arm, but it came again, harder.

"Eleanor, it's you they want. Eleanor."

She opened her eyes slowly.

"1887. You are called for examination."

Her face didn't change. Slowly, weakly, she began to get up. She wavered unsteadily on her feet, then turned and followed him. She started to ask where they were going but that took too much effort. She concentrated on putting one foot ahead of the other. It was almost Christmas. Mme. Cottin kept a little calendar. She said tomorrow would be Christmas Eve. Last Christmas Eve they had gone to midnight Mass and Andre had carried Robert home, he was so sleepy. Funny, Robert would be too big to carry this year. Andre . . . how long now, more than six months since we've heard. There isn't any hope. Not anymore. Even if he'd been among the Frenchmen who embarked at

Dunkirk and she knew him too well to think he would have left them behind, even if he had, they would have heard by now. She stumbled to a stop, staring emptily ahead.

The guard looked back. "1887!"

Once again she started slowly forward, reaching out a hand now and then to brace herself against the cold damp stone wall.

The guard had to stop four times for her to rest on the way down the twisting stairs. At the bottom, he led her to an office just past the booking room.

Eleanor walked in. The door shut behind her. She looked around incuriously then walked to the straight chair and sat down and closed her eyes.

In a moment, the room in her mind was back, a warm room, fire glistening in the monkey stove, radiators hissing with heat. She had been a little too hot last year and had pulled off her robe. Andre had looked up from the gifts and she had loved the look in his eyes. They had both laughed and Robert turned from opening a package and asked, "What's so funny?" "Nothing, darling," his mother answered. "It's just that we're all so happy tonight."

The door opened. She still sat, her eyes closed, her face closed.

"Madame." The tone was harsh.

Slowly, slowly, she opened her eyes.

Maj. Krause sat down behind a table and spread open a folder "Where did you get the money, Madame?"

"Money?"

"The 25,000 francs."

She stared at him dully and pushed her hair away from her face. Oh yes, that money. The money in the potato bag. She began to laugh. The potato bag. The potato bag. "The polydore. That's who found the money, the polydore."

"Madame." The anger in his voice cut across her wild laughter.

She stopped as suddenly as she had begun and shook her head. "I'm dizzy." She had been so weak these last few days. The others had as little food as she but she knew there was something wrong with her.

She was too tired to think, too tired to move, everything happened in a gray mist.

Maj. Krause almost signaled Sgt. Schmidt to strike her. He would get her attention. Then, once again, his eyes skimmed over the report and he stopped at the line which said: Nationality—American. If he could beat the truth out of her, he would.

He looked up. She sagged in the chair, her face white, her eyes closed, her hair tumbling down onto her shoulders.

She was the one, yes, he remembered now, she was the one who had been turned in by an informer and, after they had picked her up, kept her overnight, he personally had interviewed her and she wasn't afraid. Uneasy, yes. No one but a fool wouldn't sense that horrors could happen. But she wasn't afraid. Now she must be ill. She wasn't going to be any use to him.

He read further into the report. The sister and the son had never been found.

That was the strongest evidence against her. But they could have been frightened when she was picked up, whether they were involved in an escape line or not, and sought a way to get out of France.

That could be.

But it is easier to find a way to escape if you are running an escape line.

That was the black mark. That and the 25,000 francs, though her story about the money could be true. She was a wealthy woman and she might have been squirreling money away for emergencies. "Madame, go back to the morning of November 18. Madame, listen to me."

Once again, groggily, she looked at him. She listened and numbly, expressionlessly, tried to answer. Sometimes she just shook her head. "I don't remember. Everything's vague. I don't remember."

He was exasperated after twenty minutes. The woman was an imbecile. Or sick. The thought made him impatient. She must be a weak one. It did wear them down, to put them in the Cherche-Midi, but usually just enough to make everything hurt a little more. They could still talk. He could have her put in the prison hospital. But the food wasn't much better there. If he had her beaten, she wouldn't make any more sense then.

There was another way. One more test. If this didn't turn up some answers, there might not be any answers to be found.

He nodded his head in sudden decision.

The climb back up the twisting stairs to the third floor seemed to take forever. Eleanor knew she would have been kicked and pushed by most guards but the shift had changed and the new guard was old and slow and they struggled up the steps together. When she was inside the cell, she shook her head when the others asked if she was hurt but she could just reach the bed to fall upon it.

"Eleanor," Mme. Cottin was shaking her shoulder, "You must get up. I hear someone coming. If they look in and find you lying down, you'll be taken to solitary confinement."

Eleanor wasn't quite in a sitting position when the door opened again. "1887."

"I can't," she whispered.

"Get up."

It was like trying to move through a swamp to make the simplest effort. Grimly, Eleanor pushed herself to her feet, but this time she started to topple over.

"She is ill," Mme. Bernard cried. "Can't you see that?"

The old guard frowned. He reached out, took her firmly by the elbow. "She has to come."

Eleanor moved down the halls and to the stairs like a sleep-walker. I must be sick, she thought, I must be sick. When they reached the ground floor, she had no memory of the stairs. The guard half-carried, half dragged her into the booking room.

A German guard in rimless glasses looked up. "1887?"

She nodded.

He went to a side room and returned in a moment with a little basket. Eleanor was leaning against the counter. He spilled out the basket's contents. Her wedding ring, the purse she had carried that night. Her purse had some candy in it. She remembered that. Her hands began to shake. Would the candy still be there? And the money and her ration cards?

"Sign here, Madame."

She looked blearily at the form on green flimsy paper.

"It is to show that you have not been mistreated and that all your belongings were returned to you."

She picked up the pen and scrawled her name then looked at him again. He was picking up the basket and turning away. He looked back over his shoulder. "You can go now. That's the way out," and he pointed down a narrow hallway.

Eleanor put on her wedding rings, picked up her purse. Was it going to be this easy? Was this all there was to it? Signing her name on a piece of paper and she could walk out? She stopped, reached out to brace herself against the wall. Could that have been a confession she signed? Was this some kind of trick? She shook her head. She was dizzy and weak. Maybe this was all a dream and in a moment she would wake up on that narrow filthy bed, trying to breathe the putrid air.

She pushed away from the wall and walked down the hall. No one paid any attention to her, not two secretaries drinking a cup of coffee near a stove or a private pushing a broom down a wider hall or an officer walking away from her, striking a crop against a high black polished boot. She tried to walk a little faster. It wasn't until she pushed through the door and came out in a dingy bricked courtyard that she began to believe she was going free.

Weak, sick, dizzy, no matter, she broke into a half run, half stumble and she was through the courtyard and out on the street.

She stopped on the sidewalk. Pedestrians pushed past her, heads lowered. Icy raindrops whirled in the wind and dusted the gutter with a glitter of ice. Eleanor lifted her head and breathed and breathed. She was shaking with cold, but it smelled fresh and clean and free. She began to walk, unsteadily, but purposefully. My God, she was free! It was a miracle. She didn't care how or why, but for now, this instant, she could walk down the street and the sensation was incredible and wonderful. She stopped at the corner and reached out to lean against the lamp post. Food, she needed food.

She opened her purse, rummaged frantically inside. Her ration cards, yes, there they were and money, enough money. She lifted her head, looked up and down the street. A café sign creaked in the wind a half block ahead. She would eat. It was just on four o'clock. If the café were open, she would eat dinner and then she would have the strength to get home. She would take a velocab. She would go home and get a night's sleep and then she would think what to do.

Linda was setting the table for breakfast and he came shyly and asked if he could help. She smiled at him. "We are a little informal because we never had a chance to really stock this apartment. But you can put the knives and forks around for me."

She had saved up some extras for this breakfast. Father Laurent had given back to her the first 25,000 that Eleanor had received. She still had a good store of money so, last week, she had waited several hours in line and managed to get a crock of honey and a pot of peach jam. Treasure of treasures, though it had cost the earth, she had bought a pound of real coffee on the black market.

He watched her measure spoonfuls and draw cold water. He sniffed. "Oh, I say, that can't be real coffee?"

"Yes, it is."

"That's very nice and it is nice of you to share with us."

She looked up into his blue eyes and she wondered if he could see the pain in her own eyes. Nice of her to share it—the soldiers were the only thing that kept her sane. It still frightened her to pick them up and bring them here, it always did. No matter how many times she did it, she always felt an ache in her chest and her heart thudded wildly. She hated the fear, but she needed to see them, to have them on their brief stopovers. What good is it to have coffee or gold or life, if there's no one to share with you?

"I'm glad you're here." That was all she said. She turned abruptly and put the coffee pot on the stove. When the coffee began to perk, the others filed in. They were very quiet, very reserved until breakfast was underway. Then their faces brightened and they began to talk.

"... should have seen the straw in his hair, Miss, when we dug him out of that haystack ..."

"... and the look on his face ..."

She smiled, listening to them, and drank the coffee, the real coffee, and a faint pink flushed her cheeks and she looked young and lovely.

"I say, miss," the youngest one said suddenly, "it's awfully good of you to give time away from your family to help us, especially today."

"Today?" She repeated blankly.

"Why yes, Miss. It's Christmas Eve, don't you know?"

The silence woke Eleanor. She opened her eyes slowly. The expanse of space puzzled her. Then joy swept her once again. Her own bedroom, her own wide soft comfortable bed with its thick warm layer of quilts and comforts. And to be clean.

Eleanor stretched, arched her back and felt her toes press against the footboard. Oh God, to be clean and free. The air smelt a little stuffy though she had thrown open the two broad windows last night. The smell of that cell ... a rush of nausea surged within her. She raised her head and breathed deeply, a mixture of dust and wool and the faint overlay of her perfume.

She had bathed last night. After heating pan after pan of water, and then she had splashed cologne and gloried in the sweet fresh smell.

Why was it so quiet? A sense of unease stirred her. She reached for Andre's wool robe. Her robe was of silk but that was for the long ago days when their apartment had been heated.

The apartment was ghostly, of course. She expected that, overcame it. And Paris, ever since the Occupation, had been only a shadow of herself, a gray and ancient reflection of a voluptuous woman. Still, there were noises, German staff cars, the slam of doors, pedestrians walking to work, walking to find a place in the long line at food shops.

Why was there no sound from outside?

She stood to the side of the window, looked down into the bleak street with the frozen puddles. Such an empty street. Almost like a holiday but . . . Oh. Today was Christmas Eve.

Eleanor turned away from the window. Christmas Eve and the apartment dusty and cold and quiet. Always before she had fixed hot chocolate, thick and sweet and steaming, and tiny brioches with raspberry jam. Breakfast was long and leisurely and they never counted it a miracle, Andre with his hair ruffled and his eyes tender, Robert excited and voluble. Now there was no one . . .

She measured water to boil for ersatz coffee and cut a generous slice of bread for toast. Last night the café owner had known her for what she was. He must have become used to the occasional appearance of filthy, weak, disoriented just-released prisoners. He had heaped her plate with food and sold her a fully cooked chicken and loaf of bread to take home. "All the shops will be closed tomorrow." She had tried to pay him double but he had waved it away.

As she ate, she could feel strength returning. It was lack of food which had made her weak and dizzy. It hadn't seemed to affect the others so horribly, but they all had hunched on their beds in a stupor, their minds in limbo or clinging to remembered happiness. Thank God, she had the extra food. She would be able now to reach Father Laurent. She had felt so weak and ill the night before that she hadn't been sure. But there wasn't any hurry.

After she had eaten and washed the few little dishes, she wandered restlessly around the living room. She must stop thinking about Christmas Eve. It did no good to grieve for days that wouldn't come again. She should be grateful. She was grateful. Robert and Linda must be in England by now. They might even be on a ship en route to America. Frank would take care of them and Franz, too. That was worth everything. But she couldn't rest. If she sat in Andre's chair, she looked toward the corner of the room where the tree always stood. When she moved to her own chair, she remembered the Christmas morning that Andre had come up behind her and bent down to kiss her gently and slip a lovely matched pearl necklace around her throat.

On Christmas Eve, before they left to go to midnight Mass, Andre always lifted down the huge Bible that had belonged to his maternal grandmother and read, in his clear and resonant voice, the story of that Christmas Eve so many years ago.

Eleanor walked to the glass fronted bookcase. She carried the Bible to Andre's chair and sat down. When it was opened, she began to read and she could once again hear Andre's voice and the year slipped away and a sense of peace filled her.

She was so immersed that she almost didn't hear the tiny knock, but it was so quiet, the city lay so silent beyond, that the sound quivered and hung in the still air.

When she opened the door, the concierge, tiny Mme. Sibert, slipped in like a shadow and immediately closed the door behind her. She looked fearfully around. "Are you alone?" she whispered.

Eleanor nodded.

"Oh, Madame, I am so glad you are free. I've brought you some food," and she thrust a plate with a napkin over it into Eleanor's hands. "I was afraid you wouldn't have any food here at the apartment and you can't buy any today." A footstep sounded in the hall way and she waited, rigid, her fear communicating itself to Eleanor, until it was quiet again. She bent close to Eleanor, whispered even more softly, "Did you know, Madame, they are watching you?"

"Watching me?"

"They've taken an apartment across the street. A man with binoculars stands in the window. He has been there all day. There is another man in the alleyway near the backdoor. He is cold, that one," she added with satisfaction.

"No," Eleanor said slowly, "I didn't know they were watching me."

Mme. Sibert nodded. "They do that you know. I have heard. They let you go and then they watch you and they arrest anyone you speak to. Madame, if you have friends, for God's sake, avoid them."

When the concierge had cautiously slipped away, Eleanor looked discreetly out of the front window. Yes, there, the third floor right apartment across the street. She could see the tiny silver spots that marked the field glasses and behind them a shapeless form.

She wasn't free or safe, after all. She should have known. If she hadn't been so weak, so fuzzy the night before, she would have known. Thank God, Mme. Sibert had warned her.

A watcher at the front. A watcher at the back. If she left, she would be followed. And she couldn't lose them, not in these empty streets. Her follower would take care to cling to her heels in the Metro.

She leaned against the wall and felt the fluttering of panic. Trapped. And when they were through with her, when the decoy didn't rise, they would yank her back into that filthy sickening prison.

She would rather be dead. She would, she knew suddenly, soon be dead if she went back to Cherche-Midi.

As she stood, looking down into the icy street, the street that was now a part of the trap, two nuns, their heads down against the wind, their hands folded inside their habits, came around the corner. No matter what happened in the world, this was a joyous day to them. The eve of the birth of the Christ child, and tonight, their calm faces lifted to heaven they would sing and praise God for his gift to the world. The streets would be full of worshipers. Would the Germans enforce the curfew tonight?

"Your sister would pick Christmas Eve to come."

Rene didn't answer. It wouldn't do any good to answer. Yvette wasn't angry about Denise's arrival. Yvette had grown more and more morose this winter. First, it was the lack of business, the end of the little luxuries she coveted. Then it was the gnawing fear that they would lose their little shop and all they had worked for. Now she knew the shop's failure was inevitable. He could hold on for another month, perhaps six weeks. There had been a little spurt in sales the past few weeks, a weak flicker of buying for Christmas. He had sold the last of his pipes. But the days were numbered. There wasn't any hope and Yvette's voice grew sharper, her face more pinched.

"Did you talk to Bussiere before he left town?"

Bussiere, one of their suppliers, had gone into the black market in a big way. He was getting rich. He and his family didn't have any trouble getting passes from the Germans and they were in Nice now, for Christmas.

"It didn't do any good," Rene mumbled.

"Why not?" Her voice rose. "We've been good customers. You'd think he could help us out, now that we need it."

"No credit."

They were a half block from the station now. Rene started to walk faster.

"Did you ask him to take you on? His business is booming. He must need help."

Rene shook his head, "He's got plenty of brothers and cousins and friends to work for him. He said it would be another story if I had a truck."

At one time they could have sold their business and had enough to buy a truck. But the store wasn't worth anything anymore. There wasn't any way in the world they could get enough money to buy a truck. Yvette clutched her husband's arm. "Rene, look up ahead. Isn't that the Masson woman's sister?"

Rene peered through the gloom. "It looks like her."

Yvette began to trot, pulling on her husband's arm. "Why would she be coming to the Gare de'Austerlitz? They're still hunting for her. The Gestapo, I mean. A plainclothesman checked with me just a couple of days ago. He said if she showed up to be sure and call them. He even gave me a number. Hurry, Rene, let's get up there. I'm sure that's her."

He looked puzzled. "I thought I saw a light in the Masson apartment today."

"A Gestapo agent has been staying there. She must have been a pretty big fish. She was running an escape line for English soldiers, the agent told me."

They were about ten yards behind Linda when they entered the station. It was jammed and Yvette stood on tiptoe to keep Linda in sight.

Rene touched Yvette's elbow. "Denise's train will be on track four."

"Don't worry about her. Help me keep that girl in sight."

"What for?"

She turned her sharp bitter face toward him, just for an instant. "Ten thousand francs," she whispered. "That's what they pay for turning in those who have been helping the English escape."

"Ten thousand francs?"

Yvette nodded. She surged on ahead from Rene. There she was. That was odd. She had come to the station and now she was heading for the exit. That didn't make sense.

Yvette looked back at a checkpoint, German soldiers stolidly checking identity papers. She could run to them, tell them that the blond one, that one, was wanted by the Gestapo. But the notice had said the Gestapo would pay for the name and address of the suspect. If she turned her in to the checkpoint, she might not get credit for the arrest. She looked back. My God, she was already at the door. Yvette began to run, in little sharp half steps. She would follow her, find out where she was hiding. Then, if she called and gave the address to the Gestapo, there couldn't be any doubt about who should get credit for the capture.

Yvette hurried out onto the cold dark street. There she was, a quarter block ahead. Yvette walked quickly. Ten thousand francs. Ten thousand francs. Ten thousand francs . . .

Eleanor brushed her hair, pulling the bristles through again and again. Her hair had been matted and stringy. She had washed and washed it. Now it swept down onto her shoulders. She looked in the mirror with a sense of surprise. Her hair had always been a deep glistening glowing black. Now it was streaked with white. She began to braid it, her slender fingers twisting the lengths swiftly. When she was done, she lifted the braids and curved them around her head. Coronet braids. It had been years since she had worn her hair this way. It looked odd with the clothes she was wearing. And would look odder still, she thought with a tiny smile. She wore a soft cashmere sweater of Andre's. Her wool slacks were silk lined. Over these she pulled on a pair of Andre's corduroy trousers. She had shortened the legs this afternoon. She looked again at the mirror. She took a wool skirt, folded it, wrapped it around her waist and pinned it. Now she pulled on a jacket of Andre's. The jacket hung loose. Next came her fur coat and over all of this, she added Andre's heavy winter overcoat.

She gazed with some amusement at the mirror. She looked like a short heavy man. Except for her head. She fitted on Andre's gray hat.

Perfect.

She debated whether to carry a satchel then decided against it. She took her bundle of food, the rest of the chicken, the bread and the cheese that Mme. Sibert had brought. She stuffed the bundle inside the jacket.

Now she looked like a short fat man with a very decided paunch.

The living room was dark. She stood to the side of the far window and looked out between the shade and the frame.

Night had fallen, but the street wasn't empty now. People were beginning to spill out of the darkened buildings on their way to midnight Mass. Some were old and walked alone. There were family groups of three or four.

Eleanor didn't pause to look around the darkened apartment. There was nothing here that mattered anymore. She had Andre's most recent picture hidden in the folded skirt. The rest of it didn't matter.

As she passed Mme. Sibert's door, she slipped a note underneath.

"Take whatever you can use from the apartment before the Boche strip it. I will not return. God bless you, E. Masson."

At the front doorway, she hesitated, leaning her head against the icy glass. Would the watcher with the binoculars be clever enough to remember that a short paunchy man hadn't entered the apartment house this evening? Or would the watcher be new on the shift and think the man a visitor who must have come earlier?

There was the slam of a door down the hall. Eleanor started to hurry out then decided to risk it. She stood back a pace. A young family, she knew them by sight, passed by, with a polite nod. When the father opened the door, she came right behind them, went down the steps with them, turned and kept pace up the street.

She dared not look back.

The street had never seemed so long. She tried hard to walk like a man. God, how do men walk? She stiffened her legs, kept her back straight. She probably looked like a fool.

The young father looked at her curiously but she kept right on behind them to the end of the block and then she turned to her left.

A group of girls came out of an apartment house. One of them was singing a Christmas carol. The others began to join her and their light clear young voices rose above the crunch of footsteps on the icy sidewalk.

Eleanor passed the group of girls then slipped into a narrow alleyway. She threaded her way past dustbins to the next street. She paused for a moment. No footstep sounded behind her.

No one was following her.

Nearby church bells began to ring. They were the first she had heard. But bells would ring now across Paris, calling the faithful. She plunged out into the street and turned to her right, melting into the throng of churchgoers, just another dark shape in the night.

Linda heard the bells. She had gone to bed early, trying to escape the devastating loneliness in sleep. The apartment was always its emptiest just after she had sent on another batch of soldiers. Every Tuesday night and Friday night, the apartment was at its loneliest. A bell rang nearby, the sweet thin ring as clear as a bird's call. Restlessly, Linda pushed back the covers. Christmas Eve. She had managed not to think of it the rest of the day. Where was Jonathan tonight? Had he reached England? Was he at home?

Was he thinking of her?

Linda got up. She would smoke a cigarette then perhaps it would be quieter and she could sleep. She must have left her cigarettes in the kitchen.

Christmas Eve. At home the carolers would be coming up the street. A church group, usually. She had gone caroling many times. Laughing, occasionally a little out of key, but sometimes the voices lifted and for an instant the streets of Bethlehem would seem near.

Linda stopped by the front window, cupping the cigarette behind one hand.

God seemed very far away tonight.

Did all those hurrying down the darkened street sense Him near this night? She lifted the cigarette to her mouth. Her hand checked in mid-air.

The car had slitted headlights, but even in the dark she knew it was big. The sedan roared down the street. Pedestrians jumped for safety. It squealed to a stop directly in front of the apartment house. The street was suddenly empty.

The cigarette began to burn her fingers. Linda smashed it against the sill, sweeping away the flutter of sparks. Two men got out of the back seat and began to walk, without hurry, toward the door.

Linda began to shake. It was involuntary. Her legs trembled, her hands trembled.

She had known they would come. One day. She had known in her heart. But somehow, these last weeks, she had been so cold and tense and driven, so consumed by fear for Eleanor, that the sense of inevitability had receded, that knowledge that was part of her. Now it had happened.

The Gestapo was coming for her.

Oh Eleanor, she cried, I'm afraid. I'm afraid. They will hurt me, I know they will and I am afraid and I can't bear it.

She knew too much. Father Laurent, M. Berth whose pharmacy served as a drop, Mme. Vianney who often served as a guide, Dr. Gailland who had saved Jonathan. If they tortured her . . .

She wasn't brave. She'd known from the first. She was an awful, awful coward. Tears began to slip down her face. She turned away from the window, ran toward the door.

She heard harsh rattling knocks on the doors downstairs.

Perhaps they weren't coming for her after all.

Oh God, that didn't matter. They would search the entire apartment house. The Germans always did. They had her description, a blond American girl about twenty. Her French would never be good enough to truly pass under the identity she was carrying.

Not under pressure. Frantically she grabbed up her coat, pulled it on and ran to the door.

She stopped in the hallway, leaned over the stairs.

"We are looking for an American woman." The sergeant spoke in heavily accented French.

Linda was afraid she was going to faint. They were after her. There was no doubt now. Could she slip down the stairs, hide in an ell? They would search everywhere. And someone might tell them. Someone who didn't care who the Gestapo caught might have noticed the blond woman who went up and down from the fourth floor.

There wasn't any way out.

She heard the thick clump of boots starting up the stairs.

Desperately, she turned and hurried up the narrow steep stairs to the roof. She pushed against the trapdoor. It didn't budge. It must be frozen shut. She got up under the trapdoor, put her shoulder against it. There was a crackle of splitting ice. One final heave and the trapdoor lifted.

She climbed out onto the roof, slick and icy. She shut the trap door, looked frantically around. She could hide behind one of the chimneys. But they would find her, they would. She started toward the back of the building. There were fire escapes..

The soldiers looked small from the roof. They were dropping off the truck, every hundred yards, to surround the block. At either end, everyone who passed would be asked to show his identity. If she could reach the street from one of the other apartment houses, she could fit into the streams of people now walking to church. If she tucked all of her hair under her scarf, she could show her identity card and probably get past the checkpoint. But they weren't letting anyone out of this apartment house.

The night was bitterly cold. Linda pulled the little blue coat tighter but it didn't help. Her hands were numb with cold. She couldn't climb down the fire escape. She couldn't get past the searchers coming slowly, steadily, inexorably up the stairs. When they found the empty apartment on the fourth floor, they would turn and go on up the narrow stairway to the trap door and they would reach the roof.

She was trapped.

She skirted the squat chimney and peeped cautiously over the edge.

A driver got out and went around and opened the door. In the brief flash of light from the car interior, she saw a man in civilian clothes, and, for an unmistakable instant, she saw his face. It was the officer who had come to the Masson apartment hunting for Lt. Evans.

He was as terrifying to her as a snake. She remembered his face and his cruel thin mouth and his white hands.

He would make her pay for having tricked him once.

Linda stumbled away from the parapet.

She couldn't bear to have him touch her.

A scream rose in her throat. She pressed her hands against her mouth. She ran unevenly, slipping on the ice, toward the west side of the building. She lost her balance, skidded, flailed out, fell and brought up hard against the parapet. She had almost gone over.

She lay there for a long moment, her heart thudding, her hands aching from the fall. She had almost flipped over the edge to tumble four stories down into the narrow bricked alleyway.

The nearby bells of St. Severin began to ring. The peals were so near, so loud, she wouldn't hear the searchers when they reached the roof.

Shakily, Linda got to her feet. She stepped cautiously toward the biggest chimney. This was where Jonathan had shown her a good spot to jump.

Jonathan, I love you. Are you safe now? Jonathan, we could have been so happy.

Step by faltering step, she neared the edge of the roof. Yes, just here, he had taken her arm and pointed out the way and his arm had been so warm around her shoulders.

If she could make the jump, if she could gain the next apartment house, she would be able to slip out, join the throngs of churchgoers ignoring the curfew tonight, and walk to the Church of the Good Shepherd.

She reached down, touched the parapet with a trembling hand. She didn't look down into the well of darkness, the dark cavern that stretched between her and the lower roof. The parapet was icy. She scraped the brickwork with the edge of her purse.

Were they coming up the last flight of stairs now?

Moving quickly, jerkily, before she could think, Linda stepped onto the parapet and crouched, knees bent.

Jonathan.

She called his name as she jumped.

CHAPTER 20

Linda landed hard. Her feet skidded from beneath her on the icy roof. She slammed onto her back. She lay in a twisted heap, heart thudding, waiting for shouts and shots.

The bells rang on the clear icy air.

Carefully, Linda managed to get up on her hands and knees.

Lights flickered on the roof above her.

She crawled until she was hidden behind the rusty iron work of a ventilator shaft.

Flashlights danced above her. One light pointed down into the alleyway.

"*Nein*," a man called.

In a moment, the lights were gone.

Linda hesitated. Should she stay on the roof, wait until morning? But then she would have to go out into the streets in daylight and they were looking for her. She was conspicuous with her blond hair and light blue coat.

Now was the time.

On the narrow roof stairs, she paused to brush tar and dirt from her coat and to straighten her hair. Before she could lose her resolve, she began to hurry down the stairs. On the second floor, a large family group was heading downstairs. Linda kept close behind them. On the street outside, she kept to the outside of the sidewalk then turned to her left away from the Gestapo car that still sat beside her building.

The streets echoed with footsteps. So many were spilling out of darkened buildings on their way to midnight Mass. She walked fast. Six blocks, ten, fifteen. She began to hope.

She was almost to the Church when she began to wonder whether the Gestapo was looking for Father Laurent, too. Her steps slowed. At the end of the block near the Church, she searched for a telltale Gestapo car.

There were only church goers on foot. No German cars marred the street.

Linda was swept up in the stream of people. The Church was jammed. She slipped into a crowded pew and knelt. The service began with the processional. The boys choir came first, their lovely high voices raised in a song of exultation, then the adult choir, the altar boys and finally, the clergy, in their glorious white vestments.

When she saw Father Laurent, Linda closed her eyes and rested her head on her clasped hands. He was here. She was going to be safe. Oh Jonathan, I am coming.

She understood little of the Latin mass, but the glory and exultation of the massed voices promised something beyond this night in Occupied Paris.

When the Mass ended, she followed the crowd up the aisle. Father Laurent saw her and reached out a warm hand. She bent close and whispered, "The Gestapo came." He understood at once and turned her toward the door leading down to the basement. "My office," he murmured.

It was cold in the office. Linda paced up and down, trying to keep warm and trying to ignore the fear that pulled at her.

The door opened so quietly she was caught by surprise, then alarm. Who was this plump funnily shaped man?

"Linda! Oh, Linda."

"Eleanor. Eleanor. Eleanor."

The sisters embraced, both crying and talking at once. But, when Eleanor heard Linda out, she too was worried. "Father Laurent will have to escape with us. If they came for you, they must know all about the escape line."

"Why doesn't he come?" Linda asked nervously. "Every second that we wait could bring the Gestapo closer. Oh Eleanor, I can't bear it if we are captured now."

Eleanor smiled, trying to reassure Linda, but she too listened for sounds in the corridor. The Gestapo would as soon invade a Church as anywhere.

"Eleanor, let's leave now, not wait for Father Laurent."

"Linda," she said gently, "we don't have anywhere to go. We must wait. And hope."

Linda bit her lip. This was stupid, stupid, stupid..

They both turned strained faces when the door opened.

Father Laurent hurried inside. "My daughters, how wonderful it is to see you both."

"Father, we must hurry," Linda urged frantically. "The Gestapo may be here any minute. Have you made plans?"

Father Laurent took her cold hands in his. "Don't be frightened, Linda. You are safe now."

"How can you be sure? I tell you, they knew my name. They came for me."

He was nodding. "I have talked to a friend in the Surete. They were indeed coming for you. A woman named Yvette Bizien saw you at the train station and followed you to the Latin Quarter apartment. She knew that the Gestapo had arrested Eleanor and was looking for you. She turned you in for the reward."

"That means the rest of the escape line is safe, doesn't it, Father?" Eleanor asked excitedly.

"Yes." His smile was triumphant.

Linda looked at Eleanor and the priest in a kind of wonder because the safety of the escape line meant so much to them. Nothing, to them, mattered as much as the route to freedom for trapped English soldiers. She wished she too could be as brave as they. Her shoulders sagged. She had tried, tried her best but she would never be brave.

Eleanor was smiling at her. "Did Linda tell you, Father, how she escaped?"

Eleanor described Linda's night, the coming of the car, the race up to the roof, the slipping sliding journey to the parapet and the final desperate leap.

Father Laurent looked at her with admiration. "You never cease to amaze me, mademoiselle. You are so young and so brave."

Linda looked at him and tears glistened in her eyes. She wasn't brave. Not at all. And she was very near the end of her endurance. She knew, suddenly, that she could not leave the Church. She could not walk down the streets, try to take the train, not with the hideous gray-green of German uniforms everywhere about.

She simply could not do it.

Then she heard and understood what Father Laurent was saying . . .

"The message came last night. Sister Angelique heard it on the BBC. I cannot think there could be a better moment in time for me to tell you than on this Christmas morning," he was saying softly. "She wrote down the message." He cleared his throat. "This is what the BBC announcer read in the list of personal messages, 'Robert and Franz are halfway to Pasadena and Jonathan is safe at home.'"

ABOUT THE AUTHOR

CAROLYN HART is the author of forty-nine mysteries. Hart's fiftieth mystery novel, *Dead, White and Blue*, will be published in May 2013. Her books have won Agatha, Anthony, and Macavity awards. She has twice appeared at the National Book Festival in Washington, DC. She is thrilled that some of her long-ago books are having a new life. She lives in Oklahoma City with her husband, Phil.